HANSEN'S ROCK

CREATED BY

DAN L. KING

This is a work of fiction. Characters, organizations, corporations, institutions, and locations in this novel are the product of the author's imagination, or if real, they are used fictitiously without any intent to describe their actual behaviors, affiliations, policies, or characteristics.

First Edition
Copyright © 2014 by Dan L. King
ISBN-13: 978-0-9885440-2-4
ISBN-10: 0988544024

Visit www.hansensrock.com for additional information about this novel.

Dan L. King

ANOMALY

On the evening of June 2, Captain Lars Hansen was preparing to leave the bridge of Sirius for the night. He had watched as the autopilot had slowly turned the huge ship to a heading of 108 degrees after the ship had cleared Perth, Geographe Bay, and the extension of land that marked the southeastern extreme of Australia. This course would be followed for the next 1,850 nautical miles until they made their next turn after clearing Tasmania. There they would chart a course of seventeen degrees which would take them up the east coast of Australia and toward their destination at the Bulwer Island Refinery near Brisbane. At the ET600 full-load, maximum economy, cruising speed of sixteen knots, it would be five days before they turned north toward their destination.

The weather was good with clear skies, low humidity, and only a modest breeze…about as good as it gets in the seas between Australia and Antarctica. Some Australians consider this body of water to be a part of the Southern Sea but the International Hydrographic Organization calls the waters the part of the Indian Ocean that is between the Great Australian Bight and the true Southern Ocean which they declare to lie south of the line which is sixty degrees of south latitude.

When Hansen returned to his cabin, he turned on his monitor and clicked on the program that permitted him to operate his telescope and to view and record the images that it captured. He hit the wall switch which opened the dome silo that protected the telescope from the elements.

Hansen had begun experimenting with the new telescope shortly after leaving the ship building facilities at Ulsan, South Korea while in

Hansen's Rock

the East China and South China Seas and he had mostly figured out the new software. One of the early setup items was to calibrate the magnitude measurement module. This setup was simple enough. The instructions required that Hansen train the telescope on at least three different stars with known magnitudes. Once each star was centered, the magnitude of each star was entered, and then the software would learn the brightness associated with each magnitude. The best calibration came when a very bright star, a faint star, and a star with medium brightness were used for the calibration. After the calibration, he tested it on a fourth star of known magnitude and the software interpreted the brightness exactly correctly. The telescope could resolve object magnitudes down to nineteen[a], which would be an object over 25,000 times fainter than that which the unaided human eye could see.

***

It was unusual for any working ship to permit such an arrangement but Hansen had negotiated the telescope mounted on top of the bridge deck years ago when he had agreed to defer his retirement to assist his employer, Pole2Pole Petroleum, Inc. (P2P^2), with the development and testing of a revolutionary combination oil tanker/container ship.

The telescope was a Meade MAX 20" ACF, advertised as an observatory-quality device. Hansen referred to the telescope as MAX when he spoke about it or when speaking to it, as he often found himself doing. When he included this requirement in his negotiations with his employer, he really didn't expect that they would agree as the telescope, dome, and installation costs could exceed $80,000. But, to his amazement, P2P management agreed and also promised him that he could keep the equipment as a retirement gift if he agreed to continue working until he reached his sixty-fifth birthday. They also agreed to double his pay during his last five years of working as an incentive to encourage him to guide the development and testing of the new ET600 class of ships. While the new ship was being designed and finally built, Hansen would continue to captain his older ship and then he would command the first ship of the new class when it became sea-ready. Hansen shook the hand of the P2P CEO as soon as the boss tendered the offer; he just couldn't pass on a deal like that.

***

His exploration of the sky began with the area over the South Pole since he had never had a proper telescope to explore this part of the sky before. He had been storing digital images as he went along so by the time the ship put Albany astern, he had several photos of the sky immediately over the South Pole that had been taken on the nights when weather permitted quality images.

On this night, Hansen again told the software to point the telescope at Sigma Octantis, the generally referenced southern star even though it is about a degree off of the true celestial pole's location. This had been his starting location each night he had been able to observe and he had been working his way out from this star to explore whatever the telescope could produce. Through the powerful telescope, an object the size of the Moon and 250 million miles away would appear to be the same size as the Moon does when viewed with the naked eye.

When the equatorial drive that positioned the telescope stopped moving, Sigma Octantis was perfectly positioned in the center of the image that glowed on the monitor. In the top right corner of the monitor, the software displayed data about the object giving its name; distance from Earth; celestial coordinates; visual apparent magnitude; GPS coordinates of the observation location; and various links that could be followed to see more detailed information about the body. Out of habit, Hansen scanned the data before beginning to explore around the star. But tonight he noticed an anomaly; the magnitude of σOct was not correct. He remembered the correct value to be in a range of 5.42-5.45 as it was a variable magnitude star. He checked his reference again to confirm that his memory was accurate and it was. On other recent magnitude measurements, σOct had been measured to have an apparent magnitude that fell within the expected range. But, tonight the magnitude reflected by the software was 5.40. He studied the number briefly and made a sticky note to himself to recalibrate the magnitude measurement module of the software. He stuck the note on the monitor bezel and took another picture of σOct and its neighbors before beginning his exploration to the east of the star. He carefully studied and photographed the area to the east of σOct for a couple of hours before he turned off the monitor, closed the dome over MAX, and slept.

The next day the ship encountered one of the fairly frequent late fall storms that stirred the seas south of Australia. The rain and wind, although not very severe, lasted three days before clearing around mid-day on June 5. As the cold front passed, the temperature dropped, and the humidity relented, creating perfect weather for stargazing.

After dining in the galley with the off-duty men, Hansen made a quick trip to the bridge to check the instruments to see how the ship was operating and to note the current location which was about 650 nautical miles west of the southern tip of Tasmania. After chatting with the relief skipper, he returned to his quarters to make notes in his personal log about the activities of the day and then he turned on the computer monitor and opened the viewing door in the dome housing MAX.

His first activity was to recalibrate the magnitude measurement module. As before, he chose three stars with magnitudes that were a matter of record and began the process but every star he chose was properly measured by the software so it made no changes to the algorithms that interpolated the brightness measurements. Hansen was a bit puzzled that there was no error in the magnitude measurement software but accepted the fact and went on to follow the routine he had established. He instructed the software to point MAX at Sigma Octantis and in a short time the familiar sky segment appeared on the monitor. The corner data confirmed that this was indeed σOct but the magnitude data was still flawed; tonight the software measured the magnitude at 5.27.

Again puzzled by the magnitude measurement, Hansen pointed MAX toward Chi Octantis, slightly west-northwest of σOct and the software displayed the data on this star and reflected a magnitude of 5.29[b], which was exactly correct according to the reference tables.

σOct seemed to be getting brighter! He thought about this a bit and speculated that the southern pole star might be entering some new phase. Sometimes stars get brighter just before they collapse or maybe it was just some sort of flare. He didn't worry about it too much as the change in magnitude was still quite small, only about 0.1. He would make follow-up measurements and keep a record of the changes.

On June 6, Hansen measured the apparent magnitude of σOct as 5.23 and on June 7, as Sirius neared the most southern point in its journey, passing Tasmania to its north, MAX measured the apparent magnitude to be 5.20. The data was indisputable; the star was getting brighter by the day. He also noted that the star had developed a slight bulge on its southern edge. The bulge was barely noticeable even with the tremendous resolution capability of MAX.

Hansen wondered if anyone else had noticed the changes in Sigma Octantis and whether anyone had an explanation for what was happening to the star. But due to his work duties, he wouldn't have time to investigate the matter until after Sirius was safely secured to the pier at Bulwer Island.

BULWER ISLAND

As Sirius headed to the north the weather turned poor again and it didn't clear until they were nearing Brisbane. Activity on the ship was high as the big ship began slowing and making its approach into the Brisbane River channel that lay to the north of the Port of Brisbane and to the south of the Brisbane International Airport.

Because of the extreme size of Sirius, navigation through the channel required great caution. The harbor pilot that came to operate the ship for the last few kilometers was amazed at the size of the massive ship and seemed a bit overwhelmed so Hansen stayed close to the pilot to assist as needed. Because the ship had a beam of one hundred meters, all large ships had to be held at their berths until Sirius had passed as the channel was not wide enough to accommodate another large ship when Sirius was underway. The large beam of the ship did permit its draft to be kept to less than fifteen meters, so channel depth was less an issue than channel width.

Even though Sirius was fitted with powerful bow thrusters and mid-ship thrusters which could easily move the ship sideways under most docking conditions, four tugs met the giant ship as it arrived at the Crude Dock facility that serviced the Bulwer Island Refinery. It only took about four hours to make the ship secure at the pier. At this point, the ship's mission changed to one of a floating oil pumping and storage facility.

The refinery had a production capacity of slightly over 100,000 barrels per day. On-shore storage facilities were about 2,000,000 barrels. The local crude storage capacity was being substantially augmented by a S3 class ship, S3 Australis, which was being used as a floating storage facility and had a capacity of over 3,000,000 barrels. So Sirius would be docked at the facility until its 8,000,000 barrels of crude oil could be stored or refined, which could take as long as three to four weeks. While the crude oil was being pumped into the storage tanks, standard size shipping containers would be loaded onto the deck of Sirius from smaller container ships which would raft abeam of Sirius during the transfer of the containers.

It took two full days to get the pumping facilities connected, tested, and operational. As this was the first connection to this shore facility, a few problems were encountered and had to be solved in order for the cargo lines from the huge ship to be successfully connected to the shore lines. And since there was limited experience by the crew on the piping and pumping equipment on this new ship, all operational and safety checklists were verified twice by the crew, then they were checked by the engineer put aboard by the shipbuilder, and lastly by Hansen himself. Finally, the pumps were transferring cargo on June 11.

Hansen had done little but work and sleep for the past three days during the docking and connection-making activities. After mess that evening he returned to his cabin, just yards away from the bridge, for much needed rest. But his curiosity was running high about what was going on with σOct so he woke up the computer that had been sleeping for five days, opened the door to MAX's dome, and instructed the software to find the star.

Being in port adjacent to a major city with all kinds of light pollution and air pollution created a less than desirable observing environment but Hansen knew that he would just have to endure the poor visibility. After a few minutes, MAX's motors stopped turning and the monitor displayed a hazy image of σOct.

Hansen immediately noticed the changes. It was unmistakable even with the poor viewing conditions. There was a new object in the sky that now obscured all but a small sliver of σOct. Hansen manually centered MAX on the new object to see if the software could identify it. The data display in the corner of the monitor revealed:

Observation Date/Time: 11 Jun; 10:08 GMT / 20:08 Local
Object Identification: Unknown
Distance From Earth: Unknown
Celestial Coordinates: R.A. 21h 08m 47.0s; Dec. -88° 59' 46"
Visual Apparent Magnitude: 4.95
Observation Location: S24.422147° / E153.134195°

Hansen finally understood that there was nothing happening to Sigma Octantis but rather another object was apparently approaching Earth and previously had been within the diameter of σOct. MAX was a capable piece of equipment but it couldn't tell Hansen much about the object except that it appeared to be approaching Earth from an area of space in the direction of the southern polar star. And, it appeared that the object was drifting to the south of σOct, meaning that it was heading more southerly than the twenty-four degrees of south latitude from which Hansen was observing the object.

Captain Hansen was startled by the rapid change in the magnitude of the object as it meant that the object was approaching Earth very rapidly. While studying for his Bachelor's Degree in marine transportation, Hansen had taken a sophomore elective course in astronomy since he had been bitten by the stargazing bug when he was a young teen. He pulled his text book from an adjacent shelf and searched for a formula that he couldn't remember but knew he had studied. The formula would provide the relationship between an object's apparent magnitude and its relative distance. In a few minutes of searching he found what he was looking for. The formula was:

$$m_b - m_a = 5\log_{10}(d_b/d_a) \text{ [c]}$$

Translated, this equation meant that the difference in apparent magnitudes (m) of a body at points "b" and "a" was related, logarithmically, to the ratio of the distances (d) of the body at points "b" and "a". Hansen solved the equation by inserting the apparent magnitude values on June 11 and June 2 and solving for the ratio of the distance of the object on those two dates. He had to find his old and well-used *CRC Standard Mathematical Tables*[d] which he had bought at a yard sale, to find the logarithm values for the distance ratio. When his calculation was completed, he discovered that the object was 14.9 percent closer to Earth on June 11 than it had been on June 2. Since the object had completed nearly fifteen percent of its approach in only nine days, Hansen concluded that the object could be expected to complete the remaining 85.1 percent of its approach in another 51.4 days. Hansen triple-checked his math since he was tired and since he hadn't dealt with logarithmic functions in a very long time…but the answer did not change. Earth was going to have a visitor of some sort in less than two months.

Hansen immediately recounted his facts concerning the mysterious object in an email to Kevin Randele back in the states; he tapped the send button around 02:00 Brisbane time. Randele was President of the Anaheim Astronomical Association (a club that Hansen helped start over forty years ago when he was a summer intern at the Carson Refinery). Randele was also a Councilor to the American Astronomical Society. Hansen included all his measurements, his math, and images

Hansen's Rock

from each of his five observations. He sent the information in three sequential e-mail messages so that he could include high quality images and asked Randele to study them to see what he concluded. He told Randele that he would be catching a flight back to California in a few hours and that he would contact him as soon as possible after landing in Los Angeles.

HANSEN

Lars Hansen had been born in Taarbaek, Denmark, a smallish town about ten kilometers north of the large ship docks of Copenhagen. His father had been a modestly successful merchant in Taarbaek. His family had immigrated to the United States when Hansen was six years old to escape the high taxes in Denmark. Once in southern California, his father became a distributor of the agricultural products grown near there. The family had arrived in San Diego on a cargo steamer that belonged to the main supplier of goods to his father's store in Denmark. His father had bargained for the passage which included the transportation of the family and the family's personal goods. The accommodations were cramped and simple but the cost was reasonable. They could have afforded better passage but Hansen's father was a very conservative man. He wanted to make sure that they arrived in California with enough money to get their new lives started. The journey was begun in April and the cargo ship had made several intermediate stops before transiting the Panama Canal to continue its journey to southern California. The ship was old and slow so the ten thousand nautical mile journey took over two months. Hansen's mother suffered from seasickness almost every day, but Lars loved everything about the trip. He spent endless hours in the bridge cabin chatting with the ship's captain and observing how the captain operated the ship.

Hansen had always wanted to be a sailor since watching from the roof of his father's business as the large ships sailed from the docks in Copenhagen to the sea. His passage on the cargo steamer had solidified his ambition to become a ship's captain. During his elementary and secondary educations Hansen studied hard and excelled in the subjects that captured his interest...mostly the sciences, mathematics, and geography. After graduating from high school he had pursued his interest by attending Cal Maritime and earning a Bachelor's Degree in marine transportation. Upon graduation, he passed his first US Coast Guard test and earned his Third Mate Deck License. He was immediately hired by a large container shipping company. From that beginning he continued to increase his license rank and finally earned his Master Deck License. He worked in the container shipping industry until he got offered a much higher paying job as captain of an oil tanker. He had been with Pole2Pole Petroleum for the past twenty-five years.

SIRIUS

Hansen had been given the honor of naming the first Extreme Tanker class ship and he had chosen Sirius, named after the brightest star in Earth's night sky. This was the initial working journey for the first ET600. The trip had begun with the ballast-only run from Ulsan, South Korea, where the ship had been built and fitted, to Saudi Arabia's Ras Tanura complex on the Persian Gulf. There it was loaded with 8,000,000 barrels of crude oil, filling its 600 meter long and 100 meter wide hull. The ship was touted as being virtually unsinkable and leak-proof due to its construction. Its bow had a twenty-five millimeter thick marine steel outer hull, then a five millimeter thick carbon fiber hull, and then an inner hull that was made of titanium that was over five millimeters thick. Its bow was many times stronger than even a conventional ice breaker ship and this ship had the first sonic bulbous bow. The cargo of crude was carried in eight semi-rigid Kevlar bladders that were integrated with the lateral and longitudinal stringers that stiffened the ship's hull.

After taking its load, Sirius backtracked across the Persian Gulf and the Gulf of Oman to find the open waters of the Arabian Sea and then the Indian Ocean. The ship had performed flawlessly when empty and continued to perform better than expected with its current load, the largest volume of crude oil ever transported by a single ship.

***

The bulbous bows that had been added to large ships had dominated ship construction specifications for a century. But, the rigid bulbous bows were a hindrance at some speeds and were only employed on ships that operated near their maximum speed most of the time. The latest development in this technology was the employment of a sonic bulbous bow, technically an ultrasonic cavitation bow. As the vessels that had fixed bulbous bows slowed or varied their speeds due to weather or other circumstances, they actually suffered from having that metal appendage on their bow. The marine construction leaders had challenged the ship design industry to develop a more effective and manageable bulb that could take advantage of the benefits of a bulbous bow without conceding the disadvantages. Acoustic experts suggested to the ship's developer that it should be possible to create a virtual bulb using ultrasonic waves that could be instantaneously adjusted by a ship's navigational computer to maximize the hull's effect on the water at all speeds and in all conditions. The best fluid mechanics experts, naval engineers, and electrical engineers were challenged to make this concept a reality...and they did.

The sonic bulbous bow was implemented by placing two articulating fins, one on each side of the bow, running parallel to the bow line. The fins extended from a point that was three meters above the maximum draft waterline to a point that was three meters below the minimum draft waterline. A complex, phased array of dozens of powerful, ultrasonic transducers was placed inside each fin. By manipulating the articulation of the fins and also instantaneously reconfiguring the transducers, a sonic cavitation was created in front of the bow at exactly the correct water depth and of exactly the perfect size and shape to maximize the cancellation of the bow wave and virtually eliminate the "squat" that all displacement hulls were destined to suffer. The fin and transducer manipulation permitted the transducers to produce the sonic bulb along the entire range of submersions that the bow would experience with varying loads. The frequency, power output, and polarity of the transducers was controlled by a computer that constantly measured the ships speed and fuel consumption and optimized the size and shape of the sonic bulb to optimize efficiency and performance at all speeds, not just those in the vicinity of the theoretical hull speed. This design added very little weight to the ship, actually decreased the effective wetted surface area of the ship and therefore reduced the amount of drag that the hull experienced. And as a side benefit, the cavitation bulb produced by the transducers could even break up sea ice before it contacted the leading edge of the bow. The amplifiers needed to create the power were driven by an auxiliary steam turbine and generator. This auxiliary turbine was simply added into the circulating steam system needed on the boat to keep the crude oil at the best viscosity and to provide heat, etc. for the other components of the ship, including crew space heat. Because of this, the additional turbine added very little power overhead to the ship. Since cavitation on a surface will erode the surface when the cavitation bubbles implode, the leading ten percent of the hull's surface needed protection or would eventually be damaged by the continuous and aggressive cavitation bubble implosions. This problem was solved with the addition of impact and heat resistant ceramic tiles adhered to the hull's surface from maximum water line to the keel for the leading thirty meters of the hull. This idea was adopted from the heat shields used on various space craft to protect them from the friction-generated heat that they encountered upon re-entry into Earth's atmosphere. The tiles were adhered to the hull with a special epoxy. The epoxy compound could even be applied underwater which would permit a damaged or missing tile to be replaced without hauling the ship into a dry dock. The expected life of the sacrificial tiles was expected to be twenty years or more under normal circumstances.

A side benefit of the cavitation bubbles was that they performed a cleaning job on much of the leading portion of the hull and prevented the usual barnacles and shellfish from collecting on the hull. This meant that it was not necessary to apply expensive bottom paint to any of the surface covered by the tiles. The rest of the ship's hull was kept clean by strategically placed low-power ultrasonic transducers that, in redundant pairs, were affixed to the inside of the outer hull and driven by their own much lower power ultrasonic amplifiers. The combination of the effects of the ultrasonic bulb and the smaller ultrasonic hull scrubbers was that the huge ship's entire hull would remain clean of algae and crustaceans that would attach to untreated or worn underwater surfaces on conventionally painted hulls.

The sonic bulbous bow had been recognized by the scientific community as one of the greatest advances in marine science in a century. The impact of this development was far reaching as it could be applied to all types of hulls, not just long waterline hulls that operated near cruising speed most of the time.

In addition to the unique bow design, the deck of the ship was designed to accommodate shipping containers. The ship could carry a full load of crude oil and derivatives on an outbound leg but rather than return empty or with low value product in its bladders, it could be loaded with thousands of shipping containers to be transported on its return to pick up more petroleum product. It even had its own container cranes that could move containers from the outside areas of the ship's beam to the inside spaces so that more containers could be accommodated. This was necessary since most shore-bound cranes did not have the reach to access the middle of the hundred meter beam of Sirius.

HOME FOR HELP

Since Sirius would be little more than a floating oil storage facility for three or four weeks while the small refinery transferred or processed the crude oil in the ship's bladders, Captain Hansen would fly home for a week and leave the ship in the hands of his second-in-command. Before finishing his packing and leaving for the Brisbane airport, he copied to a thumb drive all the data that he had collected and every image that might be useful in the event that his notebook computer might experience some fatal event.

Fifteen hours after the takeoff from Brisbane International Airport, his flight landed at LAX. Rather than head to his house located off Highway 76 in the foothills near Palomar Mountain, Captain Hansen headed to the frequent flyer lounge where he called Randele to discuss the information he had sent him.

When the phone rang at 6:55 a.m. on June 12, Randele picked up the phone on the first ring, "This is Kevin."

"Hi Kevin, this is Lars; I just landed at LAX. Did you get a chance to study the information I sent you?"

"Sure did Lars; I think you may have made the astronomical find of the century, maybe of the millennium. I've studied the images and agree that we have an object that is closing on Earth at an alarming rate. I contacted the boss at Jet Propulsion Lab and sent him your data. He has concluded that we will likely have a near-Earth passing by the object in a few weeks, but likely less than your calculated 51.4 days. Your assumption of a linear velocity profile isn't the way objects approach Earth. As you know, as an object approaches Earth, the gravitational pull of Earth, the Sun, and other bodies in our solar system exert more force on the approaching object, so the object

Dan L. King

speeds up exponentially. We need more data to determine the velocity curve and the arrival date.

My friend at JPL has contacted the Director at the NASA Near-Earth Object Program and has sent him your images and data. We should hear from him soon. I'll give you a call as soon as I hear anything. Do you want me to call you on your cell phone or your satellite phone?"

"Yeah, I should have realized that gravity and proximity would have a big effect on the object." Hansen chuckled and said, "I guess my tired, sixty-four year old brain isn't as sharp as it once was. Anyway, call me on the satellite phone; the cell coverage is spotty around where I live and I don't want to miss your call. I'm going to pick up my rental car and head toward my house now."

They hung up and Hansen went to the Hertz lot, picked up the Explorer he had reserved, and started the trip to his home.

***

Randele's phone rang at 8:04 a.m.; it was his friend Michael Lister at JPL. "Kevin, this is Mike. I just finished a call with Bradley Witherspoon, Director of JPL and head of the NASA NEO Program. He has a plan."

Lister explained that Witherspoon had studied the images and information that Hansen had sent and that Witherspoon had determined a course of action. Witherspoon was very concerned about the object in the images given how little lateral movement there had been over time. That lack of lateral movement meant that the object was likely headed toward a near-Earth passing, if not an impact. Witherspoon had contacted a friend who was the head of the astronomy department at the Australian National University and who had been in charge of the Australian Spaceguard Survey. ANU was the premier astronomy and astrophysics institution in Australia; many thought that their scientists were even better than the Aussie government scientists. The head of astronomy had arranged for his best operator to do some work at their Siding Spring Optical Observatory which was the best optical observatory in Australia and had the largest reflector down under. The operator was in the process of traveling from Canberra to Siding Spring, a distance of about 600 kilometers. He was expected to arrive just as the Sun would be setting at the observatory.

Witherspoon's assumption was that the object was not all that far from Earth so it might be possible to perform an optical parallax determination that would produce some useful information. The site in

New South Wales would be taking measurements as soon as possible after sunset and as late as possible before sunrise and those two timed positions would constitute the two points for the parallax study. The procedure would be repeated nightly until sufficient data had been collected to produce a good distance-to-object measurement and maybe a probable path prediction. Normally, parallax images are taken at intervals of six months to take advantage of the orbital range of Earth but Witherspoon was sure that Earth did not have six months of time with this object. He knew that this methodology wasn't the ideal method of performing parallax measurements but it might be good enough to determine if a near-Earth visitor was on the way. The data detailing the exact celestial coordinates would permit Witherspoon's other assets to employ a Doppler radar evaluation to determine size, distance, velocity, rotation, etc.

Witherspoon had ordered one of his operators from Tucson to travel to Siding Spring to assist in taking and analyzing the images and measurements that were needed. He wanted to make sure that no mistakes were made in the process and two minds and two sets of hands would make sure that they got things right.

If indeed the parallax images from Siding Spring revealed information which confirmed a nearby body, then Witherspoon would order his NEO Satellite Control Center to schedule visual band image captures, Doppler radar, and infrared measurements of the object by NEOSADS, the Near Earth Object Survey and Discovery Satellite. Since it was in a geo-stationary, equatorial orbit, it could take images from two points in space that would be nearly 53,000 miles apart every twelve hours which would provide a sufficient parallax angle to determine distance pretty accurately for an object if it was less than 500 million kilometers from Earth. Plus, the data from the Doppler Displacement analysis would confirm and refine the optical parallax conclusions.

Randele was delighted with the plan and replied, "Mike, that's awesome. What can I do to assist?"

Mike replied, "A prayer would certainly help!"

Randele bid Lister good-bye and hung up the phone. He went to his contact list and found Hansen's numbers and tapped the satellite phone number. The phone rang several times as was usual for the satellite phone network but finally Hansen answered. Randele recounted the entire update to Larsen and promised to keep him updated by sharing any new information he received.

Dan L. King

SIDING SPRING, 13 JUNE

Responding to the late night request from his boss and head of the Astronomy and Astrophysics School, Pete Martin had arisen early for his trip to the Siding Spring Observatory. Martin was ANU's senior astronomer and, until the bush fires of 2003, had headed up the research telescope work at the Mount Stromlo Observatory near the ANU campus. Since then, Martin had headed up the research and analysis of data captured by the robotic and manned telescopes located at the Siding Spring site.

Martin parked his car in front of "The Lodge", the visiting researcher's residence adjacent to the Siding Spring Observatory dome, at around 19:30 after his nearly fifteen hour drive up from his home just off of Boldrewood Street in the outskirts of Canberra. Normally the 570 kilometer trip would not take so long but rain had fallen for most of the trip snarling traffic and causing an accident involving a double road train and a passenger car on Mitchell Highway. That accident had him parked for over two hours. By the time he passed through Gowang he could see that the fog had settled over the mountains which would make for very slow travel from Coonabarabran to the observatory. Normally the not-quite thirty kilometer trip along Timor Road and then Observatory Road would take less than an hour but when the weather was poor, it was necessary to take it slowly, especially on the narrow and winding Observatory Road.

The long journey had been pretty tiring because of the weather, the truckie accident, and a near-collision with a large adult kangaroo which darted from behind a grove of trees in front of Martin's car and across the road missing the right front fender by less than a meter.

There would be no observing tonight so Martin unloaded his personal and professional equipment into the residence and adjusted the thermostat to his favorite temperature. He also unloaded what he guessed would be about a week's worth of groceries that he had purchased on his way out of Canberra.

His first action was to call his boss to report his arrival and to inform him that the weather would likely not permit any observation work tonight. He told his boss that he would set an alarm clock for 03:00 and he would check to see if the fog had cleared. If the weather had improved, he would go to work and start his photography and measurement mission.

Martin then heated one of the meat pies that his wife had packed for him and stored the others in the fridge. After consuming the heated pie, married with a bottle of St Arnou Pilsner, he crashed on the still-made single bed in the room nearest the kitchen.

14 JUNE

Martin had awakened at 03:00 to find that the cloud over the mountain was even denser than it had been when he had arrived the night before. This time, he undressed and crawled between the sheets to complete his sleep.

***

While Martin slept, Jimmy Claxton was trying to get some rest in his economy seat on the mostly packed Qantas jumbo-jet. Claxton had caught a SkyWest Airlines flight in Tucson at about 17:00 and had flown to Phoenix where he had a one hour layover until he boarded the US Airways flight that would land at LAX a little after 20:00. After his two hour layover at LAX, he had boarded the Qantas wide-body plane that was scheduled to land in Sydney at 06:10 the next morning. In Sydney he would clear customs and catch another Qantas flight from Sydney to Dubbo City Regional Airport. Dubbo Airport was the closest to the Siding Spring Observatory that still provided commercial passenger service.

Claxton was Bradley Witherspoon's best operator; he could do everything and rarely made a mental or physical mistake. He was a quick study on everything; he could enter an unfamiliar observatory and be up to speed in an hour or less. Claxton was originally from San Antonio and had grown up on a cattle ranch. He still had a lot of cowboy in him after all the intervening years. He still dressed in blue jeans and shirts that had little arrowheads at each end of the pocket openings and whenever outside he was always covered by a well-worn Stetson.

Claxton had gotten a copy of all the images and information that Captain Hansen had sent and he had carefully studied them. He knew that this mission was an important one because of the apparent path the foreign object was taking, a path that would likely be near-Earth if not terminating on Earth.

***

The flight to Sydney and then his connection to Dubbo had completed without any difficulties. The small QantasLink plane made its approach from the northeast under clearing skies and made a perfect landing on Runway Two-Three. The plane easily departed the landing pavement about two-thirds of the way down the 1,700 meter long strip. The plane came to a gentle stop on the painted cross designated for it and the turbines began their spin-down just after 09:00. The ground crew went into action unloading luggage and freight while the passengers patiently followed the leader to the terminal building.

Claxton recovered his luggage and navigated his way to the rental car storefronts. He was surprised to find that he could choose from five different rental agencies. He made his choice and checked out a mid-size car from the attractive Hertz agent. After savoring that last beautiful smile from the clerk, he rolled his luggage out the door and found his car in the parking lot. After loading his gear into the "boot", he gingerly exited the parking lot with his first-ever left turn while driving on the right-hand side of a car. His next maneuver would be the left turn onto Highway 32, locally called Mitchell Highway. He then drove four kilometers in a virtually straight line until he came to the large roundabout that joined Mitchell Highway with Highway 39, also known as Newell Highway. He turned left at the first exit of the roundabout initially headed north. He followed the road as it made a gradual turn to the east into the center of Dubbo. Newell Highway made another left hand turn between the Caltex petrol station and the Honda motorcycle store. This turn was the one that permitted Claxton to escape Dubbo and head north across country toward his destination at Siding Spring.

As he left Dubbo and headed north on the two-lane road, he passed a sign that gave the distance to Gilgandra and a sign that read:

-RESTRICTED-
ROAD TRAIN
ROUTE
DRIVERS
CHECK

Dan L. King

YOUR PERMIT

Fortunately the sign had a drawing of a road train which appeared to be a semi-type tractor pulling two trailers in tandem. Claxton would have had no clue what a road train might be if there had been no drawing of one on the sign.

Claxton got to make his first right turn in Gilgandra as the Newell Highway turned southeast. Then after a couple of bends, the highway resumed its generally northeast direction. Claxton was making good time as the weather was good and traffic was moving at or above the eighty kilometer per hour posting. The scenery along the entire route from Dubbo to Coonabarabran was almost exclusively farmland with an infrequent collection of agricultural businesses thrown in. By the time he arrived in Coonabarabran he had grown hungry again and he began to look for a place to grab a meal. As he approached what appeared to be the center of town, he spied The Lunch Box which displayed a sign that read "Eat in or take away." He stopped in front of the little diner and backed into the only empty space on the curb. He went in, scanned the menu and ordered a chicken snitzel burger and a chocolate milk shake which were served by a lady that possessed a permanent smile.

After the meal he continued down John Street another hundred meters or so until he took a left turn at the clock tower in the middle of the roundabout that joins Newell Highway and Dalgarno Street. The road sign also pointed out that this was the direction to Warrumbungle National Park and that it was a Tourist Drive. Claxton drove two blocks and then turned right onto Namoi Street just before the sign that announced that the distance to the Siding Spring Observatory was twenty-six kilometers. Three blocks later he turned left onto Eden Street which would become Timor Road and would lead to Observatory Drive and the Observatory.

Claxton arrived at the Observatory around 13:00 and parked in front of the Visitor Centre which had two other vehicles parked there. He began looking for someone who could help him connect with Pete Martin.

ASTRONOMERS MEET

The elderly woman volunteer behind the small counter in the Visitor Centre gave Claxton instructions on how to get to "The Lodge" where she said he could find Martin.

Claxton did as directed and parked his rental car beside the experienced Land Rover Defender parked in front of The Lodge. He walked to the veranda and used his knuckle to announce his arrival. In only a few seconds he heard the footsteps as they approached the door and opened it. Martin shared a large smile, shook Claxton's hand and said, "G'day Jimmy; been expectin' ya. I'm Pete Martin. Come on in mate." Martin led Claxton to the dinette table in the kitchen where his papers and MacBook were sprawled across the surface of the smallish table and two of the chairs adjacent to the one where Martin had been sitting. There was a less-than-half-full cup of coffee on the left side of the notebook Mac.

Martin reminded Claxton of the cowhands that he had grown up with when he was a kid on the ranch. Martin had a two-day old scruffy beard and was dressed in jeans and plaids. Claxton thought to himself, "I wonder if this guy ever lived in Texas?"

Martin grabbed the ragged stack of papers in the chair to the right of his and moved them to the chair on the other side of the table and instructed, "'ave a seat, Jimmy. Can I pour ya a Long Black?"

Claxton assumed that a Long Black was some variant of coffee but didn't want to experiment. It was already after noon and he never drank coffee after his double taken at breakfast so, in his slow Texas drawl, he replied, "No thanks Pete, I'm good." Claxton took a seat in the chair that Martin had cleared.

Dan L. King

"So mate, it looks like we got ourselves a bit of a puzzle to solve doesn't it. I've studied the file I was sent and this object appears to be 'eaded straight at us! I just got 'ere last night and the fog 'ad settled so I couldn't do any work before your arrival. Looks like the air is clearing so maybe tonight we can get a spy on this rock."

"Yeah, Pete, all indications are that this thing is gonna come real close to us. I'm really anxious to get a look at it through good glass and take some measurements to determine what it has in mind."

"Me too Jimmy. This mornin' I made sure that all the equipment we'll need is ready to go. If'n we can get a coupla hours of clear air we should be able to take visuals, spectrals, and angles. By mornin', we should know a lot more about this rock, maybe even 'ow far out it is if'n we can get a respectable angle. 'ey mate; did ya 'ave a chance to grab some tucker on your trip? I've got some sammie makin's in the fridge if'n you're hungry."

Claxton was clueless to what Pete was talking about until the last three words. "Thanks for the offer Pete but I ate just before I came up the mountain. I stopped at a little place in Coonabarabran called The Lunch Box and grabbed a sandwich and shake."

Martin commented, "Yeah, I know the place; they make some mighty righteous tucker in there. Jimmy, sunset arrives at 17:08 and the Moon rises at 20:22 tonight. It's gonna be a bright one too, with nearly ninety percent of the Moon's visible disk illuminated. Anyway, we 'ave about three hours before the end of civil twilight. Why don't ya unload your stuff and get settled in? I'm in that first room on the right; you can pick any other for yourself. Do ya need any 'elp with your gear?"

"OK, I'll go get my stuff. Thanks, but I don't need any help so you can get back to work if you need to."

Claxton went back to his rental car and grabbed his backpack and his Stetson, and then towed his large rolling duffle to the first sleeping room on the left of the hallway. He parked the duffle under the window, placed his hat on the pillow, and recovered his laptop from the backpack and carried it back into the kitchen. "Hey Pete, do you guys have Wi-Fi here in the cabin or do we plug in somewhere?"

"We 'ave both, actually. Wi-Fi is pretty good for every day, low bandwidth stuff but for 'eavy-duty data we have a wired LAN that will give you really good throughput. Every room has two LAN ports and 'ere in the kitchen we 'ave a terabit switch with eight ports so a gaggle of us can plug in and share. The room turns into an obstacle course if'n ya get four or five of us star geeks all wired in at the same time…wires are all over the place." They laughed.

"Jimmy, the security boss is satisfied if'n you give it our secret code, SSOO1234#. 'cept it isn't much of a secret 'cause somebody took a

Hansen's Rock

marker and wrote the secret code on the fridge door." They laughed again.

Claxton's notebook searched for wireless networks and found one called Siding. He selected that signal, entered the password, and connected. Upon connection, Claxton checked for mail to see if he had anything urgent from back home. He knew that his phone should have pinged him if it had received any flagged messages from the states, but he wanted to double check. He opened his email client, checked for messages and began catching up after his long trip. He handled a couple of leftover messages. With nothing urgent in his inbox, he right clicked on it and selected "Mark all as read" to clear the bold face from the rest of the messages.

Claxton and Martin discussed what they would do when darkness fell. They decided that as soon after dark as reasonable, they would take some images of the object and study it to see what they could learn about it. Then they discussed what they would do with the data they measured. Martin got up and walked to the large whiteboard that adorned one entire wall of the combination kitchen and day room. He picked up a marker with a long string attached to it and started to draw. At the bottom of the board he drew a large circle to represent Earth and at the top of the board he placed a tiny circle to represent the space object. He then drew a chord through the Earth between the fifteen degree intersects referenced to the line depicting the diameter. He then drew tangents from the space rock to the chord intersects with Earth's surface. He labeled the angles and entered the distances that were known. He pointed at the various elements of the drawing as he explained.

They agreed that they should take angles over a ten hour period. At the latitude of the observatory, the diameter of Earth was 10,899 kilometers. During a ten hour period, they would cover 150 degrees of Earth's rotation and the ten hour chord through Earth from the two extreme observation points would be 10,528 kilometers. So, a ten hour start-to-stop period would permit them to take observations that transit 96.593 percent of Earth's diameter at their latitude, the percentage equivalent of the Cosine of the fifteen degrees that would remain on each end of Earth's rotation. They agreed that they should take the dark hours and center their ten hour period in the middle of night's duration. Sunset on this date was at 17:08 and sunrise tomorrow would be at exactly 07:00. So, they would take their first set of angles at exactly 19:04 and their last set of angles at exactly 05:04 the following morning. They also decided to take angles at four minutes past midnight, precisely in the middle of the two extreme observations. These three measurements would form the most important sets of data for them as they tried to determine distance and speed if the object was close enough for them to get decent angles. If they could get good angles at both end points of the ten hour period, then they should be able to calculate how far away the object was at both points and therefore determine how far the rock traveled during the ten hour period. From that number, they could calculate the average radial velocity component of the object over the ten hour period. To get the final angles that they would use for distance calculations, they would need to take their azimuth readings and add them to the seventy-five degree tangent-chord angle since their viewing would be done from the tangent.

They were excited because with their planned approach, they would be able to perform the first distance calculation immediately after they had taken the first azimuth angle. And they could use the two endpoint elevation angles to determine how much directional drift they were able to see. If they could get two good elevation angles, they could use d_1 and d_2 and some basic trigonometry to get a preliminary heading for the rock. The images from Captain Hansen showed that the rock appeared to be drifting to the south but they agreed that might be because Hansen's images were taken at a variety of latitudes.

At the end of their discussion, Martin summarized, "This is all pretty crude at best but if the air stays clear tonight, and it's supposed to, we should be able to describe this rock and its rough distance, closing velocity, and direction. We are in for an exciting night, Jimmy!"

***

Martin and Claxton went back to other work and sporadically talked about their plan as some insight came to them until the Sun began to slide toward the horizon. Shortly after 17:00, Pete said, "Jimmy, I know it's still early but I suggest we take some tucker now because we will likely be real busy from the time the sky gets dark until after we capture our first angles and do our calculations."

Claxton replied, "OK, a snack would help but I didn't even think to buy food on my way up here today. Qantas gave me a couple of bags of snacks on the flight over the pond that I thought would keep me from starving but then when I got off the plane, I was told that I would have to declare it for inspection or toss it. Not wanting to go through any grief, I just threw it in the disposal bins. What's up with that?"

"Yeah, Aussie customs is real strict about food items being brought into the country; they're picky about a bunch of other stuff too. It probably would 'ave been a real 'assle to declare your peanuts so I don't blame ya for takin' the easy path. I've got plenty of food and you're welcomed to eat your fill if ya can find something ya like."

"Thanks Pete; tomorrow I'll head back to Coonabarabran and get some supplies."

Martin and Claxton chatted while Martin ate another of his wife's meat pies and Claxton ate a sandwich made from a freshly opened hundred gram package of roasted, shaved, honey ham.

By the time they had finished their brief meal and had gotten the kitchen cleaned up the Sun had set and real darkness was only minutes away. Martin cleaned up the rest of his papers and stowed them in his sleeping room while Claxton brushed his teeth. They made the obligatory visits to the toilet closet in preparation for a busy night of rock hunting. Martin grabbed his big leather book satchel with the long cross-body strap and stuffed it with his fully charged MacBook and a paper tablet while Claxton made sure that his backpack had all the necessary contents before they exited The Lodge and headed toward the observatory silo.

SEEING IS BELIEVING

After unlocking the door to the silo and entering, Martin hit the safelight switch and the room adopted the usual muted red glow along its perimeter. He locked the door from the inside to make sure that they weren't interrupted during their work. It wasn't likely that anyone would try to enter the observatory but vandals had, on occasion, hiked through the Warrumbungle to attempt mischief on the mountain. There was some speculation that vandals had caused the bush fire of 2013 that destroyed three buildings on the property, including The Lodge...but that was never proven. Anyway, Martin always played it safe.

As civil twilight was expiring, Martin hit the button to open the viewing door of the silo and punched the proper celestial coordinates of Sigma Octantis into the computer that drove the equatorial mount for the Anglo-Australian Telescope (AAT). They knew that the object should still be in the vicinity of σOct so they would start there and then they would find the new object.

***

The AAT was a 3.9 meter reflector telescope that saw first light in 1974. It was a Cassegrain design and had a focal length of 12.7 meters. It was the largest telescope in Australia and was one of the top thirty largest reflectors in the world. Typically, this telescope had been paired with a wideband spectroscope and had been used for wide field surveys.

***

Only a couple of minutes elapsed before the gears of the equatorial mount slowed to a nearly silent operation that would hold the selected celestial coordinates in the center of the viewing area as the Earth rotated. Martin had adjusted the focal length of the receiver element to a longer distance so as to cover a larger field of view. In the center of the image displayed on the primary monitor was Sigma Octantis but there was no strange object in the two degree field of view. Martin took manual control of the mount motors and manually slewed AAT due south since that had been the travel direction indicated in Hansen's images. After slewing the telescope south another thirty seconds of elevation, the unmistakable foreign object entered the bottom of the monitor. Martin continued the manual adjustment until the object was centered on the screen.

Claxton noted that the Visual Apparent Magnitude of Hansen's Rock was now 4.73. He shortened the focal length of the receiver element in order to get a closer look at the space rock. As he reduced the receiver element focal length by half, the object grew larger and its brilliance on the monitor decreased as expected. They decided that the chosen focal length was good enough for the work that they planned to do.

They noted that the rock appeared smooth and a bit oval-shaped, not like the typical asteroid which would be irregular in shape. And, the light reflection from this rock was really bright unlike a typical darker surfaced asteroid. There was no tail or corona so it didn't seem to be comet-like. The edges of the object's image were very well defined which they agreed probably indicated that the surface was solid, not gaseous. They opined that the very light-colored surface could mean that it was covered in some kind of frozen substance that could explain the white surface and the superior light reflection.

They agreed that it didn't seem that the object was going to be big enough to be an escaped planet. They speculated that it could be some sort of ice dwarf but finally decided that they just couldn't tell what it might be. Then they discussed the possibility that the object might be spinning fast enough to make it appear to be round or spherical from this distance. They decided to make an Echelle Spectrograph run to see what it might tell them about Hansen's Rock. They were skeptical about how much they would learn about the rock because so much of the light from the object would be reflected light due to the high albedo of the rock. But they were hopeful that the lines might tell them more than the optical CCD images would tell them.

The astronomers watched the object on the monitor as they prepared for the first set of parallax measurements and reviewed what they would do. Each man would separately observe and record the measurements to make sure that the 19:04 observation would be high quality. They would repeat the procedure for the 00:04 and 05:04 observations. Each man would independently perform the trigonometric calculations that would help them to determine the distance of Hansen's Rock from Siding Spring.

Just before 17:04 Martin illuminated the simple reticle feature on the monitor and adjusted the equipment so that the cross hairs were centered on the object. As the last few seconds ticked down to the scheduled observation time, Martin counted, "Five, four, three, two, one, and mark." Each man recorded the azimuth and elevation readings.

Claxton drawled, "Azimuth is 14° 54′ 53.6796″ East of reference tangent plane; elevation is 28° 0′ 49.0356″; date is 14 June; time is 19:04:00 local; observation location coordinates are 31° 16′ 23.9988″ South by 149° 3′ 51.9984″ East."

Martin acknowledged, "Roger all numbers, mate; now let's take the perimeter measurements." Claxton adjusted the equipment so that the reticle cross hairs moved to the northernmost edge along the object's vertical centerline and the two men recorded more data. Then more adjustments moved the reticle cross hairs to the southernmost edge and more data was recorded. They repeated the process for the easternmost and westernmost points along the horizontal centerline.

When all the data were recorded and confirmed by both observers, Martin instructed, "OK Jimmy, now for the fun part; let's do the math."

Both men began the trigonometric calculations that would produce the first distance and size measurements for Hansen's Rock. They approached this work very methodically, double checking each step in the process. After several minutes, Martin looked up and watched Claxton for about fifteen seconds until he too looked up to signal his completion. Martin spoke first, "OK, Jimmy let's 'ear what ya got."

Claxton drawled, "My math indicates the object to be 3,552,768 kilometers distant; the size of the object calculates to be 16.136 kilometers across and 15.205 kilometers in height. As we could see in the monitor, it is very slightly elliptical in shape. Pete, it is a civilization killer!"

"Yeah Jimmy, 'ansen's Rock is a big boy. My math confirms all your answers. So, the morning measurement is terribly important as that data will permit us to determine the average velocity of 'ansen's Rock and maybe even an indication of its direction of travel. Based on the images that Captain 'ansen took last week, we can confirm that the object is 'eaded in a direction to the south of us but we don't yet 'ave enough information to determine 'ow close it might come to Earth. Let's pray that the air is clear for the morning measurements."

"Right on Pete, so maybe we can run the spectrograph now and see what the lines tell us."

"OK, let's get it set up for the run."

The men went through the adjustments of convergence, slit width, grating angle, etc. to prepare the equipment to record the spectral data[e]. Once ready, they ran a sixty second exposure and saved the data to the primary computer. They opened the image so it would display on the monitor and began to analyze the results.

As they had speculated, the lines told them that the light from Hansen's Rock was reflected light due to the very high albedo so the spectral lines looked very much like our very own star. However, they did see a blue shift which confirmed that the rock was moving toward Earth and there was pretty severe smearing of the lines indicating a rapid rotation of the rock[f]. That smearing meant that any attempt to determine radial velocity of the rock from the spectral data would likely produce inaccurate results so it probably wasn't worth going to the effort of trying to measure the shift and calculate velocity. They decided that they would need a radar probe of Hansen's Rock to find out what it was really like inside. They decided that Claxton would need to get his boss to petition NASA to get the NEOSADS satellite repositioned for a look at the object if their optical evaluations indicated that it might be a threat. They would make that decision after they had completed their morning data capture when they would attempt to determine average radial velocity and direction.

"OK Jimmy; so, let's take a break while we wait for midnight."

"Yeah, I'm beginning to feel the pressure too."

They closed the observation door to the silo to protect the equipment. The two men grabbed red-lensed flashlights from the bin by the door and locked the access door behind them as they navigated back to The Lodge. The time was 21:30 and the Moon had risen less than a half hour ago so it was low in the east but was over eighty percent disc. By the time they finished their break and returned to the dome in a couple of hours, they wouldn't need flashlights to see the way.

15 JUNE

The scientists had returned to the silo just before midnight and had performed the 00:04 measurements which were focused on measuring and recording an accurate set of celestial coordinates[g] for Hansen's Rock that they would reference as the 15 June location. They recorded: Right Ascension: 21h 08m 50.16s; Declination: -89° 06′ 24.97″; Date: 15 June; Time: 00:04 Local; Observation Location: 31° 16′ 23.9988″ S / 149° 3′ 51.9984″ E. After that, they again walked back to The Lodge. They set alarms to awaken them at 04:15. They napped on their bunks until their trusty phones jolted them to movement. Claxton made a quick pot of coffee and each man gulped the hot brew and ate a pastry before heading back to the observatory for the 05:04 measurements.

***

"Here we go again Pete. I have to tell ya, I'm pretty nervous about what we will know in less than half an hour," Claxton slowly confessed.

"Yeah, me too Jimmy; I'm worried we might just discover what we don't want to think about."

The two men followed the same exact procedure that they had followed the preceding evening and performed the calculations independently, finishing them at around 05:25.

When both had finished their math, Claxton asked, "What are your numbers Pete?"

"I got the current distance at 3,523,968 kilometers. The width of the object is about the same as earlier at 16.139 kilometers and the height calculates at 15.151 kilometers. The elevation reading is two seconds further south than last night and the direction of travel is due south. It's 'ard to get an accurate potential path with such small changes at such great distances but it would appear that HR could be making a pretty close flyby of Earth. Without more data, I can't figure out what Earth's gravitational pull might do to this rock. But, it seems that this rock might get real close to us Jimmy. I suspect that the reason HR seems to be getting a little flatter is a result of its travel to the south giving us a tiny bit more of a view from the side than before. Whatcha think Jimmy?"

"My numbers calculate to the same as yours so your math is right on, as I would expect. You didn't mention radial velocity but I calculated the component of velocity that is directly toward Earth to be 2,880 kilometers per hour. HR closed on us at an average rate of exactly 800 meters per second last night based on the delta of the two distance calculations averaged over the ten hours of elapsed time. With only one measurement of travel it's hard to calculate the actual speed of the rock this morning but I'm pretty sure that it could be over a kilometer per second. We need estimated mass info on the rock before we can run the gravitational exponential on the path to determine how long and how close. But, I agree with your conclusion that Hansen's Rock will get dangerously close to Earth in just a few weeks. So, we really need that satellite data to determine what our future looks like, if we have one that is."

"Yeah Jimmy, I agree. Let's button up things 'ere and 'ead back to The Lodge to make our calls."

They closed up the dome, powered down those items that could sleep, locked the door to the silo, and headed back to the dormitory around 05:45. When they got to The Lodge Claxton went to his sleeping room and Martin went to the day room to prepare their reports to their bosses. When Claxton got to his bunk, he energized his notebook computer, opened Microsoft Word, and prepared his report in bullet format.

***

Bradley Witherspoon's phone rang at a couple of minutes after 11:00 a.m., "Hello, this is Brad."

"Brad this is Jimmy Claxton; I hope you're well today."

"I'm doin' fine today Jimmy; what did you guys learn last night?"

Claxton explained that the news was not good. He gave his readout of their calculations to Witherspoon by reading through the bullets that he had recorded before the call:

The distance to Hansen's Rock was a little over 3.5 million kilometers from Earth.

The rock had closed on Earth at an average velocity of about 800 meters per second during the ten hour measurement interval.

The rock had traveled about two seconds directly south over the ten hour period.

The rock's dimensions were a little over sixteen kilometers wide and about fifteen kilometers high.

The object was spinning fast enough to create a really smeared spectrum.

The spectrum was blue-shifted which confirmed that the rock was moving toward Earth.

The object had a very high albedo so most of the light that was seen was reflected light, which hid the true information about the object. He reported that they believed that the object may be covered by some sort of ice or snow which might explain the very bright surface.

The edges of the object were very distinct so they suspected that the edges were hard, not gaseous.

The best estimate that they could make of its potential path, given the limited data, caused them to believe that the rock would come dangerously close to Earth.

In order to calculate the potential path and arrival timing, they needed good data on the mass of the object to perform gravitational influence runs.

He and Martin believed that they needed to get NASA to point NEOSADS toward Hansen's Rock and perform a complete set of surveys.

They needed the results of the radar survey to determine makeup and consequently the mass of the rock.

They needed confirmation of size and speed which the satellite Doppler equipment could give them.

The satellite surveys needed to be completed ASAP.

Witherspoon reacted, "Wow Jimmy; that's not good news at all. That rock is huge; it's at least fifty percent larger than estimates of the rock that wiped out the dinosaurs. The mass could be several times larger. OK, Jimmy I'll be on the horn to NASA NEO Headquarters as soon as we hang up here. Do you need anything else from us here?"

"I don't think there is anything else we need here except for some good data to help determine what this rock is going to do."

"OK Jimmy, plan on continuing to make your optical studies and give me a daily report. It may take a couple of days for us to get NEOSADS re-oriented, get the surveys taken, and download the data for analysis. I promise to keep you informed promptly as we develop new data."

"Thanks Brad. I'll email you my written report and attach some photos as soon as we hang up."

***

Claxton hung up; Witherspoon depressed the switch hook and dialed the number for Michael Williams, the head of the NASA NEO Satellite Control Center. Williams answered on the second ring.

"This is Michael Williams speaking."

"Mike, this is Brad Witherspoon; how are you today?"

"Hi Brad, I'm doin' good. It's hump day and I'm gonna work a short week because my wife and I are headed to London to catch a week-long cruise of northern Europe. We leave late tomorrow so I'm trying to get everything cleaned up here at the office. What's up with you?"

"Mike, I need your help..."

Witherspoon recounted the data that had been collected about the space object from the notes he had made from Claxton's report.

"So, I need for you to arrange for a full complement of surveys from NEOSADS and I think we need to get it done ASAP because we believe that the rock may be headed to a near-Earth passing or worse. When do you think we can get the satellite positioned to take a look at this object?"

"You just took the joy out of my day Brad. That is a mighty big rock! NEOSADS is in the middle of trying to find and map what we believe to be the last few hundred asteroids that are fifty to one hundred meters in size. Based on what you are telling me, this rock of yours will take priority over anything we are currently doing. Since it is currently oriented to count rocks in the asteroid belt it could be as much as ninety degrees away from the object that you described so it will take us a little time to re-orient the bird but I should be able to have it take its first look by tomorrow about this time of day. Get your boys to e-mail me the celestial coordinates of the object and I will get them programmed for upload to the bird's control module for the electric positioning thrusters. Once we have a stable attitude, we will make the Doppler radar survey first and we will also do optical scans in visible and infrared and then we'll make spectroscopic images. I'll give you a call tomorrow to let you know how things are progressing." Mike paused to see if Witherspoon had more to say.

"That sounds good Mike. I sure appreciate your prompt action on this one; I have a bad feeling about this rock. I'll have Jimmy Claxton, my man in Australia, email you the coordinates on the rock within the hour. By the way, who will be in charge during your absence in the event that we need more help?" Witherspoon asked.

"Elizabeth Wilson will be sitting in my chair until I return. She is very capable and I will discuss the importance of this mission with her to make sure that you get whatever help you need. She will personally oversee our analyses of the data which, as always, will be completed before we send you the raw numbers and our conclusions. Is there anything else I can do for you today?" Mike paused after that hint to end the call.

"Nope Mike; you have given me everything I wanted. You have a great vacation and say hello to Midge for me."

"Will do Brad; talk to you tomorrow." Williams hung up the phone. As soon as the phone was in its place, he walked from his office to Wilson's office where she was reading a report that had been submitted for her signature. He closed the door behind him as he entered and sat in the chair across from her desk. He recounted his discussion with Witherspoon and instructed her to get NEOSADS repositioned and to execute a full complement of surveys on the object. He told her that he would have coordinates on the object within the hour and would email them to her as soon as he got them.

***

As soon as he hung up with Williams, Witherspoon called Claxton and told him of his discussion and asked him to send the celestial coordinates of the rock to mwilliams@nasa-neo-scc.gov. He explained that it would take at least twenty-four hours to reorient the bird and stabilize its attitude. Then the surveys would be undertaken. He promised to send Claxton a copy of the data as soon as it was available.

Claxton immediately sent the celestial coordinates of Hansen's Rock to Williams and walked back to the day room to inform Martin of the plan. Martin was on the phone with his wife who was having a bit of a problem with their teenage son who had awakened and decided that he just wasn't going to go to school today. Martin held up one finger to indicate to Claxton that he should stand by until Martin could get finished with the call. After talking directly to his son with some stern words, Martin hung up the phone and explained, "Sometimes one o' the best things in my life can be a real pain in the arse. My boy is goin' through a rough patch. Seems some of the kids at school are goin' out of their way to rub on my boy about 'is cherub-like appearance. 'e 'ates it and would avoid it if 'e could. 'e really is one good looking kid and 'e needs to 'ear that message from someone as often as the kids at school call 'im "baby face". Anyway, what did your boss have to say?"

Claxton explained the plan to Martin who was impressed that Claxton's boss could pull such long strings in less than an hour.

"Wow; now that's service!"

They discussed the surveys a bit and concluded that it would likely be at least two days before they got any information. And, if the NASA scientists made two surveys as a part of their validation methodology, they speculated that it could be as much as three days before they saw a report. They decided that they would just continue making their measurements and see if they could start adding points on the curve that the rock would follow. They concluded that they might be able to calculate a pretty good guesstimate of the path and timing once they got three or four days of data on Hansen's Rock.

Martin said, "I love a contest, Jimmy; so let's just beat them NASA guys to the answer." Martin laughed.

Claxton followed with his own laughter and said, "Ya know Pete, I bet we can come real close with measurements courtesy of that big glass mirror!" He laughed some more.

"Pete, I've got to run to town for some food. Do you want to ride along since we won't have any work to do until dark plus two?"

"Sure Jimmy, I'd love to ride along. I can direct you to the best tucker market in Australia. There's a Coles store down on Dalgarno Street that'll give you a great selection and the best prices you'll find down under."

The two scientists climbed into the rental car and headed down Observatory Road, also called Solar System Drive. In the past, someone had decided that it would be educational to place signs on the drive from the Observatory to Coonabarabran to show the relative distances to and between the planets.

They drove a little over a kilometer and came to the Mercury sign just before the big hairpin turn that would lead to the steeper part of the descent, then came the Venus sign, and just before they turned off of Observatory Road onto Timor Rd, they passed the Earth sign. The Mars sign was about halfway along Timor Rd. The Jupiter sign was the last before they entered town and headed to the Coles Store. Saturn and the other planet signs were planted on Newell Highway, south of town. The Pluto sign was in Dubbo, 190 kilometers from the Observatory[h]. Pluto was considered a major planet at the time all the signs had been installed and even after it was decided to declare Pluto a dwarf planet nobody had decided to take the sign down.

They finished their shopping and headed back to The Lodge where they unloaded and stored the food. Then they decided to get some rest before the evening measurements.

NASA NEO SATELLITE CONTROL CENTER

Elizabeth Wilson arrived at the SCC at a little after 5:00 a.m. on 17 June so she could review the findings of the series of surveys that had been taken the day before and overnight by NEOSADS. Her engineers had worked through the night to get the data downloaded and analyzed so they could get the report prepared. When Wilson hit the light switch just inside the door to her office she saw the folder sitting in the middle of her desk with a large red tag on the front of it. She knew that the red tag meant trouble. She read the note while still standing. The tag had been applied by the lead technician and read: "Liz, I have scheduled a PSC for 9:00 a.m. so you can lead a review of this report with our team. I will have all the Technology Squad Leaders in attendance. This so-called Hansen's Rock is going to be a real problem! I also usurped your classification authority and have marked this material and all the data related to it as Top Secret. I personally counseled every one of our team on this classification and stressed that they were not to discuss any part of our findings or conclusions with anyone. See you at 9:00. Jerry"

Wilson grabbed a yellow highlighter from the large mug that she had received at the opening ceremony for the NEO SCC. She would use the highlighter to mark the items that she would want to discuss at the Post-Survey Conference that Jerry had scheduled. She took a sip of the black coffee that she had picked up from the Dunkin Donut drive-through just up the street from the center. The file folder was titled "Hansen's Rock Multi-Technology Survey Report" and had a big red ink "Top Secret" stamped across the title. She opened the folder and began to study the report. The first page was a summary of key technical data. That page was followed by over a dozen pages that provided the engineers' analyses of the various data.

Dan L. King

She could see that this first set of data from the initial surveys had raised more questions than it had answered. Some of the information was simply unbelievable. The summary page for the initial surveys taken on 16 June revealed:

Equatorial Diameter: 17.05 km
Polar Diameter: 13.62 km
Structure: mixed metal core; diameter at equator = 13.21 km; pole to pole diameter = 10.93 km; frozen surface layer depth = 1.89 km at equator to 1.35 km at poles
Rotational Period: 30.05 s; Rotational Speed: 1.997 rpm
Surface Albedo: 0.97
Surface Temperature: 3.7 Kelvin [VALIDATION REQUIRED]
Magnetic Field: Dipolar; strength: 2.71×10^{-5} Tesla [VALIDATION REQUIRED]
Core Composition: 61% unknown ferrite isotope; 39% unknown neodymium isotope.
Surface Composition: solid form of unknown hydrogen isotope.
Distance From Earth: 3.454771×10^6 km
Radial Velocity: 801 m/s
Central core volume: 998.67787 km^3;
Mass $_{\text{metallic core}}$: 7.527075×10^{15} kg
Frozen surface volume: 1071.4030 km^3;
Mass $_{\text{solid hydrogen isotope}}$: 9.214066×10^{13} kg
Total Object Mass: 7.619216×10^{15} kg
Projected Maximum Proximity (MP): 968 km; Confidence Limits ±2.763817×10^5 km
Probability of Impact with Earth: 2.300% [VALIDATION REQUIRED]
Projected Time To MP: 27d 14h 4m 7s from 00:00 PDT, 17 July [VALIDATION REQUIRED]
Projected Object Velocity @ MP if impact: 15,998 m/s
Projected Kinetic Energy @ MP if impact: 1.9246×10^{21} KJ

Wilson set the Summary Page to the side so she could reference it as she read the analyses pages. She highlighted the following items from the report:

"The object shape is that of an oblate spheroid; it is shaped something like a Rugby ball. It has an equatorial diameter of approximately 17.0 km and a polar diameter of approximately 13.6 km. The perspective from Earth is along the polar axis with the rock's north magnetic pole facing Earth. The object appears to be a round disc because of its relatively fast rotational speed.

"Surface albedo is 0.97, one of the highest we have ever measured; the surface is significantly more reflective than clean, fresh snow."

"Surface Temperature is calculated at 3.7K using the results from the thermal emissions survey and applying the applicable laws of physics. The Maximum Intensity Wavelength is 783.1816 MICRONS (The engineer had capitalized the unit micron to emphasize that it was not a mistake; typically when the thermal emissions team measured maximum intensity wavelengths for bodies in space the unit was nanometers.)

"The body has an extraordinarily strong magnetic field which is probably the result of the high level of the neodymium-type isotope. Known isotopes of Nd are antiferromagnetic at temperatures near absolute zero but this isotope seems to be immune to that phenomenon. The other conclusion that could be drawn from this data is that the strength of the magnetic field of this object could be thousands of times stronger at higher temperatures where opposing alignments would return to ordered magnetism."

"The volume of this object is calculated to be 2,070 cubic kilometers; the metallic core volume is 999 cubic kilometers and the solid gas surface volume is 1,071 cubic kilometers. The solid core volume is 4.6 times the estimated size of the asteroid that caused the Chicxulub crater and that some speculate caused the extinction of non-avian dinosaurs. If this object were to collide with Earth, our data at this time suggest a release of energy that could be the equivalent of 460 teratons of TNT."

"The surface coating of this object contains 9.21×10^{13} kg of an unknown isotope of hydrogen; this volume of solid hydrogen would create 1.025×10^{18} liters of gaseous hydrogen at atmospheric pressure levels. This is a tremendous amount of hydrogen; it is equivalent to 684 billion times the amount of hydrogen carried in the external tank of the Space Shuttles."

"We estimate that the object may have a Maximum Proximity to Earth of 968 kilometers and that it will occur nearly directly over Earth's south magnetic pole. This calculation used the data point supplied by the optical observation reported from Siding Spring

Dan L. King

Observatory and our first survey measurement along with Doppler Displacement conclusions to determine the probable path of the object. We have assigned this conclusion a ninety percent accuracy probability due to the limited data and the distance of the object from Earth. More data is needed to improve our confidence in the projected path. We need at least two more days of data to improve our confidence to the ninety-five percent level. We do not yet have a handle on how much of an influence on path will be imposed by the tremendous magnetic field around this object; we have more work to do on that. Since the object is expected to arrive in the vicinity of our South Pole and the orientation of the object is that its north pole is facing Earth, there will be an attractive relationship between the two bodies. We have not yet concluded our evaluation of how strong this magnetic attraction will be and its influence on the object's path."

"Time to Maximum Proximity is highly dependent on velocity and magnetic attraction determinations. This projection needs to be updated once sufficient accuracy of the influencing factors has been achieved."

Wilson returned her highlighter to its home in the commemorative cup a little after 8:00 a.m. Her coffee had turned cold and unappealing so she headed to the break room for a cup of freshly brewed coffee. When she got to the break room she saw that about a dozen of the engineers were asleep in various places in the room. She knew that they had worked for most of the night and would need to be available for the 9:00 a.m. meeting if their bosses needed them so they had slept over as they had done many times in the past. She poured the old coffee into the sink, filled the cup with fresh brew, and returned to her office. On the way back she passed Jerry's desk to see that he was sleeping on his copy of the technical survey report.

When 9:00 a.m. came Wilson went to the conference room for the Post-Survey Conference. She had a full complement of Technology Squad Leaders sitting around the table. Jerry sat in the first chair to the right of where Wilson would sit while she conducted the review. The team discussed all the subjects that Wilson had highlighted. Wilson instructed that each person make a backup of all their data to ensure that it was not compromised. She instructed them to perform another complete multi-technology survey of the threatening object. She stressed the importance of making sure that no information relating to this object left the facility. She instituted what she liked to call "the engineer shuffle" which meant that engineers would exchange duties for the second survey and analysis to make sure that one person couldn't make the same error twice. She trusted every one of her team but this was just too important to take any chance that a simple human mistake, for whatever cause, might compromise the quality and accuracy of the findings.

Wilson asked, "So, do we know what this object is?"

Jerry Jones was one of the most educated people in the world. He had two Master's Degrees and two Doctorate Degrees from MIT, one each in Planetary Sciences and Astrophysics. He replied, "No Liz, we don't really know what the object is. But, it has a structure similar to a star. It could be a micro-star, if there is such a thing. The fundamental difference between this object and a star is that this object somehow escaped the ignition of the surface hydrogen."

Wilson mulled, "A micro-star...Hmmm."

The PSC adjourned just before 11:00 a.m.

SURVEYS TWO AND THREE

Wilson conducted the next Post-Survey Conferences with her team at 9:00 a.m. on 18 June and 19 June. The only material changes in the information were object distance to Earth which had declined to 3,245,000 kilometers and radial velocity which had increased to 814 meters per second. The time until Maximum Proximity was projected to be about twenty-five days. The key metric of Maximum Proximity distance had varied slightly and the estimated value was now 948 kilometers with Confidence Limits of ± 64,900 km. The Probability of Impact with Earth was estimated to be 9.8 percent. Only time and more data points would reduce the potential variance to an acceptable level. Until the data and models confirmed that the object would indeed miss the Earth, the operating assumption would need to be that Earth would be impacted.

At the 19 June PSC Wilson instructed her team to continue the surveys at twenty-four hour intervals and to continue the daily reports until further notice. She again emphasized that all data and conclusions must be treated as Top Secret products. She called Mike Williams' personal technical writer into her office after she adjourned the conference.

"Mary, I need for you to take the information that we have so far and turn it into a document that could be made available for public release. Do you understand what I mean?"

Mary had done this before. She knew that she would need to prepare a report that looked official and had sufficient factual information to make it look complete. Sensitive data, like the fact that path predictions were only accurate to within a range of ±65,000 kilometers would not be included but the latest model prediction of a Maximum Proximity of 948 kilometers would be included.

"Sure Liz, I know what you want; I'll have it on your desk before I go home tonight."

Wilson thanked her as Mary rose to leave the office. Wilson then turned to the telephone to call her boss's boss, Brad Witherspoon, the JPL Director. She had called him each day after her PSC to give him the latest information and to make sure that he concurred in her activities and conclusions. So the information today would not come as a surprise to him. She read him the updated information. Witherspoon recognized that after four days of observations and multi-technology surveys that it still appeared that the object posed a very real threat to Earth. He said that he needed to "take the information upstairs", meaning that the time had come for him to inform his leadership up the chain of command. He instructed Liz to send him an encrypted copy of her latest report on the object. He said that he would make an appointment with The Administrator and discuss the problem as soon as possible. He told her to just keep her team focused on this project, to keep the daily reports coming, and he confirmed that he wanted to talk with her daily as the situation unfolded. He asked her to thank everybody in the center for their great dedication and performance.

"OK sir, I'll pass along your appreciation. You should have the encrypted report within a few minutes."

Wilson hung up the phone, encrypted the report, and sent it to Witherspoon over the JPL secure, private WAN.

***

Witherspoon personally called the office of his boss, The Administrator of NASA, Charles Barrow.

"Mr. Barrow's office; this is Emily. How may I assist you?

"Hi Emily, this is Brad Witherspoon; I hope you are well today."

"Hello Mr. Witherspoon. Yes, I am having a great day, thank you. What may I do for you?

"I need a video conference with the boss ASAP."

"Well sir, his calendar is really slammed today but I can work you in at 6:00 p.m. today. Will that work for you?

"Sure Emily, that's just fine. I'll have Kathleen get the connection set up."

"OK, I have you posted. Will anyone else be attending?"

"No Emily, it will just be the two of us."

"OK Mr. Witherspoon, and what may I tell Mr. Barrow about the purpose of this meeting?

Dan L. King

"Emily, please forgive me but the purpose of the meeting is personal in nature.

"OK Mr. Witherspoon; Mr. Barrow will see you at six."

***

Witherspoon's Secretary tapped the door with her knuckle as soon as he had hung up the phone. He waved her in and she delivered the report that Wilson had promised. He advised her that he would be meeting with The Administrator at 6:00 p.m. Eastern Time so she needed to clear his calendar from 2:30 p.m. through the end of the day. He asked her to set up the video conference connection. She said she would handle everything and returned to her desk.

Witherspoon read the entire report and noted the areas that he wanted to be sure to discuss with his boss. He converted all the measurements into American units to make it easier for Barrow and others to conceptualize.

When 3:00 p.m. arrived at JPL Headquarters, Witherspoon was in his conference room with the door closed. Barrow spoke first since he was the boss.

"Good afternoon, Brad; how's that ankle recovering?" That was a reference to the severe sprain that Witherspoon had suffered during a recent attempt to learn to waterski.

Witherspoon answered, "Hi Charlie; I'm almost good as new. Just goes to show that a man can learn his limitations at any age, doesn't it?" They laughed.

Barrow asked, "So what's the purpose of our meeting today? Emily said that you had simply indicated that it involved a personal matter." He opened the box that Emily had ordered to be delivered to the conference room and started removing the paper covering on the club sandwich.

"Yes, I chose not to reveal to Emily the purpose of our meeting. I think you will understand in just a few minutes."

Barrow instructed, "OK, let's hear what you've got on your mind."

Witherspoon began from the beginning and told Barrow that about two weeks ago an amateur astronomer discovered an object in the southern sky near the south polar star. In the beginning the object was covering part of the star causing its visual apparent magnitude to appear too bright. Over the course of a few days when he could observe, the amateur astronomer discovered that there was a new object in the sky. When he saw that the object appeared to be coming directly at Earth rather than tracking across the sky, he sent his images and data to a friend in L. A. to see if others had also noticed this object.

Hansen's Rock

After Hansen's friend did a little checking, he contacted one of Witherspoon's Division Managers who in turn called him. After reviewing the images and data that the amateur sent, Witherspoon explained that he had determined that the object deserved additional attention. He explained that he had sent one of his best astronomers to Siding Spring Observatory in New South Wales, Australia to team with the scientist that Australian National University had sent. They had made optical observations and determined that indeed the object appeared to be headed toward Earth. Their conclusion was that we could have a near-Earth passing and that it appeared that the object was very large. Witherspoon explained that he had then ordered his NEO SCC to re-orient NEOSADS for a complete multi-technology survey of the object. He explained that the center had been surveying the object for three days and the conclusion drawn from the data confirmed that the very large object could make a near-Earth passing.

Witherspoon continued with a review of the data that he had selected to share with The Administrator:

- The object is currently about two million miles from Earth.
- Its current velocity toward Earth is a little over 1,820 miles per hour and the velocity is increasing exponentially.
- The data indicate that this object has some very unusual characteristics:
  - It is almost certainly extra-galactic, probably coming from one of the Octans Constellation galaxies.
  - It is extraordinarily reflective, much more than new snow; it has a layer of solid hydrogen covering its surface that averages about a mile in thickness.
  - It has a surface temperature that is only a few degrees above absolute zero.
  - It has an extraordinarily strong magnetic field, much stronger than anything they could explain.
  - It is rotating fairly quickly so it appears as a disc or sphere when viewed optically but Doppler radar reveals that it is an oblate spheroid with its equator perpendicular to its path and with its north pole facing Earth.
- Their prediction of its path brings it to a near-Earth position in about twenty-five days. The current projected centerline of the object's path has it passing Earth about 625 miles above the magnetic south pole of Earth. But, that prediction currently has confidence limits of ± 40,000 miles. They

Dan L. King

currently calculate the probability of collision with Earth to be 9.8 percent.

- Lastly, the object is nearly eleven miles across at its equator and about eight and one-half miles along the pole-to-pole diameter. It was much larger than the meteorite that cratered in Mexico and had often been credited with killing the dinosaurs. An impact of this object with Earth would be an Extinction Level Event.

Witherspoon closed his briefing with, "That is the short story, sir; I will have an encrypted copy of the latest technical paper with the survey results, conclusions, and commentary sent to you over our private secure network. We have classified this material as Top Secret."

Barrow had been silent until now, "Damn, that is a huge rock!"

Witherspoon replied simply, "Yes sir."

"The description that you gave makes this object sound like something we've never discovered or encountered before. Is that right?"

"Yes sir you are correct; we have never come upon anything like this rock before. We are working around the clock to refine our data and to incorporate the unusual magnetic influence into our projection models. We aren't yet sure how much influence this unbelievable magnetic field will have on the rock's path. Since the rock's orientation is north-pole-first and its projected passing is over our South Pole there will be a very strong attractive relationship between the rock and Earth."

Barrow had stopped eating as soon as he had heard the dimensions of the object, "Brad, as you already know, this is very serious. What do you recommend as a course of action?"

"Sir, I have tried to determine if any of our technological defense alternatives could be employed against this object. As you know, most deflection techniques require a great amount of time to accomplish a successful deflection. I don't believe indirect methods like gravity tractors can be successful with an object of this size and with such a short amount of time to effect the deflection or delay. I see no way that we could launch a mission to place thrusters on the object and deflect or delay it given the amount of time we have. I have concluded that fragmentation would be the only possible defense given the amount of time we have before potential impact. However, an object of this size would require an enormous amount of fire power to successfully fragment. It will likely require multiple explosive devices and precision delivery and detonation. I believe defense by fragmentation could create many fragments that would be large enough to survive atmospheric entry. These large meteorites could create localized extinction and probably severe, potentially broadly propagated events such as tsunamis, earthquakes, and so forth. Clearly localized extinction is preferable to planet extinction but it will be a very difficult strategy to implement successfully. However, I recommend that we prepare a fragmentation strategy and ready all necessary, or at least all available, resources. I must continue to remind myself that as of today our analysis indicates a ten percent chance of impact; that means that we have a ninety percent chance that the object will pass without impact. I need to point out that as long as Earth remains totally inside of the cone of potential paths, the probability of an impact will mathematically rise as the cone narrows. So, sir, don't be surprised if in a week I tell you that the probability of impact has risen."

"OK Brad. It sounds like your team has done a good job of sizing up this rock and its potential. I think we need to inform the President as soon as possible since we are looking at only a little over three weeks until our encounter with this rock. I will recommend to him that we prepare a fragmentation strategy. I will schedule a meeting with him ASAP to make sure that he is informed by us before other channels break the news. I am sure that it is only a matter of time before some other stargazer discovers this new light."

"Yes sir, it is only a matter of time before the existence of this rock is discovered by someone else.

"Brad, have your guys given this object a name?"

"Most of the technical folk are calling it Hansen's Rock after the man who discovered it."

"Hansen's Rock it is. Thanks for the good work by you and your team. I'll brief you after I meet with the President. I will advise Emily to expect that report within the next few minutes."

Witherspoon left the conference room and instructed Kathleen to send the report to Barrow using megabit encryption over the secure private network between NASA HQ and JPL HQ.

***

Barrow left his conference room and walked to Emily's desk, "Emily, get me the White House Chief of Staff on the phone; tell his assistant that I have an emergency."

"Yes sir, Mr. Barrow"

Barrow returned to his office and waited for his intercom to announce that the Chief of Staff was on the line, "Mr. Barrow, Mr. Rander is on the line."

Barrow picked up his phone and spoke, "Hello David, thanks for stopping whatever you were doing and taking my call."

Dan L. King

Rander replied, "Charlie, when The Administrator of NASA announces that he has an emergency, everything else waits. What's up?"

"David, my guys at JPL have been studying a newly discovered space object for a couple of days and it appears that it will make a near-Earth visit. It could be a serious threat to life here on Earth. I need to brief the President and others on this matter ASAP."

"Stand by a minute Charlie while I check the schedules of the Chairman of the JCS, and the Secretaries of Defense, Homeland Security, and State." A couple of minutes passed, "Charlie, I can get everyone together at 0600 hours tomorrow morning. The Secretary of State is currently in Israel on a relations rebuilding mission but I will arrange for him to join by secure military satellite link. We will meet in the Situation Room. Is there any special preparation that you need me to handle?"

"That sounds fine David. I will bring my discussion slides with me. David, we have declared the material relating to this subject to be Top Secret."

"Yes sir: understood. There will be no public record of this meeting and I will only discuss it directly with the attendees."

"Thanks David, I'll see you in the morning."

Barrow punched the intercom button on his phone which disconnected the line to the Chief of Staff's office, "Emily, bring me the report that Witherspoon sent and send Judy to my office."

"Yes Mr. Barrow."

Judy Thompson was Barrow's technical assistant. She knocked on his door less than two minutes after she had been summoned. Barrow explained that he would be meeting with the President and others the following morning and gave her instructions about preparing the slides that he would use to deliver the briefing. He gave her a copy of the report, emphasized that this was a Top Secret matter and that she was not to copy the report or discuss this matter with anyone but him. He told her not to load the material to Federal Cloud Storage Servers but rather to return the slides to him on physical storage media. She left and went to her office where she prepared the briefing so that it would comply with the White House Briefing Standards.

BRIEFING THE PRESIDENT, JUNE 20

Barrow, and everyone except the President, had arrived at the Situation Room at least fifteen minutes before the scheduled start time. Barrow gave the flash drive to the equipment technician who inserted it into the notebook computer which drove the rear-screen projection system. The technician made sure that the slide "TOP SECRET" was in perfect focus and that the remote control worked reliably. He placed the LED remote on the conference table where Barrow had placed his briefcase which contained enough paper copies of the technical report from the NEO SCC. The technician confirmed that the connection to the Secretary of State was functioning and exchanged a few words with the assistant in Israel who was handling that end. As soon as the Secretary of State said, "Good morning all." the technician gave a business card to Barrow and advised him that if he needed any assistance during the meeting that he should call the number on the card. The technician left the room. The men chatted until President Mornay opened the door and began to greet each of them.

President Timothy Stephen Mornay was tallish, a little over six feet, and very fit...not skinny-fit, but muscularly-fit and everyone knew it after receiving one of his firm but sensitive handshakes. He never attempted to demonstrate how strong his hands were; he only matched the demonstrated strength of any hand he was shaking. He still had mostly black hair but gray was beginning to make its appearance above his temples. He was admired for his endearing full smile which he was able to display even under the most difficult circumstances. He had a friendly, confident face that was a true reflection of his inner self. His voice was as mellow and as perfect as a top tier radio or television announcer. Mornay had been born into a family of great financial

Dan L. King

success; he grew up very wealthy. And when it came time for him to find his own way in the world he became an extraordinarily successful real estate investor and made his own billions before he decided to serve his nation and ran for the presidency.

After the greetings were concluded, he sat at the head of the table, looked at Barrow and said, "Charlie, tell us about our problem."

Barrow tapped the remote to change from the "Top Secret" slide to the slide labeled "Hansen's Rock"; he then explained the moniker. Next he switched to the "Background" slide which contained the information about when and how the object was discovered. It summarized the actions taken to date including the optical observations and the multi-technology satellite surveys. He moved next to the "Object Characteristics" slide which contained a bulleted list of the physical characteristics of the rock. The discussion of that slide created a lot of comments, questions, and interaction. The next slide was titled "Probable Path." Barrow noted the current distance from Earth, the rock's velocity toward Earth, model projections of path, confidence limits, and probability of collision with Earth. He revealed that the most recent data indicated that Maximum Proximity was expected on July 13. The members of the group probed into how the projection was made and the Chairman of the Joint Chiefs of Staff asked, "When will we know for certain that we will or will not experience a collision?"

Barrow answered, "Sir, if the projected path remains near Earth, it may only be a few days before Maximum Proximity when we will know for sure that Hansen's Rock will or will not impact Earth. Our confidence limits will improve daily as we gain more data on the actual path that HR is taking and as it gets closer to Earth. Each additional point of data helps us refine our path model based on real information rather that computer projections of path. I must point out that, mathematically, we expect the probability of impact will increase as long as Earth remains completely within the cone of possible paths. So by this time next week the probability of impact may be significantly larger than the current 9.8 percent. The probability of impact will not show a decrease until a portion of Earth begins to fall outside the cone of path possibilities."

President Mornay asked, "So what are our options and what do you recommend we do, Charlie?"

Barrow tapped the remote control again to bring up the slide that was titled "Defense Options." He discussed the various options that had been identified in the past for defending against asteroid impacts. He pointed out that the defenses for asteroids are totally applicable to Hansen's Rock even though it was not an asteroid. He explained what each defense option was, the amount of time required to launch that defense, and its likelihood of success in this specific situation. The last bullet read "Division or Fragmentation." Barrow described this defense and the fact that due to the size of Hansen's Rock he speculated, "I believe that multiple explosive devices might need to be employed to accomplish a successful division or fragmentation. A successful "division" would need to be accomplished when the rock was still significantly distant from Earth so that the divided pieces could be diverted to paths that would cross Earth's path before and after Earth passes those points." Barrow displayed a slide that provided a visual image of a successful division. "A successful "fragmentation" would require that catastrophic explosions be delivered to Hansen's Rock to explode it so completely that no fragment of Hansen's Rock could survive entry into Earth's atmosphere and remain large enough to cause significant damage. It is my opinion that these are the only feasible options for us if we ultimately expect an impact. I recommend that we prepare to execute one or both of these options if needed. I will defer to General Watson to evaluate whether we have weapons that are powerful enough to accomplish the division or fragmentation defenses."

"We will need to do some modeling to determine how we might blow that thing up so I cannot answer this question without precise details about the size, mass, and surface characteristics. Charlie, I need for you to get your guys to prepare a hologram from the data they have collected on the surface and internal structure of this rock. Mr. President, I can assure you that this will be a very difficult mission to accomplish," Watson submitted.

Barrow advised, "OK, I'll get my guys in the NEO SCC to create a hologram composite from our radar surveys of Hansen's Rock for the General's team to review."

The President spoke, "General, give this matter priority over everything else and determine if we could execute these options."

"Yes sir, Mr. President."

The President took control of the meeting and addressed James Warren, the Secretary of State, "Jim, what actions do you recommend concerning discussions with our allies around the world?"

Warren promptly replied, "Mr. President, I think that we must share much of what we know with the rest of the world. We should be rationally transparent on this matter. We might not want to tell all the details of our knowledge but we must reveal our concern about this Hansen's Rock. I suggest that you permit me to get our Ambassador to the U.N. to request an emergency joint meeting of the General Assembly and Security Council of the United Nations so that you can address those groups to make sure that every nation knows the threat that we all face together. As you know, U.N. rules require a fourteen day notice for the calling of a special meeting. Our Ambassador should request a variance to that period. It turns out that the Presidency of the Security Council this month is the Russian Federation. I am sure you know that they rarely agree to motions promoted by the US. We will likely have to explain why the time variance is necessary and that explanation will put the Russians on the inside of what is now our little secret. However, I am pretty sure that we can secure the variance for a meeting before the end of the month because the Presidency of the Security Council will rotate to the U.K. for July and I am sure that the Russians will prefer that they be in charge when you address the U.N. groups. In that way they can make sure that they will get recognized for commentary or rebuttal.

Once General Watson determines whether we have the capability to successfully divide or fragment this rock, then we need to determine if we will need assistance from other countries. If we will need assistance from other nations that have sufficient weapons and space delivery systems, then we must open discussions with those countries. If we have the capability to handle this thing alone then we must decide if that is the wisest course of action or not due to the possibility of not sufficiently fragmenting this rock. If we assume the responsibility for destroying the rock and if we are not completely successful and large fragments fall on other countries causing damage and death, then we could face an enormous backlash. Depending on which country or countries are harmed, we might even be drawn into another large scale war that pits us against the countries harmed and maybe many more. Mr. President, I think you should make the call regarding whether we go it alone or partner with the other countries that have space delivery capability."

"Thanks Jim; that all makes sense to me. So, contact our Ambassador to the U.N. and get our request filed."

President Mornay looked at William Harriman, the Secretary of Homeland Security, and instructed, "Bill, let's hear from you on this."

Harriman answered promptly, "I think that the knowledge of a potential collision will probably lead to civil disobedience and unrest around the world including rioting, looting, and other crimes. Large numbers of people may abandon their work and family duties. Acts of terrorism are likely to increase because terrorists like to take advantage of chaotic circumstances and they may see these circumstances as improving their chances of success. It is possible that some of the more unstable governments may lose control of their weapons, possibly including nuclear assets, due to widespread desertion and conflict. We, of course, would be one of the prime targets should a terrorist group gain control of nuclear or chemical weapons. For most of us, there isn't anything more imposing and disorienting than the prospect of global extinction. However, terrorists might find the situation very liberating. We will need to promptly contact all first responders and inform them of the situation so that they can elevate readiness at all levels of law enforcement. I suggest that we direct every state Governor to activate all of their National Guard and reserve military personnel. They should be prepared to deploy to the trouble spots that will develop. I will make sure that FEMA is prepared as well as it can be for the situation, including being prepared to dispatch resources to locations of localized damage due to large fragment impacts. We will make sure that the Emergency Alerting System is at the ready to issue coordinated alerts and, of course, to enable you to address the nation within a few minutes of your request."

The President smiled and said, "Good summary Bill; proceed as recommended. Larry, what is your view and plan?"

Lawrence Garrett, the Secretary of Defense, responded, "Mr. President, we will insure that all military personnel are returned to their posts if on leave; we will be at one hundred percent of our capability within a week. Our soldiers, sailors, and marines will be available to assist state forces if needed. We will beef up the security of all military assets. We will make sure that all our ships are ready to sail within hours of an order to deploy. They will be prepared to execute offensive, security, humanitarian, or any other mission that we determine to be necessary anywhere in the world. We will declare Code Red, DEFCON Level Two readiness worldwide. The Air Force will partner with your Secret Service detail and be prepared to evacuate you to a safe location in the event that a fragment is headed toward Washington D.C. Both of your planes will, as always, be available immediately when needed. Sir, you can count on your women and men in uniform to be ready to do whatever is needed of them."

The President asked, "General Watson, do you concur with SecDef?"

"Yes sir, I agree."

"OK gentlemen, this is our plan. Charlie, I want you to provide each of us with a daily technical report on the progress of Hansen's Rock. I also want you to have the proper people on your staff available to work with my staff to prepare my address to the U.N. bodies and my address to the nation immediately following my speech at the U.N."

"Yes sir, will do."

Dan L. King

The President closed the meeting, "Gentlemen, thank you for your advice and wisdom." He stood to leave and everyone else stood until he had left the room.

INFORMATION MANAGEMENT

When Barrow got back to his office after the rush hour drive across town, he called Witherspoon and gave him a summary of his meeting with the President. He instructed Witherspoon to get his SCC team to prepare a composite hologram of Hansen's Rock. He explained that General Watson would have his scientists study the 3D model of the rock to determine where explosives would need to be detonated to fragment or divide the rock in a way that diverted any large fragments away from the path of Earth.

Witherspoon called Liz Wilson and ordered the composite hologram; she told him that she would have both available by the time she delivered tomorrow's technical report on Hansen's Rock.

Later on the morning of June 20, Witherspoon called Lister and gave him the sanitized version of the data from the SCC. He did share the projected near-Earth passing of Hansen's Rock and stipulated that it was currently projected to pass about 600 miles above the geomagnetic South Pole around July 13. He did not share how much uncertainty was attached to that projected passing. He shared the measurements of Hansen's Rock and some of the other empirical data so that his report was complete enough to create believability.

Lister immediately called Randele and gave him the same information.

Randele dialed Hansen's satellite phone number, "Hello, this is Lars Hansen speaking."

Randele began, "Good morning, Lars; I hope you are enjoying your time on dry land."

"I really am having a good time. I've been working on the construction of a silo that will house my telescope after I retire," Hansen shared.

"That does sound like fun. I'd sure like to see it when you're done."

"Sure, I'll have you out for burgers, beers, and stargazing once I get that big scope delivered and installed next January. At least I hope that I can get MAX delivered by then. I can't be sure as I don't know where Sirius will be berthed when I work my last day," Hansen explained.

"Anyway, your last six months will fly by I am sure. Lars, I finally got some information back from JPL about your space rock. The NASA folk expect the rock to make a very close flyby at about 600 miles over the South Pole around July 13. By the way, they are calling the object Hansen's Rock. Sounds like you are finally getting the fame you have always deserved." Randele laughed and Hansen joined in.

"Really, I had expected them to identify that thing with a number or something, but I don't mind having my name on it. Wow, that's a pretty close passing; I hope that they have the projected path nailed down."

"My friend at JPL didn't express any concern about the projection, so it sounds like everything will be OK. He did tell me that your rock is huge; it is about seventeen kilometers at the equator and over thirteen kilometers along the polar diameter."

"Oh man, that thing is gigantic; no wonder I could see it so well through MAX."

"Yeah, it's a monster," Randele agreed, "Well that's all they told me Lars and I just wanted to make sure that I closed the loop with you."

"Kevin, I really appreciate the call. I'm shipping out late tonight. I want to be aboard Sirius when the last of the crude oil is pumped out and we get our load of containers nested for the trip back to the west from Brisbane."

"OK Lars; you have a safe trip bud."

"Will do."

UNITED NATIONS AGENDA

Secretary of State Warren returned to his office and called Stephanie O'Donnell, the U.S. Ambassador to the U.N. He told her of his meeting with the President and that she should contact the President of the U. N. Security Council, Evgeny Popov, to arrange a joint meeting of the Security Council and the General Assembly. O'Donnell immediately contacted Popov and, as expected, the reception was a chilly one. Popov demanded to know the purpose of the meeting and wanted an explanation of the urgency. O'Donnell revealed some of the information that the United States had concerning the space object and its near-Earth passing which, she explained, was by itself sufficient reason for the urgency. Popov agreed to cut the standard notice requirement in half and said he would schedule the meeting for 13:30 on 27 June in the General Assembly Room.

***

O'Donnell immediately notified Warren who in turn notified the President about the schedule. Warren recommended that due to the length of time until the meeting that the President should go ahead and contact the leaders of most launch-capable countries to reveal information concerning Hansen's Rock. He also suggested that the President should notify them that there may be a need for a joint multi-national mission to destroy or divert the object and to enlist their support. Warren recommended that they not include Israel and Iran in the joint mission. He was sure that any rocket launch in that region would create too much anxiety and uncertainty on the part of the warring nations. He also suggested that North Korea and South Korea

Dan L. King

be excluded from the coalition for similar reasons in addition to their limited successful launch experiences. Warren suggested that the President explain to the other leaders that his experts were evaluating information about the object to determine a proposed methodology for destroying, delaying, or diverting the object and that the likelihood of a collision would be better known by the time the joint session of the U. N. was conducted. The President agreed to the proposed approach but wanted to make sure that General Watson would agree that a multi-national mission was the correct approach and that sufficient launch command and control capabilities existed for such a complicated mission. So, late that evening the President was able to discuss the proposal with Watson to get his reaction; Watson agreed with the approach.

"General, when do you expect to have your analysis of the object complete so you can tell me how many explosions we need to launch at this rock and how much explosive capability each device needs?"

"I expect to receive the hologram and other data tomorrow. I should have a plan developed by late on June 23. That plan will include the number of warheads that each country would need to launch, the sizes of those warheads, and the assignments of strike coordinates for each launch-capable country."

"OK General; sooner would be better as you know so that all partner nations can get their plan together and begin mobilizing their assets."

"Yes Mr. President, I understand; I just want to make sure that our analysis is thorough and accurate."

"Of course General; I look forward to hearing from you as soon as you have a plan."

***

Before Popov took any action regarding the request for a special meeting, he contacted the President of the Russian Federation, Andrei Volkov.

Volkov was a short man, being only five feet six inches tall. He had no hair on his body due to contracting alopecia areata when he was ten years old. The incurable disease caused Volkov's own immune system to attack his hair follicles. Some with the disease had gotten relief from the symptoms through the use of steroidal drugs but those drugs had failed Volkov. Even as a child he typically wore a toupee to cover his head and he had glue-on eyebrows; these only made his non-existent eyelashes look even stranger. Because of the disease, he had been persecuted by his childhood peers as they made fun of him and called him "mangy midget", "baldy", "ragtop", and other cruel names. Since he was a small child, it was easy for other children to steal his hair pieces and taunt him. Because of this shunning by other children and many adults, he became a mean-spirited man and developed a perpetual snarl on his face. These experiences as a child had led him to be obsessively driven to achieve control over others as they had controlled him as a boy. In adulthood, he had developed a vodka belly that caused him to appear that he was "with child."

"Comrade Leader, I received a call from the United States Ambassador to the U.N. requesting an emergency meeting of the Security Council and the General Assembly. She said that the United States has detected a space object that will make a very close approach to Earth. She requested that her President address the United Nations bodies to inform all nations of the threat and the plan that the United States is implementing to deal with the threat if the object is determined to be on a collision course with Earth. She said that she did not know any of the details about the object. I told her that I would call the special meeting in seven days. I will be issuing a notice to all members of both bodies immediately after we finish our discussion."

"Thank you for calling me Popov; you did the right thing. Here is what I want you to do. Issue the call for the emergency meeting immediately. However, I will be the primary speaker at the meeting; you may show the President of the United States as a second speaker in the role of commenter."

"Comrade Leader, your proposal will not go well with the Americans and their allies."

"Popov, I did not offer a proposal, I issued you an order. So, we will not discuss this anymore. Simply delay sending the Americans a copy of the agenda until they call in search of it."

"Yes Comrade Leader, I will handle this matter as you ordered. Thank you."

Volkov hung up the phone and summoned his assistant using the intercom line on the phone, "Anya, get me the Minister of Defence immediately."

"Yes President Volkov."

The first lamp on the phone lit and Volkov watched it glow steadily and then begin flashing. He watched as the intercom lamp lit and the ringer spoke. He ignored the intercom line and punched the flashing button knowing that it would be the Minister of Defence, Vasily Bykovsky.

Without any pleasantries Volkov began, "Bykovsky, I have learned that the Americans have discovered a large space object that they predict will come very close to Earth. I will be addressing the United Nations in seven days. I want you to use all of your resources to find this object and learn everything about it. I want a complete report on this object three days from now."

"Yes, Comrade Leader; I will immediately mobilize Space Command and we will find this object for you."

JUNE 21

The NEO SCC convened its Post-Survey Conference at 9:00 a.m. The team came to the meeting with the latest data on Hansen's Rock. The key data elements were:

Distance from Earth: 3.102058×10^6 km
Radial Velocity: 833 m/s
Projected Maximum Proximity (MP): 928 km; Confidence Limits $\pm 2.791852 \times 10^4$ km;
Probability of Impact with Earth: 22.78%
Projected Time to MP: 21d 5h 27m 28s from 00:00 PDT, 21 June

The media team had constructed the holographic image and had prepared it using gigabit encryption for transmittal to General Watson. After discussion of the various data, Wilson gave the order to encrypt and transmit the technical report to the distribution list that had grown to include her chain of command plus the President, General Watson, and the Secretaries that were now in the know.

***

Pete Martin and Jimmy Claxton made their way from The Lodge to the observatory for their 05:09 measurements. Hansen's Rock was now clearly observable with the naked eye and they could barely stop watching it as they used their red-lensed flashlights to illuminate their path. The Moon had begun its ascent only a few minutes ago and offered little illumination.

Dan L. King

They pointed the big reflector telescope to the same celestial coordinates that Hansen's Rock had occupied at their last observation. When the simple crosshair reticle came to its instructed location, they could see that HR had drifted slightly south during since their last observation. They noted the new angles and measured the Apparent Magnitude at 4.01. This meant that Hansen's Rock was now one of the brightest 500 objects in the night sky as observed from Earth. They performed their calculations and determined that the approximate distance from Earth to Hansen's Rock was 3.1 million kilometers; they calculated its average radial velocity during the past ten hours at 846 meters per second. Using the fourteen position points that they had recorded so far, they calculated that the object was going to pass within 800 kilometers of Earth in about twenty days. Their calculations showed a troubling trend; their progressive predictions of Maximum Proximity were bringing Hansen's Rock closer and closer to Earth. They returned to The Lodge and prepared their emails that would report the latest observation data and conclusions to their bosses.

Hansen's Rock

BACK ON SIRIUS

As the Boeing 747 settled into its final approach to Runway Zero-One at the Brisbane International Airport, Hansen could see his huge ship from his window seat on the starboard side of the plane. There were already thousands of containers stacked inboard on the ship. Tied up next to his ship, there was one large container ship and another container barge that ferried containers from the container dock to Sirius. From the height of the fully loaded waterline above the surface of the river, Hansen estimated that the crude oil load was down to less than two million barrels. If all went well, the last of the oil would be pumped out in less than three weeks.

The tires of the Qantas jumbo jet gently kissed the runway at 06:45 as scheduled. After collecting his bags and clearing customs, he took a taxi for the short ride from the airport to the crude oil dock where his giant ship lay awaiting its captain. The driver stopped at the security checkpoint at the entry to the crude oil facility. Hansen handed his identification badge to the armed guard who compared it with the list of approved personnel. The guard found Hansen's name and his permission. He then scanned the barcode on the back of the ID and handed it back to Hansen. He gave a temporary pass to the taxi driver and told him to place it on the dash of the Toyota Camry. He further instructed that the driver must return to the guard station within twenty minutes to avoid a dock police dispatch which would result in a fine. The cabbie nodded that he understood and placed the permit as instructed.

Once inside the gate, Hansen guided the cabbie to the nearest point of approach to the crude dock where he exchanged the metered amount plus a generous gratuity for his luggage. As the taxi headed back toward the gate, Hansen rolled his two pieces of luggage to the gangplank where he happened upon one of his crew who welcomed him back and took both luggage items from Hansen so he could deliver them to Hansen's quarters.

Hansen and the crewman took the elevator to the top level where the navigation bridges and crew's quarters were located. Hansen headed for the port bridge while the crewman headed down the passageway toward Hansen's quarters which were located midway down the corridor.

Hansen pushed the button on the secure bridge cabin door to signal the Relief Captain, Peter Smith, that he wished entry. Smith glanced at the large security monitor where the top left window showed an image of Hansen waiting at the cabin door. He smiled at the image as if Hansen could see him and then pushed the button that activated the electromagnet that released the lock on the door, "Welcome back Lars; damn we missed you!"

Hansen beamed and replied, "Peter, you may not believe it but I missed you and the crew also. I even missed sleeping in that little bunk in my quarters." He laughed. "Looks like things are moving smoothly. I don't think I'm needed around here anymore."

"Lars, you will always be needed on this ship. Are you sure you really want to retire at the end of the year?"

"Yeah Peter, I'm sure. You are well beyond being ready to add that next stripe to your epaulets and I'm getting too old to spend months on end bouncing around the oceans of the world." He laughed and continued, "I promise that I will not be in your way in about six months."

"Lars, you know you have never been in the way. Anyway, yes sir things are shaping up nicely. We need to pump approximately 1.6 million barrels of oil from the bladders to finish our crude mission and we need to load another 6,000 containers in preparation for our trip back west. We don't have any problems that are causing any delays. I expect that we should be ready to sail in seventeen to nineteen days," Smith explained.

"That sounds like everything is going according to plan. I'm going to go to my cabin and unpack. Let me have the Ship's Log to review. I will see you at 1300 hours in the mess and we can visit some more." Hansen took the Ship's Log and walked down the passageway to his cabin.

Hansen's Rock

RUSHING RUSSIANS

The leader of Russian Space Command, Yury Smirnov, had ordered his technicians to enable one of their spy satellites to determine the attitude of the American NEOSADS satellite in hopes of determining where the space object was located. His technician team leader reported that the results of this spying had the American satellite aimed toward the South Pole. They estimated that the area of space being observed by the American satellite was in the region located about five degrees east and four degrees north of the South Pole.

Smirnov instructed his team to re-orient their near-Earth object observatory satellite and to scan for new objects in the southern sky. Re-orientation took several hours due to the need to conserve attitude thruster fuel on the aged satellite. Once the satellite orientation was complete, they began wide-field scans of the southern sky to be compared with the celestial charts that they had on record until they found the new space rock. The wide-field imaging technology could survey a square area with dimensions of two arc degrees on each side. They formulated a plan to scan the sky in concentric squares about the center area that they had estimated the American satellite to be focusing on. The scans and comparisons continued for thirty-nine hours before they discovered a bright object that was not expected according to their celestial maps. They immediately reported the finding to Smirnov, who was asleep in his office awaiting a find. Smirnov ordered an immediate and complete multi-technology survey of the object. He informed his technicians that he was required to make a report to the President of the Russian Federation in only a few hours. He demanded that they work quickly to learn as much as they could about this object.

Dan L. King

The Russian technicians launched optical scans in both the visible and infrared frequencies; they launched Doppler radar scans; they performed spectrographic analyses; they initiated high energy X-ray scans; and they launched laser reflection analyses. All these activities produced an enormous amount of data that required some manual analyses in addition to the automated analyses that the equipment made.

At around 18:15 on 24 June, the lead technical manager under Smirnov called him and asked him to come to the Space Command conference room for a report on the information that his technicians had developed. Smirnov left his corner office on the top floor of the building and went to the basement where the conference room was located. When he entered, he saw the lead technical manager and six technicians sitting on either side of the table with the taller, larger, end chair awaiting him.

Smirnov started with an admonition in his Siberian dialect, "You technicians are too slow. You have jobs that any Russian would be delighted to have. You have the best training and equipment that the Russian government can provide, better than anyone else in the world. And yet, you take over three days to find a space rock and measure it. I am not very impressed with your performance so far. Maybe your answers about this rock will provide redemption. Who will start?"

The lead technical manager began, "Sir, we all apologize for taking so much time to perform the work you ordered us to do. We love our jobs and know that we are very lucky to work here for you. You are the best boss in Russia and we have worked non-stop to please you. We would have been finished more quickly if we could have identified the location of this object more quickly. Once we found this object, we have completed our initial surveys in less than a day. I believe that you will be pleased with the quality of our work. However, we think that this object is one to be concerned about!"

"You THINK I should be concerned. I assume that means that you do not KNOW if I should be concerned. After over three days you still do not KNOW?"

"Yes Leader Smirnov, that is correct. However, we do KNOW a great deal about this object. May we proceed with our report, sir?"

"Proceed."

The technician in the nearest chair to Smirnov on the left side of the table began by punching the advance button on the remote control that placed the first slide on the projection screen. He explained that they had found the object by spying on the American near-Earth object satellite and determined that it was pointing toward the southern sky, not toward the plane of the solar system as would be usual for asteroid discovery. However, because of the fact that the satellite attitude was nearly ninety degrees to the left of the Russian observation satellite, determining the exact aim of the American satellite came with a large error band. He explained that they had begun with wide-field surveys of the sky to find any new object that should not be there based on their celestial maps. With some pride he explained that they finally found the object after seventeen scans and comparisons completed in about thirty-nine hours. He apologized again for this taking so long but justified the length of time by explaining that they had to survey an area of sixty-eight square arc degrees before they found the object. He told Smirnov that they had worked without sleep until they had found the object.

Smirnov interrupted, "Get on with it boy! Tell me what I need to know and quit making excuses!"

"Of course, Leader Smirnov." The technician advanced to the next slide. He discussed the data bullets, "The object we found is large; it has an equatorial diameter of about seventeen kilometers and a polar diameter of about fourteen kilometers. We estimate it's mass to be about 8×10^{15} kilograms, or 8,000 trillion tonnes."

Smirnov interrupted, "That is a very large asteroid, isn't it?"

The technician responded, "Yes Leader Smirnov it is a very large object. Technically, we do not believe the object to be an asteroid because of its location and its characteristics which I will explain.

The object is very bright with an Apparent Magnitude of 3.6 which makes it bright enough to be seen with the naked eye in a typical urban neighborhood. People in southern Africa, South America, and Australia can already see the object with the unaided eye if they look in the correct place; it is already a public object. Its current celestial coordinates place it nearly directly over the South Pole.

The object has a solid metallic core under a very thick coating of what appears to be some form of solid hydrogen. The object has some very strange properties that we cannot explain. Our equipment indicates that the surface temperature is negative 269 degrees Celsius, only four degrees above absolute zero. This temperature will support solid forms of all the hydrogen isotopes that we know of as they lose their solid character at around fourteen degrees Kelvin; that is fourteen degrees above absolute zero. The metallic core of the object has a permanent magnetic field that is thousands of times stronger than should be the case for an object with this mass.

The object was about 2.9 million kilometers from Earth just a few hours ago and exhibited a radial velocity, its rate of speed toward Earth, of 886 meters per second. That's nearly one kilometer traveled each second. We estimate that the object could be in the vicinity of Earth within less than three weeks."

Smirnov interrupts, "LESS THAN THREE WEEKS; is that as accurate an arrival estimate that you can make? I cannot tell the Minister of Defence that we can only be accurate to within a week of time. What is your best estimate of the day that this object will be nearest to Earth?"

The technician responded, "Leader Smirnov, we need more data points before we can predict the exact day that the object will pass us. However, we believe it will be around the middle of July."

Smirnov rants again, "Now you tell me your accuracy is measured in months! Enough! I must give the Minister of Defence a date so until we know different, that date will be 15 July and that is what you will put in your report. Understood?"

The technical team leader spoke this time, "Of course Leader Smirnov; the date in our report will be 15 July until we can determine the exact date after collecting more information on its path and applying our predictive models."

Smirnov replied, "Good; that is settled. How long until you will be able to accurately determine the approach date?

"Sir, we should have a very accurate estimate in three more days."

Smirnov commented, "Good. I am happy to hear that the technicians believe that the object will pass us. That makes a lot of this other information less compelling than it would otherwise be."

The lead technical manager clarified, "Leader Smirnov, my technician misspoke; he did not mean to indicate that our analyses indicate that the object will miss Earth. We simply do not yet know how close the object will come to Earth or whether it will actually collide with Earth. That will take more time to determine. However, we will have a better idea in three days when we will confirm or revise the estimated arrival date with you."

"Misspoke? How can you tolerate a technician that is so imprecise with his words? How can you have confidence that he is not imprecise with his mathematics or his analytics? Why do you keep him around? How come you choose him to speak for the group?" Smirnov paused.

There were several seconds of uneasy silence as the assaulted technician was envisioning the loss of his job or worse. The other technicians had been silent and would remain so after observing the verbal thrashing that had just been unleashed on their colleague and friend.

The team leader broke the silence, "Leader Smirnov, my technician is an outstanding worker. He has worked without sleep now for over fifty hours so that we could deliver a report in the timeframe you specified. He spoke because he is the best technician in my organization. He deserves to be praised, not belittled over a simple misspeak. Do you have any more questions Leader Smirnov?"

Smirnov glared at the team leader and then the technician who had spoken and then at each of the muted technicians. After his glare had conveyed how little he enjoyed a worker disagreeing with him, he replied, "I have no more questions. I will expect a higher quality report by 1200 hours on 26 June. I must provide a quality report to the Minister of Defence who in turn will provide that report to the President of the Russian Federation for a speech he will make about this object at the United Nations. I will not tolerate any delays. I will be in this conference room at 1200 hours on 26 June and I expect to receive a more accurate report than the information you reported today."

"Yes Leader Smirnov."

***

Smirnov took the elevator back to his office on the top floor of Space Command Headquarters Building. He settled into his chair, picked up the phone, and called the Minister of Defence at his home. The maid answered the phone and Smirnov identified himself; she put the call on hold and went into the study where Bykovsky was studying some documents that had been delivered by a courier. The maid announced that Smirnov was on the phone; she punched the flashing button and handed the handset to Bykovsky.

Bykovsky looked at the clock which revealed the time to be 19:22, "Smirnov, you are late with your report!"

"Yes Leader Bykovsky, I know that I am late. My team did the best work that they could do as fast as they could do it. It took us a long time to find the space object in the sky since we did not know where to look. The sky is a big place and we did the best that we could sir."

"Humph! Our President instructed me to report to him today and now I will not be able to do that. Give me your report." Bykovsky picked up his expensive Swiss fountain pen and began taking notes as Smirnov told all the details from the briefing by his team. Bykovsky was silent through the entire report although he visibly winced when Smirnov told him that the path of the object was impossible to predict with the limited amount of data that his team had collected and that it would by 26 June before they would be able to make an accurate prediction. "Smirnov, this object is too big not to fear. I want you to personally remain involved in the work of your technical team and I want you to call me as soon as you know more information but certainly no later than early afternoon on 26 June. President Volkov

Dan L. King

must speak to the United Nations on 27 June and I must make sure that he is prepared properly. Do you understand?"

"Yes Minister Bykovsky; I understand. I regret that I and my team have fallen late in getting this information to you but surely you still have time to report to our President."

"No, I cannot report this information today even though there are hours remaining in the day. I will report to him tomorrow morning. Is there anything else you can tell me Smirnov?"

"No sir."

"Good night, Smirnov."

Bykovsky knew that he should not call the Russian President because it was the habit of Volkov to begin drinking vodka around 16:00 every day and he was not a happy drunk. There were many tales of his President torturing men and women that displeased him after he had been drinking. Bykovsky knew that he would prefer to be admonished by his President when he was sober. So he would wait.

COALITION BUILDING

On June 24 President Mornay received the visit from General Watson that he had been awaiting.

"Good morning, Stan."

"Good morning, Mr. President."

"So Stan, how are we going to defend against Hansen's Rock?"

Watson explained that his team had developed two plans that could be implemented. He explained that which plan was implemented would depend on how close to Earth the object was when it was determined for sure that it would strike Earth. If the strike determination could be made when the object was six days or more from Earth, then the approach would be to split the object into two large pieces by detonating a number of large nukes along the center line of the object. The intended consequence of the strikes would be to divide the rock completely and send the two large pieces away from each other. One of those pieces would be propelled on a path that would have it cross Earth's path through space before Earth arrived at that point. The other piece would be deflected so that it crossed Earth's path after Earth had passed that point. Watson cautioned that there could be some collateral smaller pieces of the rock that could continue on a path that would result in strikes on Earth. If some of the residual pieces were large enough to withstand entry into the atmosphere and be capable of creating great damage, then it would be necessary to launch smaller missiles to fragment them further. He told the President that he was confident that they should have time to execute the secondary strikes. He reported that he had ordered Los Alamos to reassemble four B93 bombs as soon as possible. Those bombs were about 600 times more powerful than the ones used to end World War II.

Dan L. King

He reminded Mornay that the reassembly of these bombs would constitute a violation of the nuclear arms reduction commitments that the US had made. However, Watson expressed confidence that if the US needed to use these bombs the international community would likely forgive them and not impose penalties or sanctions. He further explained that if the bombs were not used, they would dismantle them again and the world would never know that the US had rebuilt them.

If the determination that the rock would hit Earth came within six days of its arrival, then he explained that they must implement the fragmentation option. That option would require a large number of warheads delivered to dozens of impact zones on the rock so that they would hopefully break the rock into pieces that would be small enough that none of them could cause catastrophic damage if they survived atmospheric entry. The plan would involve multiple missiles each carrying multiple independently targetable and maneuverable warheads. That plan would be the most difficult plan to implement successfully because of the complexity of the timing required. Ideally, they would guide each individual warhead to arrive at its ideal explosion altitude of about one hundred and fifty feet above the surface of Hansen's Rock at the same detonation time. Since the rock was irregular in shape and was generally the shape of a Rugby ball, each of the dozens of explosions would occur at a different distance from Earth making the programming of each of the multiple warhead delivery systems much more complicated. In this scenario, if it was determined that Hansen's Rock was not sufficiently fragmented, there might not be enough time to launch additional missiles to successfully strike the pieces that would be large enough to withstand atmospheric entry and cause catastrophic localized damage.

Watson expressed his belief that the first plan, the plan to divide the rock, could be a multi-national mission since the flight parameters and delivery requirements would be much simpler. He believed that even the follow-up missiles, if required, could be launched by different countries if desired. He stressed that he believed that the second plan, the fragmentation plan, was so complex that it would be wise for the US to execute it without the assistance of other nations. He explained how the fragmentation plan would be implemented. He said that they would need to reprogram twenty-eight of their Peacekeeper ICBMs and each would be armed with twelve W97 thermonuclear warheads. Each warhead had an explosive power of about one-half megaton of TNT, twenty-two times more powerful than the bombs that ended World War II.

Watson told the President that he had instructed the US Missile Command to arm and ready missiles for both options. He said that he

Hansen's Rock

thought that they could be prepared in about six days to perform the initial programming for the weapons.

The President was surprised at how complicated the destruction of this space rock was going to be. Mornay probed Watson about Plan A, the divide and deflect option.

"I heard you say that Plan A could be a multi-national plan but I did not hear that you recommend that it be a multi-national plan."

"No, Mr. President I did not say that I recommend a multi-national mission. You must understand that I will always choose the simpler mission to execute and going it alone is simpler. We have all the delivery and explosive assets needed to complete the mission. However, I know that you must consider the other factors that affect international relations and responsibilities and the possible consequences of collateral damage if we fail to eliminate all localized but significant damage. So, if you choose a multi-national mission, I will see that it is successful to the extent we can get the other countries to play well together. However, I must recommend that we must go it alone if we must implement Plan B."

"OK Stan; I understand. I believe that we should make this an international mission if possible. If it turns out that we cannot implement Plan A, then at least we will have built some trust with the partner nations. I will immediately begin contacting the leaders of France, Japan, India, China, and Russia. I will refer their people who will lead the execution of their part of Plan A to you. I will demand that you be the overall execution leader."

"Of course Mr. President; as always I am at your service."

***

President Mornay called the President of France, "Bonjour, Pierre. J'espère que vous allez bien."

"Merci! Oui, afin de mieux. Your French is improving Timothy!"

"I just exhausted my French vocabulary Pierre. Hopefully you will permit us to speak in English."

"Of course, I need to practice my English anyway. What can I discuss with you today?"

Mornay told the French President everything he knew about the threatening rock and about the two defense plans. The French President was shocked to find out about the threat but agreed that he would gladly partner with the United States in the defense. He would have his Air Force Commander contact General Watson to coordinate the defense.

Dan L. King

Mornay contacted the Prime Ministers of Japan and India and they also agreed to the partnership and committed to immediately begin coordinating and preparing their part of the international mission.

Mornay next contacted the President of the People's Republic of China. The President of China was non-committal saying that he needed to discuss this proposal with his Administrator of the China National Space Administration. Mornay suspected that this excuse was just a way of postponing the decision so as to provide time for the Chinese President to review his political options. Mornay didn't expect cooperation and partnership from the Chinese anyway, especially since Japan was one of the potential launch partners and relations between China and Japan had been getting worse for many years.

Lastly, Mornay made the call that he had dreaded; he called the President of the Russian Federation. When Volkov answered the phone Mornay said, "Здравствуйте Andrei. Я надеюсь, что вы делаете хорошо."

"Здравствуйте Mornay. Да, Я хорошо сегодня. Let's speak English because your Russian pronunciation is still terrible."

"Of course Andrei; yes I know my Russian is terrible but I will keep trying to improve. If only my Russian were as good as your English."

"So did you call for a language lesson President Mornay?"

"No President Volkov, I called to let you know what we have learned about a large space rock that we have discovered and that we expect to make a near-Earth passing with a possibility of impact. We just don't know yet."

Volkov interrupted, "I assume you mean that big rock that is now over the South Pole?"

"Oh, you know about the object?"

"Of course I know about this object. You must have forgotten that I have the greatest space scientists in the world. Have you forgotten that you must come to my people to send your people and equipment into space? Your predecessors became lazy about space exploration and stopped innovating, so now you must come to us for big launches."

"Yes, of course you have very fine space scientists. So how much have you learned about this rock?"

"Timmy, I do not run a school here and I don't have time to tell you what you think you already know. You Americans are so arrogant and condescending to the rest of the world. You think you are the best at everything. But you are no longer much good at anything. We Russians are on top of this rock. In fact, I have requested a special meeting of the United Nations Security Council and General Assembly where I will share my knowledge with the world. If you come to that meeting, then you will learn what we have discovered about this rock."

Hansen's Rock

Surprised again, Mornay replied, "I too had requested a special meeting to be called by the U.N. and was told that I could speak with the bodies so that I could share what we know."

"Really...well my meeting is on 27 June. I will permit you to add comments or additional information after I have addressed the joint bodies of the U.N."

Realizing that there would be no useful discussion with Volkov, Mornay said good-bye and hung up the phone.

26 JUNE

Liz Wilson convened the Post-Survey Conference at 9:00 a.m. All the data from the last surveys were reviewed. The key changes revealed:

Distance from Earth: 2.720×10^6 km
Radial Velocity: 924 m/s
Predicted Maximum Proximity (MP): 869 km; Confidence Limits $\pm 1.08839 \times 10^4$ km
Probability of Impact with Earth: 58.41%
Predicted Time to MP: 17d 2h 7m 8s from 00:00 PDT, 26 June

Wilson observed that the key finding from the last survey still indicated that the predictions for the Maximum Proximity of Hansen's Rock were still declining with every survey they made. She deduced that they still didn't have a good model of the magnetic influence. She instructed each member of the team to evaluate the modeling equations with the goal of developing a revised model that would produce more consistent predictions. She told the team that she wanted the new model by the time of their meeting the following morning. She reminded them that the President of the United States would be addressing the United Nations the following day at 1:30 p.m. and that they needed to make sure that they gave him the best information possible. She stressed that the world would be depending on them to explain what to expect from this rock."

***

Hansen's Rock

Smirnov met with his technical team at 1200 hours for their report on the object, "What has your team learned team leader?"

"Sir, the current information on the object is that it is about 2.7 million kilometers from Earth. It is approaching Earth at a velocity that is over 3,300 kilometers per hour. Our model currently predicts that the object will approach Earth to a distance of about 500 kilometers where it will be greatly affected by the gravitational field of Earth and instead of passing Earth or being sling-shot around Earth and back into space it will enter an orbit around Earth. We expect that this orbit will quickly deteriorate leading to a collision of the rock with the surface of Earth. Depending on the interaction of the magnetic fields of the rock and Earth, it could be that the rock will plunge to Earth in hours after moving into orbit rather than days; we just cannot determine that yet. We believe that we have about a fifty percent confidence in this model. We believe the rock will assume its orbital path on 12 July."

Smirnov lamented, "Damn! I was happier when I knew nothing. So you believe that there is a fifty percent chance that this big rock will hit Earth. What kind of damage will it do?"

"Leader Smirnov, a rock of this size will cause great damage. It is much larger than the asteroid that has been blamed for the extinction of the dinosaurs. If this rock collides with Earth, there will be worldwide catastrophic damage including earthquakes, tsunamis, volcanic eruptions, fires, and more. It will likely fill the atmosphere with dust that could take years or decades to settle. We will be plunged into a dust winter as the Sun's rays will not be able to penetrate the airborne dust for years, maybe decades. Those on Earth who survive the impact will likely freeze to death because there will be no sunlight to keep Earth warm. The oceans could freeze. This collision could end human life on Earth."

The room was silent for several seconds until Smirnov finally spoke, "Are you absolutely confident in your numbers and conclusions?"

The team leader answered, "Yes Leader Smirnov we are confident that we have accurate information and that our conclusions are accurate. I must remind you that there is a fifty percent chance that this object will not strike Earth. We will not know for certain until the rock is closer to Earth. We need much more data to more accurately model the path that the big rock will follow. We will use all of our energy and resources to refine our information until we can state with certainty that the rock will strike Earth or not. We recommend that a proactive defense plan be developed by our military. Although this is a big rock, it may be possible to destroy it before it reaches Earth."

Smirnov seemed much less confident and condescending to the men in the room than he had ever been before, "Thank you all for your hard work. I will report your findings to the Minister of Defence as soon as I return to my office. I want you to continue your work studying this rock. I will visit with you each day to learn what new information you have learned."

Smirnov dragged himself out of the room and to the elevator which carried him to a spot about a hundred feet from his office. He walked slowly to his office and sank into his plush leather chair. He picked up the phone and called the Minister of Defence.

"Bykovsky."

"Minister Bykovsky, this is Smirnov; I have the update that you have been waiting for."

"Good, you kept your word that I would have good information this afternoon; that is progress. Let's hear what your team has determined."

Smirnov repeated the technical team's report faithfully, but meeker than usual. His own mortality had shocked him as he had pondered it while the elevator had ascended the shaft from the basement to the executive suite.

"That is not good to hear." Bykovsky responded, "Are you sure that your team has not overstated the threat and the risk?"

Smirnov, trying to find some reason for hope and optimism responded, "Mr. Minister, I do not believe that the team has exaggerated any of their findings. They did report that there is still a fifty percent chance that the object will not find the surface of Earth. However, it could take as much as ten more days before we will be able to determine the certainty of a strike or a miss."

"Yes Smirnov that is the better way to view these findings until a more definitive conclusion can be reached. I trust that you have charged your team with applying all their intelligence and imagination to resolving the uncertainty of this rock's path?"

"Yes sir Leader Bykovsky, I have ordered them to continue to study the data that they acquire about this rock and to notify me as soon as they can produce a definitive conclusion about the path of the object. I will be meeting with them daily until we know where this rock will go."

"Do you and your team recommend an immediate effort to destroy the rock or would we be wiser to wait until we know the path of the rock?"

"Sir my team doesn't have the skill to determine whether our bombs should be sent now or only in the case of a certain collision with Earth. I think your military specialists that understand the capabilities of their missiles and bombs must determine that. We will assist their analysis in any way they request. I will make any of my resources available to support their development of a proactive defense against this rock."

Hansen's Rock

"Yes, of course the development of our plan to defend against this space rock must be done by our military minds. Many of their weapons have capabilities that are not known to anyone except those with a need to know. I will charge General Dmitriev with overseeing the development of our plan and getting all the missiles and bombs ready. Smirnov, call me daily to tell me how your analysis is progressing."

"Of course Mr. Minister; I will report to you daily."

***

Bykovsky immediately called President Volkov and recounted the information that had been told to him along with the risk assessment. He informed Volkov that he would put General Dmitriev in charge of developing a plan for the defense of Earth including an assessment of whether an immediate strike on the object was a safer alternative to waiting for a final conclusion on whether the rock would strike Earth or not.

Volkov was not happy about the bad news; he never liked bad news. He asked Bykovsky if The Federation had bombs powerful enough to destroy the rock. Bykovsky assured him that they had the bombs needed and explained that they had been secretly storing six assembled units of Khrushchev's AN602 hydrogen bomb, the ones that were called Tsar Bomba. He reminded Volkov that the AN602 was the most powerful bomb ever detonated by mankind. He assured Volkov that they had enough collective power to convert this space rock into gravel. He explained that General Dmitriev would determine how many of the bombs must be used to eliminate the threat that this rock posed.

Volkov expressed concern about whether the detonation of the large bombs in space near Earth would create a huge radioactive cloud and probed as to whether Earth could be spared from the cloud of radioactivity. Bykovsky acknowledged that the bombs would create a huge radioactive cloud but said that he didn't yet know if they could detonate the bomb far enough away from Earth to spare it from the radioactivity. He did point out that if they could reduce the space rock to small enough pieces that the pieces and the radioactive particles that they carried would burn up in the atmosphere if they approached Earth.

"That sounds good Bykovsky. You know that I will expect you to prepare my address for the United Nations and have it securely transmitted to me at my apartment in New York City. I expect it to be available when I arrive there tomorrow at 06:00 New York time."

Dan L. King

"Of course Mr. President; I will have your speech in your apartment when you arrive and I will have it updated with the most recent information from our technical team."

UNITED NATIONS SPECIAL MEETING, 27 JUNE

Volkov's plane landed around 6:00 a.m. and his limousine was promptly unloaded from the belly of the plane. The limousine ride from the airport to the apartment took about an hour. Once he arrived at the apartment by using the private elevator reserved for apartment owners, Volkov reviewed the speech that Bykovsky had prepared. He made a couple of editorial changes, strictly style issues, and placed the folder in his briefcase. He grabbed his coffee cup and walked to the balcony of his apartment on the top floor of the Plaza Hotel where he got an unobstructed view of all the little people coming and going in the area around The Pond in Central Park.

The door chimes rang at exactly 11:30 a.m. Two of the men in his security detail went to the door. The first man looked through the security glass and then nodded to the other who had one hand on the door handle and the other hand under his jacket gripping the nine millimeter Makarov PMM that rested in the quick release shoulder holster. The first guard then turned the deadbolt to the left and took two steps back from the door so as not to be in its path. He caressed his own holstered Makarov while the second man opened the door and instructed the room service attendant to leave the cart in the hallway, to enter the room, and to raise his hands so he could be searched. Once the attendant was found not to be carrying a weapon, the second man then searched the cart at its resting place in the hallway and found it also to be safe. The second guard waved to the service attendant to role the cart to the dining table. The attendant carefully arranged the silverware, napkin, and the china plate with silver serving dome on the table and then looked up at the guards who were still gripping their holstered weapons; they waved him to the door. He left and closed the door behind him. The first guard returned to the door and turned the deadbolt to the right and took one more look through the security glass to ensure that the hallway was empty.

After dining on the Kobe veal sashimi accompanied by rice and miso soup, Volkov took a quick shower, dressed, and left the apartment for the two kilometer long ride to the United Nations Building where he would address the ambassadors of most of the nations on Earth along with a variety of Presidents and Prime Ministers that had decided to attend the meeting.

***

Liz Wilson held her Post-Survey Conference at 7:00 a.m. on this date so that she could make sure that the President of the United States had the very latest information and the benefits of the improved path prediction algorithms. The new models offered a significant change in the Maximum Proximity prediction and the more recent data also showed that a portion of Earth now fell outside of the confidence limits surrounding the path prediction. This meant that the mathematical probability of impact by Hansen's Rock had, for the first time, decreased. After a thorough review by the entire team, Wilson signed her name on the front page of the technical report at 8:30 a.m. She instructed her assistant to immediately send the report to the entire distribution list.

***

President Mornay boarded Marine One on the South Lawn of the White House for the 204 mile trip to the Downtown Manhattan Heliport. Today there were five visibly identical helicopters in the air flying an ever-changing formation called the Presidential Shell Game. The trip took slightly over an hour to complete. A motorcade with escort met the President at the heliport to transport him the remaining 4.6 miles to the United Nations Headquarters Building. He arrived just before 1:00 p.m. and met the US Ambassador, Stephanie O'Donnell, in the parking deck where his security team parked the presidential limousine. O'Donnell escorted the President to the location reserved for him next to her official position in the General Assembly Hall. It appeared that nearly every one of the 191 Ambassadors was in attendance. At least two dozen Presidents and Prime Ministers, mostly from the larger nation-member countries, had also chosen to attend as the word of a space object threatening Earth had been spread quietly by those who were in the know.

***

At exactly 1:30 p.m. the Secretary-General of the United Nations delivered one strike to the sounding board using the large hardwood gavel. Everyone knew that one strike was gavel etiquette informing them that they should be seated. Those that had been standing took their seats and the room became silent within seconds.

The Secretary-General pushed the talk button on his microphone, "Thank you all for your punctuality and for your attention. We are here today to discuss a threat to all of us. This threat does not come from any of the nearly 200 nations that constitute the United Nations. This threat has originated somewhere far away in space but the threat will be in the vicinity of Earth in the near future.

Last week I was contacted by my country's President telling me of this threat and that he wanted to share what he knows and what he is doing to address this threat. Shortly after my President contacted me, I also received a contact from the Ambassador representing the United States with the same request to share information concerning this space rock. Both men will address you today and tell you what they know. I consulted with our Chief of Protocol to determine the order of presentations and he has advised that the first requestor should be the first speaker. President Volkov of the Russian Federation will speak first. President Volkov, the podium is yours." The U.N. Chief of Protocol rose with Volkov and escorted him to the rostrum. The Chief of Protocol then returned to a position near President Mornay so that he could escort him when it became his turn to speak.

Volkov began, "Fellow leaders and ambassadors of the world, I am here to deliver potentially grave news to you and all the people you represent. Several days ago my space scientists discovered a new object in the sky over the Earth's South Pole. We have been studying this object ever since its discovery attempting to determine the path that it is likely to take. We have learned a great deal about this space rock. We have measured its size as being about seventeen kilometers across at its equator and it is about fourteen kilometers thick from pole to pole. This rock is currently about two million six-hundred thousand kilometers from Earth. That sounds like a vast distance but in space terms it is not all that far away...only about seven times the distance from Earth to our Moon. This distance is less than five percent of the distance of Mars from Earth. This rock is very close. Also, this rock is approaching Earth at a speed of approximately one kilometer per second; that is about 3,600 kilometers per hour. As the object gets nearer, the Sun, our Moon, and Earth are all exerting stronger

Dan L. King

gravitational pulls on the object. This means that the closer it comes to us, the faster it will travel. We expect that the rock could be traveling at a speed of about 27,000 kilometers per hour when it reaches its nearest point to Earth. My scientists currently believe that the rock will continue its path through space until it is within about five hundred kilometers from Earth at which point they believe it will be drawn into an orbit around Earth. My scientists do not believe that this rock will possess the velocity to escape Earth's gravitational pull. They believe that, without intervention, the rock will enter a deteriorating orbit that will in time bring the object to the surface of Earth. They currently estimate the probability of a collision between this object and Earth to be about fifty percent. My scientists believe that this rock will arrive near Earth before the middle of July.

This rock is much larger that the rock that destroyed the dinosaurs millions of years ago. If this rock strikes Earth there will be widespread catastrophic damage. The immediate human casualties would likely be numbered in the billions from the sonic explosion that will travel with the object once it enters Earth's atmosphere, from the actual impact, and from the earthquakes, tsunamis, and volcanic eruptions that would be triggered by the impact. My scientists believe that this rock could propel billions of tons of dust into the atmosphere and that this dust cloud would thrust Earth into a severe winter condition. This massive dust cloud would deny Earth sunshine for tens or hundreds of years. This dust winter would freeze most everything and likely cause the demise of those who survived the first days after the impact. This rock could destroy all of mankind on planet Earth."

This dire prediction caused much commotion amongst those attending the meeting and several side discussions began spontaneously. The Secretary-General saw that the audience had diverted their attention from his leader so he sounded the gavel once more to regain the attention of the ambassadors. The room again became silent.

Volkov continued, "So, you can see that we must mount some sort of defense against this rock so that we can ensure that none of the consequences that I described will occur. I have ordered one of my Generals to devise a defense plan that will ensure success. We do not have that plan finalized as of today but we will have it soon. The Russian Federation has missile and space scientists that are second to none on Earth. We have the most sophisticated launch and control capabilities in the world. We have explosive devices that are awesomely powerful, more powerful than any other nation on Earth. We will employ all of these resources to ensure that all the people of the Russian Federation and all the people of the world are saved from this

Hansen's Rock

space rock. I will personally provide the leadership needed to make this defense plan a success for all of us; I will save our world from destruction." Secular applause followed as Volkov returned to his chair. But even the political applause was muted; Volkov had scared everyone in the room with his candid description of what could happen. Most knew that the Russian was given to bragging beyond his capabilities, so nobody felt the comfort that Volkov had thought he would give with his promise to save the world.

The Secretary-General introduced the President of the United States and the Chief of Protocol escorted him to the rostrum where Mornay placed his folder and opened it. "Thank you Mr. Secretary. Lady and Gentlemen leaders of Earth, I come to you with a heavy heart due to the threat that President Volkov has already discussed some. I also have some information about this space object and I also will tell you that I am more optimistic that this object might pass Earth without any catastrophic consequences. However, I must be honest that it is just too soon to determine exactly how close this object will come to the surface of our little planet. I respect the skill and successes of the scientists of the Russian Federation. I also respect the skill of the scientists that serve the United States of America.

Our American scientists have taken measurements that confirm much of what President Volkov told you. We agree that the object is approximately the same size as that which the Russians measured. We have determined that this rock is very unusual in that it has a metallic core that exhibits a magnetic field that is many thousands of times more powerful than that which would be expected by a rock of this mass. This rock is also covered in a thick layer of solid hydrogen. The surface temperature of this rock is barely above absolute zero. These unusual characteristics greatly complicate determining exactly how the rock will behave as it gets closer to Earth. We have never discovered a space object near Earth with these characteristics so we have had to develop new formulas to attempt to predict its behavior as it approaches Earth. However, we have just recently improved our understanding of the potential behavior of this space rock to a point where we are now 99.7 percent confident that we know where it will go.

Our latest measurements have the object about 1,650,000 miles from Earth, the same distance that President Volkov told you. We believe the object is moving at a velocity of about 2,140 miles per hour, slightly slower that the Russian conclusion. We expect the object to be in the vicinity of Earth on July 13 around sunrise here in New York City. Our current path prediction has the object passing Earth at an altitude of 335 miles above Earth's South Pole. My scientists tell me that the probability of collision has decreased for the first time since we began making path predictions. We currently believe that there is a **44.6** percent chance of collision, down from over fifty-eight percent just yesterday. We believe that the rock will be traveling at a velocity of around **18,000** miles per hour when it passes Earth and that this speed will be enough to keep it from entering a deteriorating orbit. The rock currently has its north magnetic pole facing Earth so as it nears our South Pole, the body will be attracted toward Earth. However, once it passes our South Pole and transits Earth's equator, that magnetic attraction will change into a repulsive force that will grow as the object's north magnetic pole interacts with Earth's north magnetic pole. The repulsion will act to repel the object and assist it in escaping from Earth and slingshot back into deep space.

However, there is still some uncertainty about where the space rock will go. I too have ordered my space and military scientists to devise defense plans and they have done so. They have developed two plans for dealing with this rock depending on how far it is from Earth when we determine that a collision is imminent. If we determine that the object is on a collision course with Earth when we still have six days or more to act, then we believe that a divide, advance, and delay approach is best. This involves delivering explosions to the rock that will cause it to break into two large pieces with one piece crossing Earth's path before Earth arrives and the second piece crossing Earth's path after Earth has passed. We would have enough time to launch additional missiles to fragment any residual pieces that might be large enough to cause localized catastrophic damage on Earth. I have discussed this plan with the Presidents of France, Japan, and India and they have all agreed to partner with the United States in this mission. I would also again invite China and Russia to join this mission.

If we find ourselves unable to determine that the object will collide with Earth until it is within six days of striking us, we believe that the only possible defense at that time will be to fragment the rock into as many small pieces as possible so that the number of rocks that enter the atmosphere and survive to strike Earth is mitigated as much as possible. This is a much more complicated mission and because of this complexity the American military will perform this mission alone.

I appeal to all of you to take the optimistic view of this information and to convey a sense of calm to the people of your countries. We simply do not yet know what the path of this rock will be. But it is very clear that if we permit panic to rule our nations, then there is a great probability of widespread civil unrest including rioting, looting, and other lawless activities. I appeal to all of you to paint the most optimistic image of the facts. As I have told you, my scientists believe that there currently is a fifty-five percent probability that this object will not collide with Earth and we believe that this probability will improve as the days advance.

Ladies and Gentlemen, thank you for your attention and support. Thank you Mr. Secretary. And may God bless Earth." Mornay returned to his seat.

Volkov pressed the button on his desktop signaling the Secretary-General that he wished to speak. The Secretary opened his microphone and said, "The Secretary recognizes the President of the Russian Federation; sir you may speak."

Volkov enabled his microphone and spoke, "Fellow leaders of the world, I will not partner with the American military under any circumstance as I know from past history that they cannot be trusted and will only attempt espionage against the Federated Russian people. I also encourage each of you to appeal to President Mornay not to undertake any mission to divert or destroy this space rock without the express approval of this body.

Even though I am not as optimistic as the American scientists that this rock will miss Earth without any intervention from us, I do agree with President Mornay that you must focus on the possibility that this rock will not strike Earth; chaos will not serve any country or any person. And as I told you earlier, if this rock takes aim at Earth, I will blow it from the sky for all our sakes." Volkov silenced his microphone.

Mornay pressed the button on his desktop to signify that he wished to speak. The Secretary activated his microphone and said, "The Secretary recognizes the President of the United States; sir you may speak."

Mornay enabled his microphone and responded, "President Volkov, I am disappointed but not surprised that you choose not to partner with the other nations that have launch capability. However, your refusal to partner will not deter America from doing what we know to be the best thing for the world. As you know, the United Nations is not a governing body and as such I will not seek approval from this body for any action that I determine to be appropriate to defend Earth. It is obvious from your last remark that you too do not intend to seek approval from anyone to "blow this rock from the sky". However, I still suggest that we consult with each other to share and compare the data that our scientific teams continue to refine. I will commit to you that I will share and discuss the data that my scientists produce with you and I hope that you will agree to reciprocate." Mornay disabled his microphone.

The room was silent. It was apparent that there were great tensions between the most powerful leaders in the room. After about thirty seconds of silence, the Secretary-General enabled his microphone and spoke, "Receiving no further requests to speak, I declare this 27 June emergency meeting of the Security Council and the General Assembly to be adjourned."

BACK TO WASHINGTON, D.C.

Mornay's motorcade hustled back to the heliport where Marine One was prepared to receive the President. The limousine drove to a point just outside the reach of the rotors. Mornay exited the limo, walked to the helicopter steps, looked the Marine directly in his eyes and gave him a proper salute as he always did. Mornay had always been embarrassed by past Presidents of the United States that were sloppy and disrespectful when throwing a cavalier salute as they passed the Marine warriors who attended to the presidential aircraft. After giving the single Marine the respect he deserved, Mornay boarded the chopper. The flight crew secured the door, brought the rotor speed up, and gradually adjusted the rotor pitch until a perfect lift-off was attained. Marine One joined the four decoys hovering in the sky over the East River and they began their leap-frog maneuvers as they achieved cruising altitude and speed along the course that would take Mornay back to the South Lawn of the White House.

Once aboard the chopper his aide handed him a draft copy of the speech that Mornay would deliver to the people of the United States, both houses of Congress, all Cabinet Secretaries, all Chief Justices, and the Joint Chiefs of Staff. As Mornay read the speech, he dictated a few editorial changes, additions, and deletions to the aide who marked the changes on the copy he held. The aide assured the President that the changes would be faithfully made and the new wording would be available by the time they landed at the White House. The aide logged into the secure shared server where the speech resided, made the requested changes, and hit the printer icon that would print a copy on the printer near the desk of Mornay's Personal Secretary.

When the rotors had slowed and been feathered, the pilot opened the door, lowered the steps, and stood at salute as the President unbuckled himself and arose from his leather seat. Mornay saluted the Major and descended the steps to the finely manicured grass where he found two Marines standing at salute. He turned left, made eye contact, and returned a proper salute to the young woman. He then turned right, made eye contact, and returned a proper salute to the young man. He then turned to make the short walk to the White House.

***

When President Mornay arrived at the Oval Office he turned on the television to see how the various channels were covering the discussions at the United Nations. The media had, as usual, seized on the worst case scenario as the news of the day and they were reporting that both Mornay and Volkov had told the U.N. that there was a high probability of a collision between this large space rock and Earth. International reports were filled with snippets from various country leaders addressing their constituents asking them to be calm and expressing confidence that if the space rock would threaten Earth that the launch-capable nations of the world would cooperate to destroy that threat.

But as always, some people did not place great trust in their political leaders as they remembered that they had been lied to in the past which made it difficult to believe what they were being told today. But the great majority of people in all nations wanted to believe the best outcome would happen and they wanted to trust world leaders to do the right thing to protect them from great threats. Nonetheless, many people were seizing the opportunity to take advantage of the chaos. Looting was occurring in some poor countries and a few rich countries but it did not seem to be widespread yet.

Churches, mosques, synagogues, temples, and other places of worship were shown in the news videos with standing room only. Many of these holy places had so many visitors that they had overflowed into the streets around the worship location. Mornay knew that the worst was probably yet to come.

***

Just before 7:00 p.m., Mornay decided to call Charlie Barrow, "Charlie, good evening to you. I guess by now you have seen the news coverage resulting from the UN meeting this morning."

Hansen's Rock

"Yes, Mr. President I have been flipping channels for the past hour or so. Things don't seem too bad so far so I would conclude that you did a great job of assuring the other world leaders that a collision is not a given."

"I tried Charlie. Listen, I think I would like to participate in the next Post-Survey Conference that your NEO SCC conducts. I would hope that my participation would not be disruptive and I promise to behave." Mornay chuckled.

Barrow laughed and replied, "Sir, I think that's an outstanding idea. The folk in that center have been working around the clock since Hansen's Rock was discovered. Many of them continue to sleep in the break room. I must have paid for a thousand delivery pizzas by now."

Mornay laughed again, "OK, I will stay here in Washington so you set it up by video conference. I really want to see the faces of those women and men that are carrying such a heavy burden."

"Yes sir; consider it done. I will set it up for noon our time tomorrow in the Situation Room. If you don't mind I would like to join you for that conference."

"That's perfect Charlie; have a couple of those pizzas that your guys have been surviving on delivered to the Situation Room."

"Of course Mr. President and I will have them bring us a pint or two of that Chunky Monkey ice cream you like."

"That sounds perfect Charlie. Hey while we are talking about ice cream why don't you send your SCC a couple of cases of ice cream, compliments of the President of the United States?"

"Excellent idea sir; they will really appreciate it."

***

President Mornay entered The Chamber of the US House of Representatives at precisely 9:00 p.m. as scheduled. He was always on time; he considered himself a servant to the citizens and officials of the United States and viewed late arrivals at any scheduled event as an indication of disrespect and arrogance. As always, he was anxious to get to the podium and deliver his message to the American people but the clingers and slingers in the hall were in search of their opportunity to be seen with the President or an opportunity to deliver a brief request or comment to him. Being a courteous man, he gave everyone along both sides of the aisle a little of what they wanted, often posing while a Congressperson snapped a selfie with the President or while listening to a lawmaker encouraging the President to veto this or to approve that.

After the President made it to the spot directly in front of the podium, he turned to the left, shook about thirty hands, and finally ascended the podium to a standing ovation from both sides of the aisle and all the visitor galleries. These moments always caused him discomfort; he was a humble man and viewed this display of gratitude and respect as unnecessary. He nodded his thanks and finally turned to the Speaker of the House as an indication that it was time for the sound of the gavel meeting the sounding board. The Speaker smiled at the President and pounded the gavel just once. The hall became quiet and everyone took their seats. The Speaker then announced, "Ladies and Gentlemen, the President of the United States." All rose again with applause that lasted another three minutes in spite of obvious encouragement from the President that the hall should be seated. Finally, the hall became quiet and all were seated and focused on the leader of the free world.

"Citizens and leaders of the United States and the world, I come to you tonight to inform you of a threat to our country and the world that was recently discovered. About two weeks ago, an amateur astronomer on a ship in the seas south of Australia realized that an object in the sky that he had been observing was indeed a previously undiscovered object and that it appeared to be approaching Earth. He referred that finding to friends in the United States who in turn advised the proper government agency which has been studying this object to determine if it will threaten Earth. These brilliant and dedicated scientists have made repeated surveys of the object. They have developed and refined their predictions of the path of the object. This object has some very unique characteristics. It appears to have come from a point in the universe near the south polar star. It is an extremely cold object with a surface temperature near absolute zero. It is a very large object being over ten miles across at its equator. It is on a path that will bring it close to Earth in a couple of weeks. At this time, because of its unique magnetic characteristic, no one on Earth can determine definitively if it is on a collision course with Earth. However, American space and military scientists have developed plans to deflect or destroy this object if we determine that it will collide with Earth absent any intervention. I am confident that our scientists and military can deal with this threat if a collision with Earth becomes imminent.

When attempting to solve difficult problems, various people often reach different conclusions when faced with similar information. This situation is no different. I am sure that many of you have heard by now, that I met with the United Nations this morning to inform other nations of this threat. The President of the Russian Federation also spoke to the UN this morning and announced that his scientists currently believe that this object will approach Earth and enter a deteriorating orbit which will ultimately bring the rock to the surface of Earth. I want to reinforce my earlier statement that we disagree with this finding at this time and believe that it is too early to conclude the final path of this space rock. We believe that there is a very good probability that this space rock will come very close to Earth, that it will temporarily enter a partial orbit of Earth, and that its speed and magnetic repulsion will slingshot it back into deep space without any harm to any person. But we just do not know at this point and it will be several days before anyone can conclude exactly what will happen.

I appeal to all of you to continue your daily activities as you would without knowledge of this threat. I assure you that the American space and military leadership will take every possible action to protect us in the event a collision appears to be imminent. We believe that it is possible to deflect or destroy this object if that becomes necessary and we have partnered with other launch-capable nations in the world for a joint mission if that proves to be a viable path to eliminating this threat.

I want to repeat that there is no need to panic. Panic is counterproductive and unnecessary. Panic could produce all sorts of unfortunate events that could result in loss of property and life. I encourage every person here in America and around the world to be calm and to try to calm those who are not. We will all get through this situation safely if we stay calm and confident.

Thank you and May God bless His world."

Mornay turned to shake the hands of the Vice President and the Speaker of the House and then left the podium. The audience was standing and clapping as they always did after a presidential address but the applause was not as abundant or as enthusiastic as was customary. Instead of applauding a number of those in attendance were chatting with those that were seated nearby, obviously discussing the threat situation. Mornay exited the House chambers after again attending to all those who wanted to touch him or talk to him.

28 JUNE

Barrow arrived in the Situation Room at around 11:45 a.m. to make sure that the technician had the full-duplex video link established with his NEO SCC. He exchanged pleasantries with Mike Williams who had returned from his cruise. He spoke to Liz Wilson and complimented her on the great job she had done during Williams' absence. He chatted with a couple of the technicians that he remembered from his previous face-to-face visits to the facility. Every one of the employees of the center was in attendance. The room was packed and most were standing as there weren't nearly enough chairs to accommodate every person who worked in the center. But nobody wanted to miss the opportunity to be there when the President of the United States of America and the Administrator of NASA were visiting their shop.

The President entered the Situation Room at exactly 12:00 p.m. Following him through the door was Richard Garish, the Vice President of the United States. The surprise and excitement from the crowded SCC conference room were visible and audible. The President started, "Good afternoon, Charlie; I hope you don't object to my bringing the Vice President with me. You know that Dick somehow always sniffs out any free food within the building." Everyone on both ends of the call laughed. He looked at the screen and continued, "Good morning out there in California!"

In reasonable unison, the crowd responded with, "Good morning, Mr. President." Then several of them realized it was no longer morning in Washington D.C. and mumbled that they may have screwed up.

Mornay spoke again to the crowd in the center, "Ladies and Gentlemen, I probably can't find the words to impress upon you how thankful and proud I am for what you have done since this Hansen's

Rock was discovered. Your work has been truly amazing and I am certain that it has been better than any other scientists in the world could do. I want you to know that I am personally impressed with the quality of your work and the professional candor that you have displayed in dealing with this problem. I know that you must find this Hansen's Rock to be very disturbing and disruptive to your lives. I know that you would normally be spending much more time with your families and friends than you have been able to do since this rock was discovered. I personally admire the dedication to your country that each of you has displayed. Thank you for all that you are doing." He paused for just a couple of seconds, "O.K. Charlie let's hear today's report."

Barrow responded, "Mr. President, I have asked the center to conduct their Post-Survey Conference in the same manner that they always do even though they have several visitors."

Mornay responded, "Of course, that is exactly what I expect." He looked back at the screen and instructed, "You guys just pretend that the Vice President and I aren't here."

The conference room erupted in laughter knowing that there would be no way to overlook these observers.

Barrow ordered, "O.K. Mike, let's get this meeting started."

Williams replied, "Yes sir. If you agree, I will ask Liz to lead the discussion since this has been her baby since the beginning."

Barrow approved, "Outstanding."

Wilson looked into the screen and began, "Again good morning, I mean good afternoon gentlemen. Thank you so much for joining us. This day will be a memory that none of us will ever forget." She could see Mornay nod that he appreciated her recognition.

Wilson announced that the lead technician, Jerry Jones, would deliver the report and she nodded to him that he should begin.

Jones started the report with a distinctive quiver in his speech, "Thank you Mrs. Wilson."

He normally called her Liz, as did everyone else, but he was uncertain if such an informality would be appropriate with such a distinguished audience. The others in the room smiled a bit knowing that he was scared to death. The technician standing behind him put her hand on his shoulder to let him know that he was supported by all his co-workers.

"The latest survey results are as follows: Hansen's Rock is now 2.554 million kilometers from Earth; it exhibits a radial velocity of 985 meters per second;"

Garish interrupts, "Please excuse me for interrupting; I know my boss said to pretend we weren't here but could I request that you convert these numbers into American-type units so I can understand? I'm a political science guy, not a technical science guy."

The conference room delivered another good laugh. Jerry answered, "Of course Mr. Vice President." He pulled his smartphone from his shirt pocket and opened his calculator app so that he could convert the units as he discussed each metric. "Hansen's Rock is now approximately 1,587,000 miles from Earth. It is traveling toward us at a speed of 2,200 miles per hour. We believe our confidence in being able to predict the path is 99.8 percent. We now calculate the probability of an impact with Earth to be 41.8 percent, down from yesterday's calculated probability of 44.6 percent. We calculate that the closest distance that the object will come to Earth will be 323.7 miles. The rock will reach that distance at a point nearly directly over the South Pole at around 1:00 a.m. here in California on July 13; that would be around 4:00 a.m. there in Washington, DC. Our latest survey results continue to confirm dimensional and mass metrics that were determined from previous surveys. These are the key findings from our most recent measurements."

There was a period of silence. After about ten seconds of silence Wilson realized that she was in charge, "Thanks Jerry; that was a very good report. These findings continue to reinforce our earlier conclusions. Are there any additions or corrections? She looked around the room to see if anyone wanted to contribute. She received a few terrified smiles and a couple of headshakes but no comments. Then she asked, "Mr. President, that summary concludes the material portion of our report. Do you have any questions, sir?"

Mornay replied, "Yes Liz I do have a couple of questions. I guess that you have heard that the Russian scientists believe that Hansen's Rock will enter a deteriorating orbit around Earth and will eventually fall from that orbit. Can you confirm or dispute that prediction?"

Wilson swallowed nervously and answered, "Mr. President, I must tell you that we really don't know the answer to that question. Our calculations cause us to believe that HR should slingshot around Earth and head back into deep space but the confidence limits around our path predictions at this time cannot rule out an orbital capture of the rock that might bring it to Earth." She looked at Jones for details.

He performed the calculations and spoke, "Mr. President the band of potential paths for HR range from an extreme altitude of 3,497 miles above Earth to a head-on collision with Earth."

Mornay accepted, "Thank you. So, when will we know for sure that we will be safe from this rock?"

Liz answered, "Sir we think it will be at least another week before we know; isn't that correct Jerry?"

Jones elaborated, "Sir, we believe that we will know on the morning of July 4 if we will be safe. We believe that by July 4 Earth will fall outside of the confidence range if all of our current predictions continue to receive confirmation from future surveys." Jerry looked at Liz and took a deep breath not knowing if he had overcommitted or if he should have been so candid. Liz's countenance confirmed that she was nervous about that prediction also.

Mornay replied calmly, "Excellent job Jerry and all of you out there in the SCC." He looked at Barrow and instructed, "Charlie, I will need a daily report on the key findings of each survey. I also am requesting that we set up another video conference with the SCC on July 4. I know that is an important holiday but this matter is just too important."

"Yes Mr. President we will do that."

Garish looked at the projection screen and said, "Thank you all for everything you have done. Your report today was informative and very professional. I am proud to have people like you helping to save America and the world. And thank you for dummying things down so a dummy like me can understand."

The center laughed a more relaxed laugh realizing that they had survived the meeting.

Mornay spoke one more time, "I want to again thank you for all your hard work. I know that it isn't much but I have asked Mr. Barrow to see that you have an ice cream party today compliments of the Vice President and me; hopefully it will arrive soon. Maybe that will help you add back a pound or two that you have probably lost during this long ordeal."

Wilson spoke as if she were in charge, "Thank you so much Mr. President. We really appreciate all your kind words and I promise you that by sunset today we will have consumed all the ice cream you are sending." The room had been nodding agreement as she spoke and broke into applause when she had finished. She smiled.

Mornay closed the conference, "O.K. sounds good. We'll see you again on July 4."

Barrow hit the button to summon the technician. The technician entered the room with three pizza boxes and a cooler containing dry ice and three pints of Chunky Monkey ice cream. He terminated the video connection and left the room.

Garish was the first to rise and head to the credenza where the pizza boxes rested, "What kind of pizza will it be for you today Mr. President?"

29 JUNE

The President studied his Daily Brief which began with a summary of the latest data regarding Hansen's Rock. The rock was measured to be 1,531,820 miles from Earth; it was traveling toward Earth at a speed of 2,288 miles per hour; predicted Maximum Proximity was 335 miles with a calculated accuracy of ± 2,460 miles; the probability of an impact with Earth was predicted to be 33.24%, down from yesterday's prediction of 41.76%.

The Brief cited a dramatic increase in the amount of chatter originating from regions known as terrorist strongholds and training camps. The Brief opined that there had developed a sense of urgency among the terrorist communities. The terrorists feared that they were running out of time to accomplish acts of terror against western countries. The Brief reported that the number of young men and women volunteering for suicide duty had tripled in just the last two days since the world became aware of the threat from space. Apparently these young people had begun to believe that the time that they had to become martyrs for the Global Jihad was expiring and they wanted to impress Allah before being killed by a rock. This imminent threat of death had liberated the young volunteers permitting them to be careless but focused with the last days of their lives. The NSA had detected an increase in suspicious voice and data traffic within the United States leading them to conclude that the likelihood of terror attacks from so-called home-grown terrorists could be increasingly likely. The report told that a State Department Alert had been issued to all Americans around the world, even within the borders of the United States. The alert stated that Americans should at all times remain aware of their surroundings due to the heightened risk of bombings and kidnappings. It advised against all travel abroad until the State Department formally rescinded the warning.

The Brief also noted that satellite surveillance showed a great deal of activity around several of the Russian nuclear missile launch bases. The Brief reported that at least one silo at Aleysk, Dombarovskiy, Imeni Gastello, Kartally, Uzhur, and Zhangiztobe were being readied. The silos at these bases were known to contain SS-18 Satan Mod 6 missiles. Activity was noted around the clock with large numbers of vehicles and personnel working around each silo. Typically getting ready for a launch meant simply running tests on all the equipment. Sometimes, if a payload was being modified, large trucks and heavy cranes would be used at these sites. During the recent satellite passes, each silo had several large trucks nearby and each had the arm of a large crane hovering over the open silo door. The large amount of activity was interpreted to mean that the Russians were modifying the missiles to a new configuration of some sort.

The Brief noted that there was a heightened amount of disturbing activity in Iran. Large volumes of vehicular traffic were noted going to and from the buried bunkers where, in the past, uranium had been enriched. The Brief revealed for the first time that there was limited evidence that the Iranians were now capable of building nuclear bombs, based on a confession by one individual recently detained by the CIA. The scientist had told interrogators that Iran had enough enriched material to construct as many as three nuclear bombs. The informant's facts led to a conclusion that Iran would likely be building bombs in the ten megaton explosive range. The informant indicated that these three bombs would be added to existing missiles that would be targeted at the cities of Jerusalem, Tel Aviv, and Haifa. Three bombs of this explosive power would be able to virtually destroy these three cities and would likely kill over 1,500,000 people outright. The collateral deaths from the nuclear poison that would be spread over other portions of Israel, Jordan, Syria, and maybe even portions of Iraq would likely sicken another million people, many of whom would die painfully within weeks. Possible confirmation of this coerced confession was indicated by the amount of activity around the Iranian launch facility located in northern Iran about twenty-five miles from the city of Shahrud. Surveillance photos revealed that several of the launch silos showed activity that was significantly elevated from previous levels. The Brief reported that this intelligence had been shared with appropriate Israeli officials.

The Brief reported that the Department of Homeland Security had issued a formal request to the Governors of every state to place their National Guard forces on ready status so that they could be mobilized immediately if needed. The offices of all Governors had reported that they had complied with the request. All branches of the military had canceled all leaves and all but a handful of military and civilian personnel who worked on military installations had returned to their assigned posts. Security at all military installations around the world, including those in the United States, had been increased. The level of protection included increased patrols and other access protection measures including large caliber automatic weapons "sandbagged-in" and manned around the clock at all vehicular entrances.

The Brief reported on the progress being made in getting the rescue missiles and warheads ready for launch. The first priority had been to get four of the largest missiles prepared for launch and to get the four B93 hydrogen bombs reassembled and married to the missiles. Since these bombs would be used for the divide and deflect mission, they would be needed the soonest. Progress was good and these weapons were expected to be ready by 3 July. The fitting of the W97 thermonuclear bombs in Multiple Independently Maneuverable Warhead bundles of twelve to each of the twenty-eight Peacekeeper ICBMs was progressing satisfactorily. The programming of the guidance systems to convert them from ballistic trajectories to the rescue mission trajectories was taking some time because there were so many bombs and missiles to prepare and test. The report confirmed that all the missiles would be ready by 8 July.

The Brief contained information on no-shows in the civilian and military work forces. Most businesses that were reporting this voluntary statistic, as requested by the Labor Bureau, were reporting minimal no-shows and quits so far. All military branches reported almost no desertions. There had been no reported cases of price gouging in the United States but there had been spotty reports in some central African nations and one South American country. Local governments were reported to be dealing appropriately with these rare cases.

The President placed the briefing folder in the top right drawer of his desk. He buzzed his Personal Secretary and asked her to get the Secretary of State on the phone for him.

James Warren was speaking with the President within twenty minutes, "Sir, I am sorry it took me so long to get back to you."

"That's OK Jim; I know that you were meeting with the Prime Minister. I just finished reading my Daily Brief; have you read it yet?"

"No sir, I haven't had a chance to do that yet."

"Well it reports that we have apparently underestimated the nuclear progress that Iran has continued to make even though they signed another agreement to cease enrichment activities three years ago. We have acquired statements from a former scientist who has defected. He believes that Iran has enough enriched uranium to make as many as three bombs with ten megatons of explosive power. There is also evidence that the Iranians are working feverishly to prepare missiles for launch. We have shared this information with Israeli officials. I need for you to get over there and talk to both countries to try to get this thing under control. I am afraid that Iran may try to make good on their boast that they would blast Israel off the face of the Earth. They may try to do just that before the date that they think this space rock will collide with Earth. Of course Israel will act to defend itself from this possibility. These events could plunge those two countries and perhaps neighbors into a nuclear war. I need for you to get these guys to settle down and explain to them that at this time there is more threat to humankind by their potential actions than from any space rock."

"Yes sir. I will leave London within the hour and will get appointments with both leaders if the Iranian President will agree to meet. I'll be back to you as soon as I have something material to tell you."

"Good; thanks Jim." Mornay disconnected from Warren and then punched the button that would ring into the office of the Vice President. Garish answered the call himself.

"Hello Mr. President."

"Hello Dick; are you available to visit with me now?"

"Of course Mr. President; I am about to finish a small meeting here in my office. I will be there in less than ten minutes."

"That sounds fine. This is not an emergency request so wrap up your involvement properly."

"Yes sir."

Garish arrived at the outer area of the Oval Office within the ten minutes as promised. The Personal Secretary to the President smiled, said hello, and advised Garish that he could enter the Oval Office. Garish pushed the convex door halfway open and tapped on the outside of it like he always did as if he needed to announce his arrival and wanted to be invited to enter by the President. "Come on in Dick; I hope I didn't interrupt a card game or something." Mornay laughed at his stinger.

"No sir you didn't interrupt; the lady had run out of clothing already," Garish reported.

Mornay laughed and again remembered how much he appreciated that Garish had a quick wit and instant humor during almost any circumstance. "Dick, I've been wondering if it would be wise for us to try to get out into the public a little more while we are in this rock limbo. I was thinking that America might be a little more comfortable if they were to see you making appearances on the late night comedy shows. Americans might feel better knowing that life should go on while we wait to find out how this space threat will end. You know everything we are doing and could tell what needs to be told to see that Americans are informed and reassured. What do you think?"

"Mr. President, I think that, as always, you have a shrewd and effective way of caring for our citizens. I agree that it would show that those of us here in Washington are not paralyzed or panicky over Hansen's Rock. And you know I just love to spar with those guys on the late night shows. I don't mean to brag too much but I am almost always the winner in those sparring matches." Garish grinned.

"Dick, haven't you figured out that they let you win? Man, you are the Vice President of the United States. They aren't going to knock you down and kick you!"

"Yes sir, I guess I have chosen to think it was skill on my part, not fear on their part."

"O.K. Dick you have a direct order to go have fun on the late night talk circuit. If you lose a word match with one of those guys, I promise you that you will not be my running mate again."

"Well sir, thanks for all the encouragement and confidence." They laughed and Garish left the room.

***

Trish Daly, the White House Press Secretary, opened the daily media briefing with a statement about the current information that they had decided to release on the location of Hansen's Rock. This was the first time that a title had been given to this space rock in public so she explained the origin of the moniker. She reinforced the positive news that the probability of a collision with Earth had declined overnight and was expected to continue to decline. She reported generally on the two potential defense plans and explained how they were different, providing a little more detail than the President had given in his address to the nation. When she finished her opening remarks, she paused expecting to receive questions from the reporters. And she got some.

"The Russians are predicting that this space rock, uh...Hansen's Rock, will eventually fall to Earth. The President stated that we believe that the rock will slingshot back into space. How can different space scientists using essentially the same technologies and methodologies arrive at such dramatically different conclusions?" asked the correspondent occupying the center seat in the front row of chairs.

"I am not a space scientist..." she paused as the room filled with laughter, "...as if I had to explain that to you. But, as I understand it, at

Hansen's Rock

this point every space scientist's conclusions are based on data that has a certain amount of potential error in it. Path predictions involve a lot of complex interactions where an assumption as small as one thousandth of a percent could make the difference in whether the object enters a deteriorating orbit around Earth or slingshots back into space. I think it will be at least a week before anyone in the world can predict with certainty where Hansen's Rock will go. It could even take longer than a week."

The next correspondent asked, "Unconfirmed sources are suggesting that Iran, out of nowhere, has now accumulated enough enriched uranium to make several nuclear bombs. Will you confirm the veracity of that report? And since Iran had signed an agreement that bound them to terminate their enrichment activities, do we know if they produced their own material or did they receive that material from another country?"

The Secretary paused, flipped a few pages in her briefing binder and began, "I cannot confirm the accuracy of that rumor. However, I can tell you that the President is very concerned by the instability in that region of the world and has sent our Secretary of State to the Middle East to continue discussions with critical players in that region."

A correspondent representing a major television network asked, "My producer told me that Vice President Garish requested to be invited to our late night show. What is driving that request and doesn't the Vice President have more important things to do than to exchange jokes with late night show hosts?"

"I think that if you were to check you would find that your network has repeatedly invited several White House officials to appear on their shows. These invitations have included numerous requests that Vice President Garish agree to visit with your late night hosts. So, I think that the Vice President has decided to accept the last invitation he received from your network. And of course he deals with more important things. But he knows that spending a few minutes discussing American issues with your host does not interfere with his other responsibilities. The Vice President considers it important for his constituents to see him and to hear from him. The late night circuit provides visibility to audiences that are typically much different than those that watch daytime programming."

The White House Secretary responded to several more questions from correspondents representing large and small media organizations. When she believed that most of the important matters had been addressed, she concluded the daily briefing and exited the room.

30 JUNE

It was 1:00 a.m. in Washington D.C. when the bombs exploded. Four coordinated bombs destroyed four double-decker buses preparing for departure at the Walthamstow Central Bus Station in London, England. Initial reports indicated that casualties could exceed four hundred. It was obvious that the explosions had been timed during the peak travel hour so as to create the greatest possible carnage. The bombs did considerable damage to other buses at the station and severely damaged the station itself. Local authorities suspect that backpack bombs were used by homicide bombers but more analysis would be required to determine the nature and locations of the explosives. There had been no threats made by anyone before the explosions and in the few hours after the bombs went off nobody had claimed responsibility.

***

Russian Federation President Volkov addressed his nation reaffirming the belief of his scientists that the space rock would enter a deteriorating orbit and then crash to Earth. He restated his commitment to save the world. He revealed that it would be at least another ten days before his missiles and warheads would be constructed, tested, and ready to destroy the rock.

***

It was Sunday and places of worship around the world were filled with worshipers seeking comfort from the threatening situation; trying to

Hansen's Rock

redeem themselves; or trying to connect or reconnect with their spiritual deities. Offerings were reported to be more generous than at any time in the past.

***

The USS South Carolina, a Virginia-class fast attack submarine, arrived at its assigned post in the Gulf of Oman about eighty miles due east of Muscat, Oman. It arrived with all twelve vertical launch tubes pre-loaded with Tomahawk Land Attack Missiles and a full torpedo room storing another twenty TLAMs plus eleven torpedoes. This hovering position put nearly ninety percent of Iran within the 1000 mile range of the missiles armed with a conventional 1000 pound high-explosive unitary warhead. The missiles could easily reach Iran's missile silos in Shahrud and the city of Tehran, if needed.

***

James Warren called President Mornay to inform him of the discussions that he had completed with the Presidents of Israel and Iran.

Warren reported that tensions in the Middle East were as high as he had ever seen them. He had met with the President of Iran first and he had denied that Iran had any nuclear aspirations other than the peaceful use of nuclear fuel for power generation and medical applications. He also had denied having any missiles trained on Israel. The President of Iran had told Warren that he did not fear the space rock and that he was confident that his friends, the Russians, would destroy the rock if it threatened Earth. He assured that Iran had not changed any military posture as a result of the potential threat from the space rock. He asserted that they had no plans for any preemptive military action against any country. However, he emphatically promised that if any nation were to attack any part of Iran that he would unleash every retaliatory weapon in the Iranian arsenal including "suicide bombers by the thousands."

Warren then reported on his meeting with the Prime Minister of Israel. He observed that the Prime Minister as always had a cool head. He commented that if a country had been surrounded by chaos and hatred for centuries that you would expect that the people would have to elect a cool head like their current leader. Warren reported that Israel's position had not changed. The Prime Minister simply restated that he will not permit Iran or any other nation to attack his country with nuclear or conventional weapons. He reaffirmed that he was prepared and that he would order preemptive strikes if intelligence indicated that Iran or another nation were intending to target his people. He assured Warren that the Israeli military knew where all the Iranian missile solos were located and that, if provoked, he would bomb every silo into the sand. Warren advised the Prime Minister that the US had sent another nuclear submarine to the Gulf of Oman to complement the two submarines that were already on station in the Persian Gulf. Warren assured the Prime Minister that all of the US ships were within range of the missile silos and that the US would have his back.

Mornay summed up the report as sounding pretty much as he had expected and asked Warren if he had further recommendations for actions that the US might take. Warren recommended that the President move a Carrier Strike Group back into the Persian Gulf so that both the Iranians and the Israelis were reminded that the US was serious about defending its allies in the region. Warren said that he supported the previous move of the Carrier Strike Group out of the Persian Gulf two years ago in an effort to lower tensions in that region but that he thought now would be a good time to reassert America's strength to the Iranians. The President agreed with the recommendation and said he would order General Watson to take care of it.

***

Mornay punched the intercom button and asked his Personal Secretary to get General Watson on the phone for him. Watson was on the line in less than ten minutes.

"Good morning, Mr. President; what can I do for you?"

"Stan, I spoke with Jim Warren a little earlier. He had met with the Prime Minister of Israel and the President of Iran to pursue this intelligence that Iran may have enough material to make some bombs. Nothing much new came from the talks. Iran denies the intelligence and Israel simply says that they will defend themselves. Jim suggested that we reassert ourselves in the area and move a Carrier Strike Group back into the Persian Gulf. I agree with that suggestion and think now would be a good time to send a message of strength and support for our allies in that region. What do you think?"

The General promptly replied, "I agree whole-heartedly. You probably will remember that I did not want to move those ships in the first place but acquiesced to the political importance of deescalating tensions over there. The ships will be in position within twelve hours. Along with the two Virginia-class subs we have kept in the Persian Gulf all along, we should have all the fire power we could need. What else can I do for you Mr. President?"

"I do have a question. As you have heard, President Volkov continues to promise that he will save the world with his missiles and bombs. Do you think that the Russians can actually do what he promises?"

"Yes sir, I believe that they have the bombs and missiles to do the job if they can get their missiles successfully reconfigured from ballistic mission orientation to that required for this unique mission. I'd say that they can probably be ready before the rock gets here but if they wait too long they may not be able to avoid multiple smaller collisions with Earth from the fragments of their attempt. I fear that Volkov and his military guys are planning to use a few large nukes to try to fragment this rock and that may not be successful. I think our plan to use hundreds of smaller warheads targeted smartly across the entire surface of this rock is more likely to accomplish a successful fragmentation."

"Your plan does sound more rational. I have one last question today. Since you have limited confidence that the Russians can accomplish their mission, do you think that we should intervene if they launch missiles at the rock?"

"That's a tough one Mr. President. Firstly, shooting down a missile that is coming at you is much easier than shooting down a missile that is moving away from you. The intercepting missile would have to catch up to the target which would have a head start. It is possible but we would have to be on the ready to launch interceptor missiles as soon as possible after the Russians launch their missiles. And there is another concern. I have to believe that they will be using their largest nukes and considering the target I am nearly certain that they will use proximity detonation. That means that they will program the bomb to detonate when it reaches a certain distance from the surface of the target. If we shoot one or more of their missiles down, there is always a possibility that a nuclear warhead could survive and accidentally detonate near enough to Earth to cause damage. Depending on where the bomb is when it detonates, we could have widespread death and destruction. Even if the bomb doesn't detonate over populated land we could have to deal with a huge radioactive cloud dropping nuclear contaminants to Earth for a long time. It's a very tough call." The General paused.

"Of course; I hope we don't get to a point where we have to contemplate doing that. Thanks for your excellent advice General. Good-bye for now."

"Good-bye Mr. President."

Dan L. King

HE-E-E-ER's RICHARD

The band played the first thirty seconds of the song "Dynamite", the fight song for Garish's college alma mater, as he walked from stage left to be greeted by the host of the most-watched late night show in America. Garish stood to a standing ovation while the music played. He acknowledged the audience which seemed, to a person, to be supportive and pleased that the Vice President was in their midst. When the music stopped Garish took a seat along with the host but the audience continued to applaud for another fifteen seconds until Garish appealed that they be seated.

The host spoke first, "Thank you Mr. Vice President for visiting with us tonight. I guess things must be slow at the White House these days."

Garish didn't pause a second before he replied, "Things are always pretty slow if you are the Vice President." The crowd appreciated the self-deprecation.

"Yeah, I guess that's true. I would guess that you don't have to refill the President's coffee cup very often after the evening meal."

"No, after I have pressed and laid out the President's suit for tomorrow I'm pretty much off duty until I bring him his breakfast the next morning." More laughter came from the audience.

"So what kind of important stuff did you do today?"

"Well, let's see. I cleaned up a water spill on the floor of the outer room of the Oval Office. You know we just can't have the President taking a fall while on the job." The crowd continued to enjoy the quick wit of the Veep.

"You know, of course, that the hottest discussion topic in America right now is this space rock that might end life on Earth. So is the White House concerned about this rock?"

"No, we are not concerned at all. After all, didn't you hear, the Russian President has assured us that he will save the world." The crowd laughed uneasily at this quip while Garish paused. He then continued, "But seriously, we do face a threat from this space rock, which is often called Hansen's Rock after the amateur astronomer who discovered it. However, the current predictions from our space scientists have the rock missing Earth and probably just heading back out into space. But, we have our military preparing for two potential missions to either divide and deflect it or to destructively fragment the rock if it is determined that the rock does ultimately pose a threat to Earth. I am confident that our plans will eliminate the threat and I am confident that life on Earth will continue to be as crazy as ever." The audience applauded at the reassuring message and the attempt at humor.

The host asked, "So given the enormous capabilities of all of the world's satellites, radio telescopes, optical telescopes, and the various efforts to map asteroids that might be a threat to Earth, how is it that this rock is discovered by an amateur with a store-bought telescope?"

Garish tried to explain, "Well, firstly this rock is not an asteroid from the asteroid belt that we normally think of as the source of space rock threats to Earth. Our survey efforts to map asteroids that are a potential threat have us searching our solar system mostly along the same plane that the planets and the asteroid belt are located in. This space rock is coming to us on a path that is basically perpendicular to the plane of our solar system. Also, this rock is approaching from an area near the south polar star. This means that none of the terrestrial facilities above the equator has a view of this part of space since the object would be below the horizon for land-based facilities in the northern hemisphere. Most of the highly capable terrestrial facilities in the world are north of the equator. There are a handful of capable facilities in the southern hemisphere but, as I mentioned earlier, they would most often be looking for objects that would be at higher elevations than where this rock is located in the southern sky."

The audience was engrossed in this explanation and remained mostly silent awaiting the next probe from the host.

"So doesn't your explanation point out a serious problem for us if no nationally funded facility is actually looking at these parts of space that are out of the normal study zones?"

Garish began to feel a little defensive as he could see this line of questioning leading to a criticism of his administration, "Yes, the evidence would lead one to think like that. However, we do have survey satellites that can view those areas of space that are not easily viewed from the ground. In fact, we are using one of these satellites to keep tabs on this rock as it approaches Earth. I would expect that we will broaden the range of space on which we perform continuing surveys so that in the future we will identify these celestial wanderers using government or private satellite observatories." He paused. The audience was still very interested in this line of questioning but didn't find this response fully satisfying.

"So are you saying that in the future you can assure us that we will have eyes in the sky watching for objects approaching Earth from unusual areas of space?" the host probed.

"Yes that is possible," Garish replied realizing that he couldn't and shouldn't promise that satellites would cover every bit of space in the future any more than they had covered every bit of it in the past.

"I am sure that everyone would agree that it is possible. My question was could you assure the audience and me that it will be done?" the host twisted the blade a bit.

Garish knew that his boss believed in totally honesty no matter the consequence and that he had better not deviate from that principle ever. He knew that he could not spin the facts into something that they were not. "No, I cannot provide absolute assurance that we will never again have a rock approach us from space that isn't detected by government owned or sponsored facilities on Earth or in the sky. Space is huge and there is always the possibility that even with all reasonable efforts by governments we could still have instances of objects that are discovered by amateurs rather than professionals."

"That isn't the most reassuring summary is it Mr. Garish?"

Garish promptly replied, "No, I guess not. I must admit that you have me between a rock and hard space." The audience immediately connected with Garish's witty description and roared with laughter and rewarded him with a long applause. They really did appreciate his candor and unwillingness to say all the right things that he wouldn't be able to deliver. Garish had again disarmed his opponent with his quick wit.

CHAOS GROWS

The first three days of July brought more signs of the effect that the threat of extinction was having on the people of Earth.

Only hours after the US Carrier Strike Group entered the Persian Gulf to take up its idle speed patrol as close as one mile west of the midline of the gulf, the Iranian Supreme Leader was condemning the return of the big ships as "provocative and dangerous." He said that this was a clear sign that the Americans were interested in starting another war in the region. He said that his naval and ground-based forces would blockade the Strait of Hormuz as promised by Iran's oil minister and other Iranian officials in the past. This blockade would suspend the passage of the oil tankers that supplied one-third of the world's oil that was shipped by sea. He warned the Americans that if their ships crossed the midline of the gulf that the wrath of Allah would rain down upon the ships.

Immediately after this threat was delivered to all the public media that would listen, the President of Iran ordered his most senior naval officer to align their largest frigate so as to shadow the US carrier ship wherever it might be. He ordered that the distance between the two ships should be small enough that the captain of the frigate "…should be able to read the name tags on the American sailors' uniforms." The naval leader informed his President that to get close enough to read American sailor nametags would require that the Iranian ship cross the midline and be within the perimeter of the escort ships that defended the aircraft carrier. He advised that attempting to accomplish a distance that small would not be wise as it would immediately create an international "situation" that would quickly escalate into a very short, full scale naval battle that the Iranians would most certainly lose. The

President of Iran backed down on his expectation and ordered that the frigate patrol parallel to the US ship and one kilometer east of the midline of the gulf. He ordered that sufficient ships be sent to the Strait of Hormuz so as to be able to blockade all shipping if he gave the order. Within hours two of Iran's smaller frigates and two of their submarines were patrolling the Strait of Hormuz. The submarines were in surface patrol mode so as to be visible and because the water in the area was too shallow for safe sub-surface operation. The largest frigate in the Iranian navy was quickly approaching its ordered position to shadow the US Carrier Strike Group ships.

The United States responded to the statement of the Supreme Leader of Iran with a statement attributed to the President. It said that the United States and all other nations had the right to pass through the territorial waters of Iran and Oman under the transit passage provisions of the United Nations Convention on the Law of the Sea. It went further to state that the United States would not permit a blockade of the Strait of Hormuz and would take every action necessary to maintain normal passage capability for the ships of all nations.

General Watson, after consultation with the President, ordered his naval commander to reposition one of the submarines that had been patrolling within the Persian Gulf. He instructed that the sub take up a position just west of the Strait of Hormuz to protect egress from the gulf. He ordered the newly arrived submarine to a position just south of the entrance to the Strait of Hormuz to protect shipping ingress. Both ships were ordered to assume a surface posture to make sure that they were visible to all ships in the region, including the Iranian warships.

***

There continued to be isolated terrorist bombings around the world. A Eurostar train traveling from Paris to London was derailed by an explosive placed on the tracks near Calais, France. The train was traveling at over 300 kilometers per hour at the time of the derailment. Over 300 people perished and another 200 were injured. There were six car-bombings in Fallujah and Baghdad causing many fatalities, injuries, and significant property damage. A disgruntled worker at the Hamaoka Nuclear Plant located on the southern coast of Japan about 190 kilometers from Tokyo attempted to enter the facility with a liquid-based bomb in two soft drink bottles but was discovered at the security checkpoint. He detonated the bomb killing him and several other workers awaiting clearance to go to work.

Tensions were causing an ever-increasing number of confrontations at public places like grocery stores, bus stations, gasoline filling stations, and other places. People were resorting to anger much more often than had been the norm.

Purchases of major items soared as people who had wanted an expensive toy of some sort apparently decided that they were in a "now or never" situation. Some thought that they likely had nothing more to lose if they splurged on a huge-screen TV or a red sports car since there was a good chance that the world would end before they received their billing statements.

Applications for pay-day loans and title loans soared. Some loan businesses had to hire armed guards to control the crowds that were coming to their doors each day in search of loans that the applicants expected they might not have to repay.

Slowly, people who had fled their homeland because of war were beginning to re-cross the borders leaving the refugee camps that had supported them for months or years so that they could be at their true home when the end of the world arrived.

Thousands of people in every country were migrating to religious landmarks so that they could be close to the holy place when the end came.

Isolated looting had begun to pop up in civilized nations including the United States. Local authorities and National Guard personnel typically had the situations under control pretty quickly but the trend was not good.

People were visiting family that they hadn't visited in months or years. Runaway children were returning home to be with their parents and siblings.

The sale of alcohol and illegal drugs was soaring. Many package stores had empty shelves. People were buying large amounts of beer and liquor to load into their title-loaned car...they would party until their time was up.

Sick days were being used up before they were lost. No-shows were starting to increase. Workplace revenge was growing as people who had been disciplined or disappointed for some reason were getting even with their bosses through beatings or worse.

THE FOURTH OF JULY

As the fourth of July arrived, most US cities and towns were still planning their traditional celebrations of the anniversary in spite of the warnings that the likelihood of terrorist acts was high. The National Terrorism Advisory System had been set at the "Elevated Threat Alert" level. The Department of Homeland Security would have raised the threat level to the "Imminent Threat Alert" if they had been able to discern a "specific threat" from all of the threat intelligence they were analyzing. But their own rules required that they have specific information about a threat before posting an Imminent Threat Alert. Had they posted the highest threat level, it is likely that some cities would have cancelled their celebrations.

***

It was widely publicized that the President of the United States would address the nation from the Oval Office at 11:00 a.m. The time was a little unusual as presidential addresses to the nation were typically scheduled for prime-time evening broadcasts. But, since this was a national holiday, it seemed sensible to deliver the President's message to the nation earlier in the day and before all the mid-day news broadcasts. He wanted to be able to reassure the citizens of the United States early in the day on this special anniversary.

The President began, "Fellow Americans, 247 years ago today the Thirteen Colonies in America formally adopted a document called the Declaration of Independence. On that day John Hancock, the President of the Continental Congress, applied the first of the fifty-six total signatures on the document. The Declaration of Independence explained the action taken two days earlier by the Second Continental Congress which had voted to approve a resolution of independence which declared the formal separation of the colonies from the Kingdom of Great Britain. The day that the Second Continental Congress voted to separate from the British Empire was the most important day in this nation's history; it was literally this nation's birthday. The final version of the Declaration of Independence referred to the thirteen colonies as the "thirteen united States of America." The day that the Declaration of Independence received John Hancock's signature and every anniversary of that day are called Independence Day. Today, we again celebrate that momentous day and America is still independent. I believe that our founding fathers would still be proud of what they started.

As you know, the declaration to separate from the Kingdom of Great Britain came after a difficult war between the colonies and Great Britain. The basis of the war was that Great Britain was taxing the colonies to remain a part of The Empire but had refused to give America any representation in Parliament. It was this taxation without representation that divided the colonies from Great Britain and ultimately compelled them to form the union that was the first step toward the United States of America. In 1776, America's freedom was being threatened and America responded

History shows that America has been threatened many more times since its birth and has always responded to those threats. Today we still face threats. We are still in a war with those who choose to terrorize America and it citizens. This war, which is now decades old, is different from past wars in that it isn't about a war between nations so much as it is a war on America by groups that may have no national allegiance; it is a war on the principles and ideals of America. Some of those who would bring terror to Americans are radical citizens of America. Others who bring terror to America take advantage of the welcoming freedom that America makes possible in the form of visiting visas, student visas, and the like as a vehicle for gaining entry to America so that they can strike from within. Nevertheless, America is responding again and we have been successful in discovering many of the plots against us and we have stopped nearly all of them before harm could be imposed on our law abiding citizens. We have not yet won this war; but we are not losing it.

Recently we all learned of a new threat to America and the world. The space rock that has been discovered in space over the South Pole poses a very serious threat to America and every other nation on Earth. The rock which is coming toward us and is expected to reach the vicinity of Earth late next week is large enough to cause catastrophic damage were it to collide with Earth. However, I want to assure each of you that we fully intend to deal with this threat. As in the case of all threats in the past, America is responding to ensure your safety and freedom. We have plans that will deflect or destroy the rock if we determine that it is likely to collide with Earth. As of this time, we believe that there is a probability of over seventy percent that this rock will pass Earth and continue harmlessly back into space. I want to encourage you to continue your lives as you would have without knowledge of this threat from space. I do, however, think that this threat should give all of us an opportunity to reflect on how we are living our lives. If we each were to live our life as if we only had ten days of life left, would we behave the way we have in the past? Would we be so quick to be critical? Would we remain as greedy as we might have been in the past? Would we discriminate against others on the basis of our differences rather than embrace others because of our similarities. Would we let our families dissolve over petty disputes? Would we cheat on our taxes or friends or spouses? Would we destroy the property of others simply because we are angry or bored or feel disenfranchised? Would we fear strangers or would we make them our friends? I hope that you will look inside yourself on this day of independence and find your answers to these questions.

I assure you that Earth will have many more days and that we will celebrate many more Independence Day anniversaries. I hope that each of you enjoy the independence that our predecessors entrusted to us and I hope that each of you accepts the responsibility that each of us has to ensure that the United States of America and every one of its citizens will remain independent and safe.

Thank you and may God bless America."

The red light on the camera expired and Mornay pushed his chair away from the antique wood desk. He went to the private washroom to wash the TV makeup from his face and to prepare for his meeting with the NEO SCC scientists.

Vice President Garish knocked on the door to the Oval Office just as Mornay exited the bathroom. He informed Mornay that apparently coordinated attacks on three US Embassies had been made during Mornay's address to the nation. None had been successful in breaching the security perimeters of the embassies due to the beefed-up physical barriers and the increased security personnel in place.

***

Mornay arrived at the Situation Room a few minutes before noon. He chatted with Barrow, Garish, and the technician setting up the duplex video connection. When noon arrived the technician turned on the projector which showed the image of the SCC on the rear projection screen.

Mornay spoke first, "Good morning to all of you out there in sunny California."

The room responded in unison, "Good afternoon, Mr. President." They had remembered that last time they had forgotten the time difference between Washington and Pasadena and had vowed to get it right this time.

Mornay asked, "OK who's in charge today?"

The conference room responded in unison, "You are Mr. President." Everybody on both ends of the connection laughed. It was clear that the scientists in the conference room were in good spirits. Mornay was happy to see that.

"OK, you got me on that one. Let me clarify, who is leading the discussion today?"

Liz Wilson spoke this time, "Mr. President I will start things off and I will get assistance from my team during our discussion. First of all let me say how proud we all are of the speech you made just a few minutes ago. We all watched it and agree that is was just awesome. We are always inspired after hearing each of your addresses to the nation." She paused.

"Thank you so much Liz and everyone else. I really appreciate your kind words."

"You're welcome Mr. President. We only tell the truth in this center so you can rest assured that we aren't just sucking up because you have a few more stripes than us." Everybody laughed again. "Sir, we have some good news to report to you today. I hope that you can sense that we are in good spirits and the reason for that is that our prediction of the likelihood of a direct collision with Hansen's Rock continues to decrease."

Garish interrupted, "That's great news!"

"Yes sir; we agree. Now for the numbers and more discussion: Hansen's Rock is now 1,212,000 miles from Earth. The rock is approaching Earth at a velocity of approximately 3,000 miles per hour. We project Maximum Proximity to be 311 miles with confidence limits of ± 606 miles so the range of MP is between a high of 914 miles and a low angle collision with Earth. We calculate the probability of impact at 24.37 percent but we are very optimistic that this probability will go down dramatically in just a few days. If our predictive models continue to resolve the way we think they will, we expect that by the eighth of July we will be able to report that the surface of Earth will be outside the cone of uncertainty. However, I need to point out that just because

Earth's surface falls outside of the cone of uncertainty does not mean that we are totally out of the woods. The remaining uncertainty is related to velocity, angle of attack, and the interaction between Earth's magnetic field and that of Hansen's Rock, which are still somewhat uncertain. This uncertainty has to do with what is called escape velocity. In other words, in order for the rock to pass Earth and head back into space, it must be moving fast enough not to be drawn to the surface of the Earth and fast enough to avoid going into an orbit around Earth. Technically, an orbit around Earth might not be all that bad as that could give us a significant amount of time to destroy the rock but we would have to be dealing with the rock for a long time also. The numbers break down this way. In order for the rock to pass Earth and head back into space, it will need to be traveling at a velocity of about 25,500 miles per hour. That speed is sufficient if the object approaches Earth on a line that is exactly parallel to a tangent plane at the surface of Earth. If the rock approaches at an angle that is steeper, it will need to move faster to avoid being captured in an orbital path around Earth. If the rock approaches Earth at a velocity of less than 17,200 miles per hour, it will fall to Earth without making a single orbit. Again how quickly it hits Earth will depend on the velocity and angle of attack. If Hansen's Rock reaches its maximum proximity with a velocity between 17,200 and 25,500 miles per hour, it will enter an orbital path around Earth. The closer the speed is to 17,200 miles per hour, the lower and less elliptical the orbit will be. The faster the velocity of the rock, the more elongated the elliptical orbit will be. For example if the rock is traveling at exactly 24,600 miles per hour, the rock will enter an orbit that will range from altitudes of about 300 miles to about 78,300 miles. What this means is that there is still a possibility that Hansen's Rock could initially pass Earth only to be dragged into an orbit around Earth that could eventually deteriorate and bring the rock down." She paused.

Garish asked, "So the Russians could be right about the rock entering a deteriorating orbit?"

"Yes sir, we must say that their prediction is within the realm of possibility. However, we believe that the velocity of the rock will be well above that which will keep it from falling to Earth. But, we will just not know until the magnetic and gravitational interaction between Hansen's Rock and Earth are better understood and that may require several more days of data since HR has such strange magnetic attributes. Recent data suggests that the rock is accelerating faster than we had modeled in the past. We now believe that the rock may be in the vicinity of Earth early in the morning of 12 July; that's about a day earlier than our models told us until the last survey data was input."

Garish continued, "So you told us that within a couple of days you may be able to tell us that a direct strike can be ruled out; when will you be able to tell us that the rock will not enter a deteriorating orbit?"

Wilson had expected that question and she and her team had discussed how to respond to it. "Sir, the real truth is that the rock may be very close to Earth before we can give you that information but we would hope to be able to answer that question when HR is at least two, maybe three, days away from Earth."

"That doesn't give us much time to exercise our options does it?"

"No sir."

President Mornay wrapped the discussion, "OK, continue the good work. I will anxiously await your daily reports. I would like to meet with all of you again on July 9 since you believe that you may be able to determine whether Hansen's Rock will enter a deteriorating orbit by then. If you get a breakthrough of some sort before then, immediately contact Mr. Barrow and he will get me informed or he will get us together again. Thanks again for the outstanding work. Good-bye."

"Of course sir; we will appreciate your meeting with us on the ninth. Good-bye sir."

***

Martin and Claxton finished their early morning optical survey of Hansen's Rock and returned to The Lodge to prepare their reports to their bosses. When they sat down at the table in the day room to drink their first cup of coffee and nibble on some sweet bread, Claxton proposed that they make today's observation the last. He reasoned that since Hansen's Rock was now so low in elevation that they were looking through too much atmosphere to get good images and measurements. In addition, the weather forecast was predicting several days of unsettled weather at the observatory which would likely keep them from performing visual studies. He suggested that he and Martin recommend to their bosses that they terminate surveys from the observatory. Martin agreed with the proposal and further added that the folk back in the states had much better technology on their satellites to monitor the rock anyway. They each felt confident that their bosses would agree with the recommendation. So, after sending their proposed last report, they began cleaning up The Lodge in preparation for their departure.

Claxton checked on flights out of Sydney and found one that would leave at 22:10 that evening and would take him to LAX. By the time he had finished checking on the flight availability, both bosses had concurred in the recommendation to terminate studies from Siding

Spring Observatory. Martin left The Lodge around 11:00 for his drive home and Claxton left around 13:00 for his drive to Dubbo Airport to catch the 16:55 to Sydney.

***

President Volkov summoned Anya and ordered her to have General Dmitriev come to see him immediately. Dmitriev arrived about an hour later to discover that Volkov was not in a good mood.

"Dmitriev, do you not walk when I say walk? Do you not run when I say run? Do you not jump when I say jump?"

"Yes Mr. President, I do as you instruct me to do."

"Did Anya not tell you to come to me immediately?"

"Yes Comrade Leader Anya did tell me to come immediately and that is exactly what I did. My plane had just landed at Chkalovsky when Anya called me and gave me the message. Surely you must agree that it is not unreasonable that it took me an hour to travel from the airport to your office."

Volkov realized that an hour was a reasonable travel time but he didn't care to be reasonable, "Maybe you need a better driver."

"No Comrade Leader, my driver is very capable. Why did you need to see me?" Dmitriev asked, having grown weary of his President's childish behavior.

"The President of the United States talked to his people today and told them that his scientists believe that this space rock will pass Earth and head back into space. What are my scientists telling you now that they have studied this rock more?"

"Sir, your scientists still believe that this rock will approach Earth at a speed that is too slow to propel it back into space after its near-Earth visit. They believe that it will go into an orbit around Earth and that the orbit has a good chance of deteriorating fairly quickly permitting the rock to strike Earth."

"Dmitriev, do you believe that our scientists are accurate with their forecasts?"

"Yes Comrade Leader; we have the best space scientists in the world."

"Of course we do. So how is the missile preparation coming?"

"We are facing some difficulties and setbacks. The large hydrogen bombs were not intended to be launched into space by our rockets and our rockets were not designed to carry such large payloads. We have focused our resources on getting at least one Bomba-missile ready for launch as soon as possible and then we will begin working on getting others prepared."

Hansen's Rock

"So Dmitriev do you believe that one of our Bomba-missiles is sufficient to destroy this space rock?"

Dmitriev knew that there was only one acceptable answer to this question, "Yes Comrade Leader I am certain that one Bomba-missile is enough to destroy this rock. The Tsar Bomba is the most powerful bomb ever exploded by mankind on Earth; it will be enough to destroy this little rock from space."

"Good Dmitriev; when do you expect we will be ready to launch this Bomba-missile?"

Dmitriev lied, "Comrade Leader, we expect to be able to launch our Bomba-missile in six days if we continue to believe that it is necessary to launch it."

"Dmitriev, I want you to make sure that we get this bomb ready in plenty of time to kill this rock. You must make sure that your people are working as long and as hard as it takes to get at least one bomb ready to launch before the rock gets too close to us."

"Of course Comrade Leader; I have my men working eighteen hours and only sleeping six hour per day now. I fear that pushing them harder will cause them to make mistakes."

"Dmitriev, let me explain it to you this way. If you are unsuccessful in getting at least one of these bombs ready to launch and the rock misses Earth, I will see to it that you spend the rest of your life digging potatoes at the penal camp near Krasnoyarsk in the frigid land of Siberia."

"Of course Comrade Leader; I can assure you that we will prepare your Bomba-missile in time." Dmitriev knew that if he failed he would likely die from the impact of the space rock so there was no additional risk in committing to being successful.

"Go to work General."

"Yes Mr. President."

***

Volkov summoned Anya to his office, "Anya I want you to take down a message that I want to be released to the press and the people of the Russian Federation."

"Yes Mr. President." Anya walked around the big hardwood desk until she was able to touch her hip to Volkov's shoulder. She opened the case on her electronic tablet and exposed the virtual keyboard. She placed the tablet on the desk, bent over, and placed her fingers above the keyboard and said, "I am ready sir."

Volkov smiled, rubbed her thigh with his shoulder a couple of times, and began his dictation, "I want to again assure the people of the

Russian Federation and indeed the peoples of the world that my Russian space and military scientists are working feverishly to prepare a missile that will destroy the space rock if we determine that destruction of this rock is necessary to protect the welfare of the people on Earth. I have been assured by the very highest official in our military that we will be ready to successfully execute a mission to destroy this rock if needed. Russia has the largest bombs on Earth, we have the most powerful missiles, and our missiles are able to deliver a bomb to any place in the world and to any place in the universe that we choose. My scientists still believe that this rock represents a threat and they still believe that if left alone this rock will enter a deteriorating orbit around Earth and will eventually fall to the surface. I will not let that happen. If this rock continues to threaten Earth, then at the proper time I will order the launch of one or more missiles that will destroy this rock. The Russian people should continue to go about their daily lives as if this space rock does not exist. Since you cannot see this rock from any point in the Russian Federation, you should not fear it in the least. I promise that I will save you if needed. Anya, prepare that for distribution to all the usual media and, of course, post it to my VK, Facebook, Google+, and Twitter."

"Yes sir I will distribute it immediately. As you know, your message is too long for a tweet but I will post a link on your twitter that will permit your followers to read your statement."

"Of course Anya that will be fine. Anya could we go to my apartment for lunch today; I am already very hungry."

Anya smiled and said, "Of course Mr. President, I too am famished."

Anya went back to her desk, tapped the screen on her tablet a few times to select the usual distribution list for media and others, selected the file that she had created from Volkov's dictation, and hit the send button. She then took care of all of the social media postings.

Anya was not in love with Volkov; in fact she didn't even like or admire him. But because she was agreeable she earned an income that was at least five times what a personal secretary could earn anywhere else in Russia. And she and her family had access to many things that average Russians could not access. When there were shortages of any commodity necessary for everyday life, she and her family were always granted the same access to the item that was had by the powerful people Anya worked around. Volkov shamelessly used her and she felt no shame for using him. So, she continued to be kind and agreeable to the little hairless man.

After preparing for the distribution of Volkov's message to the world, she went to her private dressing room and freshened all her

Hansen's Rock

scents, repainted her lips, and touched up the light makeup that she employed before leaving her office to go to the garage. From there she would drive her car to the secret apartment location where she would meet Volkov "for lunch."

SOME CALM, SOME CHAOS

The sale of telescopes and binoculars were soaring in Australia, Africa, New Zealand, and South America in those locations where the space rock was visible. Even though it was easily visible with the unaided eye, people still wanted to see more if they could. The apparent magnitude of Hansen's Rock was now 1.5 which made it brighter than Mars seen from Earth.

***

All around the world people had started gravitating to places held to be sacred. In Egypt, believers were congregating around most of the sacred sites along the Nile River. Temporary camps had been set up at The Great Sphinx, at the pyramids at Dahshur, at sites that lie on the path of the flight of the Holy Family of Egypt, and near the Monasteries of St. Antony and St. Paul. In Israel the faithful were gathering in Bethlehem at the Cave of the Nativity, at the Tomb of Rachel, and other sacred places. In Jerusalem people gathered around Mt. Zion, The Church of the Holy Sepulcher, and other sites. In Great Britain people were even visiting Megalithic sites like Stonehenge and nearby Neolithic sites in addition to conventional places of worship. In Rome there was a steady flow of worshipers moving through the Basilicas of St. Mary Major, St. Peter, and St. John Lateran. In Australia the Anangu Aboriginal community adjacent to Uluru was swelling and tents were being pitched to accommodate the influx of native visitors. Conventional places of worship were experiencing attendance levels that they had never seen before. The sale of religious symbolic items like rosary beads were extraordinarily active...there were certainly more Hail Mary prayers to count during these days.

***

In several schools in the United States teachers had asked students to write essays about the space rock telling their feelings about it and the way they, their families, and others were acting or reacting to the presence of the threat. To some students this would be a therapeutic exercise; to others it would only heighten their anxiety. But, in general, teachers thought that it would be good to talk about this rock and to find out what was going on in the young minds of their students. In many cases the students would read their essays before their class rather than just submitting them to their teacher. In one small town in California, essays had been submitted to the teacher and he had chosen two of them to be read by the authors and then discussed by the entire class. The instructor chose one of the essays that approached the presence of the rock from a purely technical and scientific approach discussing the mechanics of how the object might behave and how it would be destroyed by man and missile. The other essay had discussed the matter from a spiritual approach discussing how the presence of the rock might either reinforce or erode the faith of people on Earth. The young girl had fearlessly used the G-word in discussing her own faith and that of others. She opined that God would save the Earth by filling space scientists with the knowledge necessary to destroy the threatening rock. The teacher saw this as an opportunity to discuss two of the primary approaches that people take to life and to engage the young minds to investigate and to appreciate both approaches. This did indeed produce a lively discussion and most students seemed to be really engaged in trying to learn as much as they could about the roles of religion and science in explaining how people reacted to various situations like the threat of this space rock.

However, the father of one of the kids in the class filed a complaint with the school principal declaring that the teacher had violated the separation of church and state principle when he permitted the public reading of the essay that gave God credit for the good behaviors of mankind. As a result of this complaint, the teacher was required to issue a public apology to his class and to every parent in the form of a letter approved by the principal and signed by the teacher to be sent home with each student. To drive the point home that this behavior was considered improper by the school district, the teacher was suspended without pay for a week. He would be out of the classroom until after Hansen's Rock had reached the vicinity of Earth.

Dan L. King

This punishment caused division in the community and several marches of large numbers of community members. These marches produced a few cases of physical violence as the two opinions converged on the city streets. The national news reported on the classroom behavior, the subsequent punishment, the marches of support, and the marches by those who were calling for a retraction of the apology and an undoing of the punishment given the teacher. Once other teachers across the nation saw the potential penalty for discussions like this, the essay writing and discussion quickly disappeared from the classrooms of America.

***

The Russian military and space scientists were working feverishly to marry the huge sixty megaton bombs to the missiles that were never designed to be fitted with the now-ancient bombs. The bombs had been constructed to be dropped from aircraft, not propelled into space by a missile. The work was not going well and it was beginning to look as if the rescue missiles would not be ready. But none of the scientists wanted to be the one to tell General Dmitriev that they might fail. They continued to put all their efforts into getting at least one missile-bomb ready to launch. They knew that getting none of the bombs ready to launch would literally cost them their lives…if not from the space rock, then the General would see to it.

***

The Americans were making good progress. Since it appeared that the six day window needed to employ the divide and deflect option was quickly closing, they stopped working on that option and dedicated all their resources to getting the multiple warhead Peacekeeper missiles prepared for launch. They would be ready.

***

In Brisbane the crude oil dock was full of activity. The pumping of crude from Sirius was moving very smoothly and the crew would finish emptying the ship by 8 July. Loading of the containers was also progressing well and Hansen expected it to be completed by 9 July. Captain Hansen had notified Pole2Pole Petroleum Headquarters that Sirius would depart Brisbane late on 9 July.

The ship was rising in the water due to its reduced displacement since the density of the crude oil being pumped out was much greater than the density of the loads in the cargo containers. The captain had ordered the crew to start pumping ballast water from the river to keep the ship from becoming too top-heavy due to the nearly empty oil bladders and from the weight of all the containers being added to the deck of the giant ship. The beam of the ship and the careful distribution of the weights of the containers would keep the ship sufficiently stable while in port but the captain would order a healthy ballast load once he cleared the shallow channel and entered the Pacific Ocean. He preferred to ballast the ship with the cleaner water of the Pacific rather than that of the Brisbane River which had all manner of pollutants and contaminants in it. He would load the minimum amount of water needed to ballast the ship while it was being navigated to the clean waters in Moreton Bay. There he would discharge the river water and replace it with ocean water so that he would not transport the pollutants from the Brisbane River to other ports along his path back to the Mediterranean Sea.

Hansen had notified the Port of Brisbane Pty Ltd who ran the harbor, the Harbormaster, the harbor pilot, and the tug operators of his intended departure so that everything would be coordinated. Sirius would consume the entire shipping lane and all other traffic would need to be held at berth or at sea until Sirius cleared their holding positions.

9 JULY

Sirius' crew had concluded their inventory and confirmed that they had all of the Twenty-foot Equivalent Units (TEUs) that they were supposed to transport on the deck of the ship. At about 13:00 Hansen ordered the mooring lines to be cast off. Rain was pelting the line tenders on the dock. As the crew operated the huge diesel winches to recover the mooring lines from the water fore and aft, Hansen ordered his second-in-command to set the props to maximum pitch, to turn the rudders hard to port, and to engage the engines in reverse at idle rpm. He ordered portside bow and mid-ship thrusters engaged to bring the ship away from the crude oil dock.

Two tugs were in position on the southern side of Sirius when the maneuver began. As soon as the ship was approximately in the center of the navigable portion of the river the other two tugs moved into position on the northern side of Sirius. Hansen gave the order to return the rudders to the neutral position and to give pitch control to the navigation computer. The computer quickly adjusted the pitch of the four huge propellers to optimize performance at idle speed.

The Brisbane River was not wide enough in this area for Sirius to execute a turn-around maneuver so Sirius would back out of the river, assisted by the tugs. The harbor pilot took over command of the ship at this point; Hansen stayed nearby and fully engaged as the huge ship backed out of the channel at a speed of a little over one knot. Sirius traveled the six nautical miles needed to clear the Port of Brisbane facilities and reach Moreton Bay shortly before 19:00. At this point, Hansen took over command of the ship again. The harbor pilot boarded his tender and headed back to the harbor. The tugs were notified to cast off. They left Sirius and headed back to their berths in the harbor. Hansen maintained this reverse direction while staying in the channel through the mostly too shallow bay for another eight nautical miles until the depth sounders finally showed water that was 100 feet deep. The GPS units both showed the location to be approximately S27.23° / E153.27°. The charting monitor showed that the water depth at this point was sufficiently deep enough to either side of Sirius that a turn-around maneuver could be undertaken. Hansen ordered the propellers to be manually adjusted to maximum pitch and rudders to be turned to full port. He ordered the starboard bow thruster to maximum thrust. The stern of the ship slowly crept to starboard and the bow slowly crept to port. Sirius had all its lights aglow to ensure its visibility so as to avoid collision in the squally weather. The turning maneuver was continued until the bow was pointed just east of due north. Once the ship had the proper bearing, Hansen ordered his second to return control of propeller pitch to the navigational computer and to set a heading of 012 degrees at half speed. He ordered that the river water ballast be expelled and replaced with sea water. This operation took about an hour to pump enough ballast into the two tanks that ran along the outside extremes of the ship. The ballast tanks were designed on the outer reaches of the hull so that a minimum amount of ballast would create the maximum amount of stability. Just after 03:00, 10 July, the ship's main computer finally calculated that the ship had taken on enough ballast to make it safe for open sea operation and Hansen ordered the navigation computer to bring the ship up to maximum economy cruise speed. This heading would be followed for about twenty-two nautical miles as Sirius was navigated out of Moreton Bay and into the open Pacific. Once the ship was steady on the course he had ordered Hansen relinquished command to his second-in-charge and he headed to the mess deck for a quick snack before he went to his cabin for a nap.

***

President Mornay and Vice President Garish arrived at the Situation Room together and found Charlie Barrow already there as always. The technician enabled the duplex video circuit and the NEO SCC conference room lit up the projection screen. The room was filled by every employee in the center sitting or standing and chatting with one another until they noticed the image from Washington had arrived.

"Good morning everyone," the President greeted the SCC team.

"Good morning, Mr. President," returned from the SCC.

"People, I sure hope you have good news for us this morning," Mornay said.

Dan L. King

Wilson replied, "Sir, I think I can sum up what we know as some good news and some not so good news."

"OK Mrs. Wilson, let's hear what you have learned," Mornay instructed.

"OK sir. Here are the numbers from out last observations. Hansen's Rock is now about 711,000 miles from Earth. The rock is approaching at about 5,500 miles per hour. We are now 99.991% confident that HR will achieve a Maximum Proximity to Earth that is between 246 miles and 377 miles. We are now certain that Hansen's Rock will not make a direct impact with Earth." She paused for comments if any.

Garish spoke, "Awesome… that IS great news! I assume that was the good news you mentioned earlier?"

"Yes Mr. Vice President; that is the best news we have for you today. But the other news we have is not all bad. You will remember that we advised you and the President that if the rock was traveling at less than 17,200 miles per hour that it would enter a deteriorating orbit and subsequently fall to Earth. We also explained that if the rock approached with a speed of between 17,200 and 25,500 miles per hour it would enter into an orbit around Earth that could be considered stable, at least long enough to permit a mission to destroy it. If the object were to be traveling at more than 25,500 miles per hour, its path would be bent by Earth's gravitational and magnetic fields and the rock would slingshot around Earth and take a path back into deep space. Well, we currently believe that the rock will be traveling at 18,687 miles per hour when it reaches its Maximum Proximity. So, we believe that HR will be traveling nearly ten percent faster than necessary to avoid a deteriorating orbit. Of course there is still some uncertainty about the angle of attack which could alter our prediction slightly. If the Maximum Proximity turns out to be on the lower end of our confidence limits, then the orbital dimensions could change. However, if our velocity prediction is precisely accurate and if our prediction of Maximum Proximity is precisely accurate, then we believe that the rock will enter a stable elliptical orbit around Earth that will range from a minimum altitude of 311 miles to a maximum altitude of 910 miles. We now believe that the rock will reach Maximum Proximity around 3:00 p.m., Eastern Daylight Time, on 12 July. We still believe that the rock will be nearly directly over the South Pole when MP is achieved." Wilson paused again.

Mornay spoke, "So you are certain that the rock will not be slingshot back into space?"

"Yes Mr. President we are certain of that; our velocity prediction is that HR will only have about seventy-five percent of the velocity required for it to totally escape Earth."

Hansen's Rock

Mornay asked, "You indicated that your prediction of a stable orbit was good for at least a while. Do you know how long the rock would stay in this orbit before the orbit would begin to deteriorate?"

"Yes sir, the orbit would stable for a very long time but we don't know how long at the moment. The atmosphere of Earth actually goes a long way into space and this orbit would have Hansen's Rock moving between the layers of Earth's atmosphere that are called the Thermosphere and the Exosphere. The atmosphere is very thin in these areas but there are some gas molecules present. The fact that there are some gas molecules in these layers would create a minute amount of drag on the rock and over time the orbit would deteriorate but it could take years or decades, maybe even centuries, before Earth would again be threatened by this rock. If our predictions are correct, we could have a very long time to deal with this rock. However, I must mention that we do have a number of satellites that occupy this space between 300 and 1000 miles above Earth. We have weather satellites, photo satellites, military communications satellites, and military spy satellites in this area of near-space. So it is possible that there could be collisions between Hansen's Rock and one or more of these satellites. The path of the rock would not be materially altered by these collisions since the mass of HR is enormous compared to the satellites.

There is another likely occurrence while HR is in this orbit. We expect that the rock would gradually be warmed by the small amount of friction with the thin atmosphere and the constant exposure to the solar radiation. Over time the solid hydrogen surface coating would begin to melt when the surface temperature reaches about fourteen degrees Kelvin. Then it would boil and it would turn into a gas at about twenty degrees Kelvin. We measure the current surface temperature to be about four degrees Kelvin so the surface temperature would only need to rise about sixteen degrees of Celsius in order for the surface layer to begin changing from solid hydrogen to gaseous hydrogen, a process called sublimation. The rock would likely develop a trail or tail, if you will, of this gaseous hydrogen that would eventually disperse harmlessly into space. There is currently enough hydrogen captive to this rock to make an extremely large explosion. If our prediction of a long orbit life is correct, then the entire layer of hydrogen would melt and gasify exposing the metallic surface. In fact, there is the possibility that we could use this enormous hydrogen covering as the fuel to move the rock away from Earth over time. This would be done by placing a manmade satellite relatively near the object and focusing sunlight onto the surface so that the sublimation process forms a localized rocket–like thrust which could push the rock onto a new path. Over time this

Dan L. King

could accelerate the rock to the point where it would achieve escape velocity and leave Earth's vicinity.

Since the predicted orbit would likely be stable for many years or even decades, once the surface hydrogen evaporated, we might even have the technology, and the need, to mine the minerals from the rock. Over time the mining process would decrease the mass of the rock and make it easier to employ other deflection methodologies such as simply attaching a large rocket to the rock and guiding it to a path that would remove it from the orbit and away from Earth. I guess my point is that with Hansen's Rock in a stable orbit, we have many options that could be explored in a methodical way."

"Sounds more like science fiction that real science to me!" Garish quipped.

Mornay said, "OK Mrs. Wilson; thank you for the detailed description of this predicted orbit. I guess that is good news in a way. So, let me just make sure that I understand where this leaves us. Are you advising us that we should not try to deflect or fragment this space rock, that we will be safe to leave it to travel its current path and enter this orbit?"

Wilson knew that this was a crucial question and that the continued existence of life on Earth was on the balance. She looked around the room and made contact with her senior technician looking for a nod or a shake. Jones nodded in the affirmative. She then looked at her boss to get his vote; he too nodded that he agreed. "Mr. President our team unanimously recommends that America not try to divert or fragment this space rock. We believe that our science is solid and we are confident that the rock will enter a harmless orbit around Earth. Our exact predictions may not perfectly describe the Maximum Proximity and orbital dimensions but we believe that a stable orbit of some dimensions will be entered by Hansen's Rock. We will of course continue to study the rock and refine our numbers but we believe that an attempt to deflect or fragment this rock is much more dangerous than letting it follow the course that we believe it will follow."

Mornay looked at Barrow who nodded his agreement. He looked at Garish who shrugged and said, "How could I disagree with so many smart people?"

Mornay said, "OK, that's it. We will hold off on any defensive measures unless your surveys and derived data produce a different conclusion. I want to continue to receive a daily update with the survey numbers and I want a positive statement every day that defensive measures should be deferred unless your data changes and you determine that we must attack this rock."

Mornay looked at Barrow and instructed, "Charlie, if nothing material changes between now and then I want to have another video conference with the SCC at noon our time on 12 July."

"Yes sir; I will set it up," Barrow assured

"Ladies and Gentlemen in Pasadena, thank you again for your excellent work on one of the toughest challenges we have all faced in our lives. I am very proud of the way you have responded to this troublesome rock. I look forward to discussing this matter again on the twelfth. Thanks again and good-bye."

MORNAY PRESS CONFERENCE

The President decided that it would be appropriate to call a press conference so that he could share the new intelligence about Hansen's Rock with the national press and, in turn, with the people of America. His staff sent a bulletin to all the media advising that the President would conduct the press conference in the East Room of the White House at 4:00 p.m. Eastern Daylight Time.

When 4:00 p.m. arrived, the President walked into the room, took his position behind the podium, and then opened the folder that contained the talking points that he had handwritten earlier in the afternoon after his briefing from the SCC.

"Good afternoon everyone." The room remained silent.

"I have a few remarks that I want to make before opening the floor to questions. Today at noon I met with the American scientists that have been monitoring the progress of the space rock that has come to be known as Hansen's Rock. As the rock has gotten closer to Earth, this team of professional and highly talented scientists has continued to refine their understanding of the rock and their prediction of its path. I am pleased to be able to tell you today that this team has concluded that there will not be a direct collision of this rock with Earth." This statement was greeted with extremely rare applause from the press core. The President continued, "At this time these scientists believe that the rock will approach Earth within a distance of between 250 miles and 375 miles above the South Pole. They also believe that the rock will be traveling fast enough to keep it from falling into a deteriorating orbit that would eventually bring the rock to the surface of Earth. They now believe that the rock will not just pass Earth and keep going back into deep space but rather will enter a stable orbit around Earth. This stable orbit could keep the rock revolving safely around Earth for decades, maybe even centuries, barring any intervention. This stable orbit would mean that mankind would have a substantial amount of time to determine what, if anything, we choose to do about the rock. It would give us plenty of time to employ less risky methods of moving this rock away from Earth over time. We expect the rock to enter this orbit around Earth sometime on July 12th. These scientists continue to monitor the progress of this space rock and will be refining their predictions until it arrives. In any case, I am now firmly convinced that this rock presents no immediate threat to Earth at any time in the near future. I will now take some questions."

The President nodded at the correspondent in the center seat on the front row, "Thank you Mr. President. Sir, if we have the capability of destroying this rock then why haven't we already done that and why are we not planning on doing that to get rid of this threat for good?"

"That is a good question Ed and there is a good answer to go with that question. To begin with this is a very big rock as you know based on information that we have supplied in the past. To destroy this rock at this point in time would require what is known as a fragmentation mission. We would need to send multiple explosive devices to the rock that could break it into pieces so small that they could not survive passage through Earth's atmosphere and would, therefore, present no threat to us here on Earth. This is a very difficult mission to ensure that we break the big rock into pieces so that no piece is large enough to cause significant damage on Earth. The rock has been close enough to Earth for over a week to ensure that many of the fragments of Hansen's Rock would remain in the path of Earth. The vast majority would burn up when Earth's atmosphere ran into the pieces but there is no guarantee that every piece of the rock would be small enough that one or more could not cause localized catastrophic damage. So, although we have a plan to attempt this fragmentation if we deem it necessary, we have concluded that there is no immediate threat to us. Therefore, we believe it better not to attempt to destroy the rock and risk sending large pieces of it to some place here on Earth."

Hands rose all over the room; Mornay nodded to a woman in the third row, "Thank you Mr. President; the President of the Russian Federation issued a statement just a few days ago reaffirming his previous statement that his scientists believe that this rock will enter a deteriorating orbit and eventually fall to Earth. How is it that American and Russian scientists continue to arrive at different conclusions about the path of this rock?"

"Karen, predicting the path of this rock is more difficult than predicting the path of a regular rock like an asteroid. As you know this

Dan L. King

rock has an extraordinary magnetic field that is several thousands of times stronger than would be expected from a normal asteroid of the same size. It is how the scientists model the effect of this magnetic field on the path predictions that we believe is the difference between our predictions and those of the Russian scientists."

Hands go up again and Mornay nods to another questioner, "Thank you Mr. President. Given the differences in conclusions drawn by the different teams of scientists, have you spoken with President Volkov to attempt to resolve these different predictions? Are our scientists communicating with the Russian scientists to share insights about the rock so that they all could arrive at a common conclusion?"

"No Peter I haven't talked with the President Volkov since the emergency meeting of the United Nations. However, since I just earlier today received the new prediction from our scientists I have asked my office to set up a discussion with President Volkov as soon as we can get our calendars matched. I expect that we will talk within twenty-four hours."

The President nodded to another correspondent, "Thank you Mr. President. Assuming that things change and that we must employ this fragmentation mission you mentioned, exactly how many and what kinds of missiles and bombs will we use to fragment Hansen's Rock?"

"David as I indicated earlier I do not believe that we will need to launch a fragmentation mission at any time in the near future so I don't see the need to discuss the details of our mission. Further, discussing the numbers and types of bombs and missiles that we would use would violate the security classifications assigned to them."

Believing that he had accomplished his mission of informing the press and the American public of the information that he wanted to share, Mornay said, "Thanks to all of you." and he left the room.

10 JULY (WASHINGTON, D.C.)
11 JULY (BRISBANE, QUEENSLAND)

Hansen arose at 05:00 to check on the progress of Sirius. He went directly to the starboard bridge, got buzzed in, and walked to the steering position. "Good morning Peter. How did things go overnight?"

Smith reported with a smile, "Overnight? Captain, you've only been away for two hours! Everything went as expected sir; the ship is performing perfectly. The guy that designed this ship must have been a genius."

Hansen smiled at the flattery and replied, "Yeah Peter, that guy must be very smart." His attention went to the navigation panel that was populated with gauges, meters, monitors, and joysticks that could control every manageable piece of equipment on the ship. There were the two joysticks, with one located on each arm of the "steering chair" that permitted either left-handed or right-handed manipulation of the ship's "wheel". Then there were joysticks that controlled all sixteen mooring line winches; there were joysticks that controlled the four anchor windlasses; there was a joystick that permitted manual control of the ultrasonic bow if needed. There was a switched potentiometer that could control the ultrasonic hull scrubbers. There were switches to control the cargo discharge and balancing pumps, ballast pumps, and the bilge pumps from the panels in each "wheelhouse." There was a set of eight joysticks that were locked under a clear, armored glass cover which bore the label "Ship Defense Controls". Each of those joysticks controlled one of the eight ordnance stations strategically located around the perimeter of the ship's deck. Each of these joysticks could control the firing of a fifty caliber machine gun or a self-loading grenade launcher if the boat was being threatened. Each station had its own high resolution camera that could be operated in wide angle mode to give a broad view of a section of the sea around Sirius and each camera could also be operated in "siting mode" which would be used to aim the weapons. The images from each camera could be displayed on the security monitors in each bridge.

Hansen looked past all these controls and others to focus on the current heading and current position data. Both electronic compasses showed the heading to be 012°. The primary and secondary GPS devices revealed the same location, S26.97102° / E153.34948°. The GPS units also gave the ship's speed in two units of measure, 29.60 kilometers/hour and 15.98 knots, the typical economical cruising speed for Sirius. The twin radar sweeps revealed a few ships to the east of Sirius but none along its heading. The twin depth sounders showed water depth to be slightly over nineteen meters / sixty-three feet. The plotting monitor confirmed that Sirius was now about five nautical miles north of the western tip of Moreton Island and about twenty-nine nautical miles from the Bulwer Island Refinery crude oil dock. Hansen programmed NavCom (the common reference on ship for the navigation computer) with all the waypoints needed to take the ship to a spot just west of Perth. Sirius would hold the current course for another three nautical miles until it would make a turn to follow the 26.92° southern latitude line for thirty-five nautical miles. This course would ensure than Sirius had at least thirty meters of water under its keel while rounding Moreton Island. The next adjustment would take the ship to a heading of 180° to follow the east 154° longitude line which would be held for 325 nautical miles. Then the heading would be adjusted to 200° and held there for 810 nautical miles until the ship reached the 45° south latitude line where NavCom would turn Sirius to the course heading that would deliver it to the programmed location southwest of Perth. It would be about seventy-four hours before Sirius would adopt the westerly heading after clearing Tasmania.

Sirius could be operated in several propulsion modes depending on the needs at any particular time. The navigation computer normally was given complete control of engine speed, propeller pitch, ultrasonic bow wings, ballast balance, fluid cargo balance, and even control of the amplitude of the signals sent to the ultrasonic hull scrubbers. When an operating mode was chosen by the skipper, the computer optimized all the variables to produce the optimum solution for the mode selected. The most commonly used mode was "Maximum Economy" which caused the navigational computer to adjust all the variables of the ship to produce the least fuel consumption per unit of distance traveled. There was also the "Maximum Speed" mode which would achieve the fastest possible speed through the water without regard for economy. There was the "Maximum Thrust" mode which would ensure that the ship would have that greatest possible pushing or pulling power. The last option was called "Constant Speed" which would hold a speed that was manually entered by the ship's captain; this option would maintain a constant speed regardless of conditions like headwinds, tailwinds, sea height, current ship's displacement, etc.

After completing his review of the instruments Hansen bargained Smith with an offer of time off duty in exchange for a fresh cup of coffee. Smith went to the back side of the wheelhouse, took the full carafe of coffee from the warmer, and filled the large mug that had "LARS" written on it with a black marker. He delivered the mug to the Hansen who was now sitting in the big swivel chair at the steering station with his legs dangling in front of the foot rest like he often did. Smith left the bridge and headed to the galley for breakfast before he crashed in his bunk.

***

Mornay arose at 4:00 a.m. to prepare for his 5:00 a.m. telephone conference with President Volkov; the time in Moscow was 13:00. Volkov knew that this time would be awkward for Mornay and that was the reason he had said it was the only time he had available. He reasoned that if he chose an earlier time Mornay would reject it as too early and if he chose a later time, it would not sufficiently inconvenience the President of the United States.

Mornay dialed the number himself as he did not believe it respectful to have his secretary come to work at 5:00 a.m. just to dial an international call for him.

"Good morning, President Mornay," Anya cheerfully greeted in her nearly perfect English. "President Volkov will be with you in just a moment."

Mornay responded, "Good morning, Anya; I hope that you are having a good day."

"Thank you, President Mornay, and yes my day has been just fine. Sir, President Volkov is available now; I will connect you."

"Good morning, Mornay; what shall we discuss today?" Volkov was forever ensuring that the American President knew that the Russian leader had no respect for him. He was almost always gruff, condescending, arrogant, and abrupt. Mornay knew he was being tested and never fell victim to Volkov's attempts to agitate and aggravate him. Mornay always took the high road and treated everyone with respect, even when they didn't deserve it, as was the case with Volkov.

"President Volkov I want to discuss with you the latest information that I have from my space scientists and perhaps we can compare information and maybe come to an agreement on the path that this space rock will follow."

Volkov wanted to know what the latest information from the American scientists might be so he replied, almost sounding like a command, "Continue President Mornay."

"I met yesterday with our experts and they have now concluded that the space rock will not collide directly with Earth but will enter an orbit around Earth."

Volkov interrupted, "Yes, of course; my scientists have been predicting this for many days now."

Mornay clarified, "Yes, the Russian scientists have been saying that the rock would enter a deteriorating orbit for many days now. However, the American scientists are predicting that the rock will enter a stable orbit. They believe that the rock will be moving sufficiently fast and that the angle of attack will be shallow enough that the rock will enter a stable orbit, an orbit that could be stable for decades or longer."

Volkov debated, "As I recall it was just a few days ago when your experts were advising you that they thought the space rock would pass Earth harmlessly and keep on going back into deep space. They were apparently wrong then; what makes you think that they are correct now?"

"President Volkov you are correct that our scientists had been a little too optimistic in their original predictions. However, they have been improving their ability to model this unusual rock. They have been very forthright about the prospect that this rock might collide with Earth. I will admit that in my public statements I stressed the more optimistic possibilities concerning the path of this rock all the while knowing that there was a possibility of a collision. But yesterday when I met with our scientists they revealed that for the first time since they had been tracking this rock, their prediction put a direct strike out of consideration. The second bit of good news is that they believe that the speed of the rock will be about ten percent higher than is necessary to ensure a stable orbit, not a quickly deteriorating one. Granted there is only a ten percent margin between stable and deteriorating but they felt very confident in their prediction and so do I."

Volkov was sure that he had learned all that he could from the American so he returned to his usual demeanor, "You Americans are always so optimistic. You always want to believe the best. You read your children fairy tales that always end well. We Russians face life as it is, not as we wish it could be. If my scientists make a serious mistake, they pay a serious penalty. When your scientists make a serious mistake, you apparently pat them on the shoulder for admitting that they were wrong. You Americans know nothing about accountability. My scientists must be right every time or they will be replaced and they will live the rest of their lives as disgraced failures. Some even are sent to penal colonies if their mistake deserves harsh punishment. I am confident in the prediction that my people have made because they know that they will be held accountable and so they perform flawlessly. Based on the advice from my people I must reject the advice that you have received from your people. My people have not admitted to making mistakes because they haven't made mistakes. Your scientists have now come to a conclusion that is within ten percent of the conclusion that my experts came to many days ago. I must believe that given the history of the predictions that your people have made in the last two weeks that there is no reason that I should believe that they can predict this object's speed more precisely than my people. Is there anything else that you want to share with me Mornay?"

Mornay did not like being talked down to but he knew that his job was to rise above personality and anger and to get to the facts the best he could. "Yes, President Volkov, I would suggest that our two teams of scientists arrange a conference so that they could compare the detailed information that each has acquired about this rock and to discuss the various predictive modeling components to see if the two teams of scientists could come to a better agreement on the likely path of this rock."

"Mornay, it sounds as if you would like for my scientists to train your scientists on how to survey a space object and use the sophisticated tools of space scientists so they could figure out what they have done wrong. My people are busy people and do not have time to train your inferior scientists so that they will understand how to do this space science correctly. I have them working around the clock to continue to make sure that their conclusion is precisely accurate. I choose not to interrupt their important work to conduct a training class for you Americans."

"OK President Volkov; my offer for our experts to partner will stand. Call me if you want to accept my offer. Good day President Volkov."

Volkov hung up the phone without speaking.

***

Since Mornay was already at the office he moved on to other things. He checked his secure electronic mail first. It contained a report from

General Watson confirming that the multiple warhead missile preparation was nearing completion and that all work should be complete by 1500 hours on 10 July.

He had a report from Secretary Warren that the tensions between Iran and Israel had not improved. Warren reported that there was now some concern over the veracity of the intelligence concerning the Iranians possessing sufficient enriched material to construct one or more nuclear bombs. The report indicated that clandestine activities by the CIA were underway and they held some hope that they could capture another Iranian nuclear scientist from his home near the alleged enrichment facility. They would interrogate, coerce, threaten, or bride him into revealing factual information about the state of the Iranian bomb building capability.

He had a brief report from Secretary Harriman of DHS that revealed that two cells of home-grown terrorists with intentions of simultaneous attacks against Amtrak facilities had been foiled and about a dozen people had been taken into custody along with several homemade bombs.

Just before 7:00 a.m., President Mornay's Personal Secretary arrived and knocked on the door to the Oval Office just in case. Mornay knew who it would be and replied with, "Come in Susan."

"Good morning, Mr. President."

"Good morning, Susan."

Susan walked around the desk and opened the top right drawer to extract Mornay's "outbox", "I see that you stayed in the office after your call this morning and got a very early start on your paperwork today."

"Yes Susan I had plenty to do and saw no sense in postponing it."

"I hope your call with President Volkov went well this morning," Susan said, just chatting while she read the instruction notes that Mornay had put on several documents so she could get on the spot clarification if any was needed.

Mornay never revealed the nature or success of his discussions with other world leaders to Susan, "Susan it's always a mixed bag when dealing with President Volkov."

"Of course, sir." Susan left the office and closed the door behind her.

***

At 9:00 a.m. in Pasadena the NEO SCC held its Post-Survey Conference to review the latest survey information. Jerry gave the readout for the technicians:

Hansen's Rock

Distance from Earth: 838,134 km
Radial Velocity: 3,546 m/s
Predicted Maximum Proximity: 499.1 ± 67.1 km
MP Confidence Level: 99.992%
Predicted Velocity at MP: 8,291 m/s
V @ MP Confidence Level: 99.0%
Time of MP: 15:14 p.m. PDT, 12 July

"Liz, these data generally confirm the prediction that we gave to President Mornay yesterday. The only change of note is that we now project that the object will be traveling sixty-three meters per second slower. This means that the orbital path the rock adopts will be a little less elongated that we projected yesterday. This slower expected velocity has resulted in us pushing back the timing of MP by about three hours. However, this velocity is still 7.8 percent higher than that which is needed to ensure a stable orbit," Jerry summed up stating the optimistic view of the new data.

Liz reacted to the change in velocity, "The change in our prediction of velocity at MP is troubling since we now predict that the object will be traveling over two percent slower that we estimated just yesterday. I realize that there is still a seven percent safety buffer in our prediction but single digit safety margins are worrisome. And you are only showing a ninety-nine percent confidence in your velocity at MP projection. That's not very high given the small amount of time we have until MP."

"Yes ma'am; we technicians are a bit troubled also."

11 JULY (IN US)
12 JULY (IN TASMAN SEA)

Hansen's Rock had grown much brighter and now had an apparent visual magnitude of -0.23, making it brighter than all but two stars in the night sky; only Canopus and Sirius outshined Hansen's Rock. But because of its approach to Earth, every day there were fewer people able to see it as it began to quickly fall below the horizon for most of the heavily inhabited parts of the southern hemisphere. But the fact that it was out of sight did not mean that it was not wearing on the minds of people all over the globe. People were confused by the fact that just last week the American President had said that the rock would pass Earth and head back into space. Then a couple of days ago the same American President said that there was no need for immediate concern and that the rock would enter a harmless orbit around the Earth. Then the Russian President was saying that his experts were predicting that, without intervention, the rock would enter a deteriorating orbit and eventually fall to Earth somewhere. Even though the Russian President had promised to save the Earth, many worried that he might not have the capability to do that or that there might still be serious consequences caused by an attempt to destroy the rock.

People around the globe were growing restless and feeling helpless. The combination of anxiety and hopelessness were fueling an increase in lawlessness. Looting had reached historic levels on every continent on Earth. Even the governments of countries that historically had been merciless in their use of force to control riots and protests were unable to dissuade crowds from looting and burning property or from committing harsh physical crimes against their fellow citizens.

Robberies, murders, and assaults, especially sexual assaults, were drifting beyond control by conventional approaches.

The sale of illegal drugs had skyrocketed as those with a little cash attempted to escape from the threat that the space rock presented by getting high and staying that way. Overdose cases had reached levels that had never been seen before and treatment facilities were overrun with victims.

The incidence of serious health issues was growing. Reports of strokes, heart attacks, and anxiety attacks had tripled in just the past two weeks in most American cities, outpacing the capacity to treat the health events. People began to quit taking their medications and began to suffer the consequences of cessation and withdrawal.

The percent of civilians that were no-shows at work had grown and now exceeded ten percent. Children were being held home from school or were permitted by out of control parents to just do whatever they chose and often those children were not making good choices.

Because of marches and riots that left debris and damage and because many city workers weren't showing up for work, the streets of cities large and small were full of garbage and looting debris. This was leading to illness caused by the unsanitary conditions. Concerns of disease epidemics were growing amongst health professionals. City governments were pleading with their citizens to assist by reducing the amount of trash that they produced and to stay off the streets as much as possible to avoid the unsanitary conditions. Curfews were established in a few large cities that lasted from dusk until dawn and they were being strictly enforced. This strict enforcement quickly filled up the jails. Many of those arrested were being held in temporary work camps. They were being employed to clean the streets during daylight hours in an effort to catch up on the trash and debris littering the cities.

Trains seemed to be the favorite target of terrorists, thieves, and vandals. Terrorists had begun to target the city train systems in large cities around the world because the security on these lines was less robust than that on the long haul, high speed trains. The trains were usually attacked with bombs on track systems that detonated at just the right time to cause the maximum damage and death. These terrorism threats and successes led to the termination of cellphone service along the rail systems in an attempt to keep the terrorists from detonating their explosive devices with cellphones. This absence of cellphone service meant that the people on the trains were even further out of touch with first responder resources. Even on trains not targeted with bombs, single or multiple thieves would go from car to car robbing the passengers of anything valuable. Rail cops were outgunned and knew it so they typically surrendered and relinquished their weapons. The number of people riding the trains had begun to drop dramatically because riders feared for their safety; this led to a further increase in the no-shows being experienced by urban companies.

Religious hatred, that under normal conditions remained unexpressed, was now becoming more visible in the form of attacks on places of worship. Those that hated Christians were burning churches; those that hated the Jewish people were targeting synagogues; those who hated Muslims were attacking mosques. Not all attacks were destructive; some were just acts of vandalism such as spray painting signs or symbols on the property. In the more violent parts of the world where religious divergence was great, the religious wars that had been waged for centuries began to escalate.

***

President Volkov summoned Anya to his office. "Anya, get General Dmitriev on the phone as soon as possible."

"Yes Mr. President."

Anya had Dmitriev on the phone in less than two minutes and placed the line on hold while she punched the intercom line. Volkov, as usual, ignored the intercom line and picked up the flashing line knowing that it would be the General, "Dmitriev, when will my Bomba-missile be ready?"

"Comrade Leader, we are in the final testing stage and I believe we could be complete within eight hours."

"Good Dmitriev; I will leave my office a little later and fly to the launch control center to personally supervise the launch and mission."

"Yes, of course, Comrade Leader; we will certainly benefit from your leadership. We will anxiously await your arrival."

Volkov hung up the phone and buzzed for Anya to come. "Anya, arrange for my helicopter to pick me up in four hours; I will be flying to Korolyov Control Center for a missile launch."

"Yes Mr. President"

Anya went to her desk to make the phone calls and returned to Volkov's desk in less than five minutes. She walked around to the side of the desk where Volkov sat, rubbed her thigh against his arm, bent over, and placed a note on his desk that told him which of his pilots would be flying him today. She smiled and said, "Your helicopter will arrive in about three hours and forty-five minutes. Is there anything else I can do for you right now Mr. President?"

Volkov smiled back at the beautiful and agreeable Anya and said, "Maybe tomorrow Anya; today I must save the world."

"Of course Mr. President; tomorrow will be good…I promise."

The helicopter arrived and cautiously landed on the triangular courtyard of the Kremlin Senate where Volkov boarded the craft for the twenty-five kilometer trip to Russia's Main Mission Control Center. His plan was to stay at the center until the rock was destroyed.

***

A popular British red top tabloid published an interview with an amateur astronomer who opined that if Hansen's Rock hit in any of Earth's oceans it could create tsunamis around the globe that could be as much as a one and one-half kilometers high and would destroy everything in their path. He opined that the huge initial wave could travel hundreds of miles inland until it came to a mountain range sufficiently high to stop it. He further speculated that the mountain would need to be at least one and one-half times as tall as the wave to keep the wave from climbing over the mountain. He said if this were to happen, that the only places on Earth that might escape the wave would be those that were higher than two and one-half kilometers above sea level. This story was quickly syndicated by tabloids and newspapers around the world. This initiated mass exodus from low lying areas causing all manner of problems.

In the United States, extraordinarily large numbers of the people along the coastal areas decided to flee to higher ground. All commercial plane seats to cities like Denver were sold out within minutes of the tabloid story hitting the street. Charter planes were charging $50,000 or more for every seat in the plane and restricting luggage to less than twenty pounds per person. Private planes with the range to escape to higher elevations were heading to airfields located in the Rocky Mountains. It was not long before there was no room on the airport tarmacs to park planes, forcing pilots to park their planes on taxiways and any suitable grass around the runways. Eventually, pilots desperate to get on the ground because of fuel shortages were actually parking their aircraft on the ends of active runways which began to limit the size of aircraft that the runway could support as the stopping space became shorter and shorter. As runways became inaccessible, planes were running out of fuel and having to ditch in any open patch that they could find. Many just started falling out of the sky.

Those without access to airplane transportation were loading up their cars in an effort to get to the highest elevation they could before the predicted impact. In many cases like the US coastal areas along the Gulf of Mexico, relocating to a location with an elevation of 8,000 feet or more would require a very long and impractical trip. From Houston the trip would be over 1,000 miles by car. From Mobile the trip could approach 1,500 miles. So, many of those who lived in the Southeast were opting to drive to the highest ground that they could reach in the amount of time available before the predicted impact. This led many to attempt to get to places like the Great Smoky Mountains or the Blue Ridge Mountains.

These attempted escapes from low lying areas created the same type of gridlock that occurred with most evacuations before impending hurricane strikes. People ended up trapped on interstate highways and side roads. Those that had been able to reach locations near their intended destinations simply abandoned their vehicles and started walking to try to reach the higher ground they sought.

Others actually gravitated toward the beaches because they knew that they couldn't escape the big waves or because they just wanted to be in their favorite place when the waves came. Many started beach parties as a prelude to the predicted tsunami; "rock and roll" and "new wave" music were the chosen accompaniment for these impromptu parties for the obvious reason. One fellow who had been partying for a while was interviewed by a Daytona Beach TV station. He proudly showed off his plan to use his cell phone to capture the moment of the big wave with a selfie of him and the big wave in the background. He had encased his cellphone in a quart-size zip-topped sandwich bag that he had filled with as much air as he could keep in it after the zip. His plan was to activate his phone's video recorder when the wave approached and shoot his selfie through the clear plastic bag. He expected the plastic bag with his video to be carried somewhere far away to be discovered eventually and the recording of his last minutes would be preserved.

***

It was 9:05 a.m. in Pasadena and everyone in the NEO SCC had arrived in the conference room to review the latest survey data. As usual, Jerry Jones led the data review:

Distance from Earth: 436,039 km
Radial Velocity: 4,654 m/s
Predicted Maximum Proximity: 442.3 ± 21.8 km
MP Confidence Level: 99.9%
Predicted Velocity at MP: 8,106 m/s
V @ MP Confidence Level: 98.5.0%
Predicted Time of MP: 17:24 p.m. PDT, 12 July

Jerry pointed out what everyone had concluded when he revealed the numbers. The latest information had led to a prediction that Hansen's Rock would approach Earth at a distance that was over fifty kilometers closer than yesterday's prediction and that it would be traveling at nearly 200 kilometers per hour slower than previously predicted. The predicted velocity at MP was still 5.4% greater than that which was necessary to avoid an immediately deteriorating orbit. However, there was a developing sense of insecurity over the trend of the predictions as each successive prediction was of a rock that was going to approach Earth closer and slower than each preceding prediction. They knew that something was wrong with the algorithms that they were using to model the behavior of the rock as it approached Earth. They were sure that it had something to do with the magnetic interaction between Earth and Hansen's Rock but hadn't found the exact coefficients to describe the path. Due to the inaccuracy of recent predictions, the team lowered the estimated confidence levels around the Maximum Proximity and Velocity at MP.

Mike Williams spoke before Wilson and reacted to the readout, "OK team, we have got to do better than this. We only have one more survey that we can get from NEOSADS before this rock drops below the horizon as seen from the satellite. The safety of the world depends on us getting this last projection correct. I want two different teams to rebuild all the data points we have to date on HR and find out how to remove the prediction inaccuracy from the model. Liz will lead one team and Jerry will lead the other. I want each team to make a fresh start and to completely re-derive every formula and every coefficient that contributes to path and velocity predictions. Do not overlook any factor, no matter how small it might seem, that might affect our predictive models. I will meet with both teams again today at 5:00 p.m. to review the progress. If necessary, I will schedule another meeting around midnight to review any efforts taken after our 5:00 p.m. meeting. Tomorrow we will meet at 8:00 a.m. to get our act together before we provide our last briefing to the President. Everyone needs to make plans to spend the night here in the center. Are there any questions?"

***

Hansen had just left the mess deck after having breakfast and headed to the starboard wheelhouse where Smith buzzed him in. Sunrise was technically at 07:06 but even at 06:50 there was enough light to tell that the sky was clear and the seas were beginning to tame a little after the continuous rain and squalls that Sirius had endured since leaving Brisbane.

"Good morning, Peter. How are you this beautiful morning?"

"Captain, I feel great. Days on the ocean don't get much better than the one we are going to have today. The forecast is for much of the rest of the day to be just like it appears now. However, the weather is supposed to go downhill again later today with squalls and a pretty healthy wind on our nose."

"OK Peter, I think we can pay tomorrow's price for a perfect today."

"I totally agree, sir."

"So, did we experience anything worth noting last night?"

"No sir, nothing unusual. Sirius sailed herself perfectly and we covered 390 nautical miles as expected."

"OK, sounds good; I'll take over now Peter. You are officially relieved as soon as you have finished updating the ship's log."

"Already did it Captain."

"OK, then you may leave the bridge."

Smith questioned, "Captain, what's the latest on your rock?"

"The latest is that the President of the United States is now saying that the rock will enter a harmless orbit around Earth which will provide decades, maybe even centuries, to decide what to do with it."

"I guess that's good news. But I liked it better when they were saying your namesake would just do a flyby and head back out into deep space never to be seen again here on Earth."

"Yeah, me too, but as long as my rock isn't a threat, I don't really care much."

"So, it looks like we will be talking about your rock for years to come, hey Cap?"

"Could be; I might tire of the fame long before the rock is gone."

"OK Captain, I'll see you later today."

"OK Peter."

Hansen looked at the GPS readings to find that the current position of Sirius was S32.751 / E153.898 on a heading of 200°. This put Sirius slightly over a hundred nautical miles to the east of Newcastle, New South Wales. The plotting monitor showed 784 nautical miles until the next waypoint that would mark their turn to the west. The calculated ETA was a little over forty-nine hours but Hansen knew that this was an optimistic projection since the headwinds that they would face overnight and into tomorrow would slow them a good bit. The huge flat surface of the cargo containers covering the ship's deck and stacked five and six high would act like a mighty big sail and would catch a lot of wind. They could make up some time if they switched NavCom to "Constant Speed" mode. But that would consume more fuel and Sirius was too early in its journey to declare a delay in arrivals at the various ports that lay ahead. So, Hansen decided to stay the course in the most economical fashion. If a significant delay was experienced, he could always make it up since Sirius had plenty of reserve power and more than enough fuel to complete the journey. Since the cargo weight of the containers was less than half of a full crude oil load, Sirius was floating higher and using less fuel than if she were carrying a full load of crude oil.

***

Volkov's helicopter landed at an isolated portion of tarmac at the Chkalovsky Airport where three identical, ordinary-looking sedans were waiting. Two of the vehicles would carry four heavily armed men each. Volkov's heavily armored sedan would have one armed guard and the driver. The three vehicles drove to the launch control facility in Korolyov, just a few minutes from the airport. The cars parked in the under-building parking garage where Volkov and two of his personal body guards made their way to the elevator where one of the guards shoved a plastic card with an embedded chip into the reader and entered the PIN that opened the door to the elevator. The elevator took them to the main level of Russia's primary Missile Mission Control Center.

Volkov was greeted by General Dmitriev, "Good evening, Comrade Leader. Thank you for coming to lead this important mission."

Volkov knew Dmitriev was just sucking up, "Dmitriev, how are the preparations progressing?"

"Comrade Leader, everything is progressing well. I believe that we may finish our testing by midnight or early morning."

"Earlier today you told me that you would be complete with your testing by early evening; what has caused this change in getting the work complete?"

"Mr. President, we had been a little too optimistic about getting all the software updated and have found a few bugs that needed to be patched."

"Very good, keep things moving as fast as possible."

"Of course Comrade Leader; we will do that for you."

"Dmitriev, the President of the United States is still saying that his scientists believe that this space rock will enter a stable orbit around Earth and that there is no need for immediate actions by those of us here on Earth. What do my scientists tell you now?"

"Sir, the latest prediction from your scientists is that the rock will enter a deteriorating orbit and will travel part of the way around Earth

Dan L. King

to the northern hemisphere and it will crash somewhere between the 25th and 60th parallels."

"So which nation will receive the impact?"

"We cannot predict that very well as we are having some small difficulty determining how the large magnetic field of the rock will affect the path once the rock enters the northern hemisphere. However, there is a very real chance that it could reach Earth within Russia's borders since Russia covers over one-third of the circumference of the Earth at those latitudes."

"Hmmm. OK Dmitriev, have my meal brought to me in the private conference room upstairs."

"Of course Comrade Leader; your meal will arrive within a half hour."

***

Williams convened the two teams that had been trying to determine why the NEO SCC path and velocity predictions had been slightly flawed all along. He asked Wilson what her team had discovered as the probable cause for the inaccurate path and velocity predictions. She responded that they thought that they had it figured out. She explained, even though Williams already knew, that every celestial body exerts some type and strength of force on every other celestial body. Some of the affects are so miniscule that they can, for most calculations, be ignored. For those affects that cannot be ignored, there can be very complicated sets of pushes, pulls, and even twists that are exerted on a celestial body. For an object within the solar system, it can usually be expected that the nearest planets and their satellites would be the source of most of the influence on the object. She said that they had made conventional assumptions about which of the nearby bodies in the solar system would exert a measurable influence on Hansen's Rock. She explained that they had incorporated the impact of the substantial magnetic influence of HR when determining how it and Earth would interact but they had failed to incorporate the same tweaks when considering the influence of the Moon, the Sun, and all of the other planets in the solar system. She admitted that they had underestimated how much of an impact their assumption would have on the path and velocity predictions. She said that her team had consulted with Jerry's team and that they were in agreement that they had found the source of previous inaccuracies. They also had agreed on the new formulae and coefficients. She explained that they had incorporated the algorithmic changes and recalculated the data from last night's survey to produce new predictions. The new methodology had predicted a Maximum Proximity of 396 ± 18.6 kilometers and that velocity at MP would be 7,842 ± 78.4 meters per second. This meant that if the new predicted centerline path were exactly correct, then Hansen's Rock would be traveling at a speed that would be two percent faster than that needed to enter a stable orbit. She further revealed that if they applied the extreme lower end confidence limit on both MP and velocity, then the prediction would be for HR to be traveling slightly less than one percent faster than is necessary to enter a stable orbit. She summed up by stating that they believed that the worst case scenario would have HR enter a stable orbit that would range from 335.7 to 557.4 kilometers in altitude or about 208 to 346 miles in altitude.

Williams asked Jones if he agreed completely with Wilson's report and he affirmed that he did.

Williams was relieved and concerned at the same time, "Wow! I'm telling you...the fact that a one or two percent difference in our calculations means the difference in safety for the planet or certain annihilation is just scary! Liz, what do you think we need to tell the President?"

"Mike, you know the answer to that question. We have to tell him how we have been screwing up and what we currently think. We will conclude the last survey early tomorrow morning and then we will do the math based on those data. We will know at 8:00 a.m. whether our current prediction is confirmed when we apply the new formulae and coefficients to the overnight measurements. We will just have to follow the data to where it leads us."

Williams looked around the room and saw nothing but concern and embarrassment on the weary faces that were, to a person, focused on him. "OK team, good work on the new algorithms. We will not have a midnight meeting. I will see you at 8:00 a.m. If you aren't directly involved in collecting and analyzing data tonight, try to get some rest. I will need as many clear heads as I can get to make our last prediction about HR."

The members of the SCC would have one more sleep-over in the center. The managers, who had offices, would sleep at their desks; the technicians would unroll their sleeping bags in the break room or hallway one more time.

***

After Volkov finished his meal, a bottle of wine, and three glasses of Vodka, he returned to the Control Center where he learned that Smirnov and Bykovsky had arrived. He found the Control Center

Commander, Anatoly Petrowa, and asked, "How is my Bomba-missile progressing?"

"Comrade Leader we continue to make progress; we now think we will be ready by tomorrow morning, probably around sunrise," Petrowa reluctantly told Volkov.

"Why so long Petrowa?"

"Sir, we have had to write completely new test programs for this mission since the bomb was never intended to be launched on a rocket and the rocket was never designed to interface with this type of warhead. We are progressing fine at this point but it is very complicated and we do not want to make a mistake."

"Yes Petrowa, it is very important that we do not make a mistake. How long until this space rock reaches Earth?"

"We believe that the rock will enter its deteriorating orbit around Earth in about thirty-one hours; that is around 0400 on 13 July, sir."

"Good Petrowa so we will have twenty or twenty-one hours of time after the rocket is ready until the rock would arrive, is that correct?"

"Yes Mr. President, your math is perfect."

"I will sleep then until sunrise when I will return for your report of success. You will have a report of successful preparation for me at sunrise, will you not Petrowa?"

The Control Center Commander knew that there was only one acceptable answer to this question and he gave it, "Yes sir, I expect to be able to report to you that the preparation of our software and your missile has been successful."

Volkov nodded and walked to the elevator where his two body guards were waiting for the ride back to the private conference room. The guards would be stationed by the conference room door while the President of the Russian Federation slept.

12 JULY

Volkov awoke shortly after 0700 and looked up at the ceiling in the private conference room of the Mission Control Center. The ceiling was covered in pressed metal insets that displayed the seal of the Russian Space Agency held in place by painted wood trim pieces. He briefly thought to himself that it should be his likeness imprinted on each of the insets. He threw back the two blankets that he had warmed during the night, swung his feet around to meet the floor, and he arose from the tufted leather day bed. He donned the suit trousers that he had worn the preceding day, added socks and shoes, and went to the smallish bathroom located in the corner of the conference room behind a solid mahogany door. He washed his face, applied the adhesive to his skull, and stuck his toupee and eyebrows in their places. He returned to the day bed where he put on his shirt, tie, and suit jacket. He went to the door and opened it; the two guards previously sitting in chairs on either side of the door leapt to their feet and saluted. Volkov nodded at the wall across from the door; that was his way of acknowledging the salutes of the guards. After the nod, the guard nearest the elevator promptly went to the button and summoned the car. When the door opened the guard checked to make sure the car was empty. When he discovered it so, he looked back and nodded that all was OK. Volkov walked into the elevator and both guards followed. When they reached the main level of the building where the Control Center was located, they were greeted by the relief guards that would have the day shift protecting Volkov. The relief guards saluted Volkov and he gave his superior nod to acknowledge. Once he nodded, the guard nearest the door to the Missile Control Center pressed the button that would alert the door guard that access was desired. Volkov and the two men stared into the security camera above the door so that they would be recognized. The lockset on the door buzzed and vibrated, signaling that the electromagnet had retracted the deadbolt. The first guard opened the door and stood aside for Volkov to enter the room. Then both guards followed and stationed themselves near the door for their watch.

Volkov's first glance was at the large countdown clock to find it reading 12:06:24, meaning that launch was expected in a little over twelve hours. The personnel manning the dozen or so desks with monitors, switches, microphones, etc. were uneasily quiet. Volkov waved to Anatoly Petrowa that he should come immediately. Petrowa interrupted his important discussion with one of the senior technicians and walked to Volkov in response to the order.

"Petrowa, why does the clock show twelve hours remaining until the missile launch occurs? When I went to bed last night you told me that we should be ready this morning. The Bomba-missile should be ready now. I came this morning expecting to be able to push the launch button."

Petrowa, very nervously, explained, "Comrade Leader, during the night a problem was discovered with the missile and the technicians at Uzhur are attempting to fix it now. The commander of the 62nd Rocket Division assures me that they will have repairs completed so that we can launch the missile in twelve hours as shown on the clock."

"What is the problem and why is it taking so long to fix?" Volkov angrily asked.

"Sir, the nitrogen tetroxide pump in the second stage of the missile was determined to be defective and must be replaced. The reason it is taking so long is that the liquid oxidizer tank must be emptied before the pump can be replaced. Then the nitrogen tetroxide must be pumped back into the missile. I am told that they are making good progress."

"Why did the pump fail?"

"Comrade Leader, we do not know. Remember that all of our R-36M2 missiles were deployed over thirty years ago; I suspect the pump died of old age."

"Humph, old age...only people should die of old age. The technicians at Uzhur are there to keep those missiles in top operating shape. It would seem that we need a change of command for the 62nd Rocket Division. I will see to that after we destroy this space rock."

"As you wish Mr. President; we are totally ready here in the Missile Control Center. As soon as we receive the word that the pump has been replaced and the oxidizer has been reloaded into the missile, we will restart the testing process. As the clock shows, we expect to be able to permit you to push the launch button in a little less than twelve hours now."

"Humph, OK, I will go back to my office and will return at 6:00 p.m. to supervise the launch."

Petrowa lied, "Yes Comrade Leader, we look forward to your return."

Volkov instructed his lead guard to notify the pilots to prepare his helicopter for the trip back to the Kremlin Senate building. Volkov and all nine of his guards boarded the same three ordinary-looking cars and drove back to the airport where the helicopter was ready for an immediate departure. Volkov flew back to the Kremlin Senate. Later he and Anya had "lunch" at his not-so-secret secret apartment.

***

Seven hours later...

It was 21:00 and Hansen was taking his last look at the instruments as he prepared to turn the helm over to Smith for the night shift. As promised, the weather had turned for the worst and Sirius was sailing with the winds greeting the bow of the huge ship from forty degrees to port. The gale was producing winds gusting from thirty to fifty knots. The seas had begun to build, reaching twenty feet and by morning they would probably be forty feet or more. Sirius, being relatively lightly loaded, did notice the waves but due to its tremendous displacement there was almost no pitching. The only really noticeable effect of the waves was the hull slap as the waves broke on the port side of the bow sending reverberations down the length of the nearly empty hull. It felt and sounded as if someone were pounding on the hull with a huge rubber hammer.

Sirius was now located at S36.127 / E152.435, which put it about 135 nautical miles south-southeast of Sydney. The winds and sloppy seas had begun to slow the ship slightly; the current speed was just over fourteen knots, twenty-six kilometers per hour. The depth sounders show 4,833 meters / 15,857 feet of water beneath the ship.

Smith pushed the button on the passageway wall next to the cabin door to the bridge. Hansen glanced at the camera monitor and buzzed Smith into the bridge. They exchanged pleasantries, discussed the current weather, the forecast, and whether they should rig for constant speed running or continue with NavCom controlling the ship for economical sailing. They decided to continue saving fuel since they still had plenty of sailing time before they reached Perth where they would unload over 4300 TEU of container cargo. They speculated that they might pick up a tailwind along the way as the low pressure area moved east.

***

The President of the United States arose early and headed directly to the Situation Room in the basement of the West Wing shortly after six a.m. because it had the best complement of television monitors in the White House. He had turned the various monitors to different television stations to see what was going on in the world. The audio was muted on all the monitors except the one that interested him as the various news programs played their selected video snippets. He was especially interested about the mood and actions of the various people around the world. Amazingly, even though he had told the world that there was only a very small possibility of Hansen's Rock striking Earth, he could tell that most people weren't that confident and were acting more like the world would end in a matter of hours. He saw images of miles and miles of stranded vehicles on just about every highway in the United States. He saw exactly the same thing in several other countries. The situation in Japan was even worse than in most other countries due, according to the announcer, to the memories of how severe the 2011 tsunami had been, killing over 16,000 and causing extraordinary devastation.

After about thirty minutes the President took the stairs back up to the main floor and went toward the Oval Office. Susan was already in her office when he arrived, "Good morning, Susan!"

"Good morning, Mr. President.'

"You're here pretty early this morning Susan."

"Yes sir, I was worried about the traffic this morning so I thought I would get an early start to avoid whatever madness might occur during rush hour. The streets were very sparsely populated this morning sir; it was quite eerie. Also, I expected that you might be very busy today and I knew that you would need me."

"Susan, you are so right; I need your help every day. I'm glad you are here and that you didn't run into any trouble during your commute." She smiled and he continued into the Oval Office where he found a steaming cup of coffee sitting on a leather coaster on his desk. It was obvious that Susan had seen him pass the security camera that hung on the wall at the turn of the stairwell that he had just ascended.

Mornay was a hands-on guy; he almost always read his own e-mail. Susan would screen his electronic inbox and delete the junk stuff or forward to herself things that she or someone else on the floor could handle for the President. This way he could focus only on those things that he should be focusing on.

At precisely 7:00 a.m. Susan knocked on the open door and walked to the President's desk and delivered the folder with the red tag on the cover that read "Top Secret – For the President's Eyes Only." She walked behind the President who was still reading e-mail and she placed the folder in the center of the handmade leather desk protector. She said, "Your Daily Brief sir." and left. Mornay turned from the computer monitor, rolled back to his desk, and began to read the brief.

Most of what was covered in the brief simply reinforced what he had seen on the various news programs just earlier. However, it did report that surveillance satellites still showed a feverish amount of activity near the Iranian missile launch silos. The Brief confirmed that the information had been shared with the Israelis. They had verified that all batteries of the Iron Dome missile defense system were on the ready. The Israelis also had several bombers loaded with smart bombs and prepared for immediate departure in the event that the Prime Minister believed that a preemptive strike was necessary. Secretary of State Warren was continuing discussions with the Iranians and Israelis hoping to reach a peaceful end to the tensions.

The Brief reported that the Russians were continuing to prepare at least one missile in the silos at Uzhur in the Uzhursky District of Krasnoyarsk Krai. There was also a report that President Volkov had made a personal visit to Russia's Main Missile Control Center just yesterday and had left the center a few hours before the Brief was published. Mornay was worried about this development as it indicated that the Russians were still preparing for a mission to destroy the space rock so Volkov could "save the world" as he had promised. He decided to call Volkov and try to dissuade him from attempting such a mission if his meeting with the NEO SCC today would continue to confirm that the rock would enter a harmless orbit around Earth.

***

Three hours later...

After a four hour "lunch" with Anya, Volkov returned to the Kremlin Senate where he boarded his helicopter for the flight back to the Missile Control Center. When he entered the Center after the short flight and short drive he first looked at the countdown clock which showed 01:26:12. He smiled a rare smile. He waved Anatoly Petrowa to come to him.

"Petrowa, I see the clock is still running; are we going to be ready to launch when the countdown expires?"

"Yes Comrade Leader, I am confident that you will push the launch button in one hour and twenty-six minutes."

Volkov, obviously pleased, responded, "Good work Petrowa. I will be in my conference room; call me when the time comes."

"Of course, Mr. President."

***

Everyone that worked in the SCC had gathered in the conference room which would mean that most would be standing…again. Mike Williams spoke first and to the point, "Jerry, let's hear your report please."

Jerry nervously began, "Yes sir; here are the data from our most recent survey:

Distance from Earth: 237,600 km
Radial Velocity: 6,086 m/s
Predicted Maximum Proximity: 391.4 ± 6 km
MP Confidence Level: 99.99%
Predicted Velocity at MP: 7869 km/s
Velocity @ MP Confidence Level: 99.6%
Time of MP: 17:01 PDT 12 July

These data confirm yesterday's predictions after we incorporated the revised influence coefficients. We are now confident in our numbers. These data indicate that we have a 2.34% safety factor in the V@MP. We are now nearly certain that Hansen's Rock will enter a stable orbit that should range from 348 to 567 kilometers, that's about 216 to 352 miles." Jerry paused for the reaction.

Williams breathed a sigh of relief but asked, "Nearly certain?"

Jerry knew this tiny bit of uncertainty had to be explored but didn't really know how to do it, "Mike, we have done the best we know how to do. Everybody on the team has pored over the data. We did multiple separate derivations of the prediction and every person's prediction was exactly what I read out. However, these are only predictions based on the dozens of assumptions that we have had to incorporate into the algorithms. You know that predictive science isn't perfect. There may still be characteristics that this rock possesses that we haven't discovered and, therefore, not incorporated into our models. I repeat though that we believe in these numbers and we are sure that they are the best that we can develop."

Liz Wilson chimed in at this point, "Mike, I have worked through these numbers myself and I believe what the team has predicted is the best that anyone in the world can produce."

Williams looked at Wilson and quickly challenged, "Are you prepared to bet your life and the life of everyone else on the planet on these numbers?"

Wilson didn't pause even a little, "Yes sir; I am."

The room went silent for several seconds as everybody came to the sudden realization that they had taken their last step toward the final advice that they would be sharing with the President of the United States. They knew that the President would have to decide whether to accept a two percent safety cushion and just wait for Hansen's Rock to enter orbit or to try to increase the safety cushion by attempting to destroy the rock. Panic began to take hold of several of the exhausted technicians. Several wept. Some had to sit down on the floor to avoid falling to it. Others still stood with eyes wide open fearful that they might have made a mistake somewhere along the way.

Williams broke the silence, "OK, I too am willing to bet my life on this conclusion by this team...the best damn team of space scientists on the face of the Earth. Everybody take a break until we meet with the President in a few minutes."

Everybody left the conference room. Some went for coffee. Some chatted just outside the conference room door. Others went back to their work chairs to rest a little. Some went to the restroom where they threw up.

Jerry went back to his desk where he corrected a typographical error he had discovered on the numbers slide; he had inadvertently typed "km" where there should have been an "m" on the Predicted Velocity @ MP data line. He also converted all the metric units to American Standard Units for the discussion with the President.

***

The phone in the conference room rang at 19:02. Volkov picked up the receiver and said, "Yes?"

Petrowa said, "Comrade Leader, we will be prepared to launch in about ten minutes."

"Excellent Petrowa; I am on my way now."

Volkov left the conference room and the two guards posted by the door escorted him to the Missile Command Center. As he entered the room he could tell that the spirit of the technicians in the room was decidedly lighter than during his previous visits. He knew that this meant that things were going well. Petrowa had been watching the door anticipating the arrival of the President of the Russian Federation. As soon as Volkov entered the room Petrowa went directly to him with a large smile on his face, "Mr. President, we will be prepared to launch in…" he looked at the countdown clock, "…in two minutes and thirty-six seconds. We are delighted that you are here to push the final launch button."

"Final launch button? How many launch buttons are there and why?"

"Comrade Leader, we always use two launch buttons so as to ensure that a launch is not initiated by mistake. The first button push will be from the Senior Launch Officer and that push will prepare all of the circuitry for the button push that actually launches the missile. Your push will launch the missile sir."

"Very well Petrowa; show me to my button." Petrowa led Volkov to the center console in the middle of three rows of consoles that were monitoring and controlling various aspects of the ground support equipment and onboard equipment for the missile. The Senior Launch Officer stood and saluted when Volkov arrived. Volkov nodded and the Colonel sat back down to make a roll call of all the technicians at the control panels. He started, "Guidance?" The reply came immediately, "Go, sir." The Colonel continued until every desk had reported that the mission was a go. He looked at the countdown clock which showed seventeen seconds. He spoke to Volkov, "Mr. President, I will start an oral countdown at ten seconds and at the one second mark I will push my button. Sir, if you agree, you should push your button when I speak the word "zero". Sir, is that agreeable with you?"

Volkov, now excited over the prospect of the launch, actually spoke, "Yes Colonel; I will do that."

"Ten, nine, eight, seven, six, five, four, three, two, one, zero."

Volkov pushed his button and stared at the monitor which was a video feed showing the outside of the missile silo. Fire began rushing out of the silo rising dozens of meters into the dark sky. Then slowly the missile began to rise from the hole. The missile was climbing slowly because the sixty megaton nuclear warhead's weight was slightly above the missile's rated throw weight capability of 8,800 kilograms. Volkov watched as the missile finally cleared the silo and began its climb skyward with a tail of fire that was 300 meters long. The camera tracked the missile flawlessly as it began to shrink to just a smallish bright object on the monitor when an explosion occurred which surprised Volkov and he immediately was concerned. He looked at Petrowa who was still smiling. Petrowa explained, "Comrade Leader, we have a successful separation of the first stage of the missile and a successful ignition of the second stage." Petrowa smiled some more. Then Volkov smiled knowing that what he had observed was normal. Finally the smaller second stage and warhead disappeared from the monitor as it escaped the range of the camera's magnification.

Volkov asked the Colonel, "How long until the missile blows up the rock?"

"Two hours and twenty-nine minutes, sir."

Surprised by how long it would take Volkov responded, "Two hours?"

"Yes Mr. President; the space rock was almost 200,000 kilometers away at the time of launch. Our missile is now flying toward the rock at its velocity of 43,450 kilometers per hour. The rock is currently approaching Earth at about 21,500 kilometers per hour. The two objects will meet when they both reach a point that is about 143,350 kilometers from Earth. The bomb is equipped with an airburst detonation mechanism which will explode the warhead when it is thirty meters above the surface of the space rock; this distance will impart the greatest explosive force to the rock."

Volkov never thought about any of this before and found the explanation fascinating, "That is very interesting Colonel. I would have never imagined that it would take so long for our rocket to reach the rock. I would have thought that our rocket would be very fast."

"Yes Comrade Leader; even though the rock would have reached Earth in about eight hours, the rock is still a long distance away from us. Our missile is very fast; at its current speed it could cover a distance equal to the circumference of the Earth in about an hour. Our missile could have been faster if it was not carrying a payload that is so heavy but it ran out of fuel when the speed had reached about 43,450 kilometers per hour. The only fuel left on the missile at this time is for the small thrusters that we can use to adjust the attitude of the bomb payload when needed."

"Thank you for that thorough explanation, Colonel."

Volkov turned to Petrowa, "I will return to the conference room; call me when my missile gets near the space rock so that I can be here to see it explode."

Petrowa explained, "Sir, I will call you when we near the time for impact but keep in mind that we will not be able to directly watch the explosion. But, we will be able to capture photographs from one of our satellites that will be available after the data is downloaded and processed."

Volkov was obviously disappointed that he would not be able to watch the explosion but accepted it as just the way things were. He left the center to go back to the conference room.

Dan L. King

***

At precisely noon in Washington, President Mornay and Vice President Garish walked into the Situation Room and took their seats. The technician left the room as soon as the SCC conference room had appeared on the projection screen.

Mornay began, "Good morning everyone."

Williams was the only one to answer, "Good morning, Mr. President." He paused.

"That's a mighty quiet group out there in Pasadena today."

"Yes Mr. President, each of us knows how important this meeting is and everybody is a little on edge."

"I can certainly understand why everybody would be nervous today. OK, let's hear what you have for us."

Williams began, "Mr. President, I will be brief. Hansen's Rock is now slightly less than 148,000 miles from Earth. The rock is traveling toward Earth at a velocity of 13,600 miles per hour. HR will continue to accelerate and will be traveling at a velocity of 17,600 miles per hour when it enters a stable orbit with an altitude range of from 216 to 352 miles. We believe that Hansen's Rock will enter its orbit at 8:01 p.m. Eastern Daylight Time."

Realizing that Williams had paused Mornay spoke, "So, if I remember correctly, you told us that this rock had to be traveling at a speed of over 17,300 miles per hour to avoid falling to Earth"

Garish interrupted, "Mr. President, I think they told us 17,200 miles per hour; isn't that correct Mike?"

"Yes, Mr. Vice President the number is technically 17,200," Williams replied.

The President continued, "OK 17,200. So, this sounds like good news and that we can be comfortable that we do not have an immediate threat from this rock; is that correct?"

Williams answered, "Yes sir that is what we believe."

"OK that is great news. I do have a question though. My notes from out last discussion on Tuesday show that at that time you had predicted that the rock would be traveling at over 18,600 miles per hour when it approached Earth and that its orbit would range from 311 to 910 miles in altitude. Your numbers today are significantly different from the ones we discussed just three days ago. Would you explain this large variance please?"

Williams had expected that someone in the Situation Room would recognize that the current prediction was significantly different from the earlier predictions so he was not surprised when it came up. "Sir, we discovered some small errors in the way that we had accounted for the interaction of Hansen's Rock with the Sun, the Moon, and the other planets within our solar system. These changes, although individually minor, cumulatively caused a fairly significant change in our predictive model outputs. We now believe our prediction to be extremely accurate."

Garish spoke up, "Jeez man, you're telling us that we should be comfortable with this latest prediction when in the course of three days your velocity prediction changed by over a thousand miles per hour?"

Williams paused, embarrassed by the circumstances, "Yes Mr. Vice President; we are confident in our current prediction."

Garish looked at the President and it was obvious that he was going to speak again when the President shook his head to indicate that he should remain quiet.

Mornay continued, "Jerry, you are the lead scientist there in the SCC; are you confident in the accuracy of this latest prediction?"

Nervously Jerry replied, "Mr. President, I know that I am betting my life and the lives of billions of people on the numbers that we just shared with you." He paused, "Yes sir, I believe our current prediction is the best prediction anyone on Earth could make of where Hansen's Rock will go."

Mornay looked at Barrow who indicated his agreement with Jones. He then looked at Garish who shrugged as if to say "who knows?" Mornay paused to think through all the information and especially the confidence displayed by the SCC folk and finally spoke, "OK, that's it; we wait for Hansen's Rock to enter orbit at 8:00 p.m. this evening."

Mornay started to begin wrapping up the meeting when the phone at his position on the table rang. He said, "Excuse me." to his audience and picked up the phone to hear Susan report, "Mr. President, General Watson has called and says he has some very important information that he needs to discuss with you immediately."

Mornay said, "Put him through."

"Mr. President, our surveillance satellite detected a missile launch from a silo at Uzhur, Russia. Tracking indicates that it was a SS-18 Satan Mod 6 missile. It is headed into space in the direction of the space rock."

Mornay asked, "What do you recommend we do General?"

"Sir, there is little that we can do at this point except follow what happens next. We do not see activity at the other silos in Uzhur that would indicate another launch is imminent. I think this will be the Russians' only missile launch trying to intercept this space rock."

"OK Stan, keep me posted." Mornay hung up the phone.

Mornay looked at Garish and Barrow and then to the full but silent SCC conference room. He explained, "That was General Watson, the

Chairman of the Joint Chiefs of Staff. It seems that the Russians have fired a missile at Hansen's Rock." He paused, not really knowing what to do with what he knew. "Charlie, what do you think this means and what do you think we should do?"

Barrow replied promptly, "Mr. President, I do not believe that this is a good thing. I do not believe that they have a single bomb that is capable of diverting this rock given how close it is to Earth now. I also do not believe that they have a warhead or MIRV that can successfully fragment a rock of this size. I expect that if they are able to hit the rock, and that is not a given, that there will be large pieces of the rock that will come to Earth in any number of places. We might be able to launch some of our missiles to further fragment these larger pieces but it would be a fifty-fifty proposition as to whether we could do that successfully if there are many large pieces. I suspect that it could take as long as a couple of hours for their missile to reach the rock so we will not know how it goes for a while."

Mornay looked at the screen and asked, "Mike, are you guys able to observe this rock in real time? And are you able to see the missile? Will you be able to see the results of the impact?"

Williams replied, "Mr. President, in answer to your first question, we don't have real time visual, infrared, or radar images of the rock. We can instruct the equipment on NEOSADS to capture the images but then it must send the data to us here in the center where we convert the binary data into images. As you know, data from a satellite only takes a few seconds to cover the distance from the satellite to our antennae here. But, we must wait for the entire stream of data to arrive for each image taken. Following receipt of the complete data stream, our imaging computers must reconstruct the images from the data. In the best of circumstances, we might be able to see the initial images within fifteen to thirty minutes depending on the complexity of the images. If we are dealing with a single large object as we are now, then the data stream is less complex and we will be able to reconstruct the image in fifteen or twenty minutes. However, if the image is complex, which would be the case if HR is fragmented into many pieces, then it could take even longer than thirty minutes to get the first images. That is because the data stream will contain many times more binary changes and cannot be compressed as much as a simpler image can be. So, there is more data to transmit and more data to be reconstructed once it arrives.

The answer to your second question is "yes"; we will be able to see the presence of the missile but it will be in snapshot elements just like all the other images that we take.

The answer to your third question is "probably" given that the missile will arrive in two to three hours after the launch time. Hansen's Rock will likely go below the horizon of our satellite once it gets closer to the South Pole. I believe that HR will still be slightly above the satellite's horizon when we expect the missile and HR to collide, if they do actually collide. Depending on the results of the explosion, we may lose sight of many of the fragments as they fall below the horizon of our equipment."

"Mike, I want us to keep this video connection up until after we know the results of the meeting of the Russian missile and Hansen's Rock. I will need to leave the Situation Room while we wait for the missile to reach the rock but I will be available within five minutes if anything happens. I need for you guys to analyze whatever data you can collect and predict when the missile will reach the rock. Charlie will remain here in the Situation Room and will notify my office when you have determined the time of impact. The Vice President and I need to discuss the actions that we will take after the rock is hit by the missile."

Williams replied, "Yes sir, we are already on it and will advise Mr. Barrow as soon as we have a time of intercept."

Mornay and Garish headed upstairs and toward the Oval Office. When they arrived at Susan's office Mornay instructed, "Susan, have General Watson come to my office as soon as he can get here and reschedule everything I had scheduled for the rest of the day."

"Yes Mr. President."

***

At 1:43 p.m. Barrow called Susan's office, "This is Susan Barker; how may I assist you?"

"Susan, this is Charlie Barrow in the Situation Room. I need to speak to the President; he is expecting my call."

"One moment Mr. Barrow, I will tell him you are calling."

Susan buzzed the intercom. The President arose from the sofa to answer the ping and Susan advised that Barrow was on line six. He picked up the flashing line, "Hi Charlie, what have you learned?"

"Sir we believe that the missile will reach Hansen's rock at around 2:41."

"OK Charlie, thanks for the call. Stan, Richard, and I will come down around 3:00 p.m. Maybe by then your team in the SCC will have enough data processed that they can tell us what happened to Hansen's Rock."

"That's a good plan Mr. President; I'll advise the SCC of your expectations."

"Thanks Charlie."

WORLDS COLLIDE

At 21:20, the phone rang in the conference room where Volkov was sipping his vodka and watching the state run "news" channel to see what kind of coverage he was getting. He answered the phone and said, "I'll be right there."

Volkov and his guards descended to the floor where the control center was located and they entered as they had before. Volkov saw that Petrowa was still wearing a smile, so he knew that things were going well. He looked at the countdown clock that was ticking down toward the missile intercept time; it showed a little over fifteen minutes until the explosion.

Petrowa came to Volkov and explained what would be happening, "Sir as you can see we have about fifteen minutes until the bomb will detonate. When we get down to the last minute before detonation, the missile and space rock will be moving toward one another at a velocity of just under 67,000 kilometers per hour. When we get to the time that is sixty seconds until detonation the missile will be a little over 1,100 kilometers from the space rock. The SLO will begin a countdown at that point and continue until detonation."

Volkov nodded that he understood and followed Petrowa to a spot adjacent to the control panel in front of the Colonel. They all watched as the clock counted to the point where a zero replaced the one in the minute digit on the clock. The SLO started his countdown, "fifty seconds and 930 kilometers…thirty seconds and 558 kilometers…ten seconds and 112 kilometers…five…four…three…"

The technician manning the airburst detonation monitor panel interrupted, "Sir, we have detonation."

Dan L. King

Volkov smiled when the word came that the bomb had detonated. He had expected applause from the technicians. He looked at Petrowa to share his smile only to see no smile on Petrowa's face, "What is the matter Petrowa?" he asked.

"Comrade Leader, it appears that the bomb may have exploded prematurely. The technicians are attempting to confirm if that is correct. It should only take a few minutes to review the data that was being sent by the missile's warhead navigation computer to determine whether the bomb exploded prematurely or whether somehow the clock was out of sync with the position of the warhead."

Volkov nodded that he understood. The SLO was standing behind the technician that was reviewing the tracking data that had been sent by the onboard airburst control computer. After about four minutes the SLO looked up and walked to where Volkov and Petrowa were standing to report the findings.

"Sirs, we have confirmed that the bomb exploded too soon. It appears that the bomb exploded at a distance of thirty kilometers from the space rock. It was supposed to explode at a distance of thirty meters from the rock. We suspect a programming error to be the cause," he reported unemotionally.

Volkov asked, "Did we destroy the rock?"

"We do not know yet. We are in the process of acquiring images from our satellite but it will take another fifteen or twenty minutes for us to receive the image data and process it so that we can determine the result of the explosion."

Volkov was uncharacteristically quiet as the technicians were receiving the data from the spy satellite and processing it through the imaging computer. After nearly twenty-five minutes they produced two images. The first was a visual image from the satellite's onboard telescopic camera. This picture showed that the space rock was still in one piece looking very much like the images that previously had been taken of the spinning rock. The second image was created from a radar survey of the rock. It too showed the rock to still be in one piece but the rock looked different from before. The SLO requested that the technician print the last archived radar image for comparison. When he had both radar composites he had a discussion with the imaging specialists and they finally agreed on what had changed.

He walked back to where Volkov and Petrowa had been silently waiting. He held up the visual image to let them see, "As you can see from this image captured by our telescopic camera, the rock is unharmed." He then held up the before and after radar composites and said, "As you can see from these radar composites, the rock is still in one piece but its surface is different in the two images. We are pretty sure that the reason for this is that the rock flipped over as a result of the powerful force from the ion storm that was created by the bomb. This ion storm would be like a very strong wind here on Earth and we believe that this ionic wind caused the rock to flip. We also learned from the frequency displacement shown in our radar scan that the velocity of the rock has slowed greatly. The rock was traveling at a velocity of over 23,000 kilometers per hour before the explosion; now it is traveling at less than 10,000 kilometers per hour. It is now certain that the space rock will hit Earth. We need to get more data to evaluate how much the explosion changed the path that the rock will follow to reach Earth. We think that we should have more information on the path that the rock will follow in about an hour."

Volkov could no longer contain his anger, "Petrowa, go to my conference room immediately."

"Yes Comrade Leader."

Volkov walked to the back of the room where Bykovsky, Dmitriev, and Smirnov were standing. He looked at them with fire in his eyes and instructed, "Go to my conference room immediately."

Smirnov responded, "Yes Comrade Leader." The three men walked to the elevator and rode it to the conference room.

Volkov looked around the control center for someone else to punish but realized that he needed all these people to get the work done that would be necessary to determine where the rock would go. He motioned to his guards that he wanted to leave for the elevator. When Volkov reached the conference room, he told his two body guards to follow him into the room and they did. As Volkov entered the conference room the four waiting men rose to their feet. After the second guard closed the door, Volkov reached inside the jacket of the first guard and pulled the automatic weapon from the quick release holster. When he turned to face the four men they each had the look of terror on their faces.

Without hesitation Volkov began, "You men have disappointed me. You permitted your people to fail in the most important mission of our lives. You have embarrassed the people of the Russian Federation. As you know, you have had positions of great responsibility and each of you has enjoyed the great rewards that come with powerful positions. But you have proven yourselves unworthy of your positions and you must be punished. It is my belief that punishment should speak not only to the one being punished for failing but to others who might also think that failure is acceptable. Failure is not acceptable. You will pay the price for failing your country and your punishment will be an example for all others in positions of power. Volkov placed the

Makarov under the chin of Bykovsky and asked, "Bykovsky, do you agree that you have failed the people of Russia?"

"Mr. President, I did not fail the people of Russia and neither did Smirnov, nor Petrowa, nor Dmitriev. We each did the best that we knew how to do. We are all loyal to you and to the people of the Russian Federation. We do not deserve to be punished."

Volkov was not pleased that Bykovsky disagreed with him. Had Bykovsky agreed, Volkov would have taken that admission as permission to deposit a nine millimeter coin into the Bykovsky bank. But he was taken aback by the unabashed denial of guilt...with witnesses. Volkov decided that he should not be the one to inflict the final punishment on an official that pleaded innocence.

He turned to the first guard and returned the Makarov. He instructed, "Have these incompetent men delivered to the penal colony in Krasnoyarsk; they will dig potatoes until they are eighty years old if they do not die from the collision of this space rock. I will sign the formal order later." The guard acknowledged the order and tied the hands of the four men for transportation. They left the conference room for the elevator ride to the parking garage.

***

When 3:00 p.m. arrived in Washington, D.C., the Situation Room was occupied by Mornay, Garish, Barrow, Watson, and the others that the President had invited: Dave Rander, White House Chief of Staff; Bill Harriman, Secretary of Homeland Security; Larry Garrett, Secretary of Defense; and Trish Daly, White House Press Secretary.

The President looked at the conference room in the SCC surprised to find that only Mike Williams was there. He then looked at Barrow and said, "Charlie, we are all anxious to learn what happened to Hansen's Rock so let's get this report going."

Barrow replied, "Sir, the center technicians are running just a little later than I expected but I assure you that they will complete their analyses of the most recent data capture as quickly as possible and they will return to the conference room momentarily. The President replied, "Sure Charlie, we understand how difficult this must be for the technicians in your center." He turned to the screen and filled the vacuum with a question to Williams, "Mike, how's your team holding up out there?"

Williams nervously managed, "Mr. President, thank you for your concern about our welfare. We are doing OK given the circumstances. Sir, I apologize that we are running late but I assure all of you that we will have your report very soon."

While they were waiting Garish arose and went to the credenza that held the tray of tiny sandwiches that had been prepared for the group. He stole one of the quarter sandwiches filled with ham salad and cucumber and he gobbled it in one bite. Then he double dipped a cheese-stuffed celery stick in the pitcher of ranch dressing. Just as he was reaching for a chunk of cheddar that had succumbed to the toothpick through its heart, he saw people beginning to enter the SCC so he returned to his chair at the big mahogany table.

Liz Wilson had been the first to enter the room and was followed by Jones. Then the remainder of the familiar, weary faces followed and took their seats or their standing positions. Mornay noticed that nearly everyone sat or stood in the exact same spot as they had in previous meetings. He didn't believe that this was planned but rather just another example of how humans are creatures of habit and feel more comfortable in familiar surroundings.

Williams began, "Ladies and Gentlemen in Washington, as you can see we just completed our analysis of the data we have received since the Russian bomb exploded. Jerry, our senior technician, will provide a summary of the findings." Williams nodded to Jerry that he should begin.

Jerry, very intimidated by the room full of dignitaries in the Situation Room, began. His voice was a little wobbly, "We have determined from optical, infrared, and radar images that were taken since the explosion that Hansen's Rock remains intact. As far as we can tell no structural damage was done to the rock. However, the explosion did impart changes to the attitude, speed, and direction of the rock. An explosion in space will propel an energy wave made of the ionized particles that are produced by the explosive material and since there are virtually no other atomic particles in space, the wave of energized ions will travel undiminished in strength until it impacts something. In this case, the bomb exploded about 18.6 miles from Hansen's Rock. The bomb imparted an ionic wave which would be moving at approximately the speed of light. This ionic wave has significantly affected the movement of HR. The bottom line is that the wave significantly reduced the velocity of HR and because of the disproportionate distance that the bomb was from the two equatorial points most near and most distant from the bomb, the wave flipped Hansen's Rock completely over. Our last displacement data tells us that the rock was traveling at approximately 5,500 miles per hour. Before the explosion, it was traveling at about 14,400 miles per hour. Subsequent Doppler displacement information also suggests that the rock is slowing down as it approaches Earth. We do not totally understand this counterintuitive behavior but we theorize that it is because of the interaction of the extraordinary magnetic field around HR with the South Pole's magnetic field. When the rock flipped, it placed the south magnetic pole of HR facing Earth. So we now have two magnetic fields with the same polarity facing one another and this creates a repelling force between the two bodies. We believe that it is this repelling force that is overcoming the normal gravitational attraction of the bodies. The path trajectory of HR was altered so that it is now headed more directly toward Earth than before. Previously HR was approaching Earth on a path that would be along a tangent line to the South Pole and above Earth by 200 to 350 miles. Hansen's Rock is now destined to strike Earth somewhere in Antarctica. Once we are able to acquire additional data points as the rock progresses we will be able to refine our prediction of where the rock will strike Earth and when. Since the rock has slowed significantly, it will not reach Earth at the time we had previously predicted which was around 8:00 p.m. Eastern Daylight Time this evening. We can predict that it will be delayed by several hours since it is now traveling about one-third as fast as before the explosion. HR is now approximately 86,000 miles from Earth. If HR were maintaining a constant velocity equal to the last measured velocity, it would be between fifteen and sixteen hours before HR would strike Earth. If our initial conclusion that HR is decelerating is confirmed by future measurements, then we would expect impact at some time beyond sixteen hours from now." Jerry stopped.

The leaders in the Situation Room were flabbergasted over what they had just heard. Nobody seemed to know what to say. They weren't even immediately able to develop logical questions to ask. But Garish spoke anyway, "Wow; that is an unbelievably complex explanation to get one's head around. I don't even know what to think."

Mornay asked, "General Watson, can we still destroy this rock?"

Watson answered, "Maybe. As I advised before, the mission to destroy this rock has always been a maybe. As we know now, the Russians have failed; we might fail also. I think we have a better plan than the Russians ever had. However, Mr. President, time is not on our side. Further, now that the rock is headed directly at Earth, there will be a greater likelihood of collateral damage from fragments that are able to survive flight through our atmosphere. When the rock was coming toward us in an expected glancing attitude we could pretty well expect that at least half of the debris field would avoid Earth entirely because of its momentum generally parallel to Earth's surface. Now that the rock is coming directly toward Earth we would have to contend with most of the debris field. In addition, all of our missiles are currently programmed for an intercept along the previously predicted path of the rock. Our technicians will need to reprogram every one of our twenty-eight missiles to a new trajectory which will take a good bit of time. I am not even sure that we could get all that done in twenty-four hours. If we were able to reprogram and launch our missiles I fear that the intercept altitude would be extremely close to Earth, again ensuring that we would have to deal with most of the debris field. However, Mr. President, I will immediately order that we begin this effort and I will provide you with an assessment of the do-ability of this as soon as I get it back from our field leaders. I will need another path plot from the SCC just as soon as they can produce one. We can make minor tweaks up until launch time but I need their best celestial coordinate plot as soon as possible."

Williams spoke up, "We should be able to make a pretty accurate revised trajectory plot within a couple of hours."

Watson added, "OK, that's good enough."

"Thanks Mike; Stan, let's get that reprogramming work started immediately."

"Yes sir. With your permission I will step from the room for a few minutes to launch this new effort."

The President nodded that he agreed and Watson left the room. He continued, "Since we are going to have an impact in Antarctica; we need to issue evacuation orders to all our people down there and we need to notify other countries that may have researchers in Antarctica."

Harriman spoke up, "DHS will handle that Mr. President."

"Good; thanks Larry."

Mornay looked at Rander and instructed, "Dave, I will need to address the nation after we get this revised path from the SCC. I will do the address from the Oval Office; set it up for prime time coverage."

"Yes sir; will do."

Mornay looked at Daly and instructed, "Trish, you need to get your talking points together for a news conference that you should schedule in the Briefing Room immediately after my address to the nation."

"Yes sir, Mr. President."

Next Mornay looked at Barrow, "Charlie, I know that these meetings with your team at the SCC are a distraction so I will not plan on any more of them unless something significant arises that we don't expect. I want you to personally brief me around 6:00 p.m. By then the SCC should have their trajectory plot and a pretty good estimate of when this rock will strike Earth."

"Yes sir."

General Watson re-entered the Situation Room just as Mornay was preparing to wrap up the meeting. He spoke, "Mr. President, efforts to reprogram the missiles is underway and will be finalized within six hours after the time my people receive the revised trajectory plot."

"OK Stan; that sounds good."

Mornay asked one last question "Is there anything else we should be doing that we haven't discussed?" The room was quiet. "I again want to express my appreciation and admiration for the job that has been done by you outstanding people in the NEO SCC. OK, that's it, we stand adjourned."

***

When Volkov returned to the missile control center nobody in the room missed the fact that five senior officials had left the center and only one had returned.

Volkov went directly to the Senior Launch Officer, now the highest ranking person in the room beside himself. He asked the Colonel how long it would be until they knew where and when the rock would crash into Earth. The SLO indicated that they needed a few more position points before they could answer those questions. He estimated that the required analysis would probably take two or three hours; he said that they should be able to determine the path by 0100 hours. Volkov thanked him and said that he would go to his conference room for a nap. He instructed the SLO to awaken him when he had answers to the questions.

***

At 2:30 p.m. PDT, Williams and the entire NEO SCC met in the conference room for another Post-Survey Conference. Williams asked if the team had been able to produce a reliable prediction of the new path and whether they could answer the when and where questions. Wilson assured him that they had answers to his questions and asked Jones to lead the discussion. Jones explained that they had taken position and velocity measurements every twenty minutes since the bomb exploded. They had collected seven distance and velocity measurements and they had solved for the curve. The fitting software gave them an eighth order polynomial solution that seemed exactly to fit the points they had collected so far. The results from the extrapolation indicated that they could expect a soft landing of Hansen's Rock at approximately 2:57:36 p.m. PDT tomorrow. He reported that they expected the rock to land near South 70.5° / East 162.1°. The landing location would be on or near the eastern end of the north shore of Antarctica near Znamenskiy Island. He said that at the current time they couldn't conclusively predict whether the rock would land on Antarctic soil, or on the large ice shelf covering the Southern Ocean. But, if their projection were exactly accurate, the rock would land about eleven kilometers south-southeast of the southern tip of Znamenskiy Island. This location would be about five kilometers inland from the ice shelf on a very low altitude plain where the elevations are between fifteen and thirty feet above sea level.

Williams challenged Jones about his prediction that a rock this large could make a "soft landing"; he couldn't believe that could be possible.

Jones explained that he knew that their conclusion seemed contrary to most everything that would seem intuitive but that the formula indicated that because of the repelling force between HR and Earth's South Pole the rock would be moving fairly slowly when it touched down. He explained that if the rock were to hit higher in the mountains, like in the Explorers Range which is less than twenty kilometers away and which has elevations as high as 3,100 feet, then the model indicated that the velocity of HR would be about sixty-seven kilometers per hour. He cautioned that they needed to keep in mind that even though this rock would be moving fairly slowly, that it had a huge mass. Their calculations indicated that if the rock were to strike the 3,100 foot tall peak, the energy release from the impact would be 1.327×10^{15} Kilo-Joules; that would be the equivalent of 317.7 megatons of TNT. That energy release would be six times greater than the most powerful nuclear bomb ever exploded by man on Earth. If the rock landed where they predicted, the average altitude was about twenty-five feet. At that altitude, because of the slower velocity predicted by the model, the energy release would be equal to about 4.5 megatons of TNT. That would be a rather smallish energy release given the area over which it would be distributed. The rock would create a large crater but it would likely stay intact in the crater. It would push up a good bit of material at the crater's edge and would cause localized avalanches and cracks in the ice shelf. Of course, anything in the direct path of the rock would be destroyed.

There was one other very important conclusion to be drawn from their path and velocity prediction. The velocity of the rock would remain subsonic during its passage through the densest part of Earth's atmosphere. Therefore, there would be no sonic boom following the rock. A sonic boom from an object this large could produce sound waves that would be extremely strong, killing all life within hundreds of miles of its path. The sonic boom sound waves from such a large rock would destroy property hundreds of miles away. It would likely cause the ground to shake as in an earthquake. The shaking would cause avalanches on nearly every mountain in Antarctica, and would likely break up most of the ice shelf around Antarctica.

Lastly, he reminded Williams that Hansen's Rock had been about to drop below the horizon as seen from NEOSADS when it was headed directly toward the South Pole before the Russian bomb exploded. Now that the direction had been changed and HR seemed to be headed to an impact around the South 70° parallel, it would remain above the horizon as seen from the satellite. Therefore, they would be able to continue to take visual, infrared, and radar images throughout its path. The only problem was that the weather was not going to be good near the expected impact location so they would likely not get any useful visual or infrared images of HR once it entered the tops of the storm clouds. Jones clarified by explaining that they didn't expect to be able to get visuals or infrared images for the last fifteen kilometers or so, about the last ten miles of flight for Hansen's Rock.

Williams thanked the team and concluded the meeting. He then went to his office and called Charlie Barrow to give him the information so he could brief the President, which Barrow did around 6:00 p.m. as instructed.

By the time Barrow called the President, the news media were already spreading the word about the 9:00 p.m. EDT address that Mornay would be making. Speculation was uncontrolled. "Experts" were being interviewed on the twenty-four hour news channels with the usual political biases that they lived by. Some experts were guessing that it would be announced that the Russians had destroyed the rock. Others speculated that the Russian mission had failed and that Earth was only hours away from obliteration. Some speculated that the U. S. military was planning a mission to destroy the rock. Some speculated that the rock would continue on the path that President Mornay had previously told them it would follow and enter a stable orbit around Earth. Needless to say, virtually everyone in the world would be watching President Mornay's address.

***

The Senior Launch Officer rang the phone in the private conference room where Volkov was sleeping at 0113 hours. Volkov awoke immediately, answered the phone, and invited the Colonel to come to the conference room to brief him. While the SLO was traveling from the missile control center to the conference room, Volkov washed his face, stuck his hair to his skull, and put on his trousers and shirt; he did not add the tie or jacket. Volkov took a seat at the commanding end of the large mahogany conference table just as the knock sounded on the door. When the Colonel entered, the two guards followed expecting that the paranoid Volkov would want them to protect him but Volkov waved them back into the hallway.

"Comrade Leader, I have good news."

"Let me hear this good news."

"Sir, we believe that this space rock will now strike Earth in Antarctica."

The impatient Volkov interrupted, "How can this space rock striking Earth be a good thing? Does it really matter where the rock hits if it will destroy all of Earth anyway?"

"President Volkov, my good news is that this space rock will not destroy Earth. This rock is slowing down as it gets closer to Earth. This is because of the interaction of the large magnetic field of the rock and the powerful magnetic field at the South Pole of Earth. The two magnetic fields have the same polarity which causes them to push against each other. This pushing of the Earth on this rock is slowing it down so its velocity will be sufficiently slow when it strikes that it will not destroy Earth. Depending on exactly where the rock will land in Antarctica, the impact may not cause any significant damage on Earth except in the vicinity near the impact point. Since Antarctica is far from other land masses and since there are only research teams living there, we believe that the loss of life and property will be minimal. We have ordered all of our research people to evacuate all of Antarctica and they are in the process of securing their secret information so that it can be carried with them when they fly out within a few hours."

The SLO paused so Volkov asked another question, "So, when will this rock strike Earth?"

"We think the rock will strike Earth shortly after midnight tonight, less than twenty-four hours from now."

Volkov was now fully awake and skeptical, "This prediction of yours seems unbelievable. How can it be that such a large space rock can just land on Earth and not do any damage?"

"Sir, as I said earlier this rock has an extraordinary magnetic field unlike anything we have ever seen before. That enormously powerful magnetic field is capable of supporting the rock against the magnetic field of Earth at the South Pole. It is remarkable but we believe that it is true," the Colonel assured.

"This is indeed excellent news. I will need to speak to the people of the Russian Federation to share this good news. Listen carefully Colonel; this will be my story. I will tell them that we intentionally exploded our bomb at exactly the right time so that we would force this rock into this soft landing. Our mission was a huge success. We did exactly the correct thing and we saved the Earth from extinction." Volkov paused to see if the Colonel would choose to argue with this lie.

The SLO was silent for several seconds as he mentally weighed which response he would make to this fabrication. He too liked to be successful. He knew that if he took a position opposed to Volkov's lie that he too could disappear just like the other four men had disappeared. Since life on Earth would go on, he decided that his life on Earth would go on as well. "Yes Comrade Leader that is an excellent way to explain our actions. You will get the adoration that you deserve and we will make those silly Americans appear incapable again. Your solution is a brilliant solution Comrade Leader. You are a brilliant man and a flawless leader."

Volkov knew the Colonel was lying but he liked the sound of it anyway. "Good, we agree. You need to explain to your scientists that this deflection of the rock was the plan from the beginning. You can deal with any dissidents as you wish as long as they aren't permitted to leak any information that conflicts with our story. Is that clear?"

"Yes sir, that is very clear and I will handle it."

The SLO left the room and headed back to the control center. Volkov instructed his guard to have his helicopter prepare for the trip back to the Kremlin Senate. As before, the three ordinary-looking sedans traveled to the airport to meet the helicopter and Volkov arrived in his office shortly after 03:00. He picked up his phone and awoke Anya. He instructed her to contact his media officer to set up an address to the people at 09:00. He began to make some handwritten notes that he would use when he addressed the people of the Russian Federation.

***

The red light on the middle camera of the three set up in the Oval Office began to glow at exactly 9:00 p.m. EDT. "Fellow Americans, tonight I come to you with good news. It appears that Earth will be spared from any catastrophic damage that could have happened from this space rock we call Hansen's Rock. I will explain what has happened and what we believe will happen. The Russians sent a missile that we believe was intended to destroy the space rock but it failed to destroy the rock. However, the Russian bomb pushed the space rock onto a more direct path to Earth than it had previously been on and the bomb caused the space rock to flip over so that its southern magnetic pole is now facing Earth. As I told you days ago, this rock has an unexplainably powerful magnetic field. Now that its south pole is facing the South Pole of Earth, there is a repelling force between the rock and Earth. This powerful repelling force is slowing down Hansen's Rock and we expect that it will be moving fairly slowly when it impacts Earth on Antarctica. We believe that there may be substantial damage in the area of the impact but no widespread damage is expected. We do not expect it to induce earthquakes or tsunamis. The rock will be traveling too slowly to create a sonic boom like those that have been experienced from fast moving asteroids in the past. Our best minds have come to these conclusions and they now believe that there is no reason to fear this space rock any more. Our American space scientists predict that the rock will land relatively softly in Antarctica tomorrow evening around 6:00 p.m. Eastern Daylight Time.

Now that there is no threat to your safety, I appeal to each one of you to return to your lives and to begin living your life as you would have had there never been a threat from space. There is no longer any need for you to be concerned about this space rock. Thank you and good night America." Mornay looked directly into the camera that owned the glowing red light until it was extinguished.

13 JULY

At 09:00 in Moscow, Volkov was in a fresh white shirt, a solid red tie, and a freshly-pressed blue suit as he sat behind the large desk in his office. The desk had been cleared of all material except the handwritten notes he had created. When the cameraman gave him the signal, Volkov paused for five seconds for effect and then began, "My people of the Russian Federation, I come to you today to tell you again that you should be very proud of your country. As I told you many days ago, I have been taking all the necessary actions to save Earth from this menacing space rock that was destined to destroy us all. About sixteen hours ago, I pushed the button that launched a missile that flew toward this space rock. The plan was to deflect this rock and to cause it to flip over so as to expose the side of the rock where the magnetic field comes from the rock towards Earth. Since the magnetic field of our South Pole also has a magnetic field that leaves Earth and points upward, these two fields are opposing each other. Just as you have seen two toy magnets oppose each other and push each other away, Earth and this space rock are pushing against each other. This pushing is slowing the space rock and by the time it strikes Earth it will cause little damage except in the vicinity of the impact. I now expect this rock to fall gracefully to Earth in Antarctica. It will land in about fifteen hours, a little after midnight tonight, Moscow time. This was the plan of your space scientists and your military executed this plan flawlessly. I personally led the effort. As I promised you, I have saved Earth.

I am sure that many of you have by now heard the propaganda speech of the American President who alleged that our missile failed to accomplish its mission. As always, the Americans underestimate the sophistication of the Russian scientists, the Russian military, and the President of the Russian Federation. The Americans are simple thinkers, but arrogant at the same time. Their assumption was that we were trying to destroy this rock with our missile. This was never our plan. As you can tell since the Americans did not take any action against this space rock, they never had a plan at all. They simply do not have the intelligence and commitment needed to undertake such a complicated mission. The Americans choose to make bold speeches; I choose to undertake bold missions that protect you, my people of the Russian Federation."

***

Having heard the good news from both the President of the United States and the President of the Russian Federation, panic was relieved in most places on Earth. People who were trying to escape to higher ground began to retreat as soon as the gridlock began to clear. Looting ceased in most places. Those that had gravitated to religious places of worship said their last prayers and prepared to head back to their homes and jobs. Others were waiting until the rock came to rest to make sure that the predictions were correct; they remembered other predictions conveyed by national leaders that were proven to be false.

***

President Mornay called Charlie Barrow and asked if his SCC would be able to produce images of the rock as it approached Earth. Barrow explained that the SCC would be taking images as the object approached Earth but did not expect to be able to get visuals or infrared images during the last eight to ten minutes of travel by the rock because of the thick clouds that were expected to cover the landing area. Barrow also explained that although the center would be able to take images, there would be little to see once the images were produced. The images would simply show what would appear to be a kind of fuzzy disc due to the rotation of the rock. Barrow told the President that he would be happy to arrange another teleconference if desired but that there would be little interesting imagery. The President accepted this explanation but decided that he would like to have an active video conference at the time the rock was expected to land. Barrow agreed that it would be good to be connected with the SCC in real time when the rock struck Earth. He told the President that he would have the video link set up at 5:30 p.m. EDT since the rock was expected to strike Antarctica around 5:58 p.m.

Dan L. King

***

When 5:30 p.m. arrived in Washington, Mornay, Garish, Watson, Harriman, Garrett, and Daly converged in the Situation Room. Barrow had gotten there early to make sure everything would go well.

When Mornay entered the room, he saw that only Mike Williams was on the other end of the video call, "Hi Mike."

"Hello Mr. President."

"Mike, you look a little lonely out there by yourself. I assume everybody else is on the job. So tell me how our rock is progressing compared to what we expected yesterday."

"Mr. President the rock is behaving exactly as our model had predicted. In fact, I am amazed at how good the equation resolves the expected position and velocity of Hansen's Rock." Williams looked at the clock on the wall, then to his notes, and continued, "As of right now, HR will be about sixty-five miles high and approaching the targeted impact site. It should now be traveling at about 290 miles per hour."

Wilson walked to the open conference door and told Williams and all the folk in the Situation Room, "Everything is going pretty much as we expected. We are beginning to see what appears to be a vapor trail or a dust trail being emitted along the flight path of the rock. We don't know exactly what it is at this time. That's the only thing we didn't really expect. This trail seems to be getting denser as the rock approaches Earth."

Just killing time, the people in the Situation Room began discussing the speech that the Russian President had made claiming that their missile mission had gone exactly as planned and that the effect of the explosion was not serendipitous.

Garish gave his opinion, "I think Volkov is just trying to turn failure into victory by claiming that they knew exactly where to blow up their bomb so that this rock was slowed by exactly the amount needed to make a soft landing. And to believe that they were smart enough to figure out that they needed to flip this rock over to manage its descent is beyond what I find to be believable."

The others voiced their agreement. Harriman said, "I am not at all surprised that Volkov would bend the truth to bolster his ego."

Watson added, "Volkov is an egomaniac and a pathological liar."

At 5:45 p.m. Wilson interrupted the chatter when she again walked into the conference room. "Gentlemen, Hansen's Rock just broke through an altitude of forty miles; it is now traveling at about 230 miles per hour. That strange trail is still present and is getting denser. Radar is showing a very good return, almost as if it were a solid object. We still don't know what to make of it." She turned without waiting for comments or questions and went back into the working part of the SCC.

Having heard Wilson's comment, the President looked at Barrow with a quizzical look on his face. Barrow just shrugged to indicate he didn't have any explanation either.

Garish said, "I don't like it when the smartest space scientists in the world find something that they don't understand; that gives me the heebie-jeebies."

The others nodded their agreement but remained silent. There was no further discussion before Wilson came back to the SCC conference room with another report. "Gentlemen, Hansen's Rock just entered the cloud layer and we are no longer able to view it optically; we expect impact in eight minutes."

Everyone in the Situation Room looked at the big digital clock over all of the dark video monitors to note the time. The people in the room were visibly nervous. Daly was unconsciously tapping her designer writing stylus on the face of her electronic tablet until she saw that the action had gotten the attention of the President; she immediately silenced the stylus. The only action taken in the Situation Room before Wilson returned was when the Secretary of Homeland Security got up to pour himself a glass of water to wet his dry mouth.

Wilson finally entered the room and reported, "Gentlemen, Hansen's Rock has landed almost exactly where we had predicted. At the time of impact, the rock was traveling at about five miles per hour so we do not expect widespread damage as a result of the impact. We are in the process of confirming our probable damage conclusion by checking with the USGS to see what the Global Seismographic Network recorded as a result of the impact.

The only unexpected thing is that we are still seeing that strange trail that I mentioned before and it is not dissipating as a dust or vapor trail would. We would expect dust or ice crystals to settle or evaporate pretty quickly or to be dispersed by the wind, but that is not happening. Radar is still showing very solid returns from this trail. The trail seems to run from ground level all the way to the top of the stratosphere and maybe well into the mesosphere but the signature at mesospheric altitudes is too faint for us to resolve. We are trying to determine what we are dealing with. We recommend that we send reconnaissance aircraft to the region to assess damage from the rock and to investigate this trail."

The President spoke first, "That sounds like great news Liz. It would appear that we have dodged this space bullet for reasons that we don't altogether understand. But, we dodged it nonetheless. General Watson, I'll depend on you to get reconnaissance aircraft to the impact area as soon as possible to check out the damage and this trail thing and to report back to everyone here in the briefing room and to Mike Williams. Trish, I want you to hold a press briefing as soon as you can get most of your correspondents into the Briefing Room to spread the good news and to explain that we will be investigating the impact area. Charlie, keep me informed about what the SCC concludes about this strange trail from the rock. Are there any other suggestion?"

No one made suggestions so the President closed the meeting.

THE PUZZLE GROWS

Immediately after the meeting with President Mornay and the others, General Watson returned to his office at The Pentagon. He called his longtime friend, General Ryan Kelly, Base Commander of the Royal Australian Air Force Base at Edinburgh, South Australia. RAAF Base Edinburgh was home to No. 92 Wing, the RAAF Surveillance and Response Group. This wing commands the marine patrol squadrons that fly the Lockheed-built AP-3C Orion, one of the most capable surveillance and reconnaissance aircraft in the world. Kelly was, of course, familiar with the landing of Hansen's Rock and was eager to assist Watson by having his aviators fly to the site to recon the rock and the strange atmospheric trail left by the rock. Using the big map of the world on his wall, he measured the trip to the impact site to be about 4,200 kilometers. He advised Watson that it was currently 10:00, 14 July, in South Australia. The flight to Antarctica would take about six hours and it would take about three hours to prepare the aircraft and crews for the mission. Kelly advised Watson that there was no daylight at the location of the rock during this time of the year but that there was some twilight in the middle of the day. Kelly suggested a departure early the following morning so that the recon aircraft would arrive at the site when there was at least some small amount of twilight which would assist with flying and would produce better visual image captures. He said the return flight would require in-flight refueling. He expected the aircraft to return to base by no later than 19:00 on 15 July. After the usual debriefing session, the polished information from the flight would be available for sharing by 22:00 in S.A. which would be 07:00 in Washington, D.C.

Watson was pleased that Kelly would commission the flight. He thanked Kelly and told him that he looked forward to reviewing the results of the recon mission.

***

9:14 p.m. PDT…

For the first time since Hansen's Rock had been discovered, the SCC was back to normal scheduling and staffing, meaning that only two technicians were scheduled to work the night shift and management had returned to their normal daytime schedule. But Jerry Jones just couldn't go home until he could figure out what the trail of debris was that HR had created. He studied the radar data and it indicated that the trail was made of solid matter. He studied the infrared images and they indicated that the solid matter was very cold. The visual images showed something that was transparent at high altitude and very dense and thick at lower altitudes. Casting aside reality, he could interpret the data to mean that this "trail" was made of something that was frozen. If the trail had been small fragments of ice or dust that the rock had shed during its passage through the atmosphere, then they would have fallen to the ground or at least would have been blown around by the wind but this debris trail didn't move; it was fixed in place!

Then, as insight often presents itself, the possibility entered his mind. He knew that HR was extremely cold with a temperature just above absolute zero. He knew that the volume of solid hydrogen coating the rock was massive. There was a possible explanation…and it sounded preposterous. His theory was that HR had frozen the gases in the atmosphere as it had passed through them. Since the ambient temperatures in Antarctica were very cold anyway, the ice had persisted. In his head he saw a tunnel through the atmosphere that was encased in ice. He pushed back from the desk and looked around almost ashamed that he had arrived at a conclusion that might indicate lunacy. He went to the break room and got another cup of coffee. He walked down the hall to the door that led to the parking lot and swiped his ID badge across the sensor to unlock the door and register his exit. He walked out into the warm summer air that engulfed the parking lot and began to circle the center collection of parking spaces. He walked and sipped his coffee until the cup ran dry…all the while trying to develop another theory about what the trail could be. He couldn't come up with anything else. He knew that he had been working too hard for too long and that it might be affecting his ability to think rationally so he determined to go home and get a good night's sleep in his own bed. He swiped back into the SCC, packed his briefcase with his papers, and went home to collapse.

15 JULY (IN AUSTRALIA)
14 JULY (IN THE US)

7:00 a.m. PDT…

Jones showed up as always an hour before his scheduled hours were supposed to begin. Williams and Wilson were already there working on paperwork.

Although Jerry had gone home with intentions of getting a night of quality rest, he had found that sleep did not come easily and it came as a series of naps punctuated with periods of thinking about what the trail from Hansen's Rock might be. On the way through the center, he filled a cup with coffee before taking his place in his desk chair. The latest visual and radar images of the impact area processed by the night crew looked just like the ones from the day before; the trail had not moved. He was now convinced that he may understand this rock trail after all. He walked to Wilson's office and knocked on the window that looked out over the center. She waved him in with a large smile, "Good morning, Jerry. I hope you finally got some rest; you sure deserved a restful night at home."

Jones replied, skipping the pleasantries, "Liz, I have a theory about the trail that Hansen's Rock created."

Wilson smiled knowing that she was blessed to have a man like Jerry working with her, "OK, let's hear it; nobody else has a clue what it could be."

"Liz, I think what we are seeing is a tunnel of ice. I think that the solid hydrogen covering HR was so cold that it froze the atmosphere as the rock passed through it. I think the ambient temperature in Antarctica in the winter is so cold that the ice is persistent." He paused, expecting Wilson to laugh out loud and kick him from her office.

But Wilson did not kick him out of her office and she did not laugh. She remained silent for several seconds as she tried, in her mind, to put the facts that she knew together with the theory that Jerry had presented. It was a logical conclusion she thought...unbelievable, but certainly logical. Wilson didn't say a thing to Jones but picked up the phone and punched the numbers for Williams' extension.

"Williams."

"Mike I need to talk to you right away; are you available?"

"Sure. My office or yours?"

"Jerry and I will come to your office."

They walked around the center to the opposite corner where the only truly private office in the center was located. The door was open so they walked in and sat in the chairs across the desk from Williams. "What's up guys?"

Wilson started, "Mike, what Jerry is about to tell you will blow your mind so hang on tight."

Jerry went through his theory just as he had done with Wilson and when he was finished he said, "That's it Mike."

Williams was astonished, "Wow! I'm not sure what to say. Your theory is testing my ability to comprehend. How could such a thing happen? And furthermore, if you are correct what does it mean? Should we do anything or just let this thing melt. Does it pose a threat to anyone? Damn, I don't even know if I'm posing questions that make any sense." he just rambled.

Like a seasoned scientist, Jones replied, "Mike, those questions do need to be answered. There are probably many more questions that need to be answered. The first thing, of course, is to find out if indeed there is an ice tunnel through our atmosphere to Antarctica. When do we expect to get feedback from the flyby?"

Williams answered, "I don't know. All I know is that General Watson was going to arrange for it but I haven't heard anything more. I'll call Mr. Barrow and see if he can find out for us. For now let's assume that Jerry is correct. Let's study this ice tunnel to learn what we can about its characteristics. I know that is a tall order but if we assume that the thing is made from ice, maybe we can use the instruments on NEOSADS to try to determine how thick the ice is, etc. It would seem safe to assume that the tunnel diameter would be the same as the radial dimensions of Hansen's Rock. If that is true then we have a hole in the atmosphere surrounded by ice that is seventeen kilometers in diameter. Liz, didn't we determine that this trail, eh... ice tunnel, was visible all the way into the mesosphere? If that is true, then doesn't that mean that we have a virtual vacuum on one end of the tunnel and a rock covered with solid hydrogen on the other end? The solid hydrogen probably began sublimating as soon as it entered the relatively warm stratosphere and given that even Antarctica is a lot warmer than twenty degrees Kelvin, the hydrogen is continuing to go gaseous. So do we have a seventy mile tall ice tunnel that is filled with highly explosive hydrogen gas? Or what?"

Wilson answered, "Those are interesting thoughts Mike. Jerry and I will try to get some answers while we await an eyes-on survey from the recon aircraft."

***

The fully fueled Orion AP-3C plane had turned from the taxiway onto Runway One-Eight at RAAF Edinburgh at 04:13 on 15 July. Upon clearance from the tower the pilot pushed the throttles to the four Allison T56-A-14 turboprop engines, each of which produced 4,600 shaft horsepower. The plane was airborne before it even used half of the 2,600 meter runway. The plane assumed a heading of 167° which would be the most direct path to the location of the impacted space rock. The twenty-six minute climb to cruising altitude was a little bumpy but the air seemed to smooth some at 8,200 meters so the Flight Lieutenant in the left seat chose that altitude for cruising during the six hour trip. Once the plane leveled out and the autopilot was set, the crew of eight tried to relax a bit before they arrived at the work location. The size of the crew had been reduced from the usual thirteen since this would be a simpler mission than their usual patrols and it would save some weight, permitting a longer flight range before refueling.

The plane flew in clouds most of the way to the northeast corner of Antarctica. When the plane was about 200 kilometers from the target, the pilot began a gradual descent toward the site looking for the cloud ceiling. The magnetic compass was already showing a substantial deviation from the GPS heading so the pilot was ignoring the magnetic instrument. The objective of the mission was to get visual images of the impact site and the debris trail that the rock had left in the atmosphere so clear air was necessary to successfully complete the mission. When the plane was about thirty kilometers from the impact site, its speed had been reduced to patrol speed just before it broke through the clouds and into reasonably clear air at an altitude of 330 meters. Even though there would be no sunlight today at this latitude there was enough predawn twilight that the crew could see features with their dark-adjusted eyes. Even though they were thirty clicks from the target, the reaction of the crew to the view was immediate.

Hansen's Rock

The Flight Officer in the right seat uttered, "Holy crap! What the hell is that?"

The Flight Lieutenant was also distracted by the view. It was like nothing he had ever seen. There was this huge ice thing that grew from the ground and climbed into the clouds. It looked like a giant, ice covered skyscraper that penetrated the clouds and disappeared. In the back of the plane, the Flight Sergeant ordered the Sergeant to start all cameras. The full complement of cameras was directed at the ice thing by the Sergeant. They would take thirty frames per second motion pictures and the fixed image cameras would take one extremely high resolution image every five seconds. One of the cameras would take wide angle images, another would record telephoto images, and another would record infrared images. The radar was recording data that would permit the internal structure to be modeled.

As the plane got within about ten kilometers of the ice mountain, the pilot was having to exert a lot of pull on the yoke to maintain level flight so he instructed the copilot, "plus one elevator trim." The pilot was still having to pull back on the yoke so he repeated his order, "plus one elevator trim!" Not detecting any improvement on the pressure from the yoke he said, "Come on mate give me some trim!"

The Flight Officer replied, "Sir, you have three degrees of up trim; do you want more?"

By now the pilot realized that the plane was experiencing an unusual downdraft. He pushed the throttles all the way forward, pulled the yoke back, and turned left in an effort to climb out of the downdraft. The plane kept descending. When the altimeter showed 100 meters and was still unwinding the pilot commanded, "Prepare for impact mates; I think we are going down." All the enlisted men in the back of the plane assumed the head between knees position and prayed. The pilot fought the yoke as the copilot trimmed the propeller pitch to try to get a little more bite in the cold, dense air just above the ice shelf. When the plane was only about twenty-five meters above the ice, it began to make progress against the strong wind that was attempting to draw them into the icy skyscraper. The copilot looked at the airspeed indicator to see it reading approximately 280 knots but they were barely making progress over the sea ice. Slowly, the sea surface started to move behind them faster as they clawed their way away from the ice structure. Once the pilot recognized that they were making progress against the strong winds, he ordered, "Flight Sergeant, resume the photography mission." The cameras actually had never stopped humming and clicking. The Sergeant evaluating the images noticed that there was a large breach in the wall of ice just above ground level. Through this breach he could see a portion of the space rock that was smoking as if it were smoldering. It became clear pretty quickly that the strong wind was being created by this hole through the ice wall. The hole was about ten kilometers long and 200 meters high and rather jagged around the edges. The moving picture image in the top right quadrant of his monitor showed snow from the ground and clouds from above the hole being drawn into the hole.

When the plane had regained an altitude that was just below the clouds, the pilot asked, "OK, what did we learn from that?"

The Sergeant at the monitor spoke first, "Sir, there is a large hole in the wall of that ice thing near ground level and it is sucking big time. I suggest we give it a wide berth. I checked the plot of air speed and ground speed and when we were trying to escape the hole we were showing an air speed of 285 knots but a ground speed of only thirty-six knots. From that I conclude that the winds that we experienced while still about five kilometers from the ice wall were howling at nearly 250 knots. I also will note that the plane's barometer dropped to 880 millibars when our altitude was twenty-five meters; that's a seriously low reading sir!"

The copilot commented, "That damn wind nearly got us sir!"

The pilot said, "Yeah mate, if we didn't have such a damn good airplane we would'a been goners. OK, we came here to check this thing out so let's continue. I'm going to fly around this thing in a spiral up to our service ceiling to see what we can learn. Sarg, run all cameras and radars and let's map this thing from bottom to top as well as we can before we head back to meet the tanker."

"Aye, sir."

The plane flew around the circular ice column testing to see how close the plane could fly to the ice without getting caught in another wind vortex. There was a downdraft around the column, more pronounced in the air immediately above the hole, which was literally sucking the clouds down and into the hole. The downdraft gradually lessened as the plane increased its altitude until it reach 8,600 meters which was near the service ceiling of the plane. It appeared that the only dangerous portion of the structure was the hole near ground level.

After confirming all the gear in the back of the plane had performed properly and had recorded the data that was needed, the pilot spoke to the Flight Officer and said, "OK mate, take us home." The copilot punched buttons on the GPS-guided autopilot and hit the engage switch. The coordinates specified where they would rendezvous with the tanker to take on fuel before completing the mission. The pilot made some notes that he would use during the debriefing. After he finished his notes he got up and went to the lavatory in the back of the plane before stopping at the desks of the men in the main cabin who

Hansen's Rock

were working on processing the images that had been taken so that they could be used during the debriefing. After seeing that all was going well with the crew he returned to the cockpit and strapped himself back into his seat to rest a bit before the refueling operation.

The plane refueled uneventfully and landed at the base a little after 18:00. The flight crew had loaded all the data and images that had been collected onto two redundant external hard drives to ensure against a failure by one of them. The drives were packed in foam-lined, hard-sided cases that looked something like a small carry-on suitcase except without wheels. Two different men carried the cases in the event of an accident. They delivered the cases to the debriefing room where the Flight Sergeant took receipt of them and inserted one of the hard drives into an external drive bay. The external hard drive mount was connected to a notebook computer via a USB cable. The VGA output of the computer was connected to a LED projector. The crew waited for the Base Commander as they had been requested to do. Normally the Base Commander wouldn't be involved in a debriefing but since this was not a normal mission and since the Commander's friend had requested the mission, the General wanted to be personally involved. General Kelly arrived just after 19:00 and asked the men to continue with the debriefing as they normally would. Of course, Kelly found the images and data that the mission had produced to be nearly unbelievable. The debriefing took a little over an hour as each of the flight crew recounted their experiences and explained the data and images that each had been responsible for during the flight.

The administrative Aircraftman who had been operating the digital recorder that converted the debriefing dialogue into a text file stopped the recorder when the meeting had been adjourned. He had also printed and marked the images as they were discussed with the exact elapsed time from the recorder and the file number that the cameras had assigned to each image file. This would permit him to electronically insert the images into the text document at the proper places to complete the written report. In response to a question from General Kelly, the Aircraftman replied that he should have the file completed by 22:00. Kelly told the man to bring him one paper copy and one digital copy when they were ready so that he could forward the report to General Watson. The Aircraftman delivered the file to Kelly at 21:34.

15 JULY

Watson had arrived at his Pentagon office at 4:30 a.m. as usual. The encrypted debriefing report arrived in his secure email inbox at 6:52 a.m. When his computer chirped to let him know that he had new mail, he entered the decryption key, opened the file, and printed the report so that it would be easier to read. The printed report also provided him a way to make notations if he chose. He read the report, turned around to face his computer, and created an email to Charlie Barrow that asked, "What do your guys make of this?" He attached an encrypted copy of the report and hit the send button.

***

Barrow arrived at his office at 7:15 a.m. and scanned his electronic inbox while drinking his first cup of coffee. He found the note from Watson, entered the decryption key, and read the report. He immediately forwarded a copy of the report to Mike Williams adding only three question marks to the beginning of the email.

***

Williams settled into his desk chair at 6:48 a.m. and turned on the computer monitor. He opened his inbox and saw the message from Barrow. He entered the security token and opened the file. He read about half of the report before deciding to print three copies. When the printer quit shaking he collected the three copies and walked to Wilson's office to find her with her back to the door wading through an electronic mountain of mail. He knocked on the open door and Wilson turned around. "Good morning, Mike; how are you today?"

"I'm fine Liz. I got the report from the reconnaissance aircraft. Buzz Jerry and ask him to come see us."

She did as instructed and Jerry entered Liz's office about three minutes later.

Williams handed copies of the report to Wilson and Jones. He commented, "Wait 'til you read this!"

There was no discussion while they read the report. When Wilson and Jones had both looked up, Williams asked, "So what do you think?"

Jerry waited for Liz to speak since she was his boss. Wilson said, "This is unbelievable; Jerry you were right on with your theory."

Quickly, Jerry jabbed, "Why do you think it unbelievable that I could be correct about this thing." He laughed.

Wilson smiled and said, "You know what I meant; the information in the report is unbelievable."

Jones acknowledged, "Yes ma'am; I know what you meant." He continued, "Mike, I have an uneasy feeling about this big hole. According to the report, the velocity at which the winds are being sucked into this ice column could easily be approaching 500 kilometers per hour. That is a huge volume of air passing through the column. This hole means that we have a direct path from near sea level to the highest reaches of the atmosphere. The Earth has developed a leak!"

Jones explained that there could be at least two serious problems created by this leak. Firstly, the air that everyone breathed was leaking into space, obviously not a good thing. He didn't know if the rate of air loss would be alarming or not until he had cranked some numbers. The second problem was that this ice column that was spilling air into space would likely be producing some amount of thrust since the ice tube would act like a rocket engine. If the thrust was significant, over time it could affect Earth's rotation or declination. He told them that he was pretty sure that if the first concern was significant then the second concern would also be significant. He also reminded Williams and Wilson that they should not forget that there is a huge amount of solid hydrogen sublimating inside the column and mixing with the oxygen-rich sea level air, creating a very large volume of an extremely explosive mixture in the tube.

Williams ordered, "OK Jerry, get on this thing and figure out how big of a problem we have. Use anyone in the center to help if you need them. We will shuffle the techs to cover needed activities."

"Yes sir; I'm on it now."

Jones went back to his desk and packed up his notebook computer and the other material that he would need to evaluate the situation. He went to the conference room, closed the door, and set up his equipment. His first task would be to determine the area of the hole in the ice column. Using the data from the reconnaissance mission he determined that at the time of the flyby, the total area of the hole was very close to two square kilometers. The velocity of the air through the hole was 483 kilometers per hour. This meant that 966 cubic kilometers of air was escaping through the hole every hour. This was equal to 23,184 cubic kilometers of air every day. He was a little confused about why the air velocity was as high as it was since the differential pressure across the hole should be exactly one atmosphere or 14.7 psi. This pressure differential would not produce such a high wind velocity. So he knew that there must be some other process at work that was creating a wind velocity significantly higher than he had expected. Then it hit him; the large volume of solid hydrogen that was experiencing sublimation was creating an updraft that was drawing more air than expected through the hole. The extremely light hydrogen gas was racing toward the vacuum at the top of the ice tunnel. He reasoned that this effect would continue and that the effect would become more pronounced as the temperature of the rock increased which would increase the rate at which the solid hydrogen was being converted into gaseous hydrogen. So, the volume of air that would be drawn through the hole would be increasing by the hour until all the solid hydrogen had melted and turned to gas. He knew that this conversion would likely follow an exponential curve of some shape.

He went to his file of the data from the continuing observations of the impact site and studied the Doppler displacement data which would give him the change in the speed of the air that had occurred since the rock landed. He took the various velocity readings and plugged them into the curve fitting software on his computer and hit the return key to have the computer solve for the equation of the curve. The resulting equation and curve extrapolation was seriously alarming. It would only be a short time before the wind speed through the hole would go supersonic and then hypersonic. The increasing speed brought another concern. As the speed of the air increased, the friction of the air moving through the hole in the ice would begin to melt the ice border to the hole, making the hole larger and increasing even further the loss of atmosphere. The data was frightening. It showed that within a few weeks, Earth would lose enough of its air that the beaches in Miami would have air as thin as that which Denver normally had. This would make Denver's atmosphere so thin that most people would need to carry oxygen tanks with them wherever they went. It also meant that most commercial airplanes would not be able to take off from Denver and other high altitude airports as the existing runways would be too short in the thin air.

Next he started his thrust study. He started with the data from the recon. He already knew the volume of air that was flowing through the hole and the speed of the air flowing through the hole. All he had to do to determine the velocity of the air exiting the top of the ice tunnel was to distribute the air volume over the cross-sectional area of the ice tunnel. This produced a velocity of 4,258 meters per hour inside the tube or a velocity of 1.183 meters per second. Using the force equation after looking up the density coefficient of air at sea level and zero degrees Celsius, he calculated the thrust of the air exiting the tunnel to be 3.889×10^{10} Newtons or 2.8135×10^{11} lb-ft…281 billion lb-ft of thrust. This force would also increase over time as the entry velocity of air increased but the thrust would increase as the square of the velocity increase. This would create an enormous force on Earth. He studied the data from NEOSADS and determined that the ice column was tilted six degrees south from the vertical. The thrust from the tunnel was in a direction that would tend to decrease Earth's declination. Without intervention, the 23.5° declination of Earth would begin to reduce, causing shifts in seasonal patterns. Winter would become longer at the poles and summer would become longer at the lower latitudes.

Jones was sure that there would be plenty of people that would just want to get rid of the ice tunnel but he was concerned about how to do that without igniting all that hydrogen in the tunnel along with that surrounding the rock. But without some more work he couldn't describe the consequences that would come from blowing up the rock and its tunnel. He went back to the data from NEOSADS radar surveys and found the calculated mass of the solid hydrogen layer covering the metallic core. The data showed a mass of 7.527×10^{15} kilograms. He used the molar weight of hydrogen gas to convert the mass into moles and then applied the Enthalpy of Combustion coefficient for hydrogen which was 287 Kilo-Joules per mole. The math produced a total enthalpy of 1.076×10^{21} Kilo-Joules. He converted that into equivalent tons of TNT since more people could grasp the size of an explosion if it were stated in this unit term. The answer was astounding; the solid hydrogen had an energy equivalent of 2.58×10^{14} tons of TNT. This explosive power would be 129 billion times more powerful than the "Fat Boy" bomb that destroyed Nagasaki at the end of World War II. It seemed apparent that blowing up the rock was not an alternative as the consequences couldn't even be imagined.

Dan L. King

So the problem became how to stop the escalating leakage of air from Earth without blowing up the massive amount of hydrogen inside the ice column.

Jones took a break for more coffee and to clear his head which was now spinning in numbers. He took his coffee with him down the hall to the door. He swiped the door open and headed to the parking lot to think. Walking seemed to help him sort through complex things so he tried walking his way to a solution. While he walked he always looked around but often without seeing anything except the problem that he was trying to solve in his head. But today, he saw something not so common in a parking lot of mostly well-paid people. Someone had stuffed a wash cloth into the place where a gas cap would normally fit on the fender of a car, to seal the gas tank…sort of. That was when he realized that the only solution to his problem was to find a way to patch the hole in the ice column. He thought to himself, "It is one thing to plug the neck of a fuel tank but it's an altogether different thing to plug a two square kilometer hole in an ice mountain in the remotest part of the world." He realized that there was no way that anyone could carry enough material nearly to the South Pole to fill a hole this large. So if the hole was going to be filled, it would have to be filled with material that was already on or near the site of the hole. The predominant material near the hole in the ice column was more ice. During winter, the floating ice shelf covering the ocean could extend dozens of kilometers from terra firma. So, there was definitely plenty of ice to plug the hole. But, how in the world would anyone be able to get ice floating on the sea into the hole in the ice tunnel? What kind of machinery could move such large pieces of ice into place? How could the ice be broken into manageable pieces for relocation? How could humans or robots perform in the high winds that were getting stronger by the hour?

Jones hadn't noticed that it had begun to rain…not a soaking rain, but a gentle shower that was more common in that part of California. After realizing that the rain was falling he walked back to the porch in front of the door to the center. He stopped at the top of the steps in the shelter of the standing seam canopy over the porch to finish his coffee and think some more. The light rain was forming drops on the metal roof that were collecting next to the standing seams and trickling down the roof before they leapt to the ground where they crashed into the drops that had preceded them. When he saw these collisions he knew how to get the sea ice out of the water and into the hole. He laughed to himself about how crazy his idea sounded; then he thought again that maybe the concept wasn't all that crazy after all. He poured the rest of his coffee into the shrubbery and swiped the door open. He dropped by

Hansen's Rock

Wilson's office and told her that he was ready for a discussion of his findings. She called Williams and they all went to the conference room where Jones had been working.

Jones explained, "OK, I have determined that the volume of air escaping through that hole is significant. My data and the curve that fits the data predict an increasing flow of air through the hole. I am also convinced that the thrust that is being created by the flow of air exiting the ice column into space is significant and will increase by the square of the wind's velocity increase. Without prompt intervention, the loss of air will be noticeable in just a few weeks. Breathing will become difficult for a lot of mankind. In addition, over time, the thrust of this escaping air will reduce the declination of Earth causing significant seasonal impacts as winters get longer at the poles and summers get longer at the equator. It also struck me that the thinner atmosphere will permit more meteors to survive atmospheric entry and we will experience more meteorites hitting Earth. However, I suspect that we will run out of air long before we begin to observe the impact of the lower tilt of Earth and the lowered protection from space rocks. We need to plug that hole as soon as possible to avoid these problems."

Williams exclaimed, "Plug that hole? How do we plug a hole that big?"

"I wondered the same thing but I do have an idea that might be worth investigating. It may sound a little crazy but it might be workable. I think we can use bombs to fill the hole with sea ice. The center of Hansen's Rock landed very near the land shore of Antarctica where the sea ice starts. In fact, a portion of the ice column is actual resting on ice that previously was floating on the surface of the sea before the tremendous weight of the ice column pressed the sea ice to the floor of the ocean. This compression of the sea ice is what permitted the breach to form in the ice column. The sea floor drops off fairly rapidly in this area and the water becomes hundreds of feet deep less than a mile from the breach. I think we should explore using some of those bunker buster bombs to penetrate the sea ice shelf before they explode. The explosion occurring under the ice shelf would throw enormous amounts of ice and water into the air where a lot of it would be sucked into the hole in the ice column by the high wind. Some of the smaller pieces of ice and some of the water would probably just go straight through the hole and settle on top of HR after it entered the slower moving air inside the column. However, I think a lot of the larger pieces of ice would settle on the ice inside the wall of the hole and the sea water would freeze upon contact with the surface of the ice column and start to fill the hole. Plus, I would think that in addition to throwing millions of tons of ice and water into the air, the bombs would also produce a huge wave of water and ice that would come ashore at the base of the ice column like a tsunami. Since the hole is at the bottom of the column, the waves would break into the hole and also partially fill it as the ice and water refreezes. If we could drop several bombs along the coast parallel to the hole, I think we might have a chance to substantially plug the hole."

Wilson looked at Williams with a big smile on her face, "What do you think Mike?"

He laughed and said, "I think Jerry needs to start getting more sleep. On the other hand, in theory, it just might work. By using explosives outside the column and under water, we do avoid the risk of igniting the hydrogen inside the column. And it is certain that some of the ice and water would stick in the hole. I suppose our bombers might have to make several bombing runs to get the hole mostly plugged. We could just continue to drop bombs until the hole is completely sealed. Ya know, the more I think about this crazy theory, the more I like it. We for sure know how to drop bombs and we could probably implement this plan in a matter of days. If it was successful, we could stop this air leak before it does any material damage to the atmosphere. Liz, we will be putting our credibility and sanity on the line if we propose this plan. Are you in?"

She smiled and answered, "Yeah Mike, I think this crazy theory might actually work. Let's do it."

"Jerry, write up your findings and your proposal to plug this hole ASAP; I will need to forward the report to Mr. Barrow. I will call him right away and give him a summary of your analysis and proposal. If he agrees that we should pursue this proposal, I will suggest that we get General Watson to have his bombing experts evaluate the do-ability of this proposal. I'll let you know if I'm still running this center after my chat with Charlie." Williams laughed.

Williams called Barrow and told him about the analysis that Jones had completed on the hole and that the air loss through the hole would threaten life on Earth without intervention. He also told Barrow about the theory that might permit the hole to be plugged. Barrow responded, "Mike, that proposal to plug the hole actually sounds plausible to me but I will get General Watson to evaluate it as soon as I have your written report."

Barrow called Watson and advised him of the high level findings and the proposal. Watson agreed that the USAF could perform the mission. He would have to get them to study the physical characteristics of the hole and the ice shelf to see if his ordnance experts believed that they could blow enough ice and water into the air to plug the two square kilometer hole. He suggested that the President be informed. Barrow agreed and said that he would call Mornay to inform him about the air leak and the study that was underway.

***

Susan Barker answered the phone call from Barrow, "This is Susan Barker; how may I help you?"

"Susan, this is Charlie Barrow; I hope you are well today."

"Yes Mr. Barrow; I am fine today. How may I help you?"

"I need to speak with the President."

"He's on an important phone call at this moment. I will call you back when he is available."

"OK Susan, thanks."

Barrow's phone rang about thirty minutes later. "Barrow here."

"Mr. Barrow, please hold for the President."

Mornay picked up the phone and said, "Good afternoon, Charlie; how are you today?"

"Mr. President, I am doing fine, thank you."

"What's up Charlie?"

Barrow explained, "Mr. President, my staff has evaluated the findings from the reconnaissance mission to Hansen's Rock. The recon crew found that the rock actually froze a tunnel in the atmosphere from the upper reaches of the atmosphere all the way to the ground. So, we have this huge ice column with the rock sitting at the bottom of it. There is also a large hole in the column near ground level that is drafting air from the atmosphere up through the column and venting it into space. The conclusion is that, without intervention, this venting will in just a few weeks bleed air from Earth's atmosphere to the extent that life on Earth will be threatened. My staff has come up with a proposal for plugging the hole. Stan Watson is going to get his people to determine the feasibility of the proposal. Since you had ordered the recon mission, the General and I agreed that you needed to be informed of our conclusions and actions." Barrow stopped.

"That's really strange Charlie...but I know that your staff knows what they are doing. I want to reassemble the team that we had in the last video conference for another one as soon as General Watson has completed his feasibility study. I need to better understand the findings about this air leak and our plan to fix it. Work with Susan to get it set up," Mornay ordered.

"Yes sir; will do."

THE PLAN

16 July…

Watson called Barrow at 6:00 a.m. EDT to advise that his ordnance experts had evaluated the proposal and had developed a plan.

Barrow called Susan Barker's phone at 6:15 a.m. and left a message that he needed for her to set up a video meeting between the SCC and the same people that had met on July 13.

Barker returned Barrow's call at 7:00 a.m. and told him that she would set up the conference for noon in the Situation Room. She asked if Barrow would notify the SCC of the meeting which he agreed to do. She told him that she would contact everyone else.

Promptly at noon the President entered the Situation Room and took his regular place at the head of the table. "Good afternoon…make that good morning for the folk in Pasadena." Everyone returned the greeting. "OK, here is what I would like for us to do. Since I haven't seen this report from the SCC, I want someone in the center to tell us about the salient findings from the analysis. Then let's discuss what the plan is to solve the problems that have been discovered."

Williams answered, "Yes sir, Mr. President. I want Jerry Jones to present the findings since he personally performed the analyses and came up with the potential solution."

The Vice President quipped, "Jerry, do you do all the work in that center out there?"

Jones laughed and said, "No sir; I just get all the nasty assignments." He began, "When the Australian reconnaissance crew arrived at the site where Hansen's Rock had landed it discovered that the trail that we had been seeing on all of our images was not a trail in the conventional sense. What they discovered was that Hansen's Rock had actually frozen the atmosphere around its path as it approached Earth. As you will remember, we had measured the surface temperature of the rock to be barely above absolute zero. This ice column is very thick at ground level and tapers at the higher altitudes due to the thinner air up there. Further, the team discovered that there was a large hole in the ice column at ground level on the side of the column that faces the sea. This breach was caused when a portion of the ice column wall came to rest on the shelf of sea ice covering the ocean. When the weight of the ice column rested on the ice shelf, it squeezed the sea water out from under the shelf causing the ice shelf to sink. This sinking of support for the ice column permitted the breach to form. This hole is approximately ten kilometers long and averages about 200 meters in height. This hole is permitting air from our atmosphere to escape into space. The speed of the wind at the time of the flyby was approaching 500 kilometers per hour. This great wind speed is being produced by the updraft created by the sublimation process that the solid hydrogen covering of Hansen's Rock is going through. Sublimation is the name of the process when matter changes directly from a solid to a gaseous form. As you know, hydrogen is the lightest element that we know of. The very light hydrogen gas is racing toward the top of the ice tunnel and is creating a deep vacuum that is sucking air into the column. I expect that as the rock begins to warm faster and faster, that this updraft will accelerate and the loss of Earth's atmosphere will also accelerate. I believe that, without intervention, the Earth will lose significant amounts of its atmosphere. I believe that in just a matter of a few weeks, the air at sea level could become as thin as that normally experienced at higher altitudes. This situation would significantly affect most activities of living things on Earth.

In addition, this rapidly escaping air through the tunnel is acting like the thrust of a rocket engine and is trying to push the Earth into a different tilt. The technical name for this tilt is declination and Earth's normal declination is about 23.5 degrees. This rocket effect is acting to reduce the angle of tilt. Over time the effect of this would be that winter would become longer near Earth's poles and summer would become longer near the equator.

One other potential problem that would result from the thinner atmosphere is that we would begin to see more meteoroids survive their travel through our atmosphere and actually hit Earth.

All of these are significant problems. However, I believe that the effect of air loss will become important faster than the seasonal impact or the lowered protection from meteoroids.

Dan L. King

Obviously we need to get rid of this ice column and the first reaction would be to just blow it up. But there is a problem with that. The tunnel is filled with hydrogen gas which is highly explosive and the rock is still surrounded by a thick layer of solid hydrogen. By my calculations, this hydrogen mass could have an explosive power more than 100 billion times that of the bombs dropped on Japan at the end of World War II. So, we cannot destroy the ice column until most of the hydrogen has completed the sublimation process and escaped into space via the tunnel.

To me, this means that the only solution available to us is to plug the hole in the ice column and to wait for the sublimation process to finish before destroying the ice column. I came up with a proposal that might permit us to seal the hole. General Watson and his experts have been evaluating my proposal to determine if it is workable. Are there any questions for me about what I have reported?"

Everyone was anxious to hear the plan so nobody asked any questions of Jones.

The President looked at Watson and asked, "Stan, can we plug this hole?"

Watson replied, "I am not sure that we can plug the hole but I am sure that we can implement the proposed methodology of doing it. The proposal from the SCC is to drop bombs just offshore of the rock that will penetrate the sea ice before exploding. When the bombs explode, ice and water will be blown into the air where it would be sucked into the hole by the strong wind entering the hole. My ordnance experts believe that we can do this using our largest bunker buster bombs. These are our GBU-57 bombs that can penetrate up to 200 feet of material before being detonated. Each bomb contains five thousand pounds of high explosives. They are GPS guided so we will be able to ensure that they go where we plan for them to go. We believe that if we explode these bombs at intervals of about every 500 meters along the face of the hole that we will toss several times more ice and water into the air than that which would be needed to plug the hole. We would also create a huge wave of ice and water that would rush along the surface of the sea like a tsunami and this too would reach the hole. What we cannot predict is how much of the ice and water would actual stick inside the hole. However, we do believe that we could at least partially close the hole."

The President asked, "How do we deliver the bombs?"

"These bombs would be carried by our B-2 Spirit bombers. Each plane has already been modified to carry two of these bombs. This means that we would need to send ten of these bombers to complete the mission. They are stationed at Whiteman Air Force Base in

Missouri. They would fly from Whiteman to be refueled in-flight in the airspace near Hickam Field at Pearl Harbor. Then they would land at the Royal Australian Air Force Base at Edinburgh, South Australia. They would refuel there and the pilots would rest while preventative maintenance is performed on all the bombers. The bombers would fly out of Edinburgh and they would return to Edinburgh after dropping the bombs."

Vice President Garish exclaimed, "Ten bombers? That is a bunch of planes and pilots!"

Watson explained, "Yes sir that is a lot of planes. We looked at having a smaller number of planes make several trips back and forth to the mission site but we believe that the explosions need to happen with only a small amount of time between each one so that we basically are tossing all the ice and water at the hole at one time, overwhelming it if you will. By detonating all the bombs at nearly the same time, we will be able to direct more of the material that is tossed into the air into the hole because of the interactions between the debris fields of each bomb."

The President asked, "So, if these first twenty bombs don't do the job, how long would it be before we could launch a second mission?"

Watson answered, "There can be no second mission with these types of bombs as our entire inventory is twenty; we will use every one of these super bunker busters in the initial mission. If these bombs are incapable of doing the job, then we have no conventional bombs that can do the job and we don't have any nuclear bombs with buster casings."

"So we get one chance to seal the hole? That's a little scary!" Garish observed.

Mornay asked, "How long will it take us to get the planes down there and complete the mission?"

"I think we could have the bombs loaded onto the B2 bombers in about eight hours since the B-2s have already been modified to carry them. The trip from Whiteman to Hickam airspace would take about eight hours. The flight from Hawaii airspace to Edinburgh will take ten to twelve hours depending on the winds. So, the bombers will require about twenty to twenty-three hours completing the trip.

Then they will need to wait for the ground crews to arrive. We will be sending two C-17 Globemaster aircraft with maintenance crews, tools, spare parts, and so forth. The C-17 doesn't have the range of the B-2 so they will need to stop three times to refuel. The C-17s will fly from Altus Air Force Base in Oklahoma to Whiteman where they will be loaded with all the forward support gear and ground crews. From there they will fly to Travis for fuel, then to Hickam, then to Nadi

International Airport, a civilian facility, and then into Edinburgh. That trip will take about thirty-six hours total. Once the maintenance crews are at Edinburgh, they will give all ten of the bombers a full maintenance checkout and perform whatever work is needed to make sure that the bombers are in perfect condition to complete the bombing mission. So, I think we could be ready to commence the mission within forty-eight hours from the time I give the order."

Mornay asked, "So what do we do if we have cracks or smaller holes left after the bombs are dropped?"

The room was silent for a few seconds until Jones decided to speak, "Mr. President, I have an idea. I think we might be able to seal smaller cracks or holes by spraying water into them. The water would freeze upon contact and close the holes. If we could get a ship with large pumps pretty close to the ice tunnel, I think we could probably seal the smaller holes with the water spray."

Mornay reacted, "So we just get a ship with large pumps to suck water out of the ocean and shoot it toward the holes? I suppose that makes sense."

Jones clarified, "Sir I don't think we could pump water from the sea and shoot it at the holes in the ice because all the chunks of ice in the sea water could foul the pumps pretty quickly. Also, there would be a good chance that the sea water would just freeze in the inlet or outlet pipes or even in the pumps themselves. I think it would be better if the ship had its own supply of water to shoot at the fractures in the ice plug."

Mornay looked at Watson and asked, "Do we have a ship with pumps capable of doing this and do those ships have their own water tanks capable of carrying enough water for the job?"

Watson quickly replied, "No sir; our Navy doesn't have anything like that. The closest we have would be some old fuel tankers that were used in the days of diesel ships but we haven't used them in decades since most of our ships now have nuclear propulsion systems."

Garish piped up, "How about a commercial oil tanker? They have huge tanks that could carry water rather than crude oil. Would they have pumps that could get the spraying done?"

Watson replied, "That's a pretty good idea Dick. Crude oil tankers do have huge pumps for on-loading and off-loading their cargo. It might be possible to fashion nozzles for those pumps to spray water instead of pump oil. Since water is not nearly as dense as crude oil, those pumps could probably move a lot of water."

Rander spoke up, "Sir, a while back I read about a new super tanker that was supposed to take its maiden voyage a few weeks ago. It is supposed to be the biggest ship on the ocean and the press said that it is virtually spill proof because of the extraordinarily strong hull structure. I think its first trip was going to be from somewhere in the Middle East to somewhere in Australia. It was built for Pole2Pole Petroleum Company. Maybe we could do an eminent domain seizure or something to get use of that ship?"

Mornay replied quickly, "Dave, that's an interesting idea. General do you think we could make that ship work?"

"Perhaps sir; I read about that tanker also and was intrigued by the size of it. I believe at the time I determined that the tanker had a deck that is over twice the size of the deck of the USS Nimitz, and the tanker had a displacement that was nearly twenty times the displacement of the Nimitz. If my memory is correct, that ship could carry a lot of water."

Mornay ordered, "Dave, find out where that ship is located."

Rander began to make a note when the President spoke again, "I mean right now Dave; you may leave the room."

"Yes sir; I'll be back in a few minutes."

Mornay looked at Watson, "Stan, give the order to mobilize the bombers."

"Yes sir." Watson didn't wait to be ordered to leave the room.

Mornay gave another order, "Let's take a fifteen minute break and reconvene after that."

***

When Mornay returned to the room everyone had already arrived. He looked at Watson first. Watson didn't wait for a question, "Sir, the planes and crews are making preparations."

Then Mornay looked at Rander and asked, "Where is that ship Dave?"

"Sir, the ship is somewhere south of Australia. It left Brisbane on the 11th which would be the 10th here in Washington. It is estimated to be about half way between Tasmania and Perth. I will be able to get more specific information on its location a little later today."

Mornay began, "Dave, I don't even know if eminent domain could be applied to ships in foreign waters so before we make this exercise too legalistic, find me the phone number for the CEO of Pole2Pole Petroleum. I will call him and see if he will agree to loan us his ship for this mission."

"Yes sir." Rander left the room again.

General, I have another worry. Jerry tells us that we do not want to blow up this ice column because of the trapped hydrogen. I am worried that Volkov might launch some sort of attack to try to save the world again. I want you to order your carriers and subs in the Indian Ocean to shoot down any missile that the Russian Federation might launch toward Hansen's Rock. If we detect any kind of military aircraft leaving Russia and headed in the direction of Australia or Antarctica, have them intercepted and turned back. If they want to fight, give them everything we have."

"Yes sir." Watson left the room again and stood in the hallway outside while he gave the order directly to Admiral Hayes, Chief of Naval Operations and Commander in Chief of the United States Fleet. He reentered the room and nodded to Mornay that the order had been given.

Mornay asked, "Is there anything else we need to talk about?"

Trish Daly asked, "Sir, what do we tell the press?"

"Nothing!"

"Understood sir."

Mornay looked around for additional questions or suggestions and saw that none were coming so he closed the meeting.

17 JULY IN THE INDIAN OCEAN

07:30...

Sirius had completed a little over half of its crossing between the tip of Tasmania and Perth when Hansen's satellite phone rang, "This is Captain Hansen speaking."

"Good morning, Lars; this is Jack Anderson. It is morning over there isn't it?"

Anderson was the CEO of Pole2Pole Petroleum and was the man who had made Hansen the very attractive offer to help develop the ST-600 line of ships.

"Good morning, sir; yes, it is 0730 hours here in the Indian Ocean."

"How's everything going with your ship?"

"The ship is a dream to pilot sir."

Anderson removed his casual face and got to business, "Lars, I just spoke to the President of the United States a couple of minutes ago. He has a problem and he thinks your ship might be the solution. He has requested to borrow Sirius for a military mission and I have agreed to that loan. It hasn't been made public but when that space rock you found entered Earth's atmosphere, it apparently was cold enough to freeze the atmosphere along its path forming an ice tunnel from space to the ground where it landed. But, there is a big hole in the tunnel at ground level that is bleeding air from Earth and discharging it into space. That hole needs to be plugged. The President has sent a group of bombers down there to try to get the job done by blowing up a bunch of sea ice and seawater that they hope will be sucked into the hole and plug it or, more likely, partially plug it. The second part of the plan is where our ship gets involved. They think that the holes or cracks remaining in the ice after the bombing can be sealed by spraying seawater into them until they freeze closed. They want to load our ship with sea water, reconfigure the discharge pumps to spray water, and go to the site to finish the sealing job. They will be sending a crew from Japan to crew the ship through the mission. You should receive a call from Captain Jean Cork, an aircraft carrier captain, within the next hour or so explaining how the crew exchange will be made."

Hansen had been making a few notes as Anderson spoke. He had recorded the mission commander's name as Captain Gene Cork. "Sir, I don't think we should completely turn over our ship to a crew that has never trained to operate it. I know aircraft carriers are large ships too but Sirius is a totally different kind of ship. I want to stay with Sirius and assist the new captain; some of my crew may also want to stay with the ship."

Anderson had expected this and had told the President that this likely would be the case. The President had said that he would appreciate the service of any of Sirius's crew if they volunteered for the mission. The President had agreed that Hansen could make the decision to stay or leave, but Cork would need to be the in-charge officer. "You didn't surprise me Lars; I knew you would feel that way. You can stay aboard and serve Captain Cork in any way that you are permitted to serve. You can also permit any of your crew who want to volunteer for the mission to stay aboard."

"OK, good." Hansen approved, "So, I suppose I need turn this ship around and head to Antarctica."

"You do need to turn the ship around but I am not sure how the exchange will happen. Captain Cork will give you details on that."

"OK sir; I'll initiate the turn and will await contact from Captain Cork."

Hansen punched in the coordinates that would take the ship back to the 45th parallel south of Tasmania. NavCom slowly turned the big ship to a heading that would take it to the new waypoint. The ship had nearly completed the turn when the satellite phone rang again, "This is Captain Lars Hansen speaking."

The female voice on the other end of the link said, "Captain Hansen, this is Captain Cork of the USS Enterprise." The Enterprise was the newest carrier in the US Fleet. It was the third Ford-class super carrier. Its service date had been advanced in order to have a more modern ship in the Pacific Fleet that could be quickly dispatched to patrol the Indian or Pacific Oceans. The ship was receiving its final touches and was in the process of expanding the crew beyond the ferry-sized crew that had delivered the ship to its base station at Yokosuka,

Hansen's Rock

Japan. "Good morning, sir. Have you spoken with your boss this morning?"

Hansen, surprised by the female voice answered, "Aah...yes, I spoke to my boss a few minutes ago."

"Good; did he describe the mission that I have been ordered to lead?"

Having gotten his speech back Hansen affirmed, "Yes Captain, I got an overview of the mission."

"Good, the first part of the mission will be the crew exchange which will occur by helicopter southwest of Tasmania. I will have two Blackhawk choppers that will ferry me and my crew to your ship. Do you have a large flat space on your deck suitable for a chopper landing? The helicopters are about sixty-five feet long so, although we could land in a smaller space, I'd like to have a spot at least a hundred feet square."

Hansen explained, "Yes, we have a space at the bow of the ship that is several times that size. In fact we probably have space for both aircraft to land at the same time if needed and if the weather is good."

"Excellent. We will perform the crew exchange at sea at approximately South 44.50 by East 145.50. I was told that some of your crew may want to volunteer for the mission. I need to know how many of your crew will leave the ship and what their specialties are. I will put together a crew here in Yokosuka to replace those specialties plus others that I think are needed for the mission. Each of the Blackhawks can ferry eleven men. Do you expect to have more than twenty-two crewmen to leave the ship?"

Hansen explained, "Our entire crew, including me, is twenty-three so two choppers will be plenty. I will not know how many will leave the ship until I poll the crew. I will do that within the hour and contact you with the results of the poll if you will give me a contact number."

Cork gave Hansen a phone number and they concluded the call. Hansen gave the "all hands on deck" order and the entire crew, except for Smith who stayed on the bridge, assembled on the mess deck. Hansen explained the mission and that anyone who chose to leave could do so and he explained the crew exchange process. He encouraged all hands with wives and children to seriously consider leaving. He told them that they hadn't signed on for military duty and had absolutely no obligation to volunteer. Nine men decided that they would take some time off in Australia instead of volunteering for the mission.

Hansen went back to the bridge and told Smith that he could leave with the others if he wanted and Hansen promised that if he chose to leave that it would not in any way affect his career with P2P Petroleum.

Smith elected to stay and help as he could. Hansen called Cork and gave her the number and the specialties of the men that would be leaving the ship. She thanked him and asked when he would be at the meet point. Hansen did a little math based on choosing the "maximum speed" mode of operation which should produce about nineteen knots of speed. "Captain, we should arrive at the meet point at approximately 2100 hours on 20 July."

Cork confirmed, "2100 hours; 20 July. Captain Hansen I will be back in touch with you around 1500 hours on the twentieth to get your ETA once you are closer to the meet point."

They concluded the call and Hansen gave Smith the order to move NavCom into "Maximum Speed" mode and he adjusted the waypoint to the coordinates of the meet point.

MOSCOW NOTICES

08:00; 17 July…

General Dmitriev called the office of the President of the Russian Federation. Anya answered, "Good morning. This is Anya. How may I help you?"

"Anya, this is General Dmitriev. I need to speak with President Volkov; it is important."

Anya punched the intercom button. Volkov ignored the intercom light and picked up the flashing incoming call. "This is Volkov."

"Comrade Leader, this is Dmitriev. Overnight, our satellites noticed an unusual amount of activity at the American Whiteman Air Force Base in Missouri. This base is where the Americans home all their B-2 bombers. It appears that as many as ten of these bombers were loaded with new ordnance and have been leaving the air base every fifteen minutes or so. They appear to be heading west but once they reach an altitude that is comfortably above commercial traffic, about 12,000 meters, they are going into stealth mode and we can no longer track them."

Volkov, surprised by this news, asked, "Do we have any idea where they might be headed?"

"No, Comrade Leader we currently have no idea. I assume that they are spacing the planes sufficiently so as not to draw attention to them when they are visible from the ground. The fact that they are going into stealth mode means that they do not want to be seen. The range of this bomber is about 11,000 kilometers so if they are coming to any strategic target in Russia, they will need to refuel before they reach Russian airspace. Otherwise, they will not be able to return to international air space without running out of fuel. They could use air tankers for in-flight refueling or they could land somewhere to refuel. If they refuel in-flight they will use large tanker aircraft that are not stealth capable so our satellites will be able to see the tankers. If they choose to refuel by landing, then we will see them as they disengage stealth mode when they enter commercial traffic altitudes."

Volkov ordered, "Alert all our anti-aircraft and missile forces along all our borders; have them ready to shoot down any aircraft that intrudes into our air space. Give me an update when we are able to find the planes again."

"Yes, Comrade Leader."

***

16:00; 17 July...

Dmitriev called Volkov to report the sighting of the bombers, "Mr. President, a short time ago our satellite identified five air tankers that were refueling the American bombers near Hawaii. It is clear that the bombers are not heading to targets in Russia or they would have taken the polar route. We still do not know where they are going but we do not believe that they will threaten Russian air space."

"Good Dmitriev; keep me informed."

GETTING THERE

The two C-17s were ready to fly within an hour of getting the order. They flew from Altus AFB to Whiteman AFB to pick up the ground maintenance crews, tools, spare parts, and other support material. The crews and loads were split between the two aircraft to protect against the possibility of an accident. The C-17s then flew to Travis AFB where they topped off their fuel tanks. From there they flew to Joint Base Pearl Harbor-Hickam Field where they again refueled. From Hickam they flew to Nadi International Airport in Fiji and refueled again. From there they flew to RAAF Edinburgh.

The B-2s were each loaded with two of the huge bunker buster bombs with a total weight of 60,000 pounds, 10,000 pounds more than the normal maximum payload of the plane. To make up for this, each bomber took on 10,000 pounds less fuel than its maximum capacity. They flew from Whiteman, one plane every fifteen minutes to be less conspicuous than a formation would have been. They flew until they were near Hawaii where they were met by five KC-135 Stratotankers flown by the 96th Air Refueling Squadron. Each tanker was carrying a full load of 200,000 pounds of fuel. Each B-2 was fed 100,000 pounds of fuel through the refueling booms. The fuel transferred at about 6500 pounds per minute so each B-2 had a nearly full tank of fuel in a little over fifteen minutes of refueling. When each KC-135 finished with its first recipient, it leap-frogged backward five B-2s and loaded the remaining 100,000 pounds of fuel into the second bomber. The bombers then had more than enough fuel to complete the trip to Edinburgh.

***

Dan L. King

Captain Cork and her hand-selected crew of fifteen flew out of Narita International Airport on Qantas Airlines to Sydney where they had a two hour layover before boarding a QantasLink flight to Hobart International Airport, Tasmania. They ate lunch in the food court before leaving the terminal at HBA to take taxis to the nearby Cambridge Aerodrome where they found the pair of Blackhawks that General Kelly had promised. The choppers were fully fueled and ready for the departure order from Captain Cork.

Although it was a little earlier than she had promised, Cork dialed up Hansen anyway. Hansen answered promptly, "This is Captain Lars Hansen speaking."

"Captain Hansen this is Captain Cork; how are you today?"

"I'm doin' just fine Captain. We are making a little better time than expected due to a tailwind so I expect to be at the meet point by 1900 hours."

"That's great Captain. I and my guys are in Hobart and have loaded our gear onto the choppers. Technically, we are in Cambridge and that puts us about 250 kilometers from the meet point. I am told that the flight from here to there should take about an hour so we will be departing at around 1800 hours. We will raise you on the VHF when we get within a few clicks of where we will meet. How's the weather out there in the roaring forties?"

"The weather isn't too bad considering where we are. We have winds out of the west at a solid twenty knots gusting to thirty at times. I don't think your pilots should have any trouble landing on the deck since they have so much room."

"Roger that Captain. We will see you in about four hours."

***

Sirius arrived at the meet point at 18:42 to find an empty sky. Hansen slowed the four huge engines to idle speed and manually made a gradual turn in the direction of Antarctica since he didn't yet have the waypoints needed to sail to the landing site of the rock. He turned on all navigation lights and the normal deck work lights to make sure the ship could easily be seen and so that the deck space where the choppers would land had sufficient lighting. He ordered all the crew that would be leaving the ship to take their gear to the lowest level of the tower and wait for orders.

At 19:04 the VHF radio came to life, "Blackhawk Leader to Sirius; come back Sirius."

Hansen replied, "This is Captain Hansen on Sirius."

Hansen's Rock

The Flight Lieutenant advised, "Captain, this is Blackhawk Leader. We have a visual of your ship and we will be on deck in five minutes."

"Roger Blackhawk Leader; I will meet your party on the foredeck." Hansen grabbed one of the hand-held VHF radios in case he needed it and clipped it on his belt. He donned his Arctic parka to ward off the freezing temperatures on deck. He left his "oilies" hanging on the peg in the passageway since it was not raining and Sirius carried so much freeboard that ocean spray was not an issue. He took the stairs down from the bridge to deck level and ordered the departing crew to follow him. He walked to the foredeck where he could see the navigation lights and the landing lights on the two helicopters. Since Sirius was now on a south-southeast heading and the wind was still blowing from the west, the choppers approached from off the port bow. The first chopper proceeded to a spot near the starboard railing before setting the struts on the ship's deck. The second chopper followed the first and landed on the port side of the foredeck.

After the pilot of the first chopper feathered the rotors, Hansen approached the helicopter as the door was opening. He walked to within ten feet of the door and heard Captain Cork shout, "Request permission to come aboard sir."

Hansen was a little surprised by the formality but, nonetheless, shouted, "Permission granted."

As soon as he had granted permission, the amazingly attractive Captain Cork jumped to the deck and walked over to Hansen and offered her hand. Hansen welcomed her aboard.

Cork thanked Hansen and immediately turned around to see how the seven sailors from the lead chopper were coming in their efforts to get themselves and their duffle bags to the deck. The biggest of the men was carrying two duffle bags, one of which was obviously Captain Cork's. She walked over to him and, against his objections, took her duffle from him, slung the bag up to her shoulder, and nodded to Hansen. Hansen understood the nod and led Captain Cork and her crew back to the tower. Hansen's departing crew split up and boarded the two choppers, the doors were closed and Blackhawk Leader added power to increase rotor speed and when the speed was sufficient, he added pitch to lift the chopper from the deck and into the darkness on a northerly heading. The second chopper followed about 500 meters behind the first.

When inside the tower complex Hansen looked at Cork and explained, "We have a small elevator over there that will probably handle three men with their bags or we could just load the elevator with probably eight or ten duffle bags and meet them at the top by taking the stairs. The stairs to the crew quarters and bridge deck are over here.

Dan L. King

The quarters are the equivalent of about ten stories of steps away. So, how do you want to get your men and bags to the top?"

Cork didn't hesitate a moment, "We'll walk." Several of the crew groaned, drawing a glare from Cork.

Hansen offered, "Captain Cork, I'll be happy to carry your bag if your wish."

"Not necessary Captain."

Cork led the way to the stairs with her bag still resting on her shoulder. The train followed Cork to the top tower passageway; she never paused once. She stopped when she reached the corridor and waited for Hansen who was unsuccessfully trying to keep up. When he arrived she asked, "Where are the crew quarters, Captain?"

"Your crew should follow the passageway and go through the bulkhead hatch down there; the crew's quarters are then the first compartment on the right. You can use my cabin which is the first cabin door on this side of the bulkhead."

Cork replied, "Captain, I don't want to cramp you in your cabin; I can just bunk with my crew."

Hansen explained, "No ma'am, I didn't mean that we would share my cabin; I will bunk with the crew."

Cork poked, "To begin with, I am not a madam; I am a Captain. Secondly, I'm a little disappointed that you don't want to share with me."

This salty reply caught Hansen off guard. He paused to try to think through what he should say since he had an audience of fifteen sailors, "Excuse me Captain Cork; no offense was meant." Then he decided he had better redeem himself a little, "I would be highly pleased to share with you Jean but the bunk in my quarters is a single and I have been at sea for days so sharing might make me very tense. I think I should bunk with your crew." There were several snickers from the crew as they watched the two Captains spar.

"Very well Lars; I certainly wouldn't want to be the cause of unwanted tension in your life." She smiled and walked to Hansen's cabin.

Hansen laughed and followed her to his cabin to collect those things that he would need to bunk in the crew's compartment. When they arrived at the cabin door she said, "Captain, we need to get your ship on a proper course and plan a speed that will get us to the mission site at the correct time. I will drop my duffle here for now and we can sort out the sleeping arrangements later."

Hansen smiled and said, "Of course, follow me." He led her to the starboard bridge where Smith was watching over Sirius. Smith buzzed them in, introductions were made, and Cork pulled a folded nautical chart from the messenger bag she had brought aboard. She had manually plotted a course from the meet point and it showed one waypoint and the destination.

Cork pointed with her finger and explained, "The center of this rock and ice column is located at South 70.3554 and East 161.8900. So we need to clear Anderson Peninsula and then turn back to the south-southeast to reach the rock. If you agree, we should set a waypoint for this spot, at South 69.493 by East 162.203."

Hansen ordered, "Peter set our next waypoint at South 69.493 by East 162.203 and resume "Maximum Speed" mode. Smith punched the coordinates into NavCom and clicked on the Maximum Speed bubble. The four half-million horsepower engines gradually reached the RPM that would produce the maximum speed. The nose of the ship gradually settled onto a heading of 164.57°. NavCom produced the waypoint ETA at 80.56 hours.

Cork said, "I think we need to arrive so that we can execute as much of the mission as possible during twilight and daylight. According to my research there will be only 1.3 hours of daylight on 24 July and 1.7 hours of daylight on 25 July. Twilight will likely be maybe fifteen to twenty minutes either side of dusk and dawn. So on the twenty-fourth, we would have maybe two hours of light and on the twenty-fifth we would have about two and one-half hours. So my question is can we get there by say 1030 or 1100 hours on the twenty-fourth?"

Hansen got his notepad and started some math. Cork was watching as he estimated the time required to travel to the location of the rock. She noticed that Hansen had written "Captain Gene Cork" on the pad. After Hansen finished his math he explained, "If NavCom's ETA to waypoint is produced, then we would have about eight hours to travel the last fifty or so nautical miles to the vicinity of the rock. Much of those fifty miles will be ice that we will need to fragment with our ultrasonic bow or break it with the weight of the ship. The ship has never been tested in these conditions so I don't know how much speed we will be able to hold while we break the ice needed to arrive at the mission site. I believe we may be able to average five knots during the ice breaking. However, as we flood the cargo tanks during the last forty-eight hours of the trip, we will sink a good six meters and will actually be lower in the water than the designed waterline because of the container weight that normally would not be carried along with full bladders of fluid cargo. So our forward speed will slow considerably. I think it is questionable that we will be able to arrive by midday on the twenty-fourth. However, we do have four one million lumen lights above the bridge that we use when navigating in close quarters at night. They make a lot of light and they can be pointed in nearly any direction. So it may be that we could conduct the mission in darkness using those lights."

"Good; then let's keep our speed as high as possible and once we arrive we will test the lights to see if we can see well enough to run the mission."

Hansen agreed, "OK, will do."

She pointed to the notepad where he had written her name with the male spelling and teased, "You must have been a little surprised when we first spoke?"

Hansen smiled and looked directly into her shallow-water green eyes and said, "A little."

"It's no big deal; when I was told your name, I wrote down Hanson with an "o"." She thought to herself, "I should have written down handsome."

She continued, "Have you reconfigured your pumps to spray water?"

"My hydraulics technician worked on that while we were traveling to the meet point. We have installed three reducers on both of the largest discharge pumps to take the outlet diameter from one meter down to about fifteen centimeters. We believe that this should permit us to shoot a stream of water about 300 meters directly skyward and maybe further at an angle. But we have not tested the configuration yet. We can test it when we begin flooding the cargo bladders with seawater."

"Very good, Captain. Sir, do you have a head here on the bridge?"

"Of course." Hansen pointed to an unmarked door in the corner next to the inside rear wall of the bridge. Then he joked, "But, we probably left the seat up."

Cork didn't hesitate a second before she responded, "Then I will stand."

Cork closed the door behind her and Hansen went back to the steering station to check all the instruments. Smith leaned over and said, "Captain, they didn't make sailors like that when I was a "swabby" twenty years ago; that woman could have been Miss America."

Hansen smiled and added, "Yeah, the navy has come a long way; almost makes you want to re-enlist doesn't it?"

Smith laughed just as the door to the lavatory opened.

"Captain Hansen, my boys haven't eaten in nearly nine hours now. Can we get them fed before they hit their bunks?"

"Sure, let's go see how they are settling in and then I'll show everyone where the mess deck is located."

***

Hansen's Rock

After mess, Hansen and Cork went back to Hansen's cabin so he could collect the things that he would need to bunk with the men. Hansen gave Cork a clean set of linen for the bunk and got his shaving kit and a change of clothing for the next day. While he was collecting what he needed, she looked around the cabin. She found the cabin to be kept very neat considering a man lived there. She noticed the unusual monitor on the shelf above the little desk and asked what it was.

"That is the monitor that I use to view the sky through my telescope that is located on the roof deck of the bridge, pretty much directly over our heads."

Then it dawned on her, "Tell me you're not that famous amateur astronomer that originally discovered the space rock that we are going to visit."

Hansen smiled and affirmed, "Yes, I am the one. Some even refer to the rock as Hansen's Rock."

"You must have quite a telescope on top to be the first to discover that space rock. Maybe you could demonstrate it to me some time."

"Yes, the telescope is one of the best commercially available telescopes; it is very powerful and has excellent optics. I'd be happy to demonstrate it when we get a clear sky during our trip."

"I'm going to hold you to that promise, Lars."

Hansen took his things and left his cabin. He turned right through the bulkhead hatch, went to the crew's sleeping compartment, and selected an empty bunk.

21 JULY

General Kelly had volunteered to send one of his AP-3C aircraft to photograph the mission and to take images after the bombing so that a complete evaluation of the effectiveness of the bombing could be made during the post-mission debriefing. Because the cruising speed of the AP-3C was significantly lower than the B-2 bombers, it taxied onto Runway One-Eight a few minutes after 0400 hours. After leaving the runway, the pilot set the heading for 167°, the most direct heading to the mission site. Including the time to reach cruising altitude and cruising at 375 knots, they would arrive at the mission location just before 1030 hours.

The first of the B-2 bombers taxied onto runway eighteen just before 0600. Once airborne, the plane banked right to a heading of 235°. The plane would fly that course for about forty-five miles over Gulf St. Vincent until it turned left to a heading of 167° which it would hold until arrival at the mission site. This circuitous path was necessary to comply with the agreement that the air base had reached with the city of Adelaide to mitigate the noise that its jet aircraft would make if they flew directly over the city. The bombers would arrive at the bombing site in just under five hours. The planes departed at intervals of three minutes.

When the bombers reached a distance of seventy miles from their target field, they would slow from 485 knots to 165 knots and assume a separation of one kilometer. This would put each plane about twelve seconds behind the one in front of it. They would fly the mission at an altitude of 10,000 feet. Each plane would drop the first GPS-assisted MOP (Massive Ordnance Penetrator), commonly called bunker buster bomb, and then six seconds and 500 meters later they would drop the

Hansen's Rock

second one. The sequence would be initiated when the lead plane reached its first drop coordinate. If the mission was executed perfectly, every one of the ten bombers would reach their first drop coordinate at exactly the same time and consequently they all would reach the second drop coordinate at exactly the same time. All twenty bombs would detonate within a six second window.

The AP-3C surveillance plane was flying at 165 knots parallel to the bomber formation. It was flying twenty-five seconds behind the last bomber, and it was flying at an altitude of 350 meters. It was about one kilometer east of the bomber formation and had all cameras running. Twilight had arrived and the men on the plane could see a little of the ice tunnel. The high aperture, high resolution, telescopic cameras saw all the landscape perfectly.

The bombers assumed their position in a line formation at the 10,000 foot altitude; the planes were only about five minutes from the north end of the hole in the ice column. Once the formation leader crossed over the last plane's drop coordinate, it would only be one minute and forty-eight seconds until each plane reached its first drop point.

When the formation leader approached his first drop coordinate he started the countdown, "Five, four, three, two, one, first bomb away." He immediately started the second countdown, "Three, two, one, second bomb away." About twenty-five seconds after the first bombs were released they completed their fall, penetrated the ice, and detonated, throwing ice and water hundreds of meters into the air. Then only six seconds later the second ten bombs detonated filling the air with more ice and water. Much of the airborne ice and water was propelled toward the hole and was drawn into it. Following the airborne ice and water was a huge wave over fifty feet high that rolled ashore, some of it splashing into the hole in the ice column.

After all the bombs were dropped, the formation leader ordered the pilots to follow him to an altitude of 1000 feet. They gracefully reduced their altitude as the leader led the formation south another thirty kilometers before making a hard turn back to the north so that the entire formation could view the results of their work when they passed the ice column. They were impressed. From their distance of about two kilometers from the ice column, in the dim twilight, it appeared that the hole had been successfully plugged. The formation leader said, "Congratulations to all. It appears that our mission was a success. Let's head home. Follow me to 40,000 feet, assume a speed of 485 knots, set your heading to 347, and hold a minimum separation of ten miles."

The AP-3C flew as close as it dared to the now mostly plugged hole in the ice column to get detailed images of any unfilled areas. The crew in the back of the plane could see on the camera monitors that most of the hole had been filled except for a fairly large hole on the south end of the original hole.

The bombers returned to RAAF Edinburgh just after 1730 hours. The AP-3C arrived at 1940 hours after refueling on the return leg. The mission debriefing was led by the Flight Commander who had been the formation leader for the bombers. General Kelly attended the meeting but for the most part was just an observer. The meeting began at 2130 hours after all the data from the Orion aircraft was backed up and transferred to portable hard drives that would be accessed during the meeting. The flight crew had selected several images of the ice column and had constructed a high resolution panoramic composite. They had color-enhanced the areas where the hole was not completely plugged. For the most part, the gaps were relatively small except for one opening that was approximately 110 meters long and twenty meters tall. The large opening was at the south end of the initial hole in the ice column and the bottom edge of the remaining hole was about twenty meters above sea level. The crew reviewed the visual images and radar images that showed that the thickness of the newly deposited ice seemed to be sufficient to not only plug the hole, but to add structural strength to the ice column. The Doppler radar displacement data showed the wind was now being sucked into the remaining hole at a velocity of 1146 kilometers per hour, less than one hundred kilometers per hour below the speed of sound at sea level. The bombing mission was declared to be an overall success.

The admin Aircraftman supplied by Kelly documented the meeting and the salient results from the recon aircraft including key images showing the success of the mission along with images that showed the gaps that would need to be plugged by Sirius. He encrypted the data and prepared it for transmittal to the team of sailors on Sirius across the Maritime GX service. The transmission began at 0020 hours, 22 July.

22 JULY

Hansen was buzzed into the starboard bridge at a little before 0500 to find Captain Cork and Smith chatting over coffee. At the chart table in the middle of the bridge area were two young sailors with weather-hardened computers glowing in front of them. Hansen spoke first, "Good morning everybody."

Cork and Smith returned the greeting; the two sailors snapped to attention and returned the greeting in unison. They stood at attention until Hansen nodded that they could relax. "What's going on?" Hansen asked.

Cork explained, "Overnight we received the report from the bombing mission. My men have taken the file from your receiver and decrypted it. They are now preparing the findings for our review."

"OK; sounds good. Peter, why don't you grab some breakfast and some sleep?"

"Yes sir; the helm is yours Captain." This exchange was much more formal than was usual from Smith. Hansen smiled at Smith as if to say, "so you're trying to impress the lady, eh?"

"Captain Cork, we have the material prepared for your review," said the tall, thin sailor wearing the eagle over one red chevron.

Cork walked to the chart table followed by Hansen after he took a look at the radar sweep which showed nothing around Sirius for fifty nautical miles in all directions.

The sailor pointed to the first image which was the panoramic composite and began, "Captains, it appears that the bombing mission was very successful. Nearly all the hole has been filled. There are a couple of dozen small areas that need to be closed. They are shown in red on this image and they should pose no problem to our water spray method. As you can see, there is one large opening on the south end of the old breach that will prove harder to fill. The report says that this remaining hole is about 110 meters long and twenty meters tall and it is located from twenty to forty meters above sea level. Wind velocity through this hole has been measured at over 1100 kilometers per hour; that's over 600 miles per hour."

Cork commented, "Thanks PO Carter; very good summary." She looked at Hansen and asked, "Captain, do you think we can plug that big hole with a stream of water?"

Hansen was quick to reply, "I don't know. We should have plenty of water to do it if it will stick to the sides of the hole rather than be sucked inside the column by those high winds. Once we flood the cargo bladders completely we will have eight million barrels of water that we can spray. That's about forty-five million cubic feet of water which is well over a million cubic meters. The hole has an area of 2200 square meters so we should have plenty of water if it will just stick."

"OK, sounds like we have an achievable mission. Carter, print us close ups of the various sites where we need to close gaps and make sure that the GPS coordinates, including elevation, are posted by each gap that needs water. Place the images in order from north to south," Cork ordered.

"Yes Captain; will do."

"Captain Hansen, what's our ETA now?" Cork asked.

"GPS shows just over fifty-one hours and 1,129 nautical miles from our next waypoint. But I'm about to start loading seawater so we will slow down substantially as the water sinks the ship. I really don't know how Sirius will perform under these unusual conditions."

"OK, I guess we will find out in the next couple of days."

***

When 1800 hours arrived, Smith showed up to take his shift in the captain's chair. Hansen said, "Peter, before I leave the bridge I want to test our improvised water cannons now that we have some water in the cargo bladders."

Smith took his position in the pilot chair while Hansen sidestepped a couple of paces and stopped in front of the control panel that supported the joysticks for the cargo discharge pumps. He said, "OK, here we go." He hit the switch next to the joystick that was labeled "Hi-Cap Cargo Discharge Pump - Port." He gradually increased the flow rate from zero to maximum and watched as the ejected stream of water grew to extend well ahead of the bow of the ship. He maneuvered the stream up and down and then left and right. He smiled and observed, "Works great." He looked at Cork'; she smiled and nodded her agreement. He went through the same procedure for the starboard pump with similar results. "Peter, turn on the crude oil heaters and set them at max temp. I think we may get better performance if we heat the seawater so that it doesn't freeze as quickly once it is discharged from the pump nozzles." Smith flipped the eight switches that controlled the heaters in each cargo bladder and then twisted the temperature control knobs to the right end stop.

"OK Peter; you own the helm."

Hansen and Cork went to the mess hall for food and found both crews there eating, joking, and generally killing time. They visited with the crew who were kidding around about this being a mission that might have been in a Star Wars or Star Trek movie. The sailor with no insignia joked that Carter should be C3PO for Carter, 3rd Class Petty Officer. Carter struck back saying the kid with no rank should be R2D2 for Rank to be Determined, second time around. They got a bit bolder and realized that it was destiny that Captain Cork was the captain of the USS Enterprise just like Captain J. T. Kirk was in Star Trek. They asked her if her middle initial was T. She disappointed them when said her middle initial was "A". They teased that Hansen could have been Han Solo since he looked so much like Harrison Ford. Cork hadn't noticed that before but once her crew pointed it out she realized that there was a striking resemblance.

Hansen asked Cork, "So these guys are the best the navy has to offer, eh?"

They all laughed and she explained, "They are a bunch of jokers for sure. But when they do get serious, they are seriously good at what they do."

The crews cleaned up after themselves and headed back to the crew quarters.

When the galley was nearly empty, Hansen asked, "What's the story with the kid who has no rank insignia?"

Cork explained, "He is one of the best communications technicians in the navy but he has a hot head. He got into a scuffle with a fellow sailor a couple of weeks ago and I busted him back to Seaman Recruit. That was the second time I've busted him for the same reason. He is a great kid, just a hothead. I hope he can grow out of that because he could be a great sailor."

By now it was after 1900 hours and it had been dark for three hours. Hansen recalled that Cork had wanted a demonstration of his telescope when the weather cleared. He said, "When we left the bridge, the weather looked to be perfect for stargazing. How would you like to go to my cabin and see my telescope?"

Dan L. King

She laughed and said, "I've had plenty of offers to go to a man's quarters before but I must admit nobody has ever asked me if I wanted to see their telescope."

Hansen laughed, "Well, I don't get out much so I don't know any of the contemporary lines."

She smiled and teased, "I would love to see your big telescope Lars."

They went to Hansen's cabin and he turned on the monitor and opened the software that managed the telescope and mount. Hansen went to several different objects. He started with Alpha Centauri, a binary star that is the third brightest star in the sky as seen from Earth. They viewed a very near neighbor to the binary stars which was a red dwarf star called Proxima Centauri. He explained that it was the nearest known star to our Sun and that it was only a little over four light-years away. He pointed the telescope at several nebulae that had very different appearances. They looked at planetary nebulae like the Ant Nebula, the Powder Blue Nebula, and the Retina Nebula. They looked at a Globular Cluster designated as NGC 6752 which was 13,000 light-years distant. They looked at Abell 3627 which was a giant cluster of galaxies 220 million light-years away from Earth. They found all kinds of interesting things in the sky and chatted about their appearance and their distance from Earth, etc.

When he glanced at his watch, he discovered that it was 2314 hours. He realized that they needed rest so he said that they had seen enough for the night. Cork objected as she had been amazed by what could be seen through Hansen's telescope. The most powerful magnification she had ever used to look into the sky was from the ten power binoculars that were used on the bridges of her ships. Hansen assured her that there would be other nights that would provide them with viewing opportunities. He said he needed sleep and he told her that he really had enjoyed stargazing with her. She said she had had a great time too. He wished her a good-night, went to the crew quarters, and turned in.

13 JULY

Hansen was buzzed into the starboard bridge at 0530 hours to find Cork already there sipping on her black coffee and standing next to Smith, who was obviously enjoying her company.

"Morning Jean, Peter."

They returned the greeting.

"How are we coming with loading the seawater?"

Smith answered, "Sir, we are forty-six percent complete with the seawater loading. We are currently riding about two feet below designed waterline. We are making fourteen knots and our position is approximately South 57.4 by East 148.5. We are shown to be 802 nautical miles from our next waypoint. NavCom estimates the ETA to be 57.1 hours but that is likely an optimistic prediction as we will slow as our displacement increases. I estimate that we will arrive at the waypoint in about sixty-five hours. That would be around 2300 hours on 25 July."

Hansen smiled at the unusually complete report by his assistant. Obviously he was still showing out for Captain Cork. "Excellent report Peter." Smith glowed with the compliment and knowingly returned the smile.

Hansen walked to the counter at the back of the bridge, filled his cup with coffee, and returned to stand just behind the pilot's chair. He studied all the instrumentation even though Smith had just given him most of the information he needed. The twin radar sweeps showed nothing within fifty miles. He looked at the ship's log to find that Smith had already completed his shift report which, aside from position, speed, etc., simply reported "nothing additional to report." After seeing that all was in order, he told Smith that he was ready to take the helm.

Smith acknowledged and slid out of the captain's chair and onto the floor. He looked directly at Cork, smiled, and told her that he had really enjoyed chatting with her. Then he left the bridge.

Hansen and Cork stood their posts, mostly chatting since there was little to do as they plied the uninhabited waters. They explored each other's past without being intrusive. Hansen learned that Cork had been in the navy for her entire adult life. She had lived only a few miles from Annapolis from the time she began elementary school as her father had been a civilian instructor at the US Naval Academy. When she graduated from the public high school, she had attended the Academy, earned her rank of Ensign, and went directly to sea upon graduation. She had climbed the rank ladder and had been captaining an aircraft carrier for six years.

Hansen told his story about immigrating to the US and recounted his education and how he finally ended up as the skipper of an oil tanker.

They talked about the unique nature of Sirius. They talked about Cork's new ship, the USS Enterprise, designated CVN-80. They compared the ships. They generally got to know a little more about each other until Smith returned just before 1800 hours. Hansen noted the essentials in the ship's log before leaving the bridge to Smith.

Cork and Hansen headed to the ship's galley to dine with the crew again. Once they had gotten their food and had seated themselves in vacant chairs at the end of one of the long dining tables, CPO Carter asked, "Captain Cork, when do you trade that bird for your first star?"

Although it didn't come from Cork, her crew had apparently learned that she had been recommended for promotion. Since she had nearly thirty years of officer experience, they knew it could only be a matter of time. "You are a curious one aren't you Carter? I don't have a clue if I will ever get another bump. Since they just gave me a new ship, it seems unlikely that it would be anytime soon."

Carter wagered, "Captain, I bet you will never ship out on our new ship. We have a little wager 'mongst us blackshoes and I'm bettin' that you will be Flag Officer before the end of this year. That is of course if we don't screw up this mission to save the world." He laughed.

Cork laughed and said, "We still have a chance to screw up; just look at this bunch of jokers that I picked to save the world. If my boss knew that I had chosen you and your buddies to save life as we know it, I'm pretty sure that my judgment would be called into question and there would be no way that I would ever be awarded a star." The whole table laughed.

25 JULY

Hansen got buzzed into the starboard bridge at 0545. As he expected, Cork was already there with only half a cup of coffee remaining. Smith was sitting erect and was chatting with Cork. Hansen noticed that Peter had turned on the two outermost searchlights.

"Good morning," Hansen said and the greeting was returned.

Hansen first filled his cup and then went to the pilot's station to check the instrumentation readings. Speed was thirteen knots; GPS showed the position of Sirius to be South 69.929 by East 158.190; distance to next waypoint was 176 nautical miles; ETA to next waypoint was 13.58 hours.

"So Peter, how did things go last night?"

"Everything went fine Captain. We just passed the Antarctic Circle about twenty minutes ago and we are eighty-six percent complete with the seawater loading. We are riding low now; we are floating a little over three feet above the designed waterline. We are beginning to run into some small icebergs that didn't show up on radar so I chose to light up our path so we don't get surprised by a large floater."

"OK Peter, all that sounds like what we had expected. So, assuming we don't slow a lot more as we top off the cargo tanks with water, we should arrive at the next waypoint by 2000 hours. Then we will be about fifty nautical miles from the wall of the ice column. Once we make our turn at the waypoint, we should encounter the ice shelf pretty quickly. We will probably have about thirty-five nautical miles of ice to break before we get to our first hole in the ice tunnel. I'm guessing that it will take us somewhere between seven and eleven hours to get to the mission start point depending on how easily we can push through the ice shelf. So, we should arrive there between 0400 and 0800 hours tomorrow. I see you have already made your log entry so go get some sleep. I want you back here on the bridge to relieve me at 1500 hours. Then I will try to get a little sleep and I will return to the bridge by 2100 hours when we should begin the slog through the ice shelf. We will both be on duty from that point until we get the mission complete. So, go get some sleep; it could be a long time before you get to sleep again."

"Roger that sir." Peter left the bridge.

Hansen turned to Cork and asked, "Jean, would you get a couple of your best gamers to report to duty at 0300 hours. I need a couple of men that have great hand-eye coordination to jockey the water cannon joysticks."

"Will do, Captain." She left the bridge and headed to the crew quarters where she picked a pair of her crew that could handle the joysticks and told them to report to the bridge at 0300 hours the following morning.

***

2100 hours...

Hansen showed up on the bridge with the sound of ice sliding around the hull of the ship and nothing but ice visible in front of them. Smith had all four of the one million lumen searchlights shining into the path of Sirius. A moderate snow was falling but it was nowhere close to being one of the whiteout storms that are common to this part of the world. The twin radars, both on the fifty mile range, painted identical images of the mountains of Anderson Peninsula to the West, Explorers Range to the south, and the unmistakable ice column showing in between the two natural land features. The ice column was just west of due south from Sirius and the wall was about thirty-five nautical miles distant.

The ultrasonic bow still seemed to be working well even though Sirius was floating five feet lower than it was designed to float. Smith had taken manual control of the ultrasonic wings and had enabled all the transducers along the entire length of the wings. He had also turned the volume of the ultrasonic energy to the maximum that the transducers were capable of producing. The solid ice on top of the seawater was being transformed into sleet-like pellets that slid along the hull easily and without damaging the ultrasonic wings on the bow. Sirius was gradually slowing but was still moving at a respectable pace of about six knots. When the ice became about three meters thick, Hansen shifted NavCom into "Constant Speed" mode at five knots.

Hansen's Rock

26 JULY

0200 hours...

Hansen could hear the four big engines labor as they pushed the overloaded Sirius through the ice that was now about fifteen meters thick. Suddenly, the audible alarm sounded and a message flashed on the NavCom monitor that read, "US Wings Retracted! The Ultrasonic Wings have experienced an overload and have retracted to protect their integrity."

The deceleration could be felt immediately as the ship was now breaking the ice by brute force since it no longer had the benefit of the ultrasonic waves fragmenting the ice near the ship's bow. NavCom automatically adjusted the pitch of the four propulsion propellers in an effort to maintain the constant speed that had been set earlier. Sirius continued to proceed through the ice successfully. The ice column was now only five nautical miles away.

***

0300 hours...

The two men that Captain Cork had selected to operate the discharge pumps arrived as they had been instructed to do and were buzzed into the starboard bridge. Sirius approached the ice column slightly north of the first breach that needed to be patched and gradually turned its nose to the south to pass less than a hundred meters from the base of the ice tower. Hansen was at the helm. Smith was operating the search lights and had the center two lights pointing

Dan L. King

up at the ice wall while the two outer lights continued to illuminate the path of the ship.

The falling snow made it easy to identify the breaches in the ice column as the column was sucking the snow into each of the holes. As the first hole came within range, the jury-rigged water cannons were given their first test. Peter gave the "fire" order to the two pump jockeys and they hit the switches on the console and then steered the six-inch streams of water to the vicinity of the hole. The wind sucked the water into the hole as it had done with the falling snow. As the thousands of gallons of water began to freeze, the sucking motion became less visible and eventually it stopped. Peter gave the order to stop. The first breach had been successfully filled. The two operators exchanged "high-fives", Peter smiled, and Captain Cork teased the two young sailors, "Bet you never thought that all those Call of Duty gaming sessions were going to actually come in handy, did you?" They all laughed.

Hansen punched the "Maximum Thrust" button on Navcom and manually operated the throttles to keep the big ship moving slowly down the face of the ice column. Peter kept referencing the photographs with the GPS coordinates of the remaining holes so that he could illuminate them. The water cannon operators kept filling the holes until they quit sucking.

***

1000 hours…

The team finally filled the last of the small breaches and Sirius was approaching the large breach which was a gigantic hole and it was sucking snow so fast that it looked like a milky cloud flowing into the hole. In the dark, illuminated only by the search lights, it was the strangest sight that any of them had seen before. Hansen slowed the ship as much as possible but kept it barely moving. He knew that it would take a long time to fill such a large hole with the water cannons. Forward speed was 0.1 knots and the engines were straining.

The bow of the ship was beginning to ride up onto the ice in front of it since the ice was so thick. It took all the weight of the heavy ship to break the ice in front of it. Hansen was beginning to worry about not being able to escape the ice if and when they got their job done. The ship was beginning to list to the right which confused Hansen for a while until he remembered that the space rock was highly magnetic. It was this magnetic pull on the ship and all those metal containers on the deck that were being attracted to the magnet.

The two sailors were pouring water into the hole but it just seemed to be disappearing. Cork suggested that they focus on the edge of the opening and see if the water would stick there. This helped a little but after about twenty minutes Hansen called a halt to the spraying of water. "I can't tell that we are doing much good with the water cannons. The wind is just moving too fast and the hole is too big. I don't think we can fill the hole with water." The disappointment in this conclusion was obvious on the faces of everyone in the bridge cabin.

Hansen thought about what they might do to fill the hole for what seemed like an eternity, but was actually only a few seconds, until it finally struck him. They were carrying what would plug the hole but it was not the seawater cargo inside the hull of the ship. It was the cargo outside the hull of the ship that might do the job. They were carrying over 13,000 TEUs of containers which should be more than enough volume to close the hole.

Sirius had a unique method of racking and securing containers on deck. At deck level there were hydraulically-driven twist locks. Each container had pre-assembled units attached to each end that acted like modular cell guides performing the same function as the permanent cell guides used inside the hulls and on some deck stacks of single purpose container ships. The module also had pre-tensioned cross lashing rods. The modules were held in place by twist-locks at the corners of each container. The bottom container had the bottom of the stack module held in place by the deck-mounted, hydraulically operated twist-lock which fitted on the end of a turn-able shaft inside the modular cell guide. The bottom corners of the container stacked atop the lower container were held the same way; a twist lock was inserted into the cell guide at each corner. So it was possible to undo all the twist-locks in an entire stack by operating the deck-imbedded screw via remote control from the deck management computer located in the "wheelhouse.

Hansen revealed his plan, "I think that if we unleash the containers from the ship that the huge magnetic pull along with the high winds should suck the containers into the hole and they should magnetically stick to the rock and build up enough to permit us to plug the hole. I think we should unleash them by forty foot sections since that is how they are stacked and twist-locked, and we can do the entire operation from here. By doing it a single stack at a time, we can assess how the containers are depositing in the hole and we can move the ship gradually so that we fill the hole from one end to the other. We can fill in any gaps using seawater delivered by the water cannons as we go so that we don't have to make two runs in this difficult-to-break ice."

Dan L. King

"Peter, drop both stern anchors and let them settle. Manage the windlasses so that the chains don't run out until extra length is needed but so that the chains don't hold us back any more than necessary. Hopefully that will permit us a retreat path if the ice gets too difficult to break."

Smith did as instructed and the two huge seventy-five ton stern anchors were slowly lowered by the gigantic diesel windlasses which slowly fed out the chain links. Each link in the huge chains was nearly four feet long and weighed over a ton. When the anchors were resting on the bottom and another hundred feed of chain had been fed by each windlass, Peter placed the diesels in neutral so that they would be ready to drive the huge chain gypsies immediately when needed.

"Anchors deployed sir."

"OK Peter. I want you to operate the deck management computer and to release each stack when I give the order."

"Aye Aye, sir."

"Since our bow is well into the length of the hole, we will begin releasing containers from the aft end of the stacks. The first we will cut loose is stack S-1. OK Peter, unlock stack S-1."

Peter punched in the command to reverse twist the deck lock for stack S-1. It took the hydraulic screw about five seconds to complete the twist. As soon as the twist-lock hit the neutral position in the cell guide, the stack of six containers took off like huge kites and flew into the hole. A couple of them banged into the edge of the ice hole but were recaptured by the wind and magnetic force and were quickly drawn into the hole. Once inside the ice column, the wind speed dropped significantly and the containers were quickly drawn toward the hydrogen shell on the magnetic space rock and they stuck.

They all quickly studied what had just happened and immediately decided that the operation was a success. Hansen ordered, "Peter, cut loose stack S-18."

Smith released S-18 and those six containers passed through the hole and deposited near the first six.

"Peter, release S-36."

The next six containers entered the hole and began filling the hole toward Sirius. They continued this operation near the northernmost end of the hole until the hole was mostly filled with containers.

"OK, use the water cannons to fill in the gaps between the containers," Hansen ordered.

The two young sailors activated the water cannons and began depositing ice on the containers until it was clear that they had a solid surface on the first fifty feet or so of where the opening had been.

Hansen ordered containers to be released further forward on the ship until the next deposits had nearly filled another fifty or so feet of the hole. The water cannon operators followed up and filled the gaps that remained. This last spray operation was approaching the maximum range of the cannons. Hansen needed to move the ship forward some so he nudged the throttles on the four big engines and the ship began to crawl forward. "Peter, be sure to mind the anchor windlasses and release enough chain to follow our progress."

"Aye Captain; I am on it."

Sirius crept forward another hundred feet or so and began to ride further up onto the ice in front of it as the weight of the ship became diminished by the ejection of containers and the gradual emptying of the cargo bladders. When Hansen reached the spot where he wanted to perform the next series of container ejection, he slowed the engines to a speed that would hold their position on the ice shelf. The process was repeated again and again until there was only about a hundred feet of the hole left to fill.

Daylight had finally arrived and everything would be visible for nearly two hours before night returned. Hansen pushed the throttles to move Sirius forward another hundred feet but he discovered that the ship no longer had sufficient weight to break the ice. Instead, the bow of the large ship began to rise skyward and the stern began to sink into the mixture of water and broken ice behind them.

Hansen pushed the button on the ship's intercom and alerted all crewmembers to don their personal flotation devices and to prepare for the unexpected since he wasn't sure what would happen next. The bow continued to rise until it dropped again when Hansen reached the spot where he wanted to perform the last container ejections. Sirius was now balanced on the edge of the unbreakable ice and the propellers had lost their bite as the top of the props were now above the surface of the water. The ship was now sitting on top of the ice shelf in front of the remaining hundred feet of hole.

"Peter, stop the windlasses."

"Aye sir; all stopped."

Balancing as they were on the edge of the ice was a strange feeling. They could look down at the ice beneath the ship which was over a hundred and fifty feet below the bridge deck. They were now fifty feet higher than they had been just a short time ago. Everyone on the bridge could see what had happened and were wondering if the ship would break or if it would be sucked toward the hole. Before they could launch the next round of container ejections, the ship began to slowly slide toward the hole.

"Peter, shorten aft anchor chains to see if we can stop the drift toward the hole."

Smith tightened the chains on the aft anchors until they were tight enough that they just began dragging the ship backwards so he stopped. Still, the ship was slipping sideways toward the hole.

"Peter, drop the port bow anchor and hold the chain once the anchor is on the ice."

Peter followed the order and the ship's drift slowed but did not stop.

"Peter, disable all hull scrubbers."

Peter turned off all the hull scrubbing transducers and the ship promptly stopped.

Hansen ordered, "OK, let's dump containers in stack P-55."

Smith ordered the deck management computer to untwist the deck lock on P-55; the stack came apart and the six containers were drawn into the hole. They continued the container jettison operation until the hole was filled with containers settled helter-skelter in the hole. The sailors pumped water into all the cavities and gaps between the containers until there was a thick coating of ice over the entire surface and the containers were no longer visible through the ice. When Hansen ordered the sailors to stop the water spray, the cannon jockeys exchanged more high fives. Hansen, Cork, and Smith smiled.

Cork told her sailors, "Men, I'm very proud of the work you did; looks like I won't face a court martial for picking you guys to save the world after all." She shook their hands and patted their backs. She told them that they should go get some food and sleep.

As soon as the sailors left the bridge, Hansen got back to business, "Let's see if we can get out of here now. Peter, haul the bow anchor and start both stern anchor windlasses to see if we can pull ourselves off this ice."

Smith hit the switch that hauled the port bow anchor up and into its stowed position which automatically stopped the windlass. He also started both the aft windlasses and the ship's bow began to climb toward the sky before the ship slipped back into the chunky mixture of seawater and broken ice. Hansen left the engines in neutral so the propellers would not be damaged as the ship's wineglass stern began breaking the new and relatively thin ice that had closed in behind Sirius as it had slowly made its way around the ice column. When the anchor chains became nearly vertical Hansen ordered, "Peter haul both aft anchors."

"Aye sir, hauling anchors." Several minutes passed until the anchors cleared the seawater and finally self-stowed when the anchor flukes reached their pads on the outside of the ship's hull. "Anchors secured, sir."

Hansen turned the rudders to full port and hit the switch to see if he could reactivate the ultrasonic transducer wings on the bow to help dissolve the ice in the path of Sirius. Fortunately, since the ultrasonic wings were in the wake that the ship had made while being pulled astern by the anchors, there was enough seawater in the wake to keep the wings from automatically retracting for self-protection. The transducers began their work of turning the chunks of sea ice in their path into sleet-sized pellets. Hansen held the rudders hard to port and engaged the starboard engines while the port engines idled in neutral. Sirius began to slowly turn and the forward speed gradually increased to approximately one knot. When the GPS showed a heading of eight degrees which would be the most direct path back to the offshore waypoint, Hansen engaged the port-side engines and returned the steering joystick to the center resting position. The going was slow for the first several miles until they began to escape the thickest of the sea ice. Hansen studied all the data being produced by NavCom looking for any indication of problems that may have developed during the ice breaking exercise and the time when Sirius climbed from the sea onto the ice shelf. Everything was looking normal. "Peter, let's jettison the remaining seawater and establish a proper ballast for the remaining load of containers."

"Yes sir; will do." Peter began emptying the cargo bladders of the seawater and distributed the ballast water to make up for the lop-sided load of containers. All the containers on the starboard side of the ship had been sent into the hole and about half of the inboard containers on the port side of the ship had been ejected which left the ship with an outboard port load. So the starboard ballast tank was filled and the port ballast tank was left empty to enable the ship to sail with a nearly level attitude.

It took about eight hours for Sirius to escape the ice shelf and enter the mostly seawater environment to the east of Anderson Peninsula. Sirius now had over three thousand feet of water under her hull.

Hansen gave his last order of the day, "Peter, it looks like everything is operating normally now. Why don't you go get four hours of sleep and then return to the bridge to relieve me?"

Smith smiled and said, "OK skipper; I'll see you at 0100 hours."

This left only Cork and Hansen on the bridge.

Cork walked over to stand beside Hansen who was sitting in the captain's chair looking over the bow as the four huge spotlights lit up the sea in front of Sirius. "Lars, that was an impressive display of decision making and leadership back there at the ice tunnel. I have never seen any better display even having sailed through three wars."

Hansen laughed and teased, "Seems you're easily impressed Captain Cork."

She was quick to reply, "I am definitely impressed by you, Lars." She stood close enough that her arm touched Hansen's shoulder just to make sure that he knew she was taken by him.

Hansen didn't miss the gesture and reached for her hand which he placed palm down on the arm of his chair and placed his hand of top of hers. They stayed like that for nearly an hour until Cork said, "I wish I didn't have to move but I've got to report back to my boss and I think we should get a com sat service window in a few minutes." She stepped aside and checked the signal meter on her satellite phone. She watched it for several minutes until it showed three bars at which time she executed the call to Rear Admiral Leonard Marshall. She reported that the mission had been a success, that they had been able to free the ship from the ice shelf, and that they were on their way back to Australia. Hansen decided to wait until after he had gotten some sleep to call his CEO to tell him the good, and bad, news.

27 JULY

Smith arrived outside the bridge at precisely 0100 hours and hit the buzzer to request entry. Hansen activated the electronic lock and Smith entered the bridge cabin. Hansen asked, "So how was that four hours of rest?"

Smith answered quickly, "I was asleep before my head hit the pillow. And I cursed that alarm when it went off." He laughed.

"I can tell you that I am sure looking forward to a few hours of shut-eye; I'm tired," Hansen admitted.

"I bet you are."

"Peter, the helm is yours. We are only a few miles from the waypoint where we will turn north and head back toward civilization. I'll see you by no later than 0600 hours."

Hansen and Cork left the bridge, went to their bunks, and slept.

***

Their alarms startled Cork and Hansen awake at 0530 hours. They dressed, got a quick breakfast from the always cheerful "Cookie", and headed to the bridge to arrive as promised by 0600 hours. Peter left the bridge to get a proper amount of sleep. Finally, life aboard Sirius was nearly back to normal.

Hansen checked all the instruments and everything was as it should be. He looked at Cork and said, "Well, I guess I have put off talking to my boss as long as I can. I've got to catch the next com satellite window and tell my CEO that I deposited about three quarters of his customers' containers in Antarctica. I'm not sure how he will take the news since I am sure that our insurance does not cover intentional destruction of customer cargo." He laughed. "Heck, I may be retiring sooner than I had planned." Cork laughed too.

Hansen monitored his satellite phone until it showed that it had a handshake with the communications satellite. When he began to dial his CEO's number, Cork walked to the back wall of the bridge, refilled her coffee cup, and then walked to the other side of the bridge to give Hansen a little more privacy.

"Mr. Anderson's office," the pretty voice announced.

"Hello, this is Lars Hansen calling from near Antarctica. Is Mr. Anderson available?"

"Good afternoon, Captain Hansen. Mr. Anderson has been anxiously waiting for you to call. He is currently in a meeting with his senior officers but he told me to interrupt him when you called. Please hold while I announce your call."

Hansen listened to the silence for three or four minutes while Anderson left his conference room and returned to his office to take the call.

"Good afternoon, Lars...or is it morning over there?"

"Sir, it is early morning here in the Southern Ocean, but good afternoon to you. I'm calling to fill you in the results of our mission."

"That's great Lars. Earlier today I got a call from the President of the United States telling me that your mission had been a success and that he wanted to personally thank me and Pole2Pole Petroleum for the important role we had played in plugging that hole that was sucking our breathing air out into space. Congratulations Lars; you are a hero to the world now. I can't tell you how many thank you phone calls I have gotten from around the world. And the folk who are calling are giving us more than their thanks; they are giving us their orders too. Our volume of business for future deliveries has doubled in just the past eight hours. You and your crew have made P2P a name that every household and business in the world knows; we could never have accomplished that with any kind of paid advertisement." Anderson was obviously delighted.

Lars hated to put a wet blanket on the flame of success but he had to tell the rest of the story, "Mr. Anderson, there is good news and some news that will not be welcomed. We did plug that hole in the ice tunnel and we did it without any damage to the ship as far as I can tell. However, we were not able to plug the hole by just spraying seawater into it as we had hoped. There was one very large hole that could not be closed in that manner so I ordered the release of cargo containers from the deck. Those containers were picked up by the huge draft and drawn into that hole by the wind and the large magnetic field around that space rock. We had to release about three-quarters of the containers that we had on deck in order to deposit enough volume in that hole to get it mostly closed. We then were able to use the cargo pumps to throw water into the small openings that remained after the containers settled. The seawater spray finally filled the hole completely." Hansen paused and waited for the reaction.

Anderson began slowly, "Really Lars, you plugged that hole with the containers that we had contracted to deliver?" Hansen knew that was a rhetorical question so he remained quiet and waited for the rest of the boss's thoughts. "That's really quite ingenious Lars. That's really thinking outside the boxes...pun intended!" Anderson laughed.

Hansen had not expected that reaction; he had expected the boss to be irate but Anderson seemed not to be even a little angry.

Anderson continued, "I guess I'm going to have to get our General Counsel to devise a settlement process for the customers that lost property...but we will work that out. Lars, I am very proud of the fact that you did what you needed to do to get this very important mission concluded successfully. And your company is the most famous company in the world, at least for a while. I can't imagine how our image would have suffered had you chosen to save your cargo rather than save the world. Somebody was going to close that hole and I am glad that we did it. We will need an inventory of what was lost so I need for you to get your Chief Mate to prepare that for us with all the detail we will need to work with our customers to compensate them properly."

Hansen assured, "Yes sir, we will have that inventory completed in a few days after we compare the TEUs that remain on board with the master cargo inventory that we recorded before leaving Brisbane."

"That sounds great Lars. Thanks again for your great work and the great work of your crew. When you get back to the Middle East and start loading your next shipment of crude, I want you to take a few days off and fly back to the states. I want you to come visit me and my senior staff. We will want to hear every detail of how you tamed that breath taking dragon."

"Of course, sir; I will be happy to do that."

"OK Lars, I will see you then." Anderson hung up.

Hansen looked at Cork and said, "Wow, I never expected that my CEO would be so pleased with losing nearly a shipload of containers." He laughed.

***

Later in the day when communications satellite coverage had become more regularly available, Cork contacted General Ryan Kelly and arranged to have two Blackhawk choppers available to meet the ship on 31 July, time to be determined when the ship was closer to the meet point.

Hansen began contacting his crew members who were on furlough somewhere in Australia and advising them to report to the Cambridge Aerodrome airfield near Hobart first thing on 31 July so that they could be returned to the ship. One of the men said he would not be returning as he had met a woman that he wanted to spend his life with and he was trying to figure out how to do that.

***

After Smith arrived at 1800 hours to take his night shift on the helm, Cork and Hansen went to the mess hall to dine with the crew and afterwards went back to Hansen's cabin where they spent several hours exploring celestial bodies.

WRAPPING UP

The next three days were pretty ordinary as Sirius began to finally re-enter the world where normalcy was normal. Since the communications satellite was now available nearly all the time at the lower latitudes, the phones began to ring more often with friends of Hansen and Cork calling to congratulate them and tell them that they were now famous, etc. The weather was good and Sirius was making good time with her light load of cargo and fuel and only a gentle wind abeam from the west. The length of the days was growing quickly to produce a normal amount of daylight.

When 31 July arrived and arrangements had been made to meet the helicopters for the exchange of crew, it became heavily apparent that this would be a sad day. Hansen arrived on the bridge deck at around 0530 hours to find Cork already there chatting with Smith. Hansen got buzzed in and went directly to the coffee station and filled his cup before walking over to the steering station where the other two were waiting. "Good morning, Jean, Peter." They returned the greeting.

Hansen checked all the instruments to find that they were only four hours from the meet point and that everything was performing properly. He told Smith that he could leave the bridge once he had made his entry in the ship's log. Smith said that he preferred to stay on the bridge until after the crew exchange was complete. It was apparent that he wanted to spend as much time as he could with Cork; Hansen wanted the same.

Just after 1000 hours the VHF crackled to life, "Sirius, this is Blackhawk Leader; come back Sirius."

Hansen picked up the microphone and answered the call, "Blackhawk Leader, this is Captain Hansen of Sirius. You are cleared to land."

"Sirius, this is Blackhawk Leader. Roger that, we have clearance to land. Our ETA is five minutes."

"Roger, ETA is five minutes."

Hansen picked up the ship's PA microphone and told the crew to prepare for the personnel exchange. He ordered the temporary crew to muster on the main deck level of the ship.

Hansen said, "Well, the time is here. I will give the two of you a few minutes of privacy before Captain Cork and I head down to main deck."

Hansen left the bridge and waited in the passageway while Cork and Smith said their good-byes. When the door buzzed and Cork came into the passageway, Hansen could barely contain his emotions knowing that he only had seconds left with the woman he had grown to need. He was unsure of what he should do at this moment. But he didn't have to make a decision. Cork walked right up to him and put her arms around his neck and pulled him down as she stood on her toes. She kissed him in a way that he had never been kissed before. Hansen was amazed at how soft her lips were; they were softer than anything he had ever encountered. They were not pursed; they applied absolutely no pressure. It didn't feel like she was giving him a kiss; it was as if their two pairs of lips had become a single pair. It was as if their lips had united in a marriage that was perfect. He couldn't believe how powerful the effect was from such a gentle kiss. It was the perfect kiss. It was not trying to conquer him, but it did. It was not trying to change him, but it did. Her lips tasted delicately sweet and perfectly seasoned by the tears that gravity had delivered. His body wanted to hold her tight to his but his mind insisted that a tight hug would not fit with such a tender kiss. He found himself holding her gently. His large hands were spooning the muscles of her back just above her waist and the tips of his fingers had found a natural meeting in the cleavage of her back. He thought that he could feel her heart beating through his fingertips. But then he realized that it was his heart that he was feeling. It was pounding blood through his body and his fingertips were literally pulsing with each contraction of his heart. He was happier and sadder than he had ever been. The kiss encompassed a lifetime of need but ended after only a few seconds. When their lips separated, Hansen held Cork tenderly for several seconds while she rested the side of her head on his pounding chest.

They slowly realized that they could not stay entwined as they were. They were people of duty and their duties remained incomplete. They had to get back to work and descend to the main deck. Hansen released his hands and arms reluctantly and Cork sank back to the steel decking, tears streaming down her face. She looked tenderly into his eyes and Hansen could feel his soul discovered. He had never felt so transparent at any time in his life. She didn't say a word. She had planned for this moment; she took a tissue from her pocket and wiped her eyes dry. She headed for the stairway and began the descent. Hansen followed her to the landing zone on the bow of Sirius with her crew in tow.

The first chopper landed on the port side of the ship with its nose pointed west into the wind and the second chopper landed on the starboard side of the deck. The regular crew jumped to the deck, took their gear from the helicopters, and walked to Hansen where they shook hands and exchanged pleasantries with their captain and Cork. As soon as the permanent crew had begun to clear the foredeck, the military crew came to Hansen and shook hands, exchanged pleasantries, and a couple even saluted him as a sign of the respect that they had grown to have for the civilian leader. Then, one by one, they climbed into the two helicopters and stowed their gear. When all the sailors were on the choppers, Cork turned to Hansen, saluted him, and turned to climb into the lead chopper. Once she had settled into her seat and buckled up, she gave the "wind 'em up" signal with her finger and the blades of the lead chopper began to spin faster. After a few seconds, the chopper lifted from the deck and headed off to the northeast. The second helicopter followed about 500 yards behind the first.

The sound of the choppers evaporated quickly as they achieved cruise speed and altitude. Hansen found himself all alone on the nearly empty deck of the large ship. He had never felt so alone in his entire life. He felt as if he was without purpose. He felt as if a piece of him was missing. He found himself just walking the deck, looking but not seeing. He was in a world without sound, without purpose, without comfort... without Jean.

LIFE GOES ON

Sirius was about thirty-six hours out from Perth when Hansen's satellite phone rang.

"This is Lars Hansen."

"Lars, this is Jack Anderson; how are you today?"

Hansen was a bit surprised to hear from the CEO again; it was very unusual to get a call from the big boss when things were normal. Usually he would hear from the Chief Operations Officer of P2P, if from anyone. "I'm fine sir." Not wanting to be too brief, he rambled a bit, "It is a great day to be at sea. The Sun is shining, the sea is calm, and the ship is performing perfectly."

"That's great Lars; I'm happy to hear that you are having a good day. Listen, I'm going to get right to the point. I've talked with our General Counsel about the container loss that we experienced. We have determined that arriving at fair settlements with our many customers will be a very time-consuming and complicated business. It will require dedicated attention from many people. I have decided to establish a new officer position to be in charge of that. It will be a corporate vice president position and I want you to take that job if you are willing. Of course, it will mean a big increase in your pay and some retirement perks that you would not otherwise receive if you retire at your current title. The promotion would become effective when you arrive back here at headquarters. So, what do you say Lars?"

This offer took Hansen totally by surprise. He had very mixed feelings about it but quickly realized that his career as a ship captain was going to end in five months anyway and that if he could better his retirement benefits he would be smart to do so. Hansen was a smart man and accepted the offer, "Yes sir, Mr. Anderson, I do want that job.

Thank you very much for offering me such an important position. I have just one stipulation and that is that you promote Peter Smith to Captain of Sirius and give him the authority to choose his second-in-command. He will be an outstanding captain and he knows everything there is to know about this ship."

"That's terrific Lars. I'm really happy that you have accepted. And I was hoping that you would recommend Smith to be your replacement; I have never heard anything but compliments about him and his work. Is he on the bridge with you now?"

"No sir; he is sleeping at the moment."

"When he wakes up, have him call me for the official offer to be your replacement."

"He will be very excited about his promotion so I will go wake him and have him call you in a few minutes."

"That's fine Lars. Now here is what I want you to do. When you dock at Perth, hire a packing crew to remove your telescope and crate it for shipment back to your home as I had promised you. Then, catch the next flight back from Perth and report to my office when you get back and settled in. I will have your new office ready for you to add whatever personal items you wish. It is on the twenty-eighth floor and you have a terrific view of the San Diego Bay, North Island, and the Pacific Ocean beyond that."

"Yes sir; I will do that. Thanks again Mr. Anderson. I will have Peter call you in just a few minutes."

***

Cork's crew members had been correct. Cork would not take her new ship to sea as she was promoted to Rear Admiral upon her return to Japan. She received her star on the deck of the USS Enterprise in front of her entire cheering crew. Cork was appointed to the position of Deputy Commander, US Third Fleet. She would be stationed at Point Loma in San Diego, California.

***

The next few weeks were hectic as Cork and Hansen settled into their new jobs but neither of them could forget about the other. Finally on September 6, Cork decided to call Hansen to catch up. She dialed the number that belonged to Hansen's satellite phone.

"This is Captain Smith."

"Is that you Peter; this is Jean Cork."

"Oh wow! I don't believe it. Yes Jean, this is Peter. Wow, I think about you all the time."

"Peter, it's good to talk with you again too. I miss our early morning visits. From the way you answered the phone, I see that you are now the captain of a ship; which ship is it?"

"I'm still on Sirius; I'm just the boss now."

"What happened to Lars? Is he OK?"

"Yes, Lars is fine. He got promoted to a fancy title back at the home office in San Diego. He's a Vice President now."

"Wow, that's great news. Sounds like everybody got a bump after our little adventure to Antarctica."

"Did you get that promotion that your crew said you would?"

"Yes, they were right. I'm now the Deputy Commander of the Navy's Third Fleet."

"Sounds like you have a desk job now; do you like that or do you miss the sea?"

"I do miss the sea and the independence of being a ship's captain. Here I have two other officers that outrank me. But I love my new job too, so I'm OK."

"Hey that's great; I'm glad you are happy."

"Peter, do you have a telephone number for Lars? I'd like to catch up to him also."

It became instantly clear to Smith that Cork hadn't called to visit with him. She had called to catch up to Hansen and didn't know, of course, that Hansen had handed down his company satellite phone to Smith when he had left the ship. He gave Cork the number for Hansen's cell phone since he didn't know his office phone number.

"Thanks Peter; you be careful out there."

"OK, I will; good-bye Jean."

***

At a little after 5:00 p.m. on Friday the phone in Hansen's pocket vibrated several times while he was meeting with the General Counsel and a few of his staff. They were discussing the release terms and language that would become the boilerplate terminology for the settlements to be made with P2P customers whose containers were "lost" in Antarctica. The General Counsel was making the case for including language that would grant P2P all salvage rights for the containers that had been jettisoned. Hansen was able to deal with complexity but preferred that things be as simple as possible to execute and still accomplish the objective. He argued that there should be no salvage rights language in the settlement agreements. He had the opinion that there would be little of value that could be salvaged and that a salvage operation would be virtually impossible anyway, so he argued that there was no practical reason why they should complicate the settlement process. Since the loss was deliberate, the insurance carrier would not accept a claim so P2P should meet the terms of the insurance agreement with the customer just as if the property loss had been covered by the cargo insurance carrier. P2P would compensate the customers at the basic per pound value specified by the insurance carrier. Since the customer had agreed to those terms prior to P2P accepting possession of their container, then that should be the settlement value with no other stipulations. Hansen's staff agreed with him and they finally convinced the General Counsel to relent.

Hansen got back to his office just before 7:00 p.m. He stacked his files in the bottom right hand drawer, collected his jacket from the tree in the corner, and took the elevator to the ground floor. He walked under the covered causeway to the parking garage, entered his car, and drove for an hour before he arrived at his home. When he got home, he changed into clothing that would be more comfortable while he made dinner, which would be a ham and egg sandwich.

When the sandwich was ready he remembered that someone had tried to call him during his meeting. He pushed the button on his phone to see that the call he had missed was from a phone listed to Jean Cork. He was excited to see that she had tried to contact him. He entered his PIN and tapped the number and listened while it rang...and rang...and rang. Just as he was sure the phone switch would decide that the number was not going to answer, he heard her voice.

When Cork had gotten to her cell phone, she had seen the incoming number was listed to Hansen, "Hello Lars, this is Jean."

"Jean, it's great to hear your voice. I'm sorry I didn't take your call earlier today; I was in a meeting at the time."

"I was sure that either you were busy or you just didn't want to talk to me so I didn't pester you with additional attempts."

"Trust me Jean; I couldn't wait to talk to you once I saw that I had missed your call. How have you been and how is your new ship working out?"

"I've been fine. I didn't get that new ship after all. The Navy decided that I should be given a desk job. I am now the Deputy Commander of the Third Fleet."

"Hey that's great. Your crew was right that you would never ship out on the USS Enterprise. Did you also get the promotion that they predicted?"

"I did; I am now a Rear Admiral. Technically, I am a Rear Admiral Lower Half which is a one-step promotion from Captain."

"Congratulations Jean, that's just great. Doesn't the Third Fleet have some of their fleet officers here in San Diego?"

"Yes, currently all the senior command officers are stationed at Point Loma, including me."

"No kidding. I can see Point Loma from my office down town. We have got to get together. Do you have to work this weekend?"

"I have a little work that I need to do in the morning but I should be done by noon."

"Outstanding; would you like to come out to my place in the hills near Palomar Mountain? If you'd rather just meet some place, that would be OK too. Whatever you want to do will be fine with me; I just need to see you again."

"I would love to come see you and your ranch in the hills."

"It isn't much of a ranch but I do have a few acres; no livestock though. If it is OK with you, I'll just cook us up something on the barbecue grill."

"That sounds awesome; what time would you want me to arrive?"

"I would love to see you as soon as you finish with work but you can come any time you want to."

"OK, I'll see you around mid-afternoon then and we can catch up on everything."

"Outstanding, I'll see you then."

***

Hansen was up before sunrise to get his bachelor place cleaned up for his company. He made a run to the local supermarket and bought steaks and lobsters; he wanted to impress her as much as possible. Cork showed up a little before 2:00 p.m.; she told him she just couldn't wait any longer. They walked and talked. They sipped some wine and ate the steaks and lobsters. They talked and sipped some more. When 11:00 p.m. arrived, Hansen suggested she just stay over so she wouldn't have to drive back in the dark, etc. She surprised him when she told him that she had packed a bag just in case. She had even brought the uniform she would wear to work on Monday. That weekend they rediscovered that they were meant to be together. They became inseparable thereafter, spending all their free time with one another. They were the perfect couple!

Hansen's Rock

IT'S TIME

On October 16, just after 9:00 a.m. PDT, Jerry knocked on Liz Wilson's office window that looked out over the NEO SCC. She looked up and waved him in. "Liz, I think it's time. We finally got infrared thermography readings that indicate that there are no areas inside Hansen's Rock or the ice tunnel that are cold enough to sustain solid or liquid hydrogen. The sublimation process appears to be complete. It should now be safe to dismantle the ice tunnel."

"OK, I'll tell Mike and he'll pass the news along to Mr. Barrow. That should get the wheels moving. Just to make sure that everyone is perfectly clear about it, I will remind Mike that the ice column needs to be destroyed from the top to the bottom to avoid another possible hole in the bottom of the column that would put us back to losing air."

Barrow advised General Watson that the time had come to take the ice column down. The plan had been developed weeks ago. Watson would order the USS Enterprise aircraft carrier stationed in Yokosuka, Japan and the USS Delaware, a Virginia-class submarine cruising in the north Indian Ocean, to make way to the mission location. The distance to the mission site was over 6600 nautical miles for the carrier and nearly 7000 nautical miles for the submarine. Each ship would require about 220 hours of travel to arrive at its station offshore of the ice tunnel.

When the Commander of the US Pacific Fleet got the call from Chairman Watson to dispatch the two ships to destroy the ice tunnel, he immediately called Jean Cork and invited her to accompany the USS Enterprise on its mission. He said that she would be welcomed on the ship and that since she had been instrumental in taming the ice column, he felt it only appropriate for her to be there to see it destroyed. She immediately asked for approval to invite Lars Hansen also since he had discovered the rock and had been just as important in plugging the hole in the ice column. The Commander agreed and Cork immediately called Hansen to invite him.

***

The navy-owned Gulfstream G650 left Halsey Field, North Island Naval Air Station, at 1800 on October 18. It would carry Cork and Hansen the 4,830 nautical miles to Narita International Airport in ten hours of flight time. They would then meet the waiting driver who would deliver them to the USS Enterprise docked at Yokosuka, Japan.

The USS Enterprise had just finished final fittings and testing and had finally reached fully-manned status. This would be its first real mission. As soon as Cork and Hansen had been welcomed aboard, the captain of the aircraft carrier gave the order to cast off.

***

The USS Enterprise and the USS Delaware arrived at their combat positions around 0800 hours on 28 October. They were each located approximately fifty miles due north of the ice column. The plan was to use the aircraft on the carrier to deliver the ordnance needed to take the ice tunnel apart. The submarine would be a backup in the event its Tomahawk missiles were needed to finish the job.

The workhorse for the mission would be F-35C aircraft launched from the four catapults on the USS Enterprise. The first two aircraft would be launched from the two bow catapults and would each carry four AGM-158 Air-to-Surface missiles. Each missile carried a 1,000 pound penetrator warhead. The first sortie would take place at the 60,000 foot service ceiling for the fighters. Because the ice thickness at that altitude was only about three hundred feet, it had been determined that two warheads launched from each aircraft on opposing sides of the column might be sufficient to create a fracture that would cause the ice above the fracture to fall into the sea. If the four warheads proved to be insufficient to do the job, the initial planes would make a second run and each would launch another two missiles. The strategy was to deliver the warheads so that the fracture would be made at an angle of about thirty degrees to the horizontal encouraging the upper section of ice to simply slide off the lower portion toward the seaward side of the column and fall directly down until it crashed into the ice shelf and seawater below.

Assuming success with the initial sortie, the next two flights would deliver strikes at 50,000 feet and 40,000 feet. Each of these sorties would deliver four missiles simultaneously from each of a pair of F-35s delivering their ordnance on opposing sides of the column.

Subsequent sorties would engage four fighters with two planes delivering their full load of AGM-158s to opposing sides of the ice column every 5,000 feet until there was less than 5,000 feet of ice tunnel left.

***

The Orion AP-3C arrived on station at 0900 hours. It had refueled mid-flight to ensure that it had sufficient fuel to stay on station until the ice column had been destroyed. It would use its high resolution cameras to take motion pictures and still images of the mission. It would remain just north of the ships until after all the ice above its service ceiling had been sent into the ocean. After that it would move in closer to get better quality images of the mission activities. It would stream real-time video to the aircraft carrier and the submarine so they could view the progress being made by the missiles.

Mission control would come from the USS Enterprise. The first two F-35C aircraft had locked into the electromagnetic catapults on the bow of the ship just as the AP-3C had arrived on station. The first plane applied full thrust, the nose squatted, and then the pilot gave the nod to the deck crew. Within five seconds, the catapult sent the fighter off the end of the deck and it began to climb out toward the ice column. The second plane followed less than two minutes later and followed the first plane as they climbed to their service ceiling in a spiral path around the ice column at a distance of about twenty miles from the structure. When the planes reached 60,000 feet, the second plane adjusted its speed so that the two planes were positioned on opposite sides of the ice column. When the two planes were approaching the east-west chord through the structure, the control tower gave the "commence run" order. The two planes immediately turned toward the ice structure and five seconds later the lead pilot counted down...two...one...fire. Each plane released two missiles into the ice column.

As soon as the missiles were away, each plane banked sharply, applied full thrust, and flew directly away from the ice structure to make sure that they would avoid the ice that would fall from above them. The missiles hit their targeted location, penetrated fifty feet into the ice and detonated. As the fighters screamed away from the falling ice, accelerating to a speed near Mach 1, the operators in the control tower carefully watched the radar to see what the falling ice would do.

The fall did not start instantaneously as they had expected. Several seconds passed as the fracture spread around the diameter of the ice column before the sixty miles of ice tunnel above the 60,000 foot level began to move. But the ice column above the fracture did not slide toward the ice shelf. Instead, a large wedge of ice separated and fell from the ocean-facing side of the tunnel. The upper section of the ice column began slowly tilting and then began to fall as a tree would fall. The bottom of the top section of ice stayed pretty much in place as the top portion of the column leaned further and further toward the ocean. The total piece of upper ice column did not separate from the bottom section until it reached the horizontal. There was now a sixty mile long ice column falling through the air in a horizontal attitude. And, it was falling directly toward the USS Enterprise!

The sophisticated electronics on the aircraft carrier and the submarine made the path of the falling ice tube very clear to those on each ship. The captain of the aircraft carrier gave the "all-ahead-full" command and started turning the ship to an easterly heading in an effort to escape the trillions of tons of ice that were falling toward it. But, it would only take about four minutes for the ice to fall from 60,000 feet to sea level and the ship would not be able to escape it.

The submarine commander saw the predicament from its position that was outside of the expected impact area. The commander ordered the launch of Tomahawk missiles from vertical launch tubes one through four. He told the seamen that were responsible for guidance to guide the missiles so that they would intercept the falling ice column directly above the USS Enterprise before the ice fell into the sea and on top of the carrier.

On the USS Enterprise, the captain, Cork, and Hansen were on the bridge watching the action. The captain of the ship was focused on a strategy of flight...get out of the way of the ice if possible. Cork saw the Tomahawk missiles exit the sea and head directly up toward the ice column. She intervened, "Captain, I suggest you send your two in-flight F35's to see if they can intercept the falling ice and use their remaining missiles to destroy as much ice as possible directly over our heads. Also, I suggest you launch the other two F35s that are locked in the waist catapults and give them the same order."

Hansen asked, "Doesn't this ship have anti-aircraft missiles? Shouldn't we launch them too?"

Rear Admiral Cork said, "Yes we do carry anti-aircraft missiles," and then she ordered "captain, man the ship's VLS complex. We need to fragment the ice that is directly over our heads as much as possible if we will have any chance of surviving the impact."

Hansen's Rock

The terrified new captain ordered all four of the F35s to intercept the ice column directly overhead of the ship. He ordered the two Mk 48 Vertical Launch Systems into action and they launched their RIM-162 Evolved Sea Sparrow Missiles as rapidly as was possible. He also ordered their small RIM-116 Rolling Airframe Missiles launched in rapid succession toward the falling ice. He had now employed all the significant anti-aircraft weapons that the ship carried.

The F35s that had finished the initial mission were inbound when it was discovered that the column was falling over rather than falling down. Once they received the order from flight control, they immediately unleashed full throttle plus afterburner power, pulled the noses of their planes vertical and raced directly toward the ice until they were within three miles of it when the lead pilot gave the order to release all missiles. The four missiles had barely left their pitons when the pilots turned their aircraft as hard as they could without passing out from the multi-G forces that their bodies felt.

The two F35s that launched from the waist catapults never backed off of afterburner thrust after clearing the catapults. They too went vertical and screamed toward the falling ice over the ship. When they were about two miles from the ice the lead pilot gave the order and they discharged all eight ASMs toward the ice and then made six-G turns to race away from the debris.

The anti-aircraft missiles launched from the ship were chipping away at some of the ice even with their relatively small warheads intended to disable agile aircraft rather than destroy billions of tons of ice.

As soon as the guidance techs on the sub had the first four Tomahawks on guidance toward the falling ice, the commander gave the order to fire four more missiles and the guidance techs worked feverishly to get them on flight paths that would take them directly overhead of the aircraft carrier and toward the falling ice. As soon as the second volley of Tomahawks was away the sub commander gave the, "Dive, Dive, Dive" command and instructed the sailor manning the helm to "Zero Nine Zero" and "Full Ahead" speed. He instructed the helmsman to take the ship to 1000 feet of depth. He knew that when the massive amount of ice hit the ocean that it would create huge waves of water and he wanted to get under the waves as much as possible to avoid extraordinary damage or sinking from the trillions of tons of water that would be in motion.

The first volley of Tomahawks were the first to intercept the ice column and all detonated perfectly blowing huge portions of the ice column into small pieces that were thrown in all directions. The four missiles launched from the first pair of F35s were the next to intercept the ice and the hard-headed missiles penetrated to the designated depth and exploded separating the ice column into two large pieces with the separation being directly above the aircraft carrier.

The eight air-to-surface missiles from the two F35s that were the last to escape the carrier catapults caused the next explosions which further separated the two large pieces of ice column as more ice was blown away from the space over the carrier. It was now possible to see through the break in the ice as the sky was filled with chunks of ice that had been created from the one hundred foot thick walls of the ice tunnel.

The last four Tomahawk missiles intercepted the ice when it was only about one-half mile above the deck of the USS Enterprise.

The commander of the aircraft carrier ordered the decks cleared of personnel. The horn blared and the few technicians and pilots that had been preparing the aircraft and catapults for the subsequent missions ran for cover below the ship's deck just before the ice began to rain down on the ship.

Hansen knew that when the falling ice column hit the water that it would make some huge waves that would have the power to toss around any ship, even a ship the size of the USS Enterprise. Hansen grabbed Cork and held her firmly with his left arm as he pulled her to the back wall of the bridge where his right hand firmly grasped the handrail that ran the length of the short wall next to the sealed exit door. When they arrived at the wall, Cork held onto Hansen with her right arm and the handrail with her left hand. Hansen bent over so as to protect Cork's head.

The ice storm brought ice chunks from the size of sleet to the size of tractor-trailer trucks. The ice storm began relatively slowly as the ice debris from the first missile strikes arrived. Then the intensity of the ice fall escalated fearfully fast as the ice debris created by the other missiles reached the ship. The ice was falling so fast and densely that visibility through the armored glass of the control bridge was down to zero. The sound of the ice on the surface of the ship was painfully loud; it sounded as if a continuous nuclear explosion were occurring just outside the skin of the ship. Some of the larger pieces of ice that arrived early actually pierced the deck of the ship. The two F-35s that were left in the bow catapults were flattened until there was no space for air inside the crushed metal.

The ice continued to fall in small and large pieces. Everyone on the ship expected the "coup de grace" chunk of ice to arrive at any second and had resigned themselves to dying from it.

The ice continued to collect on the huge flat deck of the ship. The layer of ice on the deck became so thick that new pieces began sliding over the sides of the ship. The ice became seventy feet thick in the center of the ship's deck and the captain feared that the ship had become dangerously top heavy. The Enterprise was floating twenty feet lower than designed because of the extraordinary weight of the ice that had collected on the deck. The captain grabbed the PA microphone and ordered everyone to prepare to ditch but to stand by until he gave the order. Everyone clustered at their emergency muster stations if they did not have an immediate emergency job to perform.

The ice fall preceded the two large pieces of ice tunnel by at least a minute. When the two large pieces of ice tunnel finally reached the surface of the sea about a thousand feet from each side of the ship they each created huge splash waves that moved toward the aircraft carrier at over three hundred miles per hour.

The captain made a quick announcement to all personnel, "Secure yourselves; we have monster waves coming." As soon as he had made the announcement, he grabbed the two short handrails to either side of his station; the helmsman did the same.

The waves were upon Enterprise nearly instantaneously. The two splash waves were at least five hundred feet high…Enterprise was caught between two deadly tsunamis. The Enterprise was propelled upward as it was violently but briefly floated upward by the two waves until the waves met directly overhead of the big ship and spent all their energy in the collision. Billions of tons of seawater fell straight down from the colliding waves onto the top of Enterprise violently pushing the great ship toward the ocean floor. Enterprise became a submarine for over twenty seconds as the water fell upon it and finally drained back into the sea. The sound of the water drenching the ship was something no one had ever experienced. The sound was like that of a hurricane but different…it was more frightening than anything any sailor had ever experienced before. When the gigantic waterfall initially hit the deck of the ship, the ship sank another thirty feet as the weight of the airborne water tried to push the great ship into the sea. But as soon as gravity had overcome the falling water, the ship leaped vertically a full fifty feet throwing most everyone on the ship toward the floor. The wave of water had washed the deck clear of the seventy feet of ice that had resided there just seconds ago.

Ice was still falling from the sky and pounding the deck of Enterprise. Before most could regain their feet, the second round of splash waves hit the ship. These waves were less than a hundred feet high and broke at about the level of the armored windows of the bridge shaking the ship from all sides. Again the deck was washed clean; even the flattened F35s that had been held in the bow catapults had disappeared as had any other equipment that was not through-bolted to the deck of Enterprise.

The ice had now stopped falling but there were two more harmonic splash waves that the ship would endure. But they were comparatively small and didn't even come close to reaching the level of the deck of Enterprise.

Thanks to the handrails, the captain was now on his feet again surveying the deck of the massive ship. He grabbed the dangling microphone and demanded damage reports from all the key operating components of the ship. Amazingly, all the vital operating elements of the ship were operable. There did not seem to be any leakage from the two huge nuclear reactors that powered the ship.

As soon as the ship finally stabilized to the point that it was safe to send seamen to the deck of the ship to inspect the elevators and catapults, a complete survey was made. The two forward catapults were damaged when the waves jerked the flattened F35s from the locking mechanisms. They would be unusable until they could be repaired in port. The waist catapults sustained minor damage but could be repaired at sea and the mechanics immediately went to work on them. One of the aircraft elevators was damaged beyond repair but there was one that still seemed to be operable. They would confirm that when they loaded it with aircraft to be raised to the deck. Several of the F35s that had been tied down in the space under the main deck were damaged when the anchoring ties broke and the planes crashed into one another. But there were still nine planes that appeared to be undamaged.

Ninety-seven sailors and four officers had been injured during the violent movements of the ship. Twelve sailors had died immediately from their injuries, mostly crushed skulls. Twenty-one sailors were unaccounted for and were feared to have been washed overboard.

When the ship had lurched down due to the falling splash waves, Cork's and Hansen's hands were torn from their hold on the handrail. Hansen instinctively took his then-free right arm and wrapped it around Cork's head and pressed it to his chest. He managed to turn their bodies in midair so that it was Hansen's back that struck the hard steel ceiling. Even though he had lost his breath when they hit the ceiling he was attempting to turn their bodies as they fell back toward the floor to ensure that he would strike the floor first so that Cork's diminutive body would not be crushed by his two hundred pound weight. He had managed over a quarter turn when his head struck the handrail. The impact with the handrail completed the half turn so that Hansen hit the floor first and Cork landed atop him. Cork's head was still held to Hansen's chest by his right arm but the arm had no power.

Hansen's Rock

Before she moved she listened carefully to his chest and could not hear his heart. She raised herself and Hansen's arm fell lifelessly to the floor. She then saw the severe damage to the right side of his head. She immediately began to check for signs of life but there was no breathing and his pulse was silent. While the other sailors on the bridge performed the emergency assessment of the ship's systems, Cork immediately began administering CPR to Hansen...ten chest pumps at one second intervals and three lung expansions. She alternated this procedure for five minutes before she accepted the fact that Hansen would not respond. Then she wept uncontrollably; she knew that her life would never again be a happy one.

Others on the bridge came to take Hansen's body to the ship's hospital but Cork refused to let them take him from the bridge. She told them that Lars would want to be on the bridge when the last threat from the space rock was eliminated. While the still flying F35s were landed and the mission to destroy the remaining ice tower was executed, Cork stayed by the man that had made her complete. She sat next to him with her back to the bulkhead and held his hand until the last of fourteen sorties finally destroyed the evil column of ice that had been created by the space rock named after the love of her life. She watched the video monitor through the tears that continued to fall for Lars until the last giant chunk of ice fell into the sea.

THE END

Endnotes:

[a] Meade Instruments Corporation, "MAX 20" ACF – Features", http://www.meade.com/max/features, (4 February 2014)

[b] Ashland Astronomy Studio, "chi Octantis (HIP 92824)", http://www.astrostudio.org/xhip.php?hip=92824, (2 February 2014)

[c] Astronomy at Western Kentucky University: The Institute for Astrophysics and Space Science, "Distance modulus and distance ", http://astro.wku.edu/labs/m100/mags.html#Distmod, (2 February 2014)

[d] C.R.C. Standard Mathematical Tables, Thirteenth Edition, 1964, Cleveland, Ohio, The Chemical Rubber Company, p. 21

[e] Australia Telescope National Facility, "Obtaining Astronomical Spectra – Spectrographs", http://www.atnf.csiro.au/outreach/education/senior/astrophysics/spectrographs.html, (13 February 2014)

[f] Australia Telescope National Facility, "Information from Astronomical Spectra", http://www.atnf.csiro.au/outreach//education/senior/astrophysics/spectra_info.html, (13 February 2014)

[g] Las Cumbres Observatory Global Telescope Network, "The Equatorial Coordinate System", http://lcogt.net/spacebook/equatorial-coordinate-system, (14 February 2014)

[h] World's Largest Virtual Solar System Drive, "Location of Planets", http://www.solarsystemdrive.com/map-planet-locations.html, (14 February 2014)

Dan L. King

www.ingramcontent.com/pod-product-compliance
Lightning Source LLC
Chambersburg PA
CBHW051422170626
46809CB00006B/2280